The Bodies
by Paul

*For Jennifer
With love from Yvonne*

Paul

© **Paul Stephens 2013. All rights reserved.**

The right of Paul Stephens to be identified as the author of this work has been asserted by him in accordance with the Copyright, Design and Patents Act 1988.

This is a work of fiction. The character Michael Slade was inspired by a friend of mine (I'll leave it to him to decide whether to reveal his identity), although I have made many changes to his characteristics and circumstances. All other characters, and all events, are fictional, and any resemblances to real people or events are entirely coincidental. Weston-super-Mare is a real town, but only some of the places described here exist in real life – for example there's a Winter Gardens, but no Clarendon pub (as far as I know). To discover which is which, visit Weston!

This book contains some strong language, and one scene where a character uses sexually disparaging comments to try to provoke a response. There are no descriptions of violence or sexual acts.

ISBN 978-1494291242

Visit us at
www.facebook.com/thebodiesinthebeach

For Yvie,
without whose love and encouragement I wouldn't
have written this book.

Chapter 1

Mary Miller swept her hair from her eyes then peeled the sticky note from her computer screen.

"BODY UNDER PIER – SEE YOU THERE."

It was from her Detective Inspector, succinct as ever. She was grateful that he hadn't hauled her in at whatever time the body had been found, even if his main consideration had most likely been his overtime budget rather than her welfare. It would probably be non-suspicious anyway, some poor drunk ending his days by the seaside like he'd always wanted to. Cold time of year to do it though.

The Grand Pier, official Jewel of the Weston-super-Mare Seafront, wasn't far from the town's police station, and Mary decided to walk over rather than risk losing her space in the station car park. She regretted it as she turned the corner into Pier Square and felt the full blast of the wind off the Bristol Channel, but ploughed on. As she reached the promenade she could see that, drunk or no drunk, the deceased was being given the full treatment. A white tent was squeezed in between two of the big iron legs that supported the Pier's walkway, and a police Land Rover was parked on the sand near it. Parked on the broad promenade pavement was a car which she recognised as belonging to the local pathologist. Near it a uniformed constable guarded the slipway to the beach.

"Over there, Sarge, under the pier." he said as Mary approached.

"Thanks." she replied, "Is the DI here?"

"In the tent, Sarge."
"OK."

Mary pulled her coat around her and started to walk across the beach. She wasn't dressed for it; damp sand was already creeping into her shoes. As she reached the underside of the pier a tent flap was raised and DI Jones emerged.

"Mary."
"Guv. What have we got?"
"One dead body. Looks young, almost certainly female."
"What, is it burnt?"
"No, buried. Just a lower arm visible. The hand of a young woman, I'd say. They're digging her out now - I've told them to go gently."
"Who found her?"
"Dog walker, about 6.30. Still dark, the dog found her by scent. The owner phoned it in from his mobile."
"Vehicle tracks, footprints?" Mary looked around her at the morass of churned sand, footprints and tyre tracks. It looked more like the aftermath of a motorised beach volleyball tournament than a carefully preserved crime scene. The DI caught her look and smiled.

"Nothing whatsoever except the dog walker's leading up to it. He watches Crimewatch, knew not to contaminate anything. Stood like a statue until uniform arrived, with the dog on its lead. It's all been photographed."

Mary hesitated, realising that questioning her boss's crime scene management might not go down well, especially at 9am on a wet beach in November. The DI came to her rescue.

"No harm in asking though."

He must have had a good breakfast.

Mary looked around her again, imagining the sand smooth from the receding tide.

2

"So whoever buried her must have done it before the tide came in last night?" She looked down the beach to the sea, its edge so far away that it was barely visible. It was hard to imagine the water right up here.

"Possibly, but that still leaves us with a problem. The tide wasn't high last night - in fact it barely came up past here. Lots of footprints up at the top of the beach, but nothing that suggests a vehicle or someone carrying or dragging a corpse."

"Then she wasn't dead when she got here? She walked onto the beach then was murdered?"

"And buried, all without anyone seeing or hearing anything, all before 11pm last night." The DI held his phone up for Mary to see. On the screen was a table of tide times for that week; high tide, reaching just a bit further up the sand, had been at 11.14. "Possible, but very unlikely."

"I don't know, Guv - not many people around on the front that late at this time of year, and this spot's hidden from the road anyway. You'd have had to be on the beach to see it, and I doubt if anyone was."

"Still doesn't work for me. What's the killer supposed to have dug the hole with - his bare hands? If not he'd have had to carry a shovel onto the beach with him, and I think our victim might have noticed that."

Mary was about to say "Not if he came up from behind her", but thought better of it. The DI clearly wasn't going with the walk-on theory, and besides, they weren't even certain they had an entire body yet, or whether it was male or female, or what the cause of death would be. It could keep for later.

Just then a paper-suited figure appeared from the tent.

"Inspector!"

The DI raised his hand, then turned back to Mary.

"OK, let's see what we've got. Get kitted up, I'll see

you in there." Seeing Mary grimace, he added "Proper crime scene procedure, Detective Sergeant", grinned and headed for the tent.

Mary went to the Police Land Rover, where a Scenes of Crime officer gave her the regulation disposable suit and overshoes. A fat lot of difference they'd make in a scene that was already contaminated with sand, seawater, the odd seagull dropping and whatever Fido the dog had left behind, but as the DI said, it was best to stick to procedure.

Climbing into the back of the Land Rover, Mary unpacked the suit and clambered into it, tucking her skirt inside. She really wasn't dressed for this, but when she'd left home an hour earlier she hadn't expected to be dealing with a body in the beach. Pulling the hat down tight over her hair, she got out of the car and joined her boss.

Chapter 2

Inside the tent it was bright and warm from the lamps. In the middle of the floor, now partially uncovered, lay a young woman, on her back in a shallow grave with her right arm extended upwards at an angle, as if she was swimming backstroke. Mary had seen a few dead bodies, but not many; the lifelessness still shocked her. The woman – almost still a girl, really, perhaps 20 or a bit older - could have been sleeping, but at the same time she very clearly wasn't. Something had gone.

The DI hadn't guessed randomly that the hand's owner was female; black nail polish, slim fingers, silver rings on three of them. Beyond the elbow, where she'd been buried, the girl looked horribly like one of the sand statues they had on the beach in Weston every summer. She was fully clothed ("Wasn't expecting that", said the DI) and from what they could see of her there were no signs of injury. One of the Forensics people was brushing sand off the girl's face with what looked like a pastry brush, while another circled round the hole, taking pictures. As the sand disappeared it revealed clear skin, an olive complexion. Her long dark hair was crimped into small waves. She'd been pretty.

"Looks Southern European to me, Guv – Spanish, Italian?"

"Or she could just be from Exeter. Let's not jump to conclusions."

The leader of the digging team explained that to go further they'd have to widen the hole so someone could dig alongside her. The DI and Pathologist nodded their assent, the DI reminding them that the tide would be back soon so there was no time to lose. Mary was glad it wasn't her having to go in and dig.

The officer who did have to dig cut himself a space in the sand, dumping the waste neatly in a pile in case it needed to be sieved later. Then he stepped into the hole and began to remove sand, quite delicately, from around the girl's body, stacking it in a new pile next to the hole. The pathologist crouched down to examine the back of her head, looking for wounds but apparently not finding any. The photographer kept shooting, the sound of the camera's shutter almost constant, accompanied by bursts of light from the flashgun. The pathologist edged round the tent to Mary and the DI.

"No signs of trauma so far, although of course we don't know what's under the clothes. We could be looking at poisoning."

"Any ideas on time of death?"

"Very difficult, Inspector. She's had the equivalent of a cold mudpack round her for the past few hours, plays havoc with the natural cooling process. I'll really need to get her on the slab. I wouldn't say she's been dead for days though."

"So she may have been killed here then buried straight away?" Mary sneaked a glance at the DI, but he didn't seem to object to her trying the walk-on theory.

"Insufficient evidence to answer that, Sergeant - as I say, I'll need to examine her properly before I can start narrowing it down." So much for that then.

Mary and the DI watched as the digger continued to uncover the girl's body. They'd arranged a sling under her arms and suspended it from a tripod gantry they'd erected over the hole, so she hung there as the sand was removed from around her. The grave was only a couple of feet deep, but already water was seeping in underneath her. The pastry brush revealed a short-sleeved cotton top, what would once have been called a Gypsy skirt ('ethnic' was the preferred term these days), bare legs, ankle socks, flat-heeled ballet-pump shoes; not exactly suitable clothing for outdoors at this time of year. Nothing else - no coat, no bag or other belongings, no visible marks on the body. Hanging there, her back supported by the sling, she looked like a life-size rag doll. Mary looked away.

"No ID, no time or cause of death," said the DI, "I think that counts as not having much to go on. Whoever put her there made sure they didn't leave any clues behind. Starting to look a bit professional to me."

Mary nodded. It was starting to look that way to her too. Too neat for the walk-on, random-killer (or boyfriend-killer) theory.

"Get back to the office," the DI continued, "set up the incident room. All hands on this. I want CCTV from the seafront, both directions, house to house, and find anyone who was out on the prom between eight and eleven last night - winter-breakers from the hotels, joggers, boozers, druggies, anyone. Someone must have seen something. And get onto Missing Persons, here and Europe. Try Italy first."

"Yes Guv," Mary appreciated the 'Italy', "But, er..."

"What?"

"Won't this one go to the Murder Squad?"

"I don't see any sign of them on this beach, do you? My guess is they're too busy with their own problems. Either way, until we hear differently it's ours, so let's make a good job of it while it is. I'll see you back there. I'll let you know if we get anything else here."

"OK - see you later, Guv."

Not ungratefully, Mary went back to the Land Rover, struggled out of the paper suit, stuffed it into a disposal bag and left the crime scene. As she reached the promenade she saw two Range Rovers parked on it, each with a satellite dish mounted on its roof. TV News. Mary thought for a moment about getting the uniforms to nick them for parking, but remembered the edict, sent from On High, that they were now a media-friendly force, and that news coverage was a vital channel through which public awareness of policing efforts could be raised and maintained.

A woman jumped out of one of the Range Rovers and shouted across at her, "Detective Sergeant, hello!" Mary recognised her as a reporter from the BBC regional news programme, who'd interviewed her on another case. The interview hadn't made it to air, but the woman had seemed straight enough. She was impressed that she'd remembered her rank, if not her name.

"Yes?"

"Hello again. Jane Thomas, BBC. We met when I did a report on the burglaries at Locking."

"Yes, I remember."

"Look, I won't waste your time. Can you tell me anything about what's happening on the beach? We've heard a body's been found."

Dispatch room leaking like a sieve as usual, thought Mary. That or uniform.

"I can't tell you anything, I'm afraid - our press office will make an announcement in due course. We can't talk to the media direct."

The reporter looked disappointed. Mary thought for a second. She quite liked her on the TV news - she was a relatively old hand, a local woman who seemed genuinely interested in the region rather than just doing her time with one eye on London. Mary lowered her voice.

"My DI's in charge and he's still on the scene. It might be worth your while to stick around. That's all I can say, OK?"

The reporter's face brightened.

"Yes, of course - thank you, er..."

"I must be off - goodbye." No need for names.

Back at the station Mary found DCs Cox and Lane already setting up the incident room. The idea that the Murder Squad might not be coming down to take over the case seemed to have occurred to them too. This hadn't taken a genius to work out, since the Chief Constable had been on TV the night before giving assurances that the Squad would henceforth be devoting their entire resources to catching whoever had brutally murdered two university students (so far) in the city of Bristol, 20 miles away.

It occurred to Mary that the girl in the beach looked young enough to be a student herself, although this one was so far from the Bristol killer's patch and modus operandi, which left all too visible marks on the body, for there to be any real likelihood of a connection. Nevertheless, she made a note to send pictures and details to the Squad when they came through.

It was after lunchtime when Mary realised she was hungry. The DI had been back to the station for the obligatory press statement, in which he'd confirmed that the body of a young woman had been found on the beach (not "in", Mary noted) early that morning, and asked for calls to the hotline, in confidence if preferred, from anyone who'd seen a dark-haired, medium-height woman aged between 17 and 23, wearing an ethnic-style floral patterned skirt, on or near the seafront any time the previous evening.

Then he'd gone back to the scene to supervise the uniforms resuming their search of the beach after the tide had gone back down. The uniform inspector had objected to continuing the search at all, saying that by now two receding tides would have washed any evidence away, but Mary had heard the DI on the phone to him, stating in no uncertain terms that he wanted them back on the sand until he said they could leave. It was all out of character for him - he was usually big on teamwork and cooperation, and would normally have been back at the office marshalling the troops by now, not leaving the organising to her. The last thing Mary would have expected him to do was hang around on a freezing beach for longer than he had to. But she remembered the tent, and the girl hung there under the lights, dug out of the wet sand. Somehow this one was different.

Chapter 3

Mary preferred the sandwich place opposite the Town Hall to the station canteen. She'd barely reached the street, however, when she heard her mobile ringing. Reaching into her bag she struck lucky first time and hauled it out. It was the DI.

"Guv." At that moment a traffic car emerged from the yard and turned its sirens on.

"Where are you?"

"Outside the station. Just going to get a sandwich."

"Well hurry up. We've got something. A mobile phone. Uniform found it about fifty yards down the beach. It's waterlogged, but I've sent it to Tech and they say they can normally get the data off. I've told them to liaise with you. If they get anything, I want it given top priority - contacts, call records, pictures, the lot. It could be our only lead."

"Where was it found exactly?"

"I told you - fifty yards down the beach."

"Under the pier?"

"No, just to the north side"

"Guv.."

"Yeah yeah, I know - it could have been dropped off the pier by a punter, could have nothing to do with the case. But on the other hand it was found fifty yards from a murder victim, and it might explain why there are no traces of the body being brought in from the top of the beach - they brought her in by boat, and the phone got dropped on the way. So unless you've got anything better, we focus on it. OK?"

"Yes, of course Guv. I'll chase Tech. When are you coming back?"

"Soon. Incidentally, have you been saying anything to that woman from the BBC? She's been chasing me round like a sniffer dog all day."

Mary decided that the truth was best.

"I just said you were in charge and it'd be worth her while to stick around. No details, honest. I just think she's OK, isn't always looking to do us over."

"OK, I know what you mean. You didn't tell her I'd talk to her, or anything like that?"

"I'm not stupid, Guv."

"No, fair enough. She's wasting her time if she thinks I will though. Right - get your sandwich and get back, Tech may be calling you. I'll see you back there."

"OK, bye."

So much for statutory meal breaks, Mary thought. If anything kicked off - data from the phone, or a worthwhile lead from the public - she'd be lucky to be home before midnight, then back in at 8am. The first 48 hours - it was a cliché, but it was true. After that memories began to fade, evidence was obliterated, trails began to go cold. As for the idea of them bringing the girl in by boat - she'd thought of it, and guessed that the DI had too, only the idea of someone cruising across the bay with a corpse in a dinghy, even under November darkness, had seemed a bit far fetched. But if the phone turned out to be the victim's, then arrival by sea was a simpler explanation of what it was doing that far down the beach than any of the others she could think of.

She bought ham salad with French mustard, and another one for later. As it happened though, the extra round of sandwiches wasn't needed.

The phone had been biked to Technical Services, 20 miles away, and when Mary rang them, a slightly tetchy technician informed her that a. it had only just arrived, b. yes it was being given top priority, but c. it had clearly been immersed in water and would have to be dried overnight in controlled conditions in order to minimise the risk of data loss.

There were a few responses from the public, but none of any value - some rang in to say they hadn't seen anyone matching the description, others to say they had, but couldn't be sure about the hair colour (or height, or skirt, and that she might have been wearing trousers, or might have been a man). The Pathologist rang to say that initial examination confirmed no injuries or trauma marks, and no signs of recent sexual activity. The best he could say on time of death was some time after eight am yesterday, although that was provisional, as was cause of death, which he was guessing would be barbiturates when the toxicology screen came back.

In summary, as the DI put it when he'd assembled the squad in the incident room, it was likely that she'd been poisoned yesterday morning then kept somewhere until late evening, when she'd been brought to the beach, possibly by boat, and buried in the sand under the pier, with one hand, either deliberately or accidentally, left sticking out of the ground. Then, to general surprise, he told everyone who wasn't detailed for evening house-to-house to go home, get a good night's rest and be back at eight am sharp, ready to put their backs into it. Neither the Pathologist nor Tech would be giving them anything else tonight, and the call handlers would log anything from the public; make the best of it while they could.

"You too, Mary." he said, as she put her head round his office door a few minutes later.

"Sure you don't want us here, going over the CCTV?"

He shook his head.

"This looks more and more like a pro job. They won't be on CCTV. Let's just hope Tech get something from the phone tomorrow."

Mary said nothing. She'd already made her views on

the phone clear, and once was enough.

The DI smiled – something between a smile and a grimace, anyway.

"Still reckon someone lost it off the pier? We'll see. Anyway, I've cleared the early finish with the DCI, so off you go."

Mary was quick on the uptake.

"You appealed to his budgetary instincts."

"I pointed out that the overtime would almost certainly prove more effective further into the investigation, yes. Which is true. So bugger off. I'll see you eight am sharp."

"Fair enough, Guv." She turned to walk away, paused for a second then turned back. "What do you make of the victim's hand sticking up like that? Significant?"

"Could be nothing. Perhaps they held on to the arm to lower her in then found it was locked in place by rigor mortis, or the tide was coming up on them and they rushed the job. The PM might tell us more."

"OK. Goodnight, Guv."

"Goodnight."

Mary went to her desk and began to collect up her things. She was unsettled by the DI sending them all home. Call her old fashioned, but on the first night of a murder enquiry the incident room should be a blaze of light, full of officers logging anything and everything they could get their hands on, while the more experienced DCs went out to find their contacts for the word on the street. Not dark and deserted, the detectives all at home watching TV. Still, it was his squad and most of the time he was a very good DI. She wouldn't want to be anywhere else.

Her phone was still on the desk; as she went to pick it up it vibrated and whistled at her. A text message. It could be from Tech, working late and telling her they'd dried out the victim's phone and found her name and all her contacts, with pictures and email addresses. However it wasn't.

"Nothing in freezer, can u pick something up on way home? Don."

Stay calm, she thought. Yes, he was perfectly capable of going to the supermarket half a mile from their house if they needed food, but no, it wasn't worth texting that back to him because then he'd point out that he'd been installing pipework since seven am and it wasn't all about her and her job, and that he'd done the last big shop on his own because she was too busy chasing car thieves. And he'd have a point. It was an argument she didn't want to have tonight, not if she had to be back here first thing tomorrow fresh and ready to go. So she'd go to the shop on the way home, even if it was the very last thing she wanted to do. She grabbed the phone, stuffed it in her bag, wrenched her coat from the stand and left the room.

Don would also have had a point about trekking all the way round the giant out of town store near their home, where a three-course dinner could take literally half a mile to assemble. Instead, Mary chose the smaller, if older and tattier, supermarket in the centre of town, a couple of streets from the station. It was crowded, as it always was early evening, being ideal for people "picking something up" on their way home from work. Mary chose some frozen lamb grillsteaks which she knew Don didn't like much, plus potato croquettes (ditto) and green beans (positively disliked), with a lemon sorbet, which he did quite like, to finish, so he wouldn't be in such a bad mood later. For good luck she added a four pack of own-brand 5% alcohol lager, which Don liked a lot, although she suspected he'd have already secured stocks of that under his own steam.

As she pushed her trolley to the checkouts she groaned – queues at all of them except one, at which a short stretch of empty belt beckoned invitingly. Then she groaned again – the checkout operator was Chatty Michael, which explained the lack of queue.

Chatty Michael (just "Michael" on his staff badge) was a man in his late thirties, an oddity in itself on the checkouts, which were mostly staffed by youngsters and their older female relatives. He was a capable checkout operator, but he had a major flaw – he not only talked too much, but worse, he tried to engage you in conversation. All other operators stuck to the prescribed minimum - "Hello", "Do you need any help packing?", "Have you got a Shopper Card?", "Enter your PIN please" - but Michael asked you how you were, whether you'd seen a particular programme on TV last night, even whether you had any children at the school that had been on the news. To the average homeward-bound customer, just wanting to get their shopping out to the car with the minimum of fuss and even less interaction, he was a nightmare. But you could get to his till quickly.

Mary weighed up the options. Queue at any other till behind a customer whose goods weren't even on the belt yet, or go straight on the belt and run the gauntlet of Chatty Michael. Despite the early let-off, it had been a hard day. She was dying to get home and put her feet up (Don was cooking those grillsteaks, like it or not – she'd probably drink one of his lagers, too). The gauntlet couldn't be that bad.

"Hello, how are you today?" said Michael, "Do you need any help with packing?"

"No thanks, I'm fine." said Mary, "Now just shut the f**k up and scan my items." The last bit was said only in her head, but it made her feel slightly better. Unfortunately it also meant that Michael hadn't heard her.

"Did you see the lunchtime news on the BBC?" he asked, running the grillsteaks expertly over his bar-code scanner.

"No".

"Terrible business, finding that young woman's body under the pier."

Mary did a mental check that she wasn't wearing anything that could identify her as a police officer. If Michael twigged that she was connected with the case she'd never get away.

"Yes." Keep it monosyllabic, don't give him anything to engage with. She'd learnt the technique from uncooperative suspects.

"The police are asking for anyone who saw a young woman on or near the seafront last night to come forward."

"Are they?" Good for them. A couple more items and she'd be out of there.

"Yes. Although it's a bit pointless," said Michael, scanning the sliced beans then dropping them deftly into a thin plastic bag, "The victim was never on or near the seafront – she was brought in by boat, probably from Birnbeck."

Mary felt a sudden chill in her stomach.

"Is that what they said on the news?" she asked, trying not to look too interested.

"No, but the media don't tell you everything, do they?" he replied, adding the sorbet to the bag containing the frozen beans, "The other thing is, whoever killed her left her mobile phone behind on the beach – either that or she was alive when they brought her in, and she managed to drop it over the side. I expect Forensics will be drying it out as we speak."

Mary almost replied "yes, they say they'll have it done by mid-day tomorrow", but checked herself in time. She stared at Michael for a moment. He returned her stare, in a way that she found quite spooky.

"Shopper Card?"

"Sorry?"

"Do you have a Shopper Card, madam? The points add up, you know. One of my regular customers got a TV with built-in DVD player last week, on the double-points exchange. Well worth the effort."

"Er, no, sorry," Mary replied, like a confused shopper who didn't understand the double-points exchange, "I must have left it behind."

"No problem. Just keep your receipt and take it to the customer services desk next time you're in. They'll add your points then."

"Fine." Mary offered her debit card, and thought hard. Chatty Michael blathering about the lunchtime news was one thing. Michael with information about boats and phones that only the police or whoever buried the girl would know was something else. She'd done her time on the hotlines, and heard plenty of would-be detectives giving vent to their theories (quite often involving aliens or a secret world government), but this one was different. He seemed so certain, so matter of fact. And, of course, he was probably right.

Out in the entrance lobby, Mary fished her phone from her bag. She looked at her shopping, the box of grillsteaks already beginning to thaw. It was no choice, really. She pressed a button, and put the phone to her ear.

"Guv? Mary. Are you still in the office?"

"Yes, what is it?"

"I've got someone who's been mouthing off about the girl on the beach. Boats, phones – he seems to know things he shouldn't. Could be nothing, but I think we should get him in for a word."

"Now?"

"Yes."

"I thought you were going home?"

"I was on my way."

"Not like you to call in for a swift one, not on your own, anyway. You'll make a detective yet."

"I'm not in the pub. I'm at the supermarket." Mary took a split second to consider the gender stereotype implications of this, then another to decide that life was too short to worry about them right now. "The guy works on the checkout."

"The checkout?" The DI seemed to be taking a moment to digest this information – possibly, Mary thought, because he wasn't all that familiar with checkouts, "And he's dishing out inside information on a murder case along with the petrol vouchers?" He seemed to make his mind up. "It's been a long day, Mary – don't take the piss."

Mary had worked with the DI for a while now. She knew that, provided you weren't actually taking the piss, it was OK to argue your corner.

"I'm not. It was the way he said it – 'she was brought in by boat', 'they left her phone behind', as if he knew it for a fact. He may have got it from someone, overheard it somewhere. I think we should talk to him."

The DI seemed to make his mind up again.

"Or he may be involved. He wouldn't be the first bit-player who couldn't keep his mouth shut. OK, your call, bring him in. I'll put the kettle on."

"Thanks Guv. No sugars."

Mary clicked the 'End Call' button, then a couple of others, typed "Sorry held up, get takeaway, save some 4 me – M", and pressed Send. Parking her trolley, she took a last glance at the grillsteaks and went off to find the supermarket manager.

Chapter 4

Michael Slade sat at the interview room table, a mug of tea in front of him. Opposite sat Mary and the DI. Michael was wearing a green waxed cotton coat, a good quality one of the kind favoured by both admirers and hunters of wildlife. It was the first time Mary had seen him without his supermarket uniform, and it was surprising how different he looked – he could almost have been a slightly down at heel solicitor or estate agent, but for a faraway look in his eyes that didn't quite fit the image.

When she'd walked to the car with him, Mary had noticed a bulge in the jacket's right-hand pocket and remembered that this was a murder case, but she'd thought better of searching him. He was, after all, a member of the public coming in voluntarily (albeit under slight protest about having to miss the rest of his shift), not a hitman from the local Mafia, and frisking him for weapons would hardly have encouraged him to cooperate. She had, however, followed guidelines and added cold water to his tea, to cool it below the temperature at which it would scald them if suddenly thrown. You never could tell.

Mary opened the proceedings. "Now Michael, just to make sure I've got my details right, you're Michael John Slade of Flat 16, 118 Birnbeck Drive, Weston, yes?"

Michael nodded.

"And is it all right if we call you Michael?" She was the checkout operator now.

"Yes, I can't see any reason why not."

"Thank you. I'm Detective Sergeant Mary Miller, and this is Detective Inspector Jones. So you're clear about everything, you haven't been arrested, you're not under caution, and this interview isn't being recorded. You're here voluntarily to help us with our enquiries, and you can leave at any time."

"We appreciate your cooperation, Mr Slade" the DI added drily.

"Can I call you Mary?" asked Michael, "It might help us to develop a rapport, make me feel more relaxed and able to trust you."

Mary and the DI exchanged quick glances.

"Er, yes of course, Michael."

"In that case, Mary, can I say again that I wish you hadn't had me taken off the checkout like that. It'll be all over the store by now that I was taken away by the police, and once that sort of gossip starts it can quickly get out of hand. It could have waited until the end of my shift, surely?"

"We're investigating the murder of a young woman, Mr Slade," said the DI, "I'm afraid that takes priority over other considerations."

Good cop bad cop, thought Mary. How original.

"Don't worry, Michael," she said quickly, "When I spoke to the store manager I stressed that you were a potential witness, and that confidentiality was essential. She'll tell your colleagues that you were called away for a family emergency."

"Oh, I see," Michael said, relaxing slightly in his chair, "Well that may be OK then."

Sensing the DI about to make another interjection, this time about how priorities in crime investigations meant it was definitely OK whether Michael liked it or not, Mary pressed on.

"Michael, we want to talk to you about the young woman whose body was found on the beach this morning."

"In the beach," said Michael, emphasising the 'in'.

"What?"

"In the beach, not on it. She was buried." Michael said it in the same matter-of-fact way that he'd talked about boats and phones at the supermarket. Mary sensed the DI mentally reaching for his handcuffs.

"Why do you say that?" she asked.

"It's obvious."

"What do you mean, obvious?" The DI's voice was the one he used for suspects, not helpful members of the public.

"It just is," said Michael, turning to give the DI the same oddly blank stare that Mary had noticed in the shop. She decided to keep him talking.

"You seem to know a lot of things about this case, Michael. When I came through your checkout, you said that the victim had been brought in by boat, and that her mobile phone had been left behind. Who told you those things?"

"No-one. I worked it out for myself."

"Worked it out?"

"Yes, observation and deduction, like Sherlock Holmes. Elementary, you might say."

If the DI had a weakness, it was a fairly short fuse when confronted with suspects acting cocky. Mary knew that Michael had just lit it.

"I think it would be a good idea if you were less cryptic with us, Michael," she said, adding to herself, "Before my boss takes a serious and permanent dislike to you". Her boss joined in the exchange.

"What the detective sergeant means, Mr Slade," he said, "is that you need to stop playing games with us right now, and start telling us everything you know and where you got it from. Unless a night in the cells appeals, along with your employers being told why you won't be making your shift tomorrow."

"I don't have a shift tomorrow," Michael replied, "I

just work Tuesdays, Wednesdays and Fridays." It sounded as if he was being obtuse, deliberately missing the point of the DI's remark. Mary, however, began to think that it might be something else.

"Michael, this is serious," she said, "You've told us information about a murder case that hasn't been released to the public. If you won't be straight with us about where that information came from we'll have to start treating you as a suspect."

"What, you think I did it? That's ridiculous."

"Accessory," said the DI, "someone who assists in the planning or execution of a crime. Good with boats, are you?"

"No. I get seasick."

"Just very observational then."

"I'm entitled to observe, aren't I?" Michael said, aroused to something like anger now, "This isn't fair. I come here voluntarily to help and within minutes I'm being intimidated with threats of detention. That'll make a good story in the Mercury, won't it?"

Wrong answer. The DI banged his fist on the table.

"Your last chance, Slade. A young woman has been murdered and her body dumped like an animal's. One more clever dick remark from you and I'll have you taken to the cells and we'll start this again in the morning, only this time you will be under caution and you will need a lawyer. Now tell us where you got this information from."

Michael blanched.

"OK, OK. I did observe it, then drew my conclusions from what I'd seen." Seeing the DI's face darken again, he put his hand up in defence. "I was walking into work along the seafront and I saw the police officer hold up the phone and shout to his colleagues. If the phone belonged to the victim, that meant that at some point she'd been further down the beach than where she ended up, which I took to be where the white tent was. That meant that she may have come in from the sea, rather than from the promenade. When I got to the pier I looked at the beach by the sea wall, which hadn't been covered by the tide last night. There were foot and wheel marks everywhere, but nothing that looked like a body being dragged – and the police wouldn't have walked and driven all over it if there had been. So – phone down the beach, no marks at the top of the beach, she was probably brought in by boat."

"Quite the detective, aren't you Mr Slade?" said the DI, not quite managing to keep a note of being genuinely impressed out of his voice.

"I enjoy detective fiction and true crime stories, yes, and I like the intellectual challenge of solving mysteries. That's not an offence either."

"What time was this," said Mary, "when you saw the phone?"

"About two o'clock. My shift started at three. I like to give myself plenty of time."

"And what about her being buried in the beach, Michael? Why do you think that?"

"I saw them taking bags of something out of the tent and putting them in the police Land Rover. From the way the bags hung down they were heavy, as if they had wet sand in them, and there were a lot of them, as if they'd been digging a large hole, big enough for a body. And they'd only be taking it away if they thought it might contain evidence. So she must have been buried."

"Any idea what time?" asked the DI casually.

"I told you, about two o'clock." Michael replied.

"I meant do you have any idea what time the young woman was buried – assuming she was buried, of course."

Good cop, bad cop and now entrapment cop, if only in a very mild form. Against her sense of duty, Mary found herself willing Michael to keep quiet and not to be drawn any further in.

"I'd say some time between 10.15 and 10.45 pm." Michael said helpfully, "High tide was at 11.14pm last night, and since the police didn't seem bothered about churning up the sand around the tent either I assume it had been smoothed over by the tide after the burial gang had done their work. I'd also assume that the gang came in as late as possible to avoid being seen, hence 10.15 to 10.45, although that's purely speculative of course."

Either he really was an innocent observer or he had nerves of steel. In his favour, his timing for seeing the phone was correct, and his logic all made sense – in fact it was pretty much exactly the logic that Mary and the DI had used to reach pretty much the same conclusions. However the DI clearly wasn't satisfied.

"Can you tell us exactly where you were on the promenade when you saw the officer on the beach holding something up, Mr Slade?"

"Opposite the Winter Gardens."

The DI and Mary looked at each other, then back at Michael.

"How could you make out that it was a mobile phone, all the way from there?" asked the DI incredulously, "He could have been holding anything up."

"No, I saw clearly that it was a phone – a BlackBerry with a QWERTY keyboard." Michael looked at the DI, then at Mary, and seemed to decide that something more was required of him. "The Bold model, I think," he added, "rather than a Curve."

For the second time that day, Mary thought, she'd found herself watching a man digging himself into a hole.

"Mr Slade, if you were by the Winter Gardens you must have been 200 metres from that officer. At that distance you wouldn't have been able to tell whether he was holding up a mobile phone or a packet of cigarettes, let alone whether it was a BlackBerry or not. Got superhuman vision, have you?"

"No, although my eyesight is very good for my age. It runs in my father's family."

Mary sensed the need to play good cop. Urgently.

"Michael, it would have been impossible for you to make out that detail at that distance. So how did you see it? And how did you see the bags closely enough to work out that they contained sand?" A possible explanation occurred to her. "Did you go on the beach and cross the police tape to get nearer? If you did, then it's better to tell us now. It won't be the end of the world."

Not unless the DI uses it as his only excuse to nick him, that is.

"I didn't cross the tape," Michael said indignantly, "I wouldn't do that. I don't know what you seem to think of me, but I respect police procedure, and the job you do. I stayed on the prom the entire time."

"Then how did you see the phone?"

Michael hesitated, then reached into the bulging jacket pocket. He pulled out a green case, opened it and withdrew a pair of expensive-looking binoculars.

"With these."

The DI reached slowly forward and took them.

"Nice glasses."

"Yes, it's worth investing in quality where optics are concerned. These ones are compact and lightweight, and they let a lot of light in too."

"I've used binoculars myself, Mr Slade – had training on them, in fact. It's difficult to keep them stable enough to see fine detail, even lightweight ones like these. Skilled in this kind of thing, are you?"

"No, but I don't need to be." Michael pointed to a switch on the side of the glasses, "These have image stabilisation, like a digital camera. It's amazingly effective."

Touché, thought Mary. Time for some more good cop.

"What do you use these for, Michael?"

"Some birdwatching – we get a few interesting species on their way to the Wetlands Trust. Mostly shipping though, to and from Avonmouth and Cardiff."

Mary could read the DI's thoughts: "and women undressing with the curtains open on Knightstone, or couples in the car park down the road from where you live."

Somehow though she didn't think so.

"And you carry them with you wherever you go?"

"Not always, no. I took them today because I'd seen the report on the lunchtime news – that nice woman from the BBC. I like her, don't you? She's been with them a long time, sounds as if she's really interested in the region. I saw you on the news too, Inspector." Michael's last sentence was said in a way which made it clear that the DI hadn't made as favourable an impression as the BBC reporter.

The DI held Michael's binoculars up.

"Do you mind if we hang on to these for a day or two, Mr Slade? Just to check a couple of things."

"I suppose not. Going to check whether I really could have seen the phone from the promenade, I assume?"

The DI looked at him with something almost like respect.

"Something like that, yes. We have to check everything, I'm sure you understand. That's how we work."

"I do understand, yes. Can I have a receipt?"

"Of course. The detective sergeant will give you one."

Mary assumed that was the end of the interview, and began to collect her things together, but the DI continued.

"Are you married, Mr Slade?"

"Yes, but my wife and I are living semi-independently at the moment."

"Why's that then?"

"We're just sorting a few things out. We think it's best to be separate while we're doing it."

"What sort of things?"

"I don't actually see that that's relevant to your investigation, Inspector, but since I'm sure you'll tell me it is, I'll tell you anyway. I'm not certain that the styles of life my wife and I want are compatible. I need to be on my own for a while."

Mid-life crisis, thought Mary. And I bet he thinks he's the only one.

"Have you got any children?"

"Two."

"And they're with their mother?"

"Yes."

"Where's that then?"

"Bridgwater."

"See them often?"

"Every weekend."

"Good."

"I think so, yes. No child asks to be born - parents should take responsibility for their actions."

"Quite so, Mr Slade," said the DI, seeming genuinely satisfied by Michael's commitment to parenthood. He hadn't quite finished yet though. "You say you just work three days a week at the supermarket. That can't cover the bills, can it, especially with a couple of kiddies to think about? Do you do any other work?"

"Yes, some software development. Mainly back-end applications."

"What does that involve?"

"I write code that interacts with databases when people log on to ecommerce websites."

"And who do you do that for?"

"Mainly financial sector - banks, insurance companies. You want to buy an insurance policy, my code aggregates data from a variety of sources then calculates the risk. Same with a loan application."

"Surely those firms have their own people to 'write code', don't they?"

"They get me in for difficult jobs. Though I say it myself, I'm very good, especially with heterogeneous data sources."

"Sounds very impressive, Mr Slade", said the DI, with just enough emphasis on "sounds" to show that he wasn't convinced either way on whether Michael was highly skilled or just delusional, "So why aren't you doing it full-time, making a fortune like all these IT consultants we read about?"

"I used to do it full-time."

"But not any more?"

"No."

"So where do you do this computer work?"

"My flat."

"You program the computer systems of banks and insurance companies from a bedsit in Birnbeck?"

"It's not a bedsit. It's got a separate living room and bedroom. It's very comfortable, actually. I've got a laptop and a broadband connection, that's all I need. I connect using point to point tunnelling protocol with 256-bit encryption, if you're concerned about security."

"Security would be the bank's concern, not ours," said Mary, "although it does seem a rather unorthodox arrangement."

"What, 256-bit PPTP? Lots of people use it these days."

"No, I mean you working from home for these big financial institutions."

"It is quite unusual, but it works. I'm known to them,

you see. I have a track record, which is what counts with corporate clients."

"Is it well paid?"

"Reasonably, yes."

"And yet you work three days a week in a supermarket?" The DI made it sound like a suspicious activity.

"That's different. I really like my job."

"Working on the checkout? My sister's kid does it weekends and hates every minute."

Mary came in again. "Do you like it because you get to meet people?"

Michael's face lit up.

"Absolutely. All sorts. I think customers really appreciate the human touch, a bit of conversation, especially the ones who live alone. For some of my regulars I'm the only human contact they get. That's terrible, isn't it?"

"Yes it is. Michael, have you ever had your IQ tested?"

The DI shot a 'what the...?' glance in Mary's direction.

"Yes, at school when I was 16."

"What was your score?"

"174."

Even the DI looked impressed.

"That's very high, isn't it?"

"Top 0.5 percentile."

"Did you go on to university?"

"No, I was bored with school by the time I did my A levels. I was interested in computers, so I got a job as a trainee programmer."

"Where was that?"

"Agricultural merchants in Taunton. I wrote their bulk feed delivery system when I was 19. It worked so well they gave me a £1,000 bonus."

"Still, can't be many people with your IQ working on

the checkouts." said the DI.

"Oh you'd be very surprised, Inspector," Michael replied, "high IQ doesn't necessarily make you a boffin, or rich for that matter. Lots of highly intelligent people do ordinary jobs. It's not their jobs that define them."

Touché again, thought Mary. Best to wrap things up quickly.

"Well Michael," she said, glancing at the DI, "I think that's all we need for now." She waited to see if the DI contradicted her, but he didn't. "Thank you very much for coming in. We've got your details in case we need to contact you again, and of course we'll be returning your binoculars. Now if you'll come with me I'll get you a receipt for them, and arrange a car to take you home – or back to work if you prefer."

"I'll walk, thanks. I don't think I'll go back to work – that wouldn't fit with the family crisis story, would it? Probably go to the pub. There might be a quiz on."

"As you wish – this way."

"Goodbye Mr Slade. Take care now."

"I will, Inspector."

Mary walked with Michael to the front desk, noting his odd, slightly loping gait as she followed him down the corridor. Suddenly she felt slightly sorry for him, dragged off his supermarket till in front of colleagues and customers, just for airing his theories like bar-room lawyers all over Weston would be doing that evening. And to be fair to him he had been right, very sharp in fact – a distinct cut above the average amateur crime expert who got his evidence from the front pages of the tabloids, along with the prejudices that pointed him towards the 'obvious' suspects. As they reached the front lobby, she held out her hand.

"Thanks again, Michael – and sorry for any embarrassment at work, but I'm sure your manager will be discreet. We'll get your binoculars back to you as soon as we can."

"You haven't given me a receipt for them yet." Michael sounded more hurt than suspicious, as if she'd broken a promise.

"Oh yes of course – I'm sorry. Just hang on here and I'll get one." There was no-one on the desk but she found a uniform PC reading a paper in the room off it. Asking him if he didn't have anything better to do (was she turning into the DI?), she searched for a printed receipt book but found nothing, so settled for a sheet of headed Constabulary stationery. Back at the desk she found Michael standing there, staring at nothing in particular with that strange, vacant look she'd noticed upstairs.

"We don't seem to have any official receipt forms, but I can write one out on this. Will that do?" She held up the headed notepaper.

"Yes, that's OK."

She put the paper on the desk and started writing. "Received from Michael Slade, one pair binoculars for examination." He stopped her and insisted that she include the make and model, which she did. She thought for a moment, then reached into her jacket pocket, pulled out a business card and offered it to him.

"My mobile number's on there – if you get any problems at work, ring me and I'll come and put them straight, emphasise that you were interviewed purely as a potential witness. I'll give them the speech about how we rely on conscientious citizens like you coming forward to help solve serious crime. You'll be the hero of the hour, don't worry."

"OK. Goodbye then, Mary."

"Goodbye."

When Mary got back to the squad room the DI was in his office, putting his things into his briefcase. He shouted to her through the open door.

"What do you think?"

Mary poked her head round the door, latching her bag closed as she did.

"Harmless, Guv."

"Or a serial killer getting his kicks by going into the opposition's lair and acting dumb."

"Well he hardly acted dumb, did he? Drew attention to his cleverness, more like."

"Weird then. Did you buy that high IQ business?"

"Yes. I remembered something in the paper about a man with genius-level IQ who sweeps the roads, says it leaves his mind free for his own thoughts. That's why I asked Michael if he'd had his tested. I've seen him a few times in the supermarket too. Some customers avoid him because he talks so much – I do normally - but the pensioners love him, queue up for their chats. He's a bit odd, but I don't see him being involved in anything like our murder."

"Check him out anyway – see if he's known in Bridgwater, check if Social Services have got an interest in the family. And find the uniform who picked up the phone, get him to stand exactly where he found it so you can check whether our local genius could have seen it."

"Will do. Anything else?"

"No, sod off home. And don't stop at any supermarkets this time."

"No chance of that, Guv. Night."

way to the beach. The white tent was gone; the tide would have washed it away if it had been left. Instead the hole had been filled in and the area left taped off, if only to stop people posting ghoulish murder scene videos on YouTube. It was guarded by two uniforms who'd at least had the shelter of the Land Rover overnight, although Mary dreaded to think what the air quality would be like in there by now.

Mary felt sorry for Durham as he made off down the beach to the place where he'd found the phone, and thought she could hear his teeth chattering when he called her to report that he was at the location, although it was hard to tell with all the buffeting from the wind. By now she and Lane were opposite the Winter Gardens pavilion, the location from which Michael claimed to have seen the phone. Reaching it, they looked across the beach. PC Durham was a tiny figure in the distance, standing two-thirds of the way down the pier, just to the right of one of the big metal pillars that supported it.

Mary passed her phone to Lane, then unzipped the binoculars case and took out Michael's glasses. She slid the switch marked 'IS' to the 'on' position, put the binoculars to her eyes and swept the beach until she found PC Durham.

"Tell him to hold his phone up." Mary stood there for a half a minute, saying nothing as she concentrated on what she was seeing through the glasses.

"OK, you have a look." She took the phone from Lane and handed him the binoculars.

Lane found Durham, looked for a few seconds, then took the glasses from his eyes.

"Strewth, it's like magic. The image is solid as a rock."
"Could you see the phone?"
"Easily."
"Well enough to see what make it was?"
"I could see the remains of young Durham's breakfast

on his teeth, Sarge, never mind the make of phone."

"Yes, same here. Looks like Mr Slade's story holds up, so far at least."

Taking the glasses, Mary focussed again on Durham, who was still standing to attention holding his phone up.

"Tell him to go up to the Land Rover and carry the bags". At this point a flaw in the plan emerged, namely that with his phone held aloft and the wind howling round him, Durham couldn't hear Lane trying to talk to him. In the end it took a call to the station and a message to Durham's radio, but eventually the young PC made it back to the tent.

Mary watched him through the binoculars as he walked from where the tent had been to the vehicle, his phone clasped to his ear this time, a spare materials bag full of sand grasped in his other hand.

"OK tell him to do it again. You watch him this time."

Lane instructed the constable, took the glasses and watched as he made the walk again.

"OK thanks, PC Durham," said Mary, "Wait there, we'll be with you soon." She turned to Lane.

"What do you think?"

"Clear as a bell, Sarge. Pretty obviously sand in the bag too."

"Yes, I thought that. OK, let's get back."

"Wouldn't mind a pair of those myself, Sarge."

"What would you use a pair of binoculars for, Tony?"

"Birdwatching, that sort of thing." He was looking across to Knightstone Island.

Mary slipped the binoculars back into their case. As they set off back along the promenade she looked around her, half-expecting to see Michael Slade watching them, but she didn't see him anywhere.

Back at the station Mary found the DI in his office, an expression of what looked worryingly like defeat on his face. She wasn't sure the news she had for him would be especially welcome, but decided to get it over with anyway.

"We checked the binoculars, Guv," she said, "Slade definitely could have seen the phone, including what make it was, and the bags being taken to the Land Rover." She decided that a bit of empathy wouldn't go amiss, and added "although of course that doesn't mean he did."

"No, it looks like he's clean," replied the DI, allowing just the tiniest hint of regret into his voice, "Cox has checked him out. His form amounts to two parking tickets, both paid on time. Bridgwater CID have never heard of him, neither have Social Services."

"So do we forget about him?"

"Not completely. He's not on the suspect list, but keep him mind. I don't like people snooping on us through binoculars."

"OK. Talking of which, Guv, can I get those glasses back to him now? Tony Lane's taken a fancy to them and I don't want them getting 'borrowed' and damaged."

"What use has Lane got for a pair of binoculars?"

"Birdwatching, he says."

"Get them back to Slade. First though you might as well read these." The DI opened his desk drawer and pulled out a thin file, removed two sets of papers from it and handed them to Mary. "Bad news or not particularly good news – take your pick."

Mary picked one at random, and found herself reading what she assumed, or at least hoped, was the bad news. It was Technical Services' report on the phone from the beach, saying that it had contained no SIM card (and thus no phone number) and that while the internal memory had dried out OK, it had been wiped in a particularly thorough way ("not just a standard user-selected factory reset") which meant they could get nothing from it, not even the IMEI number that was supposed to uniquely identify the handset. Forensics had taken a look at it on the way through, and added "no identifiable prints" to the report. Between them, some specialist gadgetry and the muddy waters of the Bristol Channel had cleaned it in more ways than one.

The other report was from the pathology lab. They'd received the toxicology results on the beach murder victim, which confirmed the cause of death as a heart attack brought on by a massive overdose of barbiturates. The report also confirmed no signs of recent sexual activity, consensual or otherwise, and noted slight bruising to the upper left arm, consistent with being grabbed roughly and possibly dragged. Time of death was now estimated at "some time" on the morning of the day before she'd been found, a more precise figure being difficult to estimate because of the effect of cold temperatures on the progress of rigor mortis. It was almost certain that she was dead before being put in the ground though.

Mary looked up and saw the DI watching her.

"They don't exactly move the investigation forward, do they?" he said.

"No Guv." Now she understood why he looked defeated.

The DI took the papers from her and put them back in the file. "We're in danger of being stuffed here," he said, "If we don't get a lead on this soon they're going to take some of the Murder Squad off the Bristol student case and send them down here. Then we'll be in the doghouse twice – once for letting them get one over on us, and again for taking resources from the case that's got the media on the Chief Constable's back."

He opened the drawer again and brought out a plastic bag with a tag on it. Inside was the phone from the beach, clearly identifiable as a BlackBerry by its distinctive shape and rows of tiny keys. It was the first time Mary had seen it.

"Tech sent this back with their report," said the DI, in a way that told her they'd put it on a bike and charged it to his budget, "they reckon there's no point in them hanging on to it. Not much use to us, either - get it booked into Evidence, will you?"

"Yes, Guv. Can we really get nothing from it?"

"You've read the report. Clean as a whistle, and done professionally."

"OK, I'll take it down now." Mary got up, took the bag from the desk and turned to leave. As she did, the DI spoke again.

"Mary."

"Yes, Guv?"

"You're my front line on this case. Get us something - whatever it takes."

"Yes, Guv."

Mary put the evidence bag on her desk and looked at the phone inside it. The DI was right - it gave them absolutely nothing, to add to the nothing they already had from Forensics, the TV appeal, CCTV and Missing Persons. Looking up she saw Lane at the window, admiring something through Michael Slade's binoculars. She went over and took them from him, doing her best, for both their sakes, to avoid seeming like a school mistress disciplining a naughty child. Back at her desk, she fished out the notes she'd made on Slade's interview. She sat for a moment, thinking things over again, then dialled his mobile number.

"Hello, is that Michael Slade?"

"Yes, who's this?"

"Mary Miller, from Weston CID."

"Oh yes." He didn't sound over-pleased to hear from her.

"We've finished with your binoculars, Michael, so I'd like to get them back to you."

"Your tests confirmed what I told you, I assume?"

"We've done all the tests we need, for now at least. I was thinking, I have to go out anyway, so I could bring them round to you now. Are you at home?"

"Yes, but we could meet somewhere else. A cafe, perhaps."

"Oh, I wouldn't want to drag you out on your day off."

"It's no problem – I like to get out."

"Would you rather I didn't come to your flat?"

"I haven't got anything to hide, if that's what you mean."

"No, no, I'm sorry, I didn't mean that. I just thought that if I brought the binoculars to your place, then you wouldn't have to carry them round with you for the rest of the morning. They're quite valuable, and delicate I imagine."

"They're fairly robust, actually. Lightweight yet solid construction, as modern technology often is. But I take your point. OK then, bring them here. How long will you be?"

"Ten minutes."

"I'll expect you then." A slight pause. "Shall I put the kettle on?"

"Yes, that would be very nice." It meant he wasn't going to just take the binoculars and shut the door on her. "No sugars for me thanks."

"You haven't said whether you'd like tea or coffee. Some people take sugar in one but not the other."

"Oh yes, sorry Michael." She was beginning to learn this game. "Tea please."

"Tea it is then. Goodbye."

Mary kept a carrier bag next to her desk, a thick plastic one with looped handles. It advertised one of the more upmarket home furnishing chains, but had spent most of its life carrying stolen goods, other evidence and even the occasional deadly weapon back from the scenes of crimes that were too small to warrant attendance by a SOCO. Mary looked round the office and saw that no-one was paying any particular attention to her. She double checked that the DI was busy with his back to her, updating the whiteboard on his office wall. Then she paused for a moment, thought one more time, and filled the bag. Grabbing it, along with her coat and handbag, she headed out to the car park.

Chapter 6

Mary knew the Birnbeck area well, as did most police officers in Weston. Spread across the hillside at the northern end of the town, it was filled with huge, bay-windowed Victorian and Edwardian terraces, positioned to look out over the bay. At its western end was Weston's original pier, built in the 19th century to allow steamers from Cardiff to dock, a major trade on Sundays when Welsh pubs were closed.

Birnbeck Pier was now derelict though, as were quite a few buildings in the vicinity, and most of the big houses that hadn't fallen into dereliction had been converted into flats, hotels or hostels. Yet in the gaps between the terraces there were smart infill developments of modern houses and flats, and the old boarding school above the pier was being converted into luxury dwellings with magnificent views over the Bristol Channel. It was an area simultaneously up-and-coming and in decline.

118 Birnbeck Drive was old and new Birnbeck combined. The old part was a former Nurses' Home which had been turned into flats and bedsits of the kind where tenancies tended to be short and DSS payments were not only accepted but the norm. Although not technically a hostel, in practice it was used by a string of Social Services departments as a halfway house for clients who were assessed as ready to manage on their own. Mary had been there a few times for minor drug busts and the odd case of petty theft, while uniform dealt with a regular stream of domestics. Hearing Michael state it as his address had caused the DI to raise an eyebrow in a way that clearly said "suspect".

Mary found, however, that Michael's flat wasn't in the main building, but in the much newer extension on the side that came complete with double glazing and its own front door. There was even an entryphone, with a button labelled 'Slade' in clear computer printout, cut neatly to size. Mary pressed it and waited.

"Hello?"

"Hello Michael, it's Mary Miller."

"Come up – first floor, on the right."

The door mechanism buzzed, and Mary went in. Inside it was nothing like the rest of the building; while the main part of 118 was a rabbit warren of windowless corridors and heavy fire doors, here there was an open staircase and natural light. It could almost have been one of the apartment blocks that lined the seafront, but for the cheap plywood doors and pile of junk mail on the carpet.

Michael was waiting for Mary as she reached the top of the stairs.

"You found it OK then."

"Oh yes, I know this part of Weston."

"No, I meant my flat. I forgot to tell you to come to the side entrance. Most people go to the other one then get lost in the corridors."

"I was lucky, I spotted the sign on the wall as I drove up."

"Good observation – part of being a detective, I suppose."

Part of her early uniform training actually - "when attending a block of flats, make sure you get the right one, especially if you're going to force entry."

"Something like that, yes."

Michael ushered Mary through to the living room. It was pretty much what she'd expected for Mid Life Crisis Man – sparsely furnished, filled with signs of the Man's interests (computers, music and motorsport in this case), not entirely clean. It was a nice flat though, small but light, with glimpses of the sea through the main window. With a few homely touches it could be very pleasant.

There was a two seater sofa, and a chair of the kind found in old peoples' homes, with an upholstered seat and wooden arms. In between them was a low coffee table bearing an assortment of computer magazines, a laptop computer folded shut and two china mugs. Michael beckoned Mary to the chair.

"Yours is the blue one. Tea no sugar?"

"Yes, thanks very much."

Michael sat down, sinking low into the sofa so that his knees were bunched up halfway to his chest. Mary couldn't prevent her copper's instincts recording a quick description: brown leather shoes (quite large for his height – size 10 perhaps?), dark grey trousers, blue round-necked pullover with a striped shirt collar protruding, collar-length straight fair hair. He could be an off-duty accountant, or someone who'd bought the accountant's old clothes from a charity shop. It was hard to tell.

"Are you OK on that sofa, Michael? It looks a bit low for you. I don't mind swapping places."

"I'm fine thanks. This sofa came from our old house in Bridgwater – it was all we had when we were first married, so I had to get used to it. You're my guest, so you should have the chair, although if it had been your Detective Inspector I'd probably have made him sit here." Michael gave an odd nasal laugh, an old-fashioned chortling sound like something from a Boys Own paper, as if he found the idea of DI Jones sitting hunched up on the low sofa particularly hilarious. Mary said nothing, but permitted herself a brief smile.

"Here are your binoculars," she said, reaching into her carrier bag, "Thanks for letting us keep them. They were greatly admired in the squad room – I had to stop one of our DCs from running off with them." She instantly regretted the last remark, worried that Michael might interpret it literally as evidence of police corruption, but he seemed unconcerned.

"It's OK, I've secretly programmed them to send back GPS data identifying their location. I'd soon have found them." For a moment it was Mary doing the literal interpretation, until she realised that he was joining in with the joke.

"Oh, good."

There was a brief, awkward silence. Mary didn't want the interview to end, but wasn't sure about broaching the next subject. She sipped her tea, looked round the room, thought of something to say.

"Is this where you do your computer programming, or do you work in the bedroom?"

This time it was a mistake. Michael's face clouded.

"I'm not breaking any rules, if that's what you mean. I work here, as it happens" - he indicated the laptop on the table - "so this room is primarily residential with partial use for the occupant's business purposes. My landlord's fine about it as long as I don't have clients visiting the premises. Same with business rates."

"No, no, sorry, I didn't mean anything like that." She was losing control of the exchange, which wasn't like her. Deep breath, start again. "I was just interested. This idea of you programming those big banks' computers from your living room – I still can't quite take it on board."

He seemed satisfied.

"It's simple really. To them my laptop is a terminal, like the ones in their offices, only it happens to be connected via the Internet instead of a local cable. In terms of what I can do on it, it makes no difference whether it's in the City of London or Birnbeck – or India, for that matter."

"Oh. I still find that amazing. Mind you, I'm not that good with computers. I get one of our DCs to do any complicated stuff."

Mary realised, to her own astonishment, that she'd sounded close to playing the helpless woman. This was heading off the rails; perhaps she should go.

Michael smiled. "The one who wanted to make off with my binoculars, or a different one?"

"Pardon?"

"The DC you get to do the computer work? Is it the same one who liked my binoculars?"

"No, someone else. Look, thanks for the tea, I'd better be..."

Michael cut across her, not roughly but distinctly all the same.

"Are there any developments in the murder case? BBC News seem to have gone quiet about it. I suppose you can't tell me, even if there are."

Subject broached, but it was Michael, hunched on the sofa, who seemed to be controlling the conversation. Mary hesitated. This might not be necessary after all - the DI might be back at the station right now with the big breakthrough that would solve the case. Or he might not. Whatever it takes.

"Actually, Michael, I did want to talk to you about the case – to show you something, in fact. But before I do I need you to promise me that you won't tell anyone you've seen it, or that I've discussed it with you. Not your friends, or your family, and least of all anyone at the supermarket. If it got out I could be in big trouble." She'd thought of saying 'we', but she was learning not to play at psychology with Michael Slade.

"What is it you want to show me?"

"A piece of evidence. I shouldn't show it to you because..."

"I'm a suspect?"

"because you've been interviewed as a potential witness. The defence would say we'd coached you to recognise it. Even if it had no impact on the case the judge might still rule a mistrial – they're so sensitive these days."

"OK, I won't say anything to anyone. You have my word."

Mary knew how much faith the DI would have in Michael's word, but it was all she had, and despite the unsettling circumstances her instinct still told her to go ahead. She reached into her carrier again, and pulled out a transparent evidence bag.

"I assume it's the phone I saw your officer pick up on the beach?" said Michael. Mary nodded. "Why do you want me to look at it?"

"Because we can't get anything from it. There's no SIM card, no prints or fibres, apparently they've even wiped the serial number. Here's the report from our labs." She looked at him carefully, then handed him the papers. Goodbye career if she was getting this wrong.

"I still don't see why you want to show it to me, especially if you're not supposed to. Someone with a suspicious mind might think you were trying to get my prints on it, or something like that."

From his perspective, Mary thought, it was a fair point.

"No, honestly Michael, it's nothing like that. We don't do things that way in Weston. I'll be completely straight with you – we don't have anything, not even the victim's identity. I just thought, well, you seem very good at spotting things and working things out from them. Observation and deduction, as you put it. I was hoping you'd spot something on this phone."

"That the police haven't?"

"Something like that."

Suddenly Mary saw Michael transformed into a schoolboy who'd been given his dream Christmas present, eleven months early. She didn't know if this was good or bad.

"Can I take it out of the bag?"

"No – in fact wear these gloves even to handle the bag." She fished a pair of disposable gloves from her handbag.

Michael pulled the gloves on, and Mary gave him the evidence bag. He peered through the polythene at the phone inside, and pressed some of its buttons.

"It is the Bold, as I thought. 9900, by the look of it" He glanced down at the report, "I'm not surprised they wiped the IMEI code – that's the first thing anyone would do." He saw Mary's puzzled look. "International Mobile Equipment Identity - the serial number. Useless scheme, put up by the hardware manufacturers to avoid the cost of burning a serial number permanently into the silicon. Instead they stick it in Flash memory and you can wipe it using a laptop."

Like the one sitting on your table, Mary thought, but chose not to dwell on it.

"According to your labs, they've done a thorough job on it – wiped the internal memory to Department of Defense standards, the lot. I don't expect I could get anything from it, even if I could plug it in. I'm sure your technical people know what they're doing."

Mary thought of the tetchy nerds at Tech Services and wasn't so sure, but didn't dwell on that either. It looked like being a wasted journey; she just hoped it wouldn't turn out to be an expensive one.

"Oh well, thanks for looking at it. Just remember what I said about keeping it to yourself, please."

Michael didn't respond. He was still examining the phone through the polythene, pressing its buttons.

"I can tell you one thing about this phone though,

Mary."

"What's that?"

"Whoever's been using it typed a lot of text, in a language that probably wasn't English."

Mary felt the hairs rise on her neck.

"What makes you say that?"

"The big thing about BlackBerrys is that they have physical keyboards – real buttons, a separate one for each letter." He angled the bag so Mary could see the front of the phone, "I find them fiddly, but a lot of people still prefer them to things like the iPhone, where the keys are just images on a touchscreen, with no tactile feedback. One downside of real keys, though, is that they wear out if you use them a lot."

He stretched the polythene over the phone's keyboard so the keys were clearly visible, then continued.

"It's the letters and numbers on the keys that wear off first, before the actual contacts. But they don't all wear at the same rate."

Mary had a good idea why the keys on a keyboard didn't all wear at the same rate, but sensed that Michael would enjoy telling her anyway.

"Why is that?"

"Because the letters of the alphabet aren't all used with the same frequency. Depending on the language, some letters get used a lot more than others. For example, if you analyse a typical piece of English text you'll find that Es account for around 12% of all the letters - significantly more than any other letter, including the other vowels. So if a keyboard has been used a lot to type in English, you'd expect the 'E' key to have worn off before any other letter."

"And that isn't how this one's worn?"

"No, look." Mary leaned forward and peered through the polythene. "You can see that the A and I are at least as worn as the E, if not more so. That's not what you'd expect from English use."

"Any idea what language it has been used for?"

"Not off the top of my head, no. Not French or German, because they use E even more – 17% in German." He thought for a moment, then lifted up the lid of his laptop computer. "But I know where we can look."

Mary was side-on to the computer so couldn't see it properly, just the light reflecting on Michael's face as it came to life. He typed in some text, hands darting over the keys at impressive speed. Then he turned the computer sideways so that they could both see the screen. On it was a table of figures, with columns headed by names of languages, and rows labelled with the letters of the alphabet.

"Here we are – Polish. 'E' 6.9%, 'I' 7%, 'A' 8%. That matches the wear pattern on this phone perfectly."

Mary was agog. Somehow in about 45 seconds they'd gone from a no-clues phone in a plastic bag to an Internet page telling them what language its owner had written their messages in.

"Polish?"

"Yes. That is only a guess though – there could be other factors, such as the way the user holds the phone. They might even have been typing in other character sets, Japanese or something. Polish is the simplest explanation though."

Elementary, my dear Watson.

"Why didn't our tech people spot this? Why didn't I spot it, for that matter? It seems obvious, now that you've explained it."

"No, it's easy to miss", he replied, holding up the phone again, "you see, the 'E' is worn, as you'd expect - it's just not any more worn than the 'A' or 'I'".

"And you didn't miss that."

"Ah well, I've got a special interest in letter

frequency."

Two days earlier, Mary wouldn't have believed that anyone outside of a secure unit would actually say something like that.

"Why, Michael?" she asked, hoping she'd kept the thought out of her voice.

"Cryptography – it's been an interest of mine since I was at school. Frequency analysis is the first step to breaking a simple code, especially if you know what language it represents. The first modern computers were built for code breaking, of course - Bletchley Park, all of that – so it all fits together for me."

"But do you really carry the frequency of letters of the alphabet around in your head?"

"Only the vowels, and only some languages." Michael smiled. He might have been joking with her, but she was too distracted by Polish letter frequencies to tell. "German was a fairly significant language in World War II code breaking circles – on this side of the English Channel, at least." He paused for a brief chortling laugh, "Frequency analysis was no use against the Enigma machines, but it worked with lower-grade ciphers. Being so E-heavy helped at lot. Would you like more tea?"

Mary declined the offer of more tea. She had work to do, urgently, back at the office. She asked Michael if he could see anything else about the phone that might be relevant, and when he said no, thanked him very much for his help, repeated her request that he tell no-one about it, put the gloves and evidence bag back in her carrier and left the flat. As she walked down the road to her car she looked back and saw him watching her from his window. He waved; she raised her hand in acknowledgement, and turned away. Driving back across the seafront, she remembered how she'd visited an osteopath a few years earlier with back trouble, and left each session of kneading, pulling and twisting feeling shaken up but hopeful that it had done some good. She felt roughly the same about her session with Michael, only the manipulation had been mental rather than physical.

Chapter 7

When Mary reached the station she went straight to the basement and booked the phone into the Evidence store. The date and time were recorded, but it was barely an hour since the DI had handed it to her, well within the bounds of having simply had other things to do first. On her way upstairs she visited the Ladies and dumped the disposable gloves in the bin, dropping some paper towels in after them. It was lunchtime, and the squad room was half empty, but the DI was in his office. As she reached her desk he called through to her.

"Where have you been?"

From the DI's tone, Mary guessed that he hadn't got a big breakthrough while she'd been away. She went to his door to answer him. This might not be a conversation she wanted heard by anyone else.

"Getting those binoculars back to Michael Slade, Guv, like you said."

"You took them to him? I meant leave them at the front desk, not deliver them to his front door. We're not UPS."

"It was a chance to get a look inside his flat, suss him out a bit more."

The DI considered this and his manner changed to cautious approval.

"Fair enough. What was it like?"

"Classic split-up bachelor pad. Not much furniture, not much cleaning, probably a stack of takeaway cartons in the kitchen."

"Probably?"

"I only saw the living room. I put my foot in it asking him where he did his computer work, and he thought I was after him for business rates. The guided tour was off after that. The flat's in the modern extension bit, not the old building – sea view and everything. Nice little place really."

"Are you thinking of renting one or something?"

"No."

"So what's your view of Mr Slade now you've seen him in his natural habitat?"

"I still think he's harmless. A bit odd, but that goes with the high IQ thing. Basically an amateur sleuth with a good pair of binoculars and an above-average ability to put two and two together." She stopped, not wanting to lay it on too thickly.

"Hmm, I'm still not convinced. Shame you didn't get to see the rest of his place. We still keep him in mind, OK?"

"Yes, Guv."

Mary went back to her desk and switched on her computer. The big Constabulary symbol flashed onto the screen, and with it a message asking her to log on. Leaving a copy of your password in your desk was a disciplinary offence; Mary searched the pockets of her bag until she found the slip of paper, then typed the code in and put the paper back in her bag. She knew what she had to do, but had little idea of how to do it – the truth was that she was, indeed, fairly helpless when it came to computers, although she put that down to the generally poor design of IT systems rather than her own capabilities. Nevertheless, after taking the risk of showing the phone to Michael Slade, she had to chase the one possible lead he'd given her, that the victim might be Polish. The obvious place to start was Polish Missing Persons, which she knew they could access online under an EU-wide cooperation initiative. She'd just have to do her best.

After a quarter of an hour getting nowhere, Mary weighed up the situation. As she'd said to Michael Slade, she normally got one of her DCs to do things like this. The DC in question, Pete Cox, was sitting ten feet away from her, his lunchtime sub roll just finished. Cox was as good with IT systems as he was on the phone (even better, in fact). He'd be logged into Polish Missing Persons in less time than it would take her to get the weather forecast for North Somerset, but getting him involved, especially in something as unusual as an international missing persons search, would make it very likely that the whole thing would get back to the DI, which she didn't want to happen unless the search produced a result. On the other hand, if she didn't get Cox's help, there probably wouldn't be a search at all. Whatever it takes.

"Pete."

"Yes, Sarge?"

"Can you give me a hand with something? Bring your chair."

As Cox approached, Mary wheeled her chair back so he could put his in front of her desk.

"What's up?"

"Can we access international missing persons from here – EU, that is?"

"Yes, I'm pretty sure we can. Soon find out, anyway."

"Good. Can you give it a try?"

"Sure – where shall I start? France, Germany?"

"No, Poland."

"OK. Is this for the murder - have you got a lead, Sarge?"

"Just a hunch. Something someone said."

Cox was already at Mary's keyboard, working his way through a series of screens and menus. They were still at an English-language website called the European Criminal Intelligence Gateway, but as far as Mary was concerned it might as well have already been in Polish.

"We might have to get the DI to log in for this," said Cox, then seeing her quizzical look added, "authorisation level."

Mary suppressed a stab of panic. If accessing the Polish database needed the DI's authorisation code, should she abort it - in which case what did she tell Cox? - or face explaining to the Guvnor why she wanted to search Polish records for a girl of Mediterranean appearance found buried in an English beach?

"No, it's OK," Cox's voice brought her attention back to the screen, "your credit's good, Sarge. We're in."

This time the website really was in Polish, which neither of them understood. Cox managed to find his way through the menus though, to a screen filled with passport-sized images of people, some evidently taken from holiday snaps, others more official. A row of numbers above the photographs indicated that this was the first of many pages. They began to scroll through them.

At the bottom of the screen, a time display indicated how long they'd been logged into the system. Exactly three minutes and forty-six seconds after reaching the Polish Missing Persons database, on page 18 of 104, they were looking at the unidentified woman whose body had been recovered from the beach, only now she had a name.

Chapter 8

"Katya Czwisnjowski, Guv."

"Katya who?"

"Ka-chiz-knee-ovski," said Mary, spelling the surname out phonetically, "reported missing in Gdansk a week ago. It's definitely her – identifying marks match the Path report."

The DI looked up from the computer printout Mary had given him. He didn't look quite as pleased as she might have expected.

"Gdansk?"

"Poland, Guv."

"I know where it is". He looked down at the printout again. "And where did this come from?"

"Polish Missing Persons database – Pete Cox helped me access it."

"It's all in Polish – at least I assume it's Polish."

"Cox fed it through some Google Translate thing on the Internet. The English version's on the next page. It's pretty rough but the essential details are there."

"How do you know how to pronounce her surname?"

"Cox got that from the Google thing too."

Mary was expecting the next question to be "and how the hell did you come to be searching a Polish missing persons database?", but it didn't come. Instead the DI seemed satisfied with what he'd heard.

"Have you contacted the Polish police?"

"Cox is on it now, Guv."

The DI looked out into the squad room and, seeing Cox off the phone, beckoned him across. The young DC appeared in the office doorway.

"What have you got, Pete?"

"Sir, Sarge - I got through to the police in Gdansk, and they're sending the file across. It's in Polish, so we may need a translator."

"Can you try putting it through that Google Translate thing?" said the DI. Never one to miss a budget-saving opportunity, thought Mary. Cox looked worried, like a messenger who didn't want to be shot.

"Sorry, sir, it's coming by fax, and some of it may be handwritten. They don't have everything computerised like we do."

Mary suddenly thought the Polish police sounded rather good. The DI, however, seemed less impressed.

"Oh, right. Well if it's necessary."

Cox brightened. "I did get quite a lot of information from the contact I spoke to in Gdansk, sir. He spoke English."

"Shame we'll still have to pay a translator so we've got a complete file copy of the documentation then, isn't it?" replied the DI, "So what did your English-speaking friend tell you?"

Cox looked deflated. "The victim's father runs an import-export firm in Gdansk," he said, "She worked for him. The mother reported her missing exactly a week ago - said she'd just disappeared, no message or anything."

"So she was definitely reported as missing from Gdansk, not from the UK?" asked Mary.

"Yes Sarge. She had her own flat there. When she didn't turn up for work the mother went round and found it empty, daughter gone, all her clothes still there. Local police turned it over, no signs of forced entry or struggle."

"Sounds like she was snatched somewhere else," said the DI, "assuming she didn't go of her own accord."

"That's what they think. Possibly the night before – there were no signs of her having slept there or had breakfast."

"And then she turns up buried in our beach. A long way from home."

"Yes Guv."

"Did you ask them about identification?"

"He seemed to think the father might come over - they're getting back to me on it. Shall I chase up the translator?"

"Yes - no need for them to come here though. We'll send it to them, in a traffic car if necessary. OK, good work, Pete - let us know anything new as soon as it comes in."

Cox took his cue to leave.

"Looks like we're getting somewhere at last," said the DI, although still with not quite the undiluted enthusiasm he might have been expected to display. Mary considered her options. It was likely - very likely - to come out at some point that it had been Michael Slade who'd given her the idea that the victim might be Polish, in which case she'd be better off telling the DI about it straight away. On the other hand, if she spoke to Michael first, they might be able to come up with an explanation for his leap of insight that didn't involve her showing him the victim's mobile phone at his flat when she should have been getting it locked away in the evidence store.

She was shocked to find herself even considering such a collusion. On the other hand these were desperate times, and one desperate measure all too often led to another. There was, however, a third possibility - that the DI, who'd just been handed a priceless breakthrough, wasn't going to ask too many questions about where it had come from. So far it looked like he was going for that option. No need to steer him off course.

"I'll go and make sure Cox doesn't book the translator

into a hotel" she said, slyly playing to the DI's cost-conscious instincts. She was shocked again at how easily it came to her.

"Mmm." He replied, still studying the computer printout. She got up to leave.

"Inspired guess, wasn't it?"

"What, Guv?"

"Poland. Did you search any other countries before it?"

He'd be able to check with Cox, and would know it was unlikely that she'd searched anywhere else without him.

"Er, no."

"Just went straight for it then. I'd almost call that a work of genius, Mary. And of course you'd just got back from having a chat with one, hadn't you?"

"Guv?"

"Michael Slade. IQ of 174, well into genius territory. And a suspect in this case."

"Well, not actually a suspect, Guv." The DI was no fool; it was as good as an admission that the Poland idea had come from him.

"As near as matters. Sounds to me like Mr Slade knows even more about this case than he let on last night, only while I might be prepared to give him the benefit of the doubt over observing phones and sandbags through his magic binoculars, it'll take a hell of a sight more to convince me that he worked out Poland all on his own, IQ or no IQ. Why didn't you tell me this just now? And how come you didn't bring him in?"

Mary tried to think fast, even though everything seemed to be slowing down in a hideous, car-crash way. The DI obviously thought that Michael Slade had volunteered the idea that the victim was Polish, just as he'd volunteered the idea that she'd been buried in the beach during their interview the night before. He seemed to have no inkling that Mary had given Slade any assistance. Despite knowing that it would almost certainly be better in the long run to come clean about showing Slade the mobile phone, it was still a big, counter-intuitive step for Mary to take. For the second time that day she felt an interview spinning out of control, and the common factor was Michael Slade.

She started speaking without actually knowing what she was going to say.

"Well Guv, I um…"

She was saved by Tony Lane, who suddenly appeared in the office doorway where Cox had been a couple of minutes earlier.

"We've got something from CCTV, Guv," said Lane, with evident excitement, "Lone male walking away from the scene, around the right time. Clear enough for ID. It's on my computer."

"Good. Let's see it." Giving Mary a "we'll continue this later" look, the DI got up and followed Lane out into the squad room. Mary followed too.

"It's from one of the café bars on the front between the Arch and Knightstone," said Lane, "The CCTV kit's new, top of the range stuff with remote control – the owner's son's a bit of a tech wizard and installed it himself. Luckily for us he was playing about with it and decided to zoom across the road onto this chap walking along the prom."

Lane clicked the 'Play' button on the computer display, and the picture began to move. At first they saw a wide angle shot including the café forecourt, bustling in summer but empty on the cold November night. In the distance, beyond the road and across the bay, the outline of the Pavilion at the end of the Grand Pier was picked out in coloured lights. On the seafront promenade, about fifty yards away, a small figure could be seen walking northwards towards them, away from the Pier.

Soon the camera began to zoom in, panning left to stay on the walker, then smoothly right to keep the figure in frame as he drew closer. The café owner's son was clearly a skilled remote-control cameraman, and zoomed right into the figure's head and shoulders, adjusting his pan speed to keep his subject in frame. Lane clicked the pause button, and the video froze. The street lighting on the promenade was good, and the camera was, indeed, top of the range; in front of them was a perfect, full-detail image of the man's face.

"Well, well," said the DI.

Mary's heart sank.

She'd seen enough when the picture was still showing the walker full-height: the waxed cotton jacket, the collar-length hair, the odd, slightly loping gait. Zoomed into the face, there was no doubt whatsoever.

"Michael John Slade," the DI said, the middle name making it sound like a charge sheet, "now I wonder why he didn't mention this last night?"

Mary's eyes were fixed on the screen. The timestamp in the corner of the frozen picture read 22:51, when the tide would have just crept over the buried corpse. Here was Michael Slade walking away from it. There was no law against walking along the seafront, but not to mention, during questioning, that you'd been near the crime scene at the time of the crime looked bad, whichever way you viewed it. The DI's words came back to her – "Or a serial killer getting his kicks by going into the opposition's lair and acting dumb." Had she been in Slade's lair that morning, showing him their evidence?

"I think we'd better have another chat with Mr Slade," said the DI, "right away."

"I'll bring him in," said Mary. This time she'd have a look round the rest of his flat, too.

"No," the DI shot back. "Lane – you get him. DS Miller will give you the details. Caution him, and if he won't come, arrest him."

"What for, Guv?"

"Obstructing an enquiry. I've got a briefing with the DCI – put Slade in an interview room with a uniform, and none of you go near him until I get back." He looked pointedly at Mary.

Chapter 9

Michael Slade sat behind the interview room table, fidgeting with a piece of paper he'd pulled from his jacket pocket.

"Interview with Michael John Slade. Present are Detective Inspector Jones and Detective Sergeant Miller. OK, Mr Slade, you've been informed of your rights. This interview is taking place under caution and is being recorded. Just to recap, anything you say may be used in evidence, and if you fail to mention something now which you later use in court, it may harm your defence. You've been advised of your right to legal representation, but have waived it for now. You can ask for representation at any time. You haven't been arrested, and are free to leave if you wish, although if you decide to do so we may arrest and detain you. Is that all correct and understood?"

Michael nodded.

"For the tape please, Mr Slade."

"Yes."

The full PACE treatment, thought Mary.

"Why have I been brought here again?" Michael asked, "I thought we'd covered everything last night and this morning." He threw a glance at Mary.

This morning. He was going to bring up the business with the phone, Mary was sure of it. What would happen then was anyone's guess, although she could hazard a couple of fairly likely ones.

"Let me show you why, Mr Slade," said the DI. He opened the laptop computer which sat on the table, and turned it sideways so all three of them could see the screen. It came to life, the frozen image of Michael's face filling the display.

"Is this you, Mr Slade?" Michael nodded again. "For the tape, please."

"Yes, of course it's me."

"And would you have any idea where this was taken?"

Michael said nothing.

"OK, let's wind it back a bit and all will be revealed." The DI clicked the Rewind symbol, then Play. The recording began from the wide angle shot of the café forecourt.

"This is you walking along the seafront, and as you can see from the date and time in the corner, it's the night the young woman was buried in the beach under the pier you're walking away from, just after the time we think she was buried. Would you care to comment on that?"

"Not really." This was a different Michael Slade, thought Mary – not chatty at all, but sullen and uncooperative, like an unmasked culprit.

"You were interviewed informally here last night," the DI continued, "and during that interview you displayed a knowledge of the location of the body, and the approximate time it was put there. But you didn't mention that you'd been near that location at that time, nor did you mention it when you spoke to DS Miller this morning. Why not?"

Michael shrugged and pulled a "don't know" face. Still sullen, but, Mary realised, more the aggrieved infant than culprit.

"Michael, this is serious," she said. "This video places you near a crime scene at or around the time of the crime. If you don't explain it, it could count towards proof of guilt. People have gone to prison on this much evidence."

Suddenly Michael sat up in his chair. Mary saw the DI

tense, ready to counter any attack, but the anger was expressed in purely verbal form.

"This isn't fair. I didn't mention it because it wasn't relevant. I had nothing to do with the murder or burial of that poor young woman. I was just walking home from work. And for your information," he said, turning to the DI, "I may have been walking 'away from the pier', as you put it, but I was never actually at or close to the pier that evening. I cut through town and came out onto the seafront by the Cabot. It's my normal route and I'm sure you'll find me on endless CCTV recordings to prove it. I'm disappointed, Mary. I thought you'd know me better than this after our talk this morning."

Here it comes, Mary thought – he's going to blab about the phone. My own fault.

The DI was on to Mary's visit straight away.

"What about your talk with DS Miller this morning, Mr Slade? What did you talk about, exactly?"

"The case in general. We went over what I said last night. Mary didn't say specifically that your tests had proved I was telling the truth about my binoculars, but it was obvious that they had. I assumed, wrongly it seems, that you'd stop hassling me after that."

Nothing about the phone. Not yet, anyway. The DI would be asking Michael what he'd said about Poland next though, and that would lead to it. But Mary had spotted something in Michael's explanation of his seafront walk. Checking it out would delay the inevitable, and it needed asking anyway.

"You say you were walking home from work when this video was taken?" she asked, getting in quickly before the DI could continue.

"Yes, that's right."

"The thing is, Michael, the next evening, when I asked your manager when you'd be finishing work, she told me 11pm – that you were on three to eleven shift this week. So if you didn't finish work until eleven, what were you doing on the seafront at 10.51?"

It was a good point, and the DI looked interested. Michael said nothing at first, a reaction which both detectives had seen before from suspects trying to think up a story on the spot. Eventually he spoke.

"Perhaps the time stamp on the video is wrong. They probably forgot to change it when British Summer Time ended."

Mary was almost disappointed. An IQ of 174 and that was the best he could come up with. And it meant he did have something to hide. The DI went in for the kill.

"Oh come on, Mr Slade, don't sell yourself short. You're Mr Super-Observant, able to spot a BlackBerry phone at 200 metres – are you seriously asking us to believe that you've been looking at that video for the past five minutes and hadn't noticed until now that the time on the screen was wrong?"

"We can verify the time of the recording anyway," Mary added, "a statement from the camera operator, trace the number plates of cars that went past if necessary. We are used to dealing with CCTV evidence, Michael."

"And with people who lie under questioning," said the DI. "Don't mess with us, Mr Slade."

Michael looked from one to the other. Mary noticed how dilated his pupils were – fear, arousal, drugs, what? It made his eyes seem blank, like a shark's.

"All right, I left work early, but it wasn't official."

"Not official? I'm afraid you'll have to elaborate on that one."

"I'm sure even you've bunked off early now and then, Inspector," Michael replied. He seemed to be recovering his self-assurance. "The store closes at ten, and the extra hour is to get the customers out, cash up our tills and generally clear up. It was a quiet night, and there wasn't much to do. When it's like that we take turns to go early. It was my turn."

"But that wasn't official?"

"No, strictly against company policy. My checkout supervisor could be sacked if they found out."

It was a plausible explanation, thought Mary, but then they often were.

"What time did you leave the supermarket, Michael?" she asked.

"About ten. Karen – my supervisor – let me close my till at 9.45 and cash up. There were only about three customers left by then."

Now it was the DI's turn to spot a flaw.

"Sure it was ten, Mr Slade?"

"Yes, I checked my watch as I left."

"In that case, how come it took you until 10.51 to get to here?" He pointed at the computer screen, still showing Michael's image. "It can't be more than fifteen minutes walk for a fit man of your age, twenty at the most."

"I didn't say I walked straight there. I went for a quick pint."

"Where?"

"Between the Lines."

The DI sat back, a look of theatrical amazement on his face.

"Between the Lines? I wouldn't have thought that was the kind of place for a man of your intellect, Mr Slade. It's not even a proper pub."

Mary was familiar with Between the Lines, for purely professional reasons. It was, as the DI said, not really a proper pub. By day it was the on-platform buffet at Weston's railway station, selling pies and sandwiches that harked back to an earlier age of British railway catering. At night the door to the platform was closed, the door to the station car park was opened, and it became a watering-hole favoured by residents of the cheap housing that surrounded the rail tracks. The proprietors were a local couple who remembered the days of steam; entertainment included regular Country and Western karaoke nights and a meat raffle on the first Thursday of each month. It was difficult to imagine why anyone with an IQ of 174 and an interest in cryptography would go there.

"They serve a good pint," said Michael, "proper cask conditioned ale, gravity fed straight from the barrel."

This was true; they did indeed serve their ale straight from the barrel, a virtue born of necessity as the building had no cellar.

"So that's the attraction is it?" continued the DI.

"One of them, yes. You also meet some interesting people there."

Mary had met some interesting people there too, normally while accompanied by uniformed backup. She wondered if they were the same ones.

"So would you say you were known there?" she asked.

"Probably, yes. I've done the karaoke a few times."

"What, the Country and Western?" said the DI incredulously.

"I like to steer it subtly towards Celtic folk."

"But if we asked whether anyone saw you there on Tuesday night, someone would remember, would they?"

"Highly likely, I'd think. I had a discussion with Billy the landlord on the merits of Johnny Cash. He's a big fan."

"Anyone else?"

"Colleen, the woman with black hair who runs the takeaway on the other side of the roundabout. She can't stand Johnny Cash, said so as I was going to the toilets. Anyway, none of that matters, does it?"

"Why not?"

"Because I'll be on the CCTV you seem to place such store on. The camera on the station approach will show me arriving and leaving, assuming it was working. Then there must be dozens of them between the station and the Cabot."

The DI leaned back in his chair and fixed Michael with an appraising stare.

"All right, let's look at that," he said. "What time did you arrive at Between the Lines, and when did you leave?"

"I got there at about eight minutes past ten, and left just after half past. As I said, it was a quick pint."

"Not much time to talk about Johnny Cash then?"

"I didn't say it was an in-depth discussion, Inspector. The jukebox was playing 'Folsom Prison Blues' when I arrived, and Billy extolled its virtues while he served my drink. It was Marstons Pedigree, incidentally, served in a straight glass. From Burton on Trent, travels very well."

"I'm pleased to hear it, Mr Slade." The DI seemed almost to be enjoying the exchange, but Mary knew that what he really enjoyed was letting suspects relax so they'd be off guard. She also knew that to the DI Michael's apparent confidence could just be the sign of a well-rehearsed alibi.

"And can you remember what route you took from the pub to the seafront?"

"Yes – it was the one I always take. Back over the roundabout, on to the next one, left at the Bristol Hotel, down Alexandra Parade, past the Dragon, right into the High Street where it's pedestrianised, all the way through, left at the end, round past the college and onto the seafront opposite the Cabot."

It sounded convincing, but the DI evidently wasn't ready to buy.

"You say you walk past the Bristol Hotel? That's well out of your way, isn't it? Why not cut through the supermarket car park like everyone else?"

"Everyone else isn't bunking off from the supermarket, are they? I didn't want to meet anyone from work. And they've got high-resolution CCTV on the petrol station forecourt. I know, I've worked there. And as I said, it's my regular route. I like to keep to it."

It was a good point, or a well-rehearsed one, or just someone capable of thinking very quickly.

"And you're sure you turned right into the precinct, didn't just keep going straight down Regent Street to the pier? Think carefully, Mr Slade, and remember you're still under caution. There are cameras on that stretch too, so we'll find out if you did."

"Completely sure, Inspector. "

"Why go that way? Why not just go to the pier and along the front?"

"Habit. I like the area between the college and the theatre. Sometimes I have a pint in the Brit, or the karaoke bar opposite the Royal Hotel. Or sometimes there's someone playing jazz in the French café."

That, at least, made sense. From the college to the Playhouse theatre was only a couple of streets, but it held the nearest thing Weston had to a bohemian quarter, with, in fact, two theatres, plus a museum, an indoor flea market and a smattering of trendy bars and cafes. Mary could imagine Michael sharing his theories on cryptography in one of those, more easily than she could in Between the Lines.

"And did you stop off for a pint there on Tuesday?"

Michael smiled. "Evidently not," he said, pointing to the computer screen, "otherwise I wouldn't have been here by 10.51, would I?" Mary wished she'd had a chance to warn him not to get cocky with the DI again. "I did have another pint though, in the Clarendon a few minutes after this was taken. They'll remember me there, it's my local."

If the DI was irritated by Michael's manner, he didn't show it. He did bite back though.

"Drink a lot, do you Mr Slade?"

Michael seemed indignant at this. "I don't call two pints after an eight hour shift a lot, Inspector."

"Seven," came the reply.

"Pardon?"

"A seven hour shift – you were paid for eight but you only did seven, unless you started early. Did you?"

It was the tiniest chink in Michael's story, but a chink nevertheless. Mary could read the DI's mind: "Caught on the break, 1 – 0" was very probably what he was thinking right now.

"I was speaking in general terms, in response to your question about my general level of drinking. It's very rare that I get off early – only when the store's quiet, and only when it's my turn. I normally do an eight hour shift, and I typically have two pints after it. I don't consider that to be excessive alcohol consumption."

Goal disallowed. This was beginning to turn into a verbal stag rut, thought Mary, at which she was a mere spectator. In a way this was good, since the subject of her showing the victim's phone to Michael was getting delayed to the point where she might have a chance to call a break and tell the DI about it herself. The downside was that, as she was fast coming to realise, the DI would probably come off worst in any intellectual jousting match with Michael Slade, and getting him riled over that could be bad news for all of them, in a Michael in the cells, her on paperwork and the DI losing control of the investigation sort of way. DI Jones was a very good officer, but no-one liked a suspect getting the better of them.

The DI, however, kept his cool.

"All right – well we'll check out what you've told us, and if it all matches then you won't have anything to worry about."

Suddenly Michael looked worried.

"Will that have to include the supermarket?"

"Of course," said the DI breezily, "You may well be on CCTV reaching Between the Lines just after ten, but if, say, you left work just after nine, then that would leave an hour unaccounted for, wouldn't it? And it wouldn't need to be an hour - even if you only took fifteen minutes out to go and check the seafront and shine a torch to tell the boat to come in, that would still make you an accessory. So you see, we do need to be precise about the time you left the shop, and about any other little absences that may have occurred during the evening. The only way we'll get that information is to ask at your work."

No trace of cockiness now.

"Well could you just ask my supervisor, or any of the other staff who were there that night – not the store manager?"

"Why not?"

"I told you - because my supervisor could get sacked if they find out she let me go early. There's no point in asking the higher-up managers anyway – they don't work late evenings. It's only the till team who would have seen me there at that time."

"Very well," the DI tore a sheet of paper from his pad and handed it, and his pen, across the desk to Michael. "Write down the names and job titles of everyone you think saw you there, and we'll try them first, starting with your supervisor."

This was unusually accommodating on the DI's part, thought Mary. Normally he'd have treated a request not to speak to someone as grounds for making them top of his interview list - as, to be fair, would a lot of other good detectives. Or did he think Michael was double-bluffing him, pretending he wanted him to speak to his

74

supervisor, not the store manager, so that he'd do it the other way round? Or was he suddenly being Good Cop for another reason?

Michael was still writing when the DI spoke again.

"There was something else I wanted to ask you about, Mr Slade."

"What's that?" Michael looked up and handed the paper and pen back to the DI.

"Poland."

"Poland?"

OK, here came the other reason.

"Yes. What do you know about it?"

"Central European country between Germany and the former USSR, capital Warsaw."

"Anything else?"

"Also bordered by the Czech Republic, invaded by Nazi Germany in 1939, which triggered the Second World War? The Soviet Union invaded them at the same time, of course, but that got airbrushed out of history after they became our allies."

The DI leaned forward, just a little, and gazed at Michael Slade's face.

"Actually I was thinking more about Polish people – young women, in particular, who might have arrived here in the past ten days."

"I don't know any young Polish women. I don't think there have even been any through my till. Mostly Albanians around here, as I'm sure you know."

The DI ignored the comment. "The thing is," he said, "that we've had what you might call an inspired guess about the possible nationality of our murder victim. And that inspired guess came just after DS Miller here had been to visit you. Now I hold DS Miller's skills in the highest regard, but even by her standards plucking Poland, first time, from a list of, what, 50 or 60 possible countries is quite a feat, and I'm wondering if she might have had some help."

"Then I'm surprised you haven't asked her, Inspector."

Mary felt as if she was having an out of body experience, looking on helplessly as Michael and the DI played cat and mouse, with her career as the stake.

"I'm asking you, Mr Slade. Did you tell my officer that the victim was Polish, and if so, how did you know?"

Inevitable, although she had hoped to avoid the worst case scenario.

For a split second Michael looked at Mary with those blank eyes, then back to the DI.

"No, I didn't tell her that. Poland wasn't mentioned at all."

Sometimes a police officer has to make a snap judgement then act on it – they told you that in basic training. Mary made hers. Michael was lying to protect her over the phone business, just as he'd tried to lie about what time he'd arrived on the seafront in order to protect his supervisor. If it went on, he'd end up in the cells and she'd end up suspended. It had to stop.

She leant across to the DI.

"Guv, can I see you outside now?"

"What? No."

"Now Guv, really. Please."

The DI gave out an exasperated gasp, and rose from his chair.

"Interview suspended at 15.38. DI Jones and DS Miller leaving the room. Wait here please, Mr Slade, we won't be long."

Chapter 10

The DI took a few steps down the corridor then turned, making it clear that this was as far as he was willing to go in accommodating Mary's request for a word outside the interview room.

"What?" he half-snarled.

In the few steps Mary had decided that her only option was to get straight to the point; she'd only have a few seconds to get his attention, otherwise he'd be back in the interview room and going in for the kill.

"I showed Michael Slade the victim's phone."

"You did what?"

She'd got his attention, no doubt about that. Best to come fully clean now, not let him get it out of her.

"I took the phone out to his flat and let him examine it. He worked out that it had been used heavily to text or email, but not in English. It was the wear pattern on the keys – the letter 'E' should have worn off first, but it was the 'A' instead. He looked it up on the Internet, and that pointed to it being used to write in Polish."

The DI, however, hadn't got as far as letter frequency analysis yet.

"You took evidence which I'd told you to log into the store and let a suspect handle it?"

"Only through the evidence bag. I made him wear gloves too."

"Oh, good to see you sticking to procedure, Sergeant!" he spat back sarcastically, "That'll be one less charge at our disciplinary panel!"

'Our' disciplinary panel. Some DIs encouraged their officers to use their initiatives, then threw them to the wolves if things went wrong. Not DI Jones. His reputation was for backing his officers provided they stood up for themselves and convinced him they'd acted conscientiously. Mary had a chance to do that now.

"Slade wasn't actually a suspect, Guv – you'd said so yourself, and this was before the CCTV came up. We were desperate for a lead, you said that too. He'd worked out the whole story on the beach from seeing just a couple of things through his binoculars. I thought if I showed him the phone he might spot something..."

"... we were too stupid to spot." The DI completed her sentence.

"Not stupid, no, but not with the same way of seeing things as he has. And it worked – he saw something."

"How do you know it wasn't all a setup – that he already knew the girl was Polish and had that business about phone keys prepared as a cover? He builds your confidence, then gets to use you as a source of information on how we're doing."

"Strewth, Guv, he's not an evil genius."

"Ah, but he is a genius though, isn't he? IQ of 174!"

"He didn't know I was bringing the phone with me. And anyway, you should have seen him looking at it – he was like a boy who'd been allowed to drive a steam engine. It was genuine, I'd stake my pension on it."

"Well that's exactly what you could be staking – and mine too – if it turns out he really is Professor Moriarty and it comes out that we let him handle the evidence. I just hope you're right."

It was bad form for a senior officer to make a junior colleague cry, but the DI came unwittingly close to it as Mary fought to keep her reaction professional. He could have suspended her on the spot for taking the evidence out of the station against his orders, covering his back in the process. A lot of DIs would have done just that. Instead he was saying that if it went belly up he'd share the responsibility with her. His loyalty wasn't without purpose, nor did he give it to everyone, only those he knew he could trust. It paid dividends; if Mary hadn't known it was there, she probably wouldn't have shown the phone to Michael, and they still wouldn't have an identity for their victim. But it was loyalty all the same, of a kind that was increasingly hard to find among career-minded senior ranks.

Mary made sure the lump that had threatened to form in her throat was fully gone.

"I'm sure, Guv."

"Well the fact that he lied about it just now doesn't fill me with confidence."

"That was because I asked him not to tell anyone I'd showed him the phone."

The DI's face darkened again.

"And when were you going to tell me? Or were you just going to keep it a secret?"

"I was about to tell you when Lane came in with the CCTV, honest. Then you went to see the DCI and then we were straight into the interview with Slade. I would have told you as soon as I got a chance."

"Yeah, and if the Polish thing had come up blank you'd probably never have mentioned it."

Mary said nothing, but looked guilty.

"Don't look so tragic," he said, "I was a DS myself once. Right, if anyone asks where we got the Poland idea from, refer them to me. And remind your friend Slade not to say a word about the phone to anyone, otherwise it'll be me going round to his house next time."

"Thanks Guv – really."

"And for the record, I'm still not 100 percent convinced about him. Let's just hope to goodness his story checks out."

"Yes, Guv."

They went back into the interview room, where Michael sat staring vacantly at the poster on the opposite wall. As they entered, he came to life again.

"I was beginning to think you'd forgotten about me," he said, looking from one to the other.

"Oh we won't be forgetting about you, Mr Slade," said the DI, "you can rest assured of that. That's all for now though – we'll check out the times and places you've given us, and we'll get back to you if there are any further questions. Best if you don't leave the area for the immediate future."

Michael looked alarmed. "But I'll be going to Bridgwater at the weekend to see my family," he protested. "You can't stop me doing that, surely?"

"Bridgwater will be fine," replied the DI. "We can contact you there if we need to."

"Ah, all right. I'll give you the address."

"We know your address in Bridgwater, Mr Slade. Now DS Miller will see you out." The DI picked up his files. "And Mr Slade."

"Yes?"

"If you have, or come across, any further information relevant to this case, bring it to us straight away. I don't want to discover anything else involving you that you haven't already told me about. And don't ever lie to me again, because next time I will put you in the cells. Is that understood?"

"Understood, Inspector."

"Good."

Mary and Michael walked down the corridor in silence. As they reached the Station door, he turned to her.

"Your Detective Inspector can be a bit thuggish, can't he?"

Mary held the door open.

"He could have been a lot tougher than that, Michael, believe me. You should have told us you were on the seafront on Tuesday evening. And then saying that you and I hadn't discussed Poland..."

"I had to say that, Mary – I'd promised you I wouldn't tell anyone you'd shown me the phone."

"I know, and I'm grateful, really. Look, we really appreciate your help, Michael, but it was wrong of me to drag you into this, and I'm sorry. Best for you to forget about the case now, and keep well away from the investigation – don't go down on the prom with your binoculars or anything like that. My guvnor's still not sure about you, and he meant what he said about putting you in the cells. My advice is to keep well off his radar."

Chapter 11

The next morning there was a renewed air of purpose in the CID office. They now had the most important piece of information in any murder enquiry, the identity of the victim. From that would flow friends, colleagues, places worked and visited, interests – and enemies, although a young woman like Katya Czwisnjowski wouldn't be expected to have many of the those. What's more they would soon be meeting Katya's parents, for a message relayed via Divisional HQ from the Polish Embassy in London, no less, had informed them that Mr and Mrs Czwisnjowski would be arriving by car in the late morning. By Mary's reckoning that would be around 19 hours since they'd been told of their daughter's discovery, which was quick considering they lived 1,000 miles and three countries away. She guessed there couldn't be anything worse for a parent than having to make a journey like this.

Cox and Lane were checking Michael Slade's account of his walk home on Tuesday night, and were clearly keen to get it out of the way as quickly as possible, so they wouldn't miss out on the 'real' investigation which everyone seemed convinced would begin when Katya's parents arrived. Mary had to remind them to be thorough and check every CCTV source on the list, including the ones on Regent Street where it ran down to the Grand Pier, the part Michael claimed not to have walked along that night. She also detailed Cox to go and see Michael's supervisor ("Karen", she read from her notes) to check what time he'd left the supermarket, telling the young DC to be as discreet as possible. She'd have gone herself, but she was known there now, and it would do Cox good to get away from his computer screen. And she didn't want to miss the arrival of the Czwisnjowskis either.

One reason why everyone was anticipating the arrival of Katya Czwisnjowski's parents was that not much had so far been discovered about her, and they were hoping her parents would fill in a lot of gaps. Passport records showed her entering and leaving Britain via Heathrow airport on multiple occasions in the previous four years, but because she was an EU citizen she hadn't needed a visa, or to state where she was going in the UK or what she'd be doing. This information had come back quickly on no greater authorisation than Cox's login details, which meant, as the DI put it, that either she wasn't on any security watch lists or she was, but they weren't letting on.

The DI himself, meanwhile, was still practising pronouncing the Czwisnjowski's surname, and could be heard muttering "Ka-chiz-knee-ovski" to himself through his open office door. Eventually he stopped, and called Mary in.

"What we need most from the parents," he said, eyeing Cox's printout on his desk, "is what Katya was doing on all these trips to the UK. From these dates it looks as if she was actually living here, right up until the beginning of October, so she must have been doing something, working or studying somewhere."

"They won't necessarily know, Guv," replied Mary, trying not to sound too negative, "sometimes kids fly the nest and all they'll tell their parents is that they're fine and not to worry, especially if they've gone to another country. Then they run short of cash and it's 'Mum, Dad" down the phone. That could explain the return to Poland in October, and the job in the family firm."

"That sounds like personal experience?" said the DI, looking puzzled.

"My cousin's daughter," said Mary, "19, went to Spain, they hardly heard from her until the Euros ran out, then it cost them a fortune to clean up the mess and bring her back. Debts all over the place."

"Well, let's hope Ms Czwisnjowski kept in closer touch with her parents," the DI said. His pronunciation was coming on well.

At 11am, precisely, a call from the front desk informed the DI that Mr and Mrs Czwisnjowski had arrived. While they were being escorted up to the CID room, the DI did a last couple of "Ka-chiz-knee-ovski"s, then came out to greet them, alerting Mary on the way.

The Czwisnjowskis were not what the DI, or Mary, or anyone else in the Squad room, had been expecting. For a start there were three of them; a man and a woman, both extremely well dressed, the man early fifties perhaps, the woman a little younger, then another man, late thirties, still smartly dressed but not in the same league as the other two. The younger man stepped forward and offered his hand, rather formally, to the DI.

"Good morning. I am Otto Borowski, from the Consular Section of the Polish Embassy in London. May I introduce Mr and Mrs Czwisnjowski." Mary breathed an inner sigh of relief that Cox's website had given them the right pronunciation, meaning that the DI's rehearsals hadn't been in vain.

"Mr Borowski, Mr Czwisnjowski, Mrs Czwisnjowski," said the DI smoothly, "I'm Detective Inspector Steve Jones, and this is Detective Sergeant Mary Miller."

As hands were shaken all round, Mary took the chance to have a good look at the Czwisnjowskis. Mr Czwisnjowski was shortish, perhaps five feet six or eight, but anything he lacked in height he made up for in presence. He was immaculately dressed, in a brown woollen overcoat over what looked like a very expensive suit, with a red silk tie and dark brown leather shoes polished to a perfect shine. Even if he'd been wearing jeans and a T shirt, there would still have been the face, sharp-featured with cold blue eyes that looked like they would miss absolutely nothing, grey hair clipped perfectly in a style that was somehow modern and military at the same time. And then there was the handshake, the eye contact, the near-perfect English, and most of all the quiet yet firm tone of his voice. This was a man accustomed to being listened to.

No less striking was Mrs Czwisnjowski. Mary put her in her mid to late forties, her looks faded a little but still striking, to say the least. Like her daughter she looked Mediterranean rather than Polish – Italian was Mary's guess – and like her husband's her appearance spoke unashamedly, and unselfconsciously, of wealth. Mary had worked on a fur warehouse robbery once, and picked up some knowledge of the trade; Mrs Czwisnjowski's coat looked to her like Sable, worth roughly a year of her Detective Sergeant's salary. Her shoes were Prada; her jewellery hadn't come from a catalogue. Her hair and makeup had the look that only time and money, lots of it, can buy. She was like a film star from an era when film stars weren't seen in public wearing jogging pants.

It occurred to Mary that there'd been something of a communications breakdown concerning the Czwisnjowskis. Despite the information that they ran an import-export business, she (and, she guessed, the DI) had been expecting something nearer to plumbers or car washers, the Poles of the tabloid newspapers. It was clear now that there were other kinds of Polish people, and that the DCI, if not someone even higher up the food chain, should have been here to greet this couple who came with a diplomatic minder.

Thankfully the Czwisnjowskis seemed unperturbed at finding themselves in the Squad Room of a small-town CID outpost talking to a relatively junior officer, and Mr Czwisnjowski even thanked the DI for seeing them. Borowski seemed less overwhelmed with gratitude, staring rather stonily, Mary thought, as the introductions were made, but then she reflected that most of the people he gave consular assistance to were probably in trouble rather than grieving parents, so perhaps he always looked like that when dealing with local police.

The DI invited them into his office which, though comfortable for a meeting of three people, was borderline inadequate for five. Again the Czwisnjowskis seemed not to have a problem, although again Borowski looked unimpressed. Nevertheless it was a good start.

"First of all, Mr and Mrs Czwisnjowski," the DI said when they'd settled, at close quarters, around his desk, "let me say how very sorry we all are for your loss."

"Thank you," replied Mr Czwisnjowski. His wife just nodded, closing her eyes as she did so.

"Forgive me for asking, Inspector," Otto Borowski interjected, "but are you the Senior Investigating Officer on this case?" It was said politely, perhaps even with a hint of "nothing personal", but his point was clear.

The DI stayed cool.

"No, that's my immediate superior, Detective Chief Inspector Spence. I am, however, the senior officer actively investigating the case. DCI Spence supervises my team's work alongside that of the office and forensic teams.

"Then we are happy to talk to you, Inspector." said Mr Czwisnjowski, shooting a glance at Borowski, who immediately backed off. Mary noted how unquestioningly the Embassy official deferred to him.

"I should say that until there's been a formal identification we can't say for certain that the person we found is your daughter," said the DI, "although we're 99.9 percent sure, due to the details of distinguishing marks in her missing persons file. That's why we must ask you to identify her for us, if you feel you can."

"We are prepared for this, Inspector," Mr Czwisnjowski replied. Again his wife just nodded. Then he continued. "Can you tell us, please, how she died, and how she came to be found?"

The DI gave them the details; death by poisoning, the discovery by the dog walker and the excavation of the body. At one point Mrs Czwisnjowski interrupted, the first time she'd said anything except "Good morning". Even then it was brief.

"Was she clothed?"

With evident relief the DI confirmed that yes, Katya had been fully clothed, and had no injuries, although anything that could identify her – bag, purse, photographs – had been removed.

"Then how did you identify her so quickly?" asked Mr Czwisnjowski.

"It was thanks to Detective Sergeant Miller here." said the DI, "We found a mobile phone near the crime scene – it had been professionally wiped of all data, but DS Miller noticed that the pattern of wear on the keys didn't match what would be expected if it had been used for typing in English. Instead it matched use in Polish, and that led us to your country's missing persons database."

"That is extraordinary observation, Detective Sergeant," said Mr Czwisnjowski, turning to Mary, "extremely impressive." Even Borowski looked impressed.

Mary felt herself flushing. She was uncomfortable taking the credit, but could understand why the DI hadn't mentioned Michael Slade. Telling them that the British police got its key crime-solving insights from a supermarket checkout operator would hardly instil confidence.

Not wanting to waste the confidence they had instilled, the DI pressed on.

"Sir, Madam, I appreciate that this is a terrible time for you, but if you'd feel able to answer a few questions about Katya's background and recent movements, it could help us in finding whoever did this to her."

"Of course, Inspector." said Mr Czwisnjowski calmly. His wife, silent again, just nodded.

"Our records show that Katya was a fairly frequent visitor to this country, and appears to have stayed for some time on each visit. Can you tell us where she went in the UK?"

"Yes – she was a student here. She completed her degree course last summer."

Mary and the DI looked at each other.

"And where did she study, sir?"

"Bristol University – it is one of your best, I believe."

Now Mary and the DI studiously avoided looking at each other, in case they gave away too much surprise at hearing that their mystery murder victim had, in fact, been living half an hour away for the past three years.

"Indeed, sir, one of the country's best," said the DI, "In fact I'm surprised it wasn't mentioned on the Missing Persons report."

"Katya was no longer a student." Mrs Czwisnjowski's accent was unmistakeably Italian now, the "longer" stretched musically across the space of three syllables. "She had returned home to work in our business. When I filed the Missing Persons report, I thought of her only as living in Gdansk."

"But for three years she lived in Bristol, is that correct?"

"Yes, Inspector, although she came home two or three times a year, in the university vacations."

Mary noted that Mrs Czwisnjowski's English was

almost as good as her husband's, and far better than the Polish or Italian of herself or the DI. Quite a multilingual family. Not one given to displaying emotions though, if Katya's mother and father were anything to go by.

The DI pressed on. "Our records show her leaving the UK in early October this year, but the university year ended in June. Why did she stay here after that?"

"She had become very attached to England." said Mr Czwisnjowski, smoothly but firmly taking over from his wife, "She wanted a last summer here before coming home to start her career."

"And what did she do her degree in at Bristol?" An oblique, but seemingly innocent, question to break up the flow of a prepared story. Mary wondered why the DI was suddenly using an interrogation technique on a grieving parent.

Borowski was evidently wondering the same thing.

"Are these questions necessary at this moment, Inspector? Mr and Mrs Czwisnjowski have come to identify their daughter, it is a very stressful time."

"Of course they are necessary." It was Mr Czwisnjowski who answered, issuing his second slapdown to the diplomat in as many minutes, still without raising his voice. "The police must know everything possible about Katya." He turned to the DI. "Her degree was in Politics and International Relations. She achieved a 2:1, as she was expecting to do. University life is too social in the UK to expect a First."

"Thank you, sir." said the DI, not looking at Borowski, "You mention the social life at the University – did Katya have many friends there?"

"I believe so, yes, although we did not pry into her affairs. She mentioned many names, but only in passing."

"And what about boyfriends?"

Mr Czwisnjowski almost smiled. "In Poland that is

still not subject a daughter discusses with her father. My wife may be able to help you though." On cue, Mrs Czwisnjowski spoke. "No-one special, Inspector, just one or two young men she went to movies with. James, I think, and then Alexander."

James and Alexander - typical Bristol University, thought Mary. It wasn't a place famed for taking students from poor backgrounds, which many in the Force thought was the reason why the entire Murder Squad was currently working on a single case there. Probably typical Czwisnjowski though, too. Politics and International Relations sounded like a degree in networking for the children of people who were already in the network, and Katya's lifestyle that of a young woman who could award herself 'one last summer' in an expensive city before returning home to a guaranteed job in the family business empire.

Stereotypes again, Polish plumbers in reverse. Mary reminded herself that, for all her advantages in life, this young woman had been murdered and dumped in the wet sand of Weston beach, and that the wealthy couple in front of her were parents for whom the enormity of their daughter's death, and its circumstances, had probably not yet fully registered. They were entitled to the same sympathy as she'd show to a shattered family in a cardboard-walled semi in Knowle.

"Do you know if Katya knew anyone here in Weston?" she asked, trying to make her voice as gentle as possible. Mr Czwisnjowski hesitated, seeming to search his memory.

"No. I don't recall her mentioning anyone from here. Do you, Sophia?" His wife just shook her head.

"Did she ever mention coming to Weston? People often come here from Bristol at weekends."

Again a hesitation.

"No, I don't think so." Again a shake of the head from

his wife. The posh North Cornwall surfing villages had probably been more Katya's scene, Mary thought, then quickly put the thought away.

Borowski was looking impatient again, and this time the DI seemed to take his point.

"Well I think that's enough for now," he said, "If you think of anything else that might be relevant – friends, favourite restaurants, anything - please let us know." He handed Mr Czwisnjowski a card. "This has my mobile number on it. Please feel free to ring me any time, day or night."

"Thank you, Inspector."

"Now I hate to have to ask this, but do you both feel ready to come and identify Katya? Will it be both of you?"

"Yes, we will both come," said Mrs Czwisnjowski.

"OK. I'm afraid it's a half-hour drive from here, near Bristol. Our pathology services have been centralised. I've got a car ready to take you there though, and they can drop you wherever you want to go afterwards."

"We have our own car, Inspector," said Borowski. "We will follow you, but if you give us the address we will be able to find it in case we are separated."

Mr Czwisnjowski stirred slightly in his seat. "Before we go," he said, "I would like to see the place where Katya was found. On the beach, you said?"

The DI looked uncomfortable. "I'm afraid there isn't anything to see, sir. The tide has been up over the spot where Katya – where Katya was found – five or six times now, and washed away all traces of her being there."

"I wish to see it all the same if you don't mind, Inspector."

Borowski caught the DI's eye, with a look that said that any refusal to accommodate Mr Czwisnjowski's wishes would be reported through diplomatic channels as obstruction.

"Of course, sir. It's near here. We can take you there first."

"Thank you."

The DI got up and ushered the party from his office. When they were halfway across the Squad Room, he stopped and turned to Borowski.

"Where is your car, sir?"

"Outside the entrance to this building."

More likely in the Police Pound by now, thought Mary, imagining a diplomatic incident in the making.

"Very good. If you'll just excuse me for a minute, DS Miller will take you down and I'll meet you there with my car."

"Very well, Inspector."

Chapter 12

Borowski's car turned out to be a big black Mercedes with diplomatic plates and a driver who stamped out a cigarette as he saw them emerge from the station door. He and Borowski held the back doors open for Mr and Mrs Czwisnjowski, for all the world, thought Mary, like secret service agents attending to the President and First Lady of the United States. A case involving a fully-clothed body buried in a beach was never going to be straightforward, but this one was getting more disorienting by the minute.

Thankfully Mary didn't have long to wait in the cold before the DI's Audi came up the ramp from the station car park. She got in and they pulled off, the DI checking in his mirror that the Mercedes was behind them.

"Well, what do you make of them?" the DI asked as he took a left turn towards the seafront.

"Bit of a surprise, Guv."

"Expecting plumbers? So was I."

"It's the minder from the Embassy that gets me – not just the fact that he's here, but the way he treats everything the father says as law. The Czwisnjowskis must have a lot of influence somewhere. I think we should have a look at them."

"Cox is already on it. Discreetly."

"So what do you think – that Katya's murder might be political?"

"Could be anything. Right now all I think is that when someone from a background like that gets murdered, more often than not there's more to it than just random or a domestic."

"Do you think we're out of our depth, Guv?"

"Could be. If we are, someone from above will soon tell us. Until then, let's tread carefully."

The DI drove round the seafront one-way system to the pedestrian crossing by the Grand Pier then slipped the Audi through the gap in the inner sea wall and onto the promenade, pulling forward to leave room for the Mercedes. The Polish Embassy driver didn't need telling to do the same, instead mounting the pavement with a nonchalance that said he was used to doing such things under the protection of diplomatic plates. Again he and Borowski did the door-opening routine, which, with the size of the Mercedes and Mrs Czwisnjowski's sable coat, provided enough of a spectacle for passers-by to stop and stare.

It was windy again – not a howling, sand-blasting-your-face Weston gale, but enough to disturb Mrs Czwisnjowski's expensively-styled hair, and make her husband button his coat. The DI led them to the top of the slipway and pointed across to the taped-off area.

"It was there, sir, where the blue tape is," he shouted, making himself heard above the wind, "Between two of the pier uprights. I'm afraid there's nothing left there now – we had to fill the excavation in and then the tide's been over it twice a day."

"Can we go over there, Inspector?"

"Er, yes sir, of course, but the sand's very wet the under the pier."

"My wife will stay here."

"Very well, sir, DS Miller will stay with her."

Mary watched as the DI and Mr Czwisnjowski made their way across the beach, probably ruining a few hundred pounds worth of the latter's hand-made footwear in the process, although she doubted if that would worry him. Borowski had started down the slipway with them, but Mr Czwisnjowski had waved him back; again he'd deferred instantly, and now stood alongside Mary on the promenade. Mrs Czwisnjowski stood by her too, her coat pulled around her, saying nothing. Mary could think of nothing to say to her; pleasantries ("Is it this cold in Poland?", "Did you have a good journey?") would seem crass.

They saw the two men reach the pier uprights and stand there for a couple of minutes. Mr Czwisnjowski pointed to the ground, and the DI seemed to nod. Then they began to walk back across the sand.

"You are right of course, Inspector," said Mr Czwisnjowski as they reached the waiting group, "there is nothing there. I am sorry for wasting your time."

"Not at all, sir," replied the DI, "You've come all this way, I understand that you'd want to..."

"Do you have photographs?"

"Photographs, sir?"

"Of Katya, as you found her?"

Mary saw instantly where this was going, and guessed that the DI did too.

"Well, yes, but..."

"Could I see them, Inspector?"

The DI had made use of the couple of seconds' warning he'd had of Mr Czwisnjowski's request, and his reply came out firmly but compassionately.

"Sir, that isn't something we'd normally do. Crime scene photographs can be extremely distressing for families."

"But you said Katya hadn't suffered any injuries. She is not disfigured?"

"No, sir, but she is buried in the sand. It's not how any parent would want to see their child."

"Inspector, soon I have to see my daughter dead, in front of my eyes. I want to prepare myself for that. I thought that coming to this beach would help me, but I was mistaken."

Now Borowski was giving them his Diplomatic Incident look again. For the second time in two days Mary felt control of a situation slipping away.

"Of course, sir," said the DI, doing his best to sound positive, "We can go back to the station now if you like."

"Thank you, Inspector. I am very grateful."

The convoy drove back to the station, the DI dropping Mary at the entrance so she could escort the visitors to the Squad Room, Mary wondering whether the Embassy driver would dare to park his Merc like that on the pavement outside a police station in London, or even Bristol. The DI was already in his office when they got there, a file on his desk.

"Mrs Czwisnjowski, do you want to see these? I can arrange for an officer to accompany you to another room if you'd prefer."

Mrs Czwisnjowski just shook her head, eyes closing briefly as she did.

"Well I must repeat that these photographs can be extremely distressing for families. What you'll see is Katya at various stages of being exhumed from the sand. She's not marked in any way, and she is fully clothed, but she is dead. Are you sure you want to proceed?"

"Yes, Inspector." Mr Czwisnjowski, voice quiet but firm.

The DI opened the folder and took out the photographs, large prints of the images taken by the SOCO in the tent. He put the first one on the desk, facing the Czwisnjowskis.

"This is Katya when we had partly uncovered her. As you can see, there are no marks on her. For what it's worth, our pathologist is certain that she had already died when she was buried. She wouldn't have experienced any trauma."

Mrs Czwisnjowski let out something between a gasp

and a sob, quickly smothering it with a hand across her mouth. Mr Czwisnjowski just stared at the photo.

"Do you wish to continue sir, madam?"

Mr Czwisnjowski nodded.

"This is Katya when we had fully uncovered her. The sling was there to support her weight while we excavated around her, so we could remove the sand that had been in contact with her for forensic analysis."

Mary was suddenly very glad that they hadn't just rolled her over like the proverbial sack of potatoes. Borowski seemed impressed too.

"That is very thorough, Inspector."

"Our forensic service uses some of the most advanced techniques in the world, sir. If anyone left a trace of themselves in that sand then we'll find it."

Mrs Czwisnjowski's eyes opened. "What do you mean, trace of themselves?"

Mary instantly realised what she meant.

"Fibres from clothing, strands of hair, that sort of thing," she said quickly, "We all leave traces of ourselves wherever we go. The forensic tests are so sensitive these days that they can find them even in wet sand." The mother was on the edge of losing it, Mary thought. Clearly the DI did too.

"I really don't think there's any point in putting yourselves through seeing the other photos – they just show different angles on the same scene."

"Do you have one of the scene as you first found it?" It was Mr Czwisnjowski, voice still firm.

"Yes, sir, but I really do think you and your wife would find that distressing."

"Why, Inspector?" Mrs Czwisnjowski, more controlled again now.

"Because it shows just a part of her – her hand and lower forearm – projecting from the sand. It's not dignified."

"May I see it please?" Mr Czwisnjowski turned to his wife. "Sophia, do you wish to go?"

Mrs Czwisnjowski shook her head.

"Very well, sir." The DI reached into the folder, took out another photo and turned it to face Mr Czwisnjowski. "This was taken before our forensics team erected the tent and began the excavation. It's exactly how Katya was found."

The photograph, taken with flash in the half-light of morning, showed the sand, smoothed by the tide, and protruding from it the hand and lower arm of Katya Czwisnjowski, her silver rings and black-varnished fingernails visible. The camera had been angled down, but in the background was a glimpse of pier legs, leading to the forest of uprights that supported the amusement complex at the pier's end. It looked a very cold, watery place to end your life. Mr Czwisnjowski stared at it silently. Mrs Czwisnjowski had looked away.

"Thank you, Inspector." said Mr Czwisnjowski, very quietly.

The DI put the photograph back in the folder.

"It's getting late," he said, "perhaps we should break for lunch before going to the pathology centre. We have a canteen here, you'd be very welcome to..."

"That is good of you, Inspector," Borowski cut in, "but I think we may find somewhere for ourselves. Would it be convenient to meet you here at, say, 2pm?"

"Yes of course."

Mary escorted the visitors to the front desk, directing them to her best guess at a hotel that served lunches suitable for customers who arrived in chauffeur-driven Mercedes. Then she rang the DI and asked if he wanted a sandwich fetching; he gave her his order and said he'd pay for them both.

They ate in his office, glad of an hour's respite from

the stress of dealing with the murder victim's parents and their minder.

"We'll have to get the Squad in now, won't we?" Mary said between mouthfuls of ham and mustard, "Technically this is another Bristol University student found murdered."

"Technically, yes," replied the DI, "although the MO's are so different I can't see them being connected – plus, she wasn't actually a student any more. I'll ring Bristol once we've got a confirmed ID though. Better that than them seeing it flagged up on HOLMES"

Although she'd have been reluctant to admit it, Mary was glad not to be working on the Bristol student murders. It was their horrific nature, as much as their frequency, which had the city in panic, and the University's students afraid to venture out in groups of less than four. The two victims had been killed on the street, their faces disfigured, left on the pavement in pools of their blood. It looked overwhelmingly like the work of a lone attacker, jumping them from behind, knife into the lower back to disable them then the same weapon into the heart from the front and finally the carving of the faces, done seemingly for pleasure or whatever other twisted satisfaction the killer sought. By comparison Katya's murder seemed almost civilised, and almost certainly the work of more than one person, since managing the boat, the body and the burial were too much for one man. The Bristol murders bore the hallmarks of the psychopath; Katya's those of the professional.

Mary had, as planned, sent pictures of Katya's crime scene to the Murder Squad, and got the expected response; a polite thank-you, with the observation that there appeared to be no common factors linking Katya's death to the student murders. Nothing had really changed, since as the DI said, Katya was no longer a student by the time of her death. The Bristol case posed the textbook difficulty of dealing with the crimes of a psychopath – lack of motive, and thus of clues derived from it. In Katya's case, something had motivated a team of people to take on the considerable risk and effort of sailing into Weston bay and burying a body under the pier. Mary's intuition told her that Katya's parents, with their driver and minder provided courtesy of the Polish government, might have some idea of what that something was. Getting it out of them, however, might be another matter.

Chapter 13

Two pm approached too quickly for Mary, and in fact it was at 1.55 that she received a call from a flustered-sounding front desk officer asking her to come and deal with a "possible situation" at the main entrance. She rushed down to find the big Merc on the pavement, surrounded by what used to be called the press corps but was now "the media", armed with voice recorders and lightweight news-gathering cameras instead of notebooks and flashbulbs.

"The car's only just arrived – they were waiting for it," said the desk officer as Mary pressed the Exit button on the front door.

"Get DI Jones down here!" Mary shouted back, and went outside.

Borowski was already out of the car, his back to the rear passenger door, looking more than ever like a secret service agent protecting the President from unwelcome attention. On the other side of the car the driver was adopting the same position. Neither seemed very concerned about fostering good relations with the media. The reporters and photographers were mostly the local bunch, but there were a couple of faces Mary didn't recognise. They were calling for the Czwisnjowskis by name - "Mr Czwisnjowski, can you tell us why Katya was in the UK?". "The UK", not "Weston" or "The South West". They were from the Nationals, and they knew about Katya Czwisnjowski and her parents. More leaks, only now they were entering the big league.

Borowski shouted to Mary as she came out of the station. "Who told these people to be here? This is unacceptable!"

Mary had had enough of Borowski's attitude that morning, and was in no mood for him to be starting up again straight after lunch. "Clearly someone tipped them off, sir," she shouted over the din of reporters, "but have you considered the possibility that the tipoff might have come from your embassy? Some of these reporters seem to be from London-based newspapers - it's likely they got their information from a source in London."

Borowski opened his mouth, no doubt in order to complain in the strongest diplomatic terms, but at that point found himself wrestling with a photographer who was trying to push him aside to get a shot of Katya's father. In a flash Borowski had two hands on the photographer's arm and for a moment looked as if he was going to break it. Then he looked up and saw Mary watching him, took one hand away and used it, palm-first, to push the photographer off. No wonder he reminded her of a secret service agent.

By now the DI had appeared, flanked by two uniformed PCs. He didn't waste any time.

"Bring your car into our car park," he shouted to Borowski, pointing at the steel gate next to the building, then to Mary, "help me get this lot out of the way."

Mary, the DI and the uniforms went to the front of the car and began to move the reporters out of the way, a job made more difficult by the fact that threatening to arrest members of the press for public order offences (let alone under the Prevention of Terrorism Act) was strictly forbidden under the new media-friendly regime, and the media knew it. The embassy driver, however, was obviously used to situations like this, and edged the car forward in a way that hinted that his foot might slip on the accelerator at any moment, causing a deeply regrettable accident to anyone in the car's path. Those reporters who'd initially refused to budge soon changed their minds.

Mary found her bag on the front desk, smiled briefly at the thought of the DI's discomfort at carrying it through the station, and followed him to the back entrance. The Mercedes was in the car park, already turned round to head out again. The DI went to Borowski's door, and the window slid down.

"Follow me, please. Another police vehicle will fall in behind us. It'll be about twenty, perhaps twenty-five minutes to the pathology centre." Borowski nodded, and the window slid up again. Mary made for the DI's Audi, but he pointed to a big blue Vauxhall instead. It was an unmarked traffic car, she knew, complete with built-in lights and sirens, and uprated for high-speed chases.

"If we're going to play chicken with the paparazzi on the M5," he said, as the central locking thudded open, "we'll do it in the Chief Constable's wheels, not mine."

The DI drove past the Mercedes and up to the gate, which was opened by the uniforms. The reporters and photographers were still there, and clearly wrong-footed at the sight of their targets emerging in convoy from the yard. For most of them it would be game over, but Mary knew that some would have cars, or possibly motorcycles, parked nearby, and would give chase. As they pulled away from the station a marked traffic car fell in behind the Mercedes. Mary reflected that either the DI had been planning this all along, or the Vauxhall and the traffic escort had been arranged in literally a couple of minutes. Either way, the Czwisnjowskis seemed to have people jumping to attention wherever they went.

They turned right into Station Rd, and drove past the supermarket to the big roundabout by the railway station. Mary suddenly remembered Michael Slade. It was Friday – he'd be on shift at three; perhaps he was already walking along the seafront, giving himself plenty of time. She'd forgotten about him, so all-consuming had the Czwisnjowskis become.

They entered the dual-carriageway that would take them to the motorway, climbing immediately onto the bridge over the railway lines. Half a mile later they hit the tailback to the next junction, and the DI switched on the lights and sirens. The right-hand lane was empty; they were turning left at the junction but that didn't matter as they cruised up to the lights, still red, and through them onto the next stretch. It was Mary's route home, but she didn't normally drive it like this.

The speed limit on the dual carriageway was fifty miles per hour; the DI maintained a steady sixty as he cruised up the long straight section to the next big roundabout, so any paps who tried to keep up would automatically be committing a traffic offence. It didn't even occur to Mary to wonder if the Mercedes driver would be able to stay with them, and when she looked over her shoulder there it was, planted like a rock on the carriageway, exactly the right distance behind. Another traffic car was waiting in a layby as they neared the motorway; the DI flashed his lights and it pulled out, leading them onto the slip road and straight into the fast lane of the northbound M5. They cruised at a steady ninety miles per hour for around ten minutes, past Clevedon, up the hill and down the side of the Gordano Valley where the carriageways ran at different levels, then off at the next junction, the traffic car sweeping them through the lights on the roundabout and onto the Bristol road.

"Were we actually allowed to do that, Guv?" asked Mary, secretly glad that their high-speed escape run was over. The DI nodded towards the traffic car ahead of them, its light and sirens still going.

"As long as he's in front of us, yes. Plus it shows Borowski we're taking it seriously."

And of course it was great fun driving the Chief

Constable's wheels at ninety mph, thought Mary, but didn't say anything. The DI was, no doubt, even more in need of stress relief than she was.

The pathology centre was down a narrow lane, three miles or so from the motorway. Mary checked as they turned in; no-one was behind the Mercedes except the traffic car. Some of the local reporters might have guessed where they'd gone, but by the time they got there the Czwisnjowskis would be safely inside. And once Katya had been identified, shielding them from the press would be uniform's job, not CID's. Mary felt bad for even thinking that, and reminded herself again that these were bereaved parents, about to see their daughter in the worst possible circumstances. But bereaved parents didn't usually come with diplomatic minders and drivers trained in escaping from public disorder situations, and they didn't drag investigating officers round town and pressurise them into playing family albums with photographic evidence. Though it was only mid-afternoon, it seemed like it had already been a very long day, and she just wanted this part of it to end.

They went into the centre and were shown to a waiting room which Mary knew was next to the one where Katya would be laid out. The five of them sat awkwardly together, none of them saying anything. Mary had been there before, thankfully not too many times. She stole a glance at Mrs Czwisnjowski, sitting impassively next to her husband. She'd didn't seem the silent wife type, yet she's hardly said a word all day. Was she stunned by grief, bottling it all up, what? Mary still couldn't make her out.

A door opened and an attendant came in, spoke to the DI, and led them into the next room. It was larger than the waiting room, with a wide doorway in the opposite wall, suitable for manoeuvring long trolleys in and out.

In the centre of the room was such a trolley, and on it was a body, covered in a white sheet. Mary was behind Mrs Czwisnjowski, and heard her intake of breath as she saw it. She put her hand gently on her shoulder.

"Mrs Czwisnjowski, are you sure you want to do this?" she asked, "we can wait outside if you prefer."

"Thank you, I will stay," the woman replied, her eyes not leaving the white sheet.

The DI took over the proceedings. "Sir, madam, in a moment we'll draw the sheet down to reveal the young lady's face. This is a legal process of identification so I'm afraid I must ask at least one of you to look carefully enough to be certain whether or not it is Katya. Are you both ready?"

"Yes, Inspector," said Mr Czwisnjowski. His wife nodded silently, as before.

The DI signalled to the attendant, who pulled the sheet slowly down over the young woman's head, leaving it folded above her shoulders. Below it, Mary knew, would be a massive scar from chest to groin where they'd cut her open for the autopsy, but there was no need for her parents to see that. She looked paler than when Mary had seen her two days earlier, literally bloodless. Mary could see how strongly she had taken after her mother, with her full lips, round face and long dark hair, but there was a hint of her father too, especially around her eyes.

Mr Czwisnjowski took a half step forward and stared, for a full five seconds, at his daughter's face. Then he stepped back and turned to the DI.

"Yes, this is my daughter Katya." The voice was still firm, but Mary thought she could see the eyes begin to moisten.

"Thank you sir. I am most deeply sorry for your loss."

Mrs Czwisnjowski stepped forward now, looked much more briefly at her daughter and then, suddenly, began to scream at her husband in what Mary took to be Polish. Mary had no idea what she was saying, but her clenched fists, her blazing eyes and the way she spat the words at him provided their own translation; it was her husband's fault that their daughter had died. Mr Czwisnjowski raised his hand, and for second Mary thought he was going to hit his wife; the DI tensed, but Czwisnjowski just brought his hand to rest on her arm, and began to speak to her, "Sophia, Sophia" then more soothing words, still in Polish. The effect was remarkable; almost instantly Mrs Czwisnjowski became silent and regained her composure.

"I am sorry, Inspector, it is just seeing my daughter..."

"Please, Madam, there's absolutely nothing to apologise for. This is a terrible thing for a parent to have to go through."

Mr Czwisnjowski took charge again. "Thank you, Inspector. Now I think we have seen enough."

Mary was relieved to find that there weren't any press in the car park. As they approached the Mercedes, Mr Czwisnjowski held out his hand to the DI.

"Thank you for everything you have done for us today, Inspector. You have been most understanding."

"You're welcome, sir," replied the DI, "and thank you for talking to us about Katya. I know this must be a terrible time for you both." Mr Czwisnjowski nodded silently. The DI pressed on. "It may be that you can help us with more information – is there somewhere we can contact you over the next week or so?"

Mr Czwisnjowski reached into his jacket and brought out a wallet, from which he produced a card.

"This is my private mobile number. We will be at the Avon Gorge Hotel in Bristol."

There were more handshakes, then Borowski and the driver did their door-opening routine and the

Czwisnjowskis got into the car, the doors clunking heavily shut behind them. As Borowski turned to open the front passenger door, the DI called to him.

"Mr Borowski."

"Yes, Inspector?"

"A quick word before you go." The DI, standing a few feet away, made it clear he wanted this word on his ground. Borowski hesitated, then came over. The DI got straight to the point.

"What did Mrs Czwisnjowski say to her husband back there?"

"When, Inspector?"

"When she shouted at him, in the identification room."

"I'm sorry, I did not hear."

Mary and the DI looked at each other in disbelief at the blatant lie.

"You heard perfectly well," said the DI, his tone devoid of all diplomatic niceties, "you were standing three feet from her and she was shouting at the top of her voice."

"It was a private conversation between grieving parents, Inspector. It is not for me to violate that privacy. Mrs Czwisnjowski speaks excellent English, and if she had wanted you to know what she was saying then she would no doubt have used it."

"This is a murder enquiry, Mr Borowski."

The Consular Official seemed to consider this for a moment, then replied.

"My government would like to express its appreciation for the efforts you are making in this case, Inspector," he said. It was diplomatic-speak for "Don't push your luck with me, or my Ambassador will be onto your Chief Constable." There was a sting in the tail, too.

"On the matter of the investigation, I hope you do not mind me asking, but is there not a Major Crime

Investigation Unit team specialising in murder cases, which would normally deal with one such as this?"

He'd done his homework, but the DI seemed ready for the question.

"Yes, sir, based in Bristol, not far from here. But, as you may have read, they have a major case in progress in which two students at Bristol University have been murdered in violent knife attacks. They have reason to believe that it may be the work of a serial killer who will strike again, and the priority is to apprehend them before they do. As for Katya, it's normal for local CID to be involved at this stage of a murder enquiry, and now that we have her identity and the information her parents have given us, we'll be able to brief the Major Crime unit fully as and when they become involved. This case is being monitored at the highest levels within the Force, sir, and I can assure you that it's receiving proper attention. I'm highly confident that we will catch whoever is responsible for Katya's death."

Borowski seemed satisfied, as much by the DI's mastery of official tone as by what he'd actually said. The DI, however, had a sting of his own to deliver.

"Funny thing is though, we had a murder here a few years ago where the victim was a Polish citizen. Your embassy didn't seem very interested in that one, just wanted a written report afterwards. The dead man's wife had to make her own way here too - no consular officials or diplomatic cars. But then her husband was just a builder."

Borowski gave a wry smile, the first time Mary had seen him look anything but serious.

"Let us not be naïve, Inspector," he said, "Mr Czwisnjowski is a prominent figure in the Polish business community. If the child of one of your FTSE 100 CEOs had been found murdered in my country then your embassy in Warsaw would no doubt be providing similar assistance, and asking similar questions."

Touché.

"Yes, no doubt," the DI conceded.

"In the Soviet era it would have been only for a senior Party official. Today Poland is a member of the European Union, so we do it your way. It is what you wanted, is it not?"

"I wasn't personally involved in the decision-making process, as it happens."

"Which of us is, Inspector?"

Borowski bowed his head briefly, turned to walk away, then turned back.

"Inspector."

"Yes?"

"Mrs Czwisnjowski did not want her daughter to come to England. She thought it was too dangerous here."

"Thank you."

"Goodbye."

Chapter 14

The long day wasn't over yet. A press briefing was scheduled for five o'clock, at which the identity of the murder victim would be confirmed as Katya Czwisnjowski of Gdansk, Poland, although this was evidently already an open secret among the media. After that would be a squad briefing on the day's developments and assignments for the following day, Saturday being a work day in the first week of a murder case.

The DI and Mary drove back down the motorway to Weston, lights and sirens off this time, at what seemed like a sedate seventy miles per hour.

"What do you make of the Czwisnjowskis now?" asked the DI as he pulled out into the fast lane.

"I get the feeling there's a whole lot under the surface that they're not showing us, Guv," Mary replied, "I mean, stiff upper lip's one thing, but they've kept it bottled up beyond belief. Except for that one bit when she let rip at him. Even then she was buttoned up again ten seconds later."

"I'm not sure we should read too much into that." the DI said sceptically", "They're from the rich and powerful – people like that don't show their feelings in front of the hired help. The father'll probably go down the hotel gym tonight and knock seven bells out of a punchbag".

"Just as long as he doesn't knock seven bells out of his wife instead."

"Does she look to you like the kind of woman who'd take that sort of thing? She'd have his eyes out with those nails of hers – they're already painted blood red to camouflage the evidence."

Mary smiled. She'd noticed Mrs Czwisnjowski's fingernails too – no extensions for her, just long natural ones perfectly manicured and painted. "So do you think they're just grieving parents who don't show it then, nothing more than that?"

"No, as it happens," replied the DI, "I think it's overwhelmingly likely that Katya was murdered because of who she was, most likely to get at her father. The whole thing is too professional – the boat, the burial, the way her phone had been wiped. It looked that way from the start, but seeing her parents makes it a cert for me. The father's in import-export, whatever that actually means, operating in the former Soviet Bloc. There's a fair chance he does business with people who wouldn't think twice about killing his daughter as a penalty for late delivery. If so, it's odds on that he's got a good idea who actually did it."

"So we need to find out who he does his business with?"

"Exactly. Let's hope Cox has got something for us."

Cox didn't, in fact, have all that much for them on the Czwisnjowskis' business interests, which he put down to his inability to understand the contents of most of the online company registration and business databases he'd visited. Nervously he explained that the 'Google Thing' could only go so far in translating complex ownership and shareholding details from Polish to English, and that they really needed to get a translator in. That meant cost, which Cox knew wouldn't be a welcome option with the DI. But to Cox's and Mary's surprise the DI said to go ahead and get one, and to bring them in tomorrow even though that meant paying weekend rates. Taken aback by this, Cox said that they could always ask the Polish police, who seemed to have plenty of English-speaking officers, but the DI said no. Puzzled, but with no inclination to argue, Cox went off to make the arrangements.

"Why don't you want him to ask the Polish police, Guv?" said Mary, as they prepared to go downstairs for the press briefing.

"I'd just like us to know something that our friend Borowski doesn't know we know," he replied as they went down the stairs, "even things out a bit."

"Don't you trust him?"

"He's a diplomatic official, and by the look of him he's used to operating at the sharp end of diplomacy. He'll bat for his side, which right now means the important Polish citizens he's been sent down here to look after. As he said back there, our Embassy people would be doing the same in Poland."

The Press Briefing had mushroomed into a major event, with TV lights, the Constabulary backdrop and a PA system. The room was small, crammed with reporters and cameramen, and consequently hot, the air conditioning being off for the winter. Mary saw most of the group who'd been outside the station at lunchtime, plus a few more she didn't recognise. Jane Thomas, the reporter from the BBC local news, was there, and she and Mary exchanged nods.

DCI Spence introduced the proceedings, then quickly handed over to DI Jones. Mary watched from the sidelines, craning to see over the heads of the journalists.

"We can now confirm that the victim is Katya Czwisnjowski, of Gdansk, Poland", the DI said into the microphone. He'd been on the media course, and looked much more relaxed than Mary knew she'd have been. "Katya was a student at Bristol University for three years, studying politics and international relations, and graduated this summer. There must be many people who knew her at the university, and we'd ask anyone who did to contact us on the hotline number we'll be giving at the end of this briefing. We are, however, particularly interested in hearing from anyone who saw Katya in the UK in the past six weeks, since early October."

Questions were supposed to be taken at the end, but after a few more details, plus a promise that the spelling of Czwisnjowski would be in the press release, one of the reporters, a young man holding up a voice recorder, decided he wasn't waiting any longer.

"Do the police think there's any connection between the murder and the Czwisnjowski family's business interests in Russia and the former Soviet Bloc states, Inspector?" he shouted. All heads turned in his direction, but Mary kept her eyes on the DI, who seemed keen to take the question on.

"You seem to know more about this case than we do, sir" he replied, "I hope you'll share any relevant information you have with us."

The reporter laughed. "My information is privileged, Inspector."

"With respect, sir, your information is covered by section nine of PACE, which means we can apply for a court order compelling you to release it to us if it would help our investigation."

The young man's expression hardened. "Is that a threat?"

"No sir, it's a request on behalf of the community here in Weston-super-Mare for assistance in finding out who murdered this young woman, before they murder someone else. I'm sure we all share a desire to do that."

1-0 to the Guvnor, thought Mary – picking up that the young reporter wasn't local and throwing the 'community' angle at him. Quite brilliant, in fact. The reporter didn't have an answer to it, but another one, a local Mary recognised, went in with a supplementary.

"Could there be a link between those business interests and groups from former Soviet Bloc countries operating here in Weston?" It was a more provocative question than it sounded, as the reaction from other local reporters indicated. He meant the Albanians, and probably knew it would be a delicate subject for the DI.

"We'll be looking at all relevant aspects of Katya's background, but the investigation is still at an early stage. We only became aware of Katya's identity yesterday." In other words we're not saying. But it was an angle they wouldn't be able to ignore.

Q&A seemed to have started in earnest now, and the other reporters weighed in, with the DI fielding questions from all angles.

"Is this case being linked with the Bristol University murders?"

"Obviously the fact that Katya studied at Bristol means we have to examine that possibility, but the differences in the killers' methods, and the fact that she was no longer a student, point towards them not being linked."

"Was there a sexual element to the murder?"

"No, we've pretty much ruled that out. There are, in fact, no signs that Katya suffered physical violence of any kind before her death."

"Is it true that Katya's arm was pointing up out of the sand? If so, is it considered significant?" Good question, thought Mary, wondering where the reporter had got her information from.

"It is the case that Katya's body was not fully covered by the sand when she was found, but the tide had been in and out by then, and may have disturbed it." A not entirely straight answer.

"Will you be keeping control of this case, or will the Bristol Murder Squad be taking over?"

"We're in full contact with the Major Crime

Investigation Unit's Murder Team, and they're monitoring progress here, but as you know it's been assessed that there is a real danger that the Bristol killer will strike again, and officers there are fully deployed on preventing that from happening." Not entirely straight either, although the DCI was no doubt liaising with his opposite number. The media course wasn't wasted, thought Mary. She wondered if she'd ever be able to handle the press that well, although she'd have to make it to DI first.

The young reporter who'd asked about the Czwisnjowskis had backed off, but came back now.

"How did you trace Katya so quickly, when initial reports said there was nothing to identify her? Did you get a tip-off?"

The DI smiled. "No, there was no tip-off. Instead it was an exceptional piece of observation by one of our officers, who noticed that the wear pattern on the keyboard of Katya's phone was consistent with having been used to type in Polish rather than English. That led us to check Polish missing persons, and we found Katya's details there."

Mary groaned, so loudly that a photographer standing next to her turned and stared at her before directing his attention back to the DI. It had been bad enough when the DI had told the Czwisnjowskis that she'd spotted the keyboard wear, but this was potentially far worse. She just hoped it would stay at that without her being named in public, although she had a bad feeling about that too.

The rest of the briefing went smoothly enough, with the DCI stepping in at the end to assure everyone that those responsible would be found, and those present would be kept fully informed.

Jane Thomas was a few feet from Mary, talking to her cameraman. Mary pushed her way over to her.

"Hello Jane." Mary's turn to earn kudos by remembering a name, "do you know who that reporter is?" She gestured at the young man who'd asked the DI about the Czwisnjowskis.

"No, he's not local," Jane replied, winding a cable round her hand as she spoke, "I think he's from one of the nationals, a broadsheet. He was down here when the Hinkley Point enquiry was on."

"He seemed to know a lot about our victim's family."

Jane Thomas smiled. "I wouldn't take too much notice of that. If he had anything really juicy he wouldn't have let it out in front of the rest of us. I assume he's right though, that the Czwisnjowskis have got business interests in the former Soviet Union?" Now she was quizzing Mary. Mary decided she should give her something.

"They run an import-export business in Gdansk, so they may well have, although we haven't looked into it yet. We only met them today."

Jane's eyes brightened. "So you've met them personally? What are they like?"

"Grief-stricken," replied Mary, "but in general they seem like very prosperous business people. Katya's mother is Italian."

"Is she indeed?" said Jane.

"Yes, or at least she sounds it," said Mary, "but don't quote me on that, please."

"My sources are privileged," said Jane, in a jokey impersonation of the young broadsheet reporter. They both laughed, and Mary moved off to find the DI.

The DI's team briefing was, thankfully, less eventful than the one for the press. Everyone was due in the next day, which caused a few grumbles from those with Saturday commitments ("The Constabulary second fifteen will have to manage without you, Constable – they had to plenty of times in my playing days, I can assure you"), but brought the considerable compensation of overtime. The focus, the DI told them, was now firmly on the Czwisnjowskis, specifically any contacts, business or otherwise, they had in the UK who might have had a reason to murder their daughter. He'd be going to Bristol the following morning to talk to the Murder Squad about any possible link to the university killings, even though that seemed very unlikely. More usefully, they might be able to give him a head start on Katya's life at the university.

When the DI asked for any other reports, Cox piped up.

"Michael Slade, sir, the man we had on CCTV walking away from the scene – his story checks out. Twelve cameras altogether, tracking him all the way from Between the Lines to the Cabot."

A few jeers went up at the mention of Between the Lines. Cox continued.

"Plus, there are witnesses to him arriving at the Clarendon three minutes after his last CCTV appearance, just before five to eleven. He's known in there – they reckon he's a bit of an eccentric, apparently. There's no way he'd have time for any detours between the cameras – in fact he must be a quick walker to have got to the Clarendon that fast."

"Did you confirm the time he left the supermarket?" asked the DI.

"Yes, Guv. His checkout supervisor said he was there from three to ten pm, never left the building. She wasn't very happy talking to me about it, but she seemed on the level."

"All right, thanks Pete." said the DI.

"So where does that leave Slade, Guv?" asked DC Lane. "Is he on the board?"

The DI looked across at the whiteboard, actually a

transparent plastic screen which, during a major case, got covered in photographs of evidence, victims and suspects, along with connecting lines and key facts scrawled in marker pen. Today it was looking decidedly empty.

"No, not a person of interest either, but let's not forget him altogether. He wouldn't be the first one to pop back into the frame just before the final whistle."

Mary was relieved. Michael Slade was effectively ruled out of the case, which meant that the business of her showing him Katya's phone could be left to fade into the mists of time. She still felt bad about the DI not crediting him with spotting the keyboard wear, but perhaps that was for the best too. She certainly wouldn't talk to the DI about it tonight, as she'd been half-intending to do. Despite the early start tomorrow it was still Friday night, not the time to be making an issue over something that, with a bit of luck, would be forgotten anyway. Time for her to have a Friday night too, one she really needed after a draining day.

Almost as she thought it, her phone made its incoming text message sound. She checked the screen – 'Don'. If this was another instruction to go shopping on her way home, he'd be getting a very short reply. But in fact it wasn't. Instead the message read:

"Dinner on, wine in fridge. Expect u've had a tough day. Back soon?"

She smiled, remembering how Don had often done things like that when they were first together and she'd been on lates as a uniform PC. It didn't happen so often now, but if it was happening tonight she'd gratefully accept it. Inexpertly she texted back:

"Sounds lovely, leaving now"

Then quickly, before anything could stop her, she stuffed the phone into her bag, grabbed her coat and headed for the car park.

Chapter 15

The clock in Mary's car read 18:46 as she pulled onto the short concrete drive up to their garage. Don had parked his van on the road in front of the house. She read the lettering on its side: "DON MILLER HEATING" and his Gas Safe registration number, showing that he was qualified to install gas equipment. Don traded under his full name to show that he was proud of his workmanship; he could be slovenly around the house, but his van and its contents were always immaculate. It gleamed under the street lamp now. He was very good at what he did, just as she liked to think that she was a good detective.

Entering the house she smelt the food; it would be supermarket ready meals, but heating them in the oven rather than the microwave counted as proper cooking in Don's book (and, in truth, hers too). He came out into the hall to meet her.

"Hello Love, perfect timing. It's almost ready – five minutes."

This wasn't the Don who'd greeted her with a semi-comatose grunt of "All right?" from the sofa three days earlier. He'd changed out of his work clothes, and looked smart-casual in navy chinos and a denim shirt. He smelt faintly of the aftershave she'd given him for his birthday. They kissed, on the cheek. Behind him Mary could see the table in the dining area, formally laid out with wine glasses and napkins.

"This is lovely, Don. What's the occasion?"

"Nothing. You've had a tough day, that's all. I saw you earlier."

"Did you? What was I doing?"

"Fending reporters off a big Merc outside the station. You and Jones. I drove past, but you had your back to me. Looked like you were struggling to keep 'em off."

"We were." Lunchtime seemed like the distant past now. "We weren't expecting that many of them. I think someone had tipped off the nationals."

"So who was in the Merc?"

"Our victim's parents, plus a driver and a consular official from the Polish Embassy in London."

"Blimey – diplomatic incident, eh?"

"Something like that."

"Well forget it for now. It's Duck a l'Orange, your favourite. Sit down, I'll get the wine."

Mary looked down at her work clothes. It was doubtless her imagination, but she could still smell the disinfected air of the Pathology centre on them.

"Pour me one out. I just want to change out of these things. Five minutes, max – I promise."

"No rush," he smiled, "I'll dish up."

Their house was modern, the staircase made lethally steep to save space. As she often did these days, Mary noticed they weren't getting any easier to climb. The bedroom door was open, the bedside lamp left burning on Don's side. He'd made the bed. Out of habit she looked for his dirty overalls on the floor but they were nowhere to be seen; he really was going the extra mile.

Mary stretched the five minutes to accommodate a 90 second shower. She'd have liked to change into her slouch gear afterwards - jogging pants, sweatshirt, big fluffy slippers - but Don had made the effort and it seemed only right to reciprocate. She chose a grey jersey dress, smart-casual like his shirt and chinos. She'd spent the day investigating a murder, now she was making herself look attractive for her husband, tidying her hair, redoing her makeup. In twelve hours time she'd be investigating the murder again. It was hard switching roles sometimes, but she did it. She'd been very attractive once, a woman men turned to look at as she entered a room. She'd liked it, and so had Don. She didn't want to lose it altogether.

Don's response, as she entered the living room, made it worth the effort. His eyes widened, a soft smile spread across his face.

"You look lovely, love. You really do. Thanks."

"No need to thank me," she said, like an awkward teenager on a first date, "you look nice too."

"Yeah well, it's nice to make an effort sometimes, isn't it?"

She nodded. He stepped forward, and she felt his arm round her waist. They kissed, briefly but on the lips this time. He stepped back again, and took a glass of wine from the table.

"Here we are – chilled to perfection. The good stuff too - none of that three quid rubbish for my beautiful wife!"

She smiled as she took the glass.

"It used to be two quid, remember?" That was when they were first married and living in a flat over a shop, saving for a deposit. She'd been a uniform WPC, in the days when 'W' was still used to denote female officers. Don was not long out of his apprenticeship, already talking about setting up his own business. He smiled too now at the thought of it.

"Yeah, that Bulgarian Riesling that tasted like paint stripper, and we wouldn't buy the Piesporter because it was 30p extra!"

It seemed a long time ago, and so it was – sixteen years next summer. And they could still be like this together at home on a Friday night. It couldn't be all bad.

The moment was disturbed by the sound of Mary's mobile phone, coming from her bag in the hallway. She gave an agonised look.

"Let it ring," she said, keeping her back to the doorway, "I'm off duty."

"You know you can't, love," Don replied, but his voice was gentle and he was still smiling, not the angry look he'd had in recent years when her work had interrupted their lives, "You're on a murder case, there is no off duty. It's OK, really."

Not quite sure of him, but knowing he was right about the duty, she turned, went to her bag and retrieved her phone. The caller was a mobile number she didn't recognise, which meant it could be a kid on a prank, or the Murder Squad calling her in for an emergency briefing. There was only one way to find out. Walking back into the dining room, she pressed the button and held the phone to her ear.

"Hello?"

"Is that Mary?"

"Who's this?"

"Michael."

"Sorry?"

"Michael Slade. I'm on my break at work and I've just seen the end of the evening news. I didn't think you'd do that to me, Mary, steal my credit for helping you. I thought I could trust you."

Mary groaned, and looked helplessly at Don. They'd obviously run the bit from the press conference where the DI had claimed that one of his detectives had spotted the Polish connection on the phone keyboard.

"Michael, I had no idea he was going to say that, really." That wasn't altogether true, given that she'd heard the DI say it to the Czwisnjowskis earlier in the day. She hadn't expected it to come up at the press conference though.

"Yes, well, I'm not surprised he did - just like your Detective Inspector, frankly, from what I've seen of him.

Keeps me detained in a windowless interrogation room then takes the credit when I give him his crucial lead. I was foolish to expect anything better from the Police. It's very disappointing, all the same, Mary."

"It was just a passing remark, Michael. He probably didn't even think about what he was saying." Mary was still facing Don; she mouthed "I'm sorry!", but he just smiled and mouthed "It's OK" back.

"Well he'll think about it when it's all over the front page of the Mercury that Weston CID rely on help from the public to solve their crimes then steal the credit for it." That got Mary's attention. Rightly or wrongly, she was the instigator of this situation; in a PR disaster, with the Force needing a scapegoat, she'd be lucky to hold on to a job in uniform, with or without the 'W' in front of 'PC'.

Mary knew her limitations. In this situation the DI would keep spinning a line, despite that being a dangerous approach to use with Michael Slade. For her the only option was honesty, whatever the outcome.

"Look, Michael, it's complicated. The victim's parents have got someone from the Polish embassy with them, and he's been taking shots at us all day, as if he's looking for an excuse to make an official protest. If he found out that I'd shown that phone to you, having previously taken you in for questioning, he'd have a field day. The DI was probably protecting me when he said that at the press conference."

"Protecting himself, more likely, Mary."

"No, I honestly think he'd put his officers first. I know you've seen the rough side of him, but he just wants to find out who killed Katya. And he is a good boss - he backs us up, takes responsibility for what we do. Believe me, you don't always get that these days." Mary said it with such conviction that even Don looked impressed.

There was silence from the other end of the phone.

Mary didn't know if this was good or bad. Eventually Michael spoke.

"Yes well, perhaps I've misjudged him due to the difficult circumstances in which we've met. I think he misjudged me too though."

"To be fair, Michael, you gave him good reason." There was another silence. Mary wondered if she'd gone too far, but Michael's voice came back.

"All right, I suppose I did. Have they finished checking my route to the seafront on Tuesday yet?"

"Yes, I was going to ring you tomorrow about that. Your story checks out."

"Good. Perhaps your boss will remember that." Michael's brief period of penitence was evidently over.

"I'm sure he will, but if I were you I wouldn't go rattling his cage with any more startling revelations or unexpected CCTV appearances. Best to just leave it to us now, and I'm really sorry about the press conference."

"That's all right, I suppose. I'm not looking for fame and fortune. There was something else though Mary, in the news report just now. I wanted to ask you ..."

Mary swiped her forehead in frustration, and mouthed "Sorry" at Don again.

"Michael, did you hear what I just said? Leave it to us. I can't discuss the case with you any more."

"But it's only a small point," Michael persisted, "Someone said the girl's arm was pointing up out of the sand. Which direction was it pointing in?"

"I don't remember, and I couldn't tell you even if I did."

"It could be crucial, just like the wear on the keyboard was. It's the small things that often lead to the solving of crimes, you know."

"Yes I do know – I'm a detective." She was becoming exasperated now. "But do you know that it's not unknown for a murderer to get their kicks from staying close to the police investigation, or how high up the list of profiling categories for this kind of crime middle-aged men with broken marriages come?"

"My marriage isn't broken. We're just readjusting."

"You know what I mean. You're not a suspect in this case, but you still could be. You've had two strikes with us, and my DI still isn't fully convinced about either of them. Don't take a third."

"But I think the direction of the hand may be significant..."

"Michael!" She barked down the phone so loudly that Don jumped. "For your own good, keep away from the police now. Look, I'm back on duty in the morning, I have a few hours at home with my husband which I desperately need. I'm really sorry about the press conference, and I'll try to get you some recognition, honestly. But I've got to go now. Goodbye." Without waiting for Michael's reply, she pressed the red button to end the call.

"I'm so sorry love, really." Mary gave Don a pleading look as she said it. Don, however, seemed genuinely sympathetic.

"It's not your fault, love, any more than an emergency callout for a burst boiler's mine." He laughed. "See - we both serve the public don't we?" Mary laughed too. Don the diffuser of tension; you could see a new side to someone, even after fifteen years of marriage.

Mary held the phone up so he could see the screen, pressed the Menu key and chose the 'Silent' option.

"There," she said, putting the phone back in her bag, "it's not off, is it? I just may not hear it if it rings. Anyone wants me, they can text me." If they really wanted her they'd send a squad car round, they both knew that. It was a gesture, but not a bad one.

"Sorted, I'd say," said Don, "Who was that, anyway? Sounded a bit weird."

"He is. I won't bore you with the details."

"No, go on – unless you don't want to talk about it."

But she did want to talk about it. She often wanted to tell her husband about the things that had happened at work, but he often – well, almost always – didn't want to hear. "Yeah, yeah, I'm sure it's a lot more exciting than fixing gas boilers" was a favourite put-down of recent times, but there had been plenty of others in the years since her move into CID, and especially since her promotion to Detective Sergeant. It seemed as if he saw every advance of hers as a setback for him. Tonight though, it was different.

So she told him, as they dished up the dinner and poured more wine, describing the half checkout operator, half computer genius who'd seemed to know too much, how his powerful binoculars had let him spot a BlackBerry phone from 200 metres away and his even more powerful intellect had let him work out the entire crime scene from a few glimpses. When she got to the bit about the CCTV Don expressed astonishment that the DI didn't already have Michael banged up on remand awaiting trial, commenting that the small matter of the suspect being innocent had never worried him the past, a jibe which Mary chose to ignore. And when Don asked her why this not-quite-a-suspect was ringing her up on a Friday evening, she took a deep breath and told him how she'd taken the mobile phone out to show him, against various rules and the DI's orders, how Michael had spotted the keyboard wear pattern, and how the DI had then told the press conference that one of his officers had found it.

Don put his knife and fork down and leaned back in his chair.

"Well I can see why this Michael chap was upset," he said, "with your boss stealing his thunder like that. I could have warned him to watch out for Jones."

Mary chose to ignore that jibe too.

"It's like I said to him, I think the DI was probably protecting me more than himself."

"Hmm," said Don, clearly still sceptical, "So if this bloke's so useful, why were you telling him to back off on the phone just now?"

"What I said. The DI isn't convinced that he's not the murderer, or at least involved in the murder, feeding us titbits for fun."

"And are you?"

"Pretty much, yes. He's more like an enthusiastic schoolboy. You should have seen his face when I gave him the phone to look at."

"If he's as clever as you say then that could just be a front."

Mary looked at Don, the husband who not only let her talk about her work but offered opinions too. The conversation was becoming disorientingly like the one she'd had with the DI on this subject the previous day. One lapse of concentration and she'd be calling him 'Guv', and that really would not go down well.

"Fingers crossed he isn't." She looked down at her plate. "This is lovely, Don – thank you. Just what I needed tonight, couldn't be better."

If Don was relieved that the shop talk was over, he did a good job of hiding it.

"I'm glad you like it, love. When I saw you outside the station trying to clear those photographers away, it made me think how tough all this must be for you."

"It's my job, but yes it has been tough today, so this is brilliant," Mary said, with genuine gratitude, "We had to take the parents to identify the body. Never a nice thing."

"No," said Don, and looked down at the table. "Look I know I don't say it often, but I am proud of what you do, love, and I do know it's important."

Mary suppressed a smile. "I don't say it often" was something of an understatement, but now wasn't the time to dwell on it. Instead she changed the subject, opting for a topic with a good track record of neutrality.

"Has Tina heard anything about her op yet?"

Don's sister was on the waiting list for a minor operation to remove a benign growth from her foot, and after eight months was becoming impatient. Don, for a variety of reasons, found this mildly amusing.

"No," he chuckled, "she's saying that she needs all new shoes now as none of hers fit any more, and she's going to send the bill to the NHS. It's poor Dave I feel sorry for – every time they give her another brushoff she takes it out on him. Mind you, I did warn him not to marry her, so he's only got himself to blame."

Mary laughed out loud. Don was very fond of his sister, but she could be temperamental and he had, genuinely, warned his close friend Dave that she might not be the ideal bride. Mary's relationship with Tina had not always been silky smooth either, but right now she could have kissed her.

"She can borrow some of my shoes. I'm half a size bigger than her, they should fit perfectly."

Now it was Don's turn to laugh out loud.

"Oh dear. I don't quite know how to put this, my love, but I don't think your taste in footwear would satisfy our Tina's fashion requirements." They laughed together. It was true that Mary's collection of shoes didn't include any leopardskin pumps with gold lame trimming, or five-inch heel Jimmy Choo knock-offs from the Sunday market. Bless her.

The relaxed atmosphere lasted, both of them determined to keep it that way. On the sofa, close to Don, Mary felt warm and happy. Some might (and did) question how she could laugh and joke just hours after seeing a dead girl and her distraught parents, but despite being prone to guilt about other things, she'd let her training and experience teach her to feel none about this. She was working to make things as right as they could be made about Katya's death, by catching whoever killed her; to do it effectively she needed to keep it professional and take breaks from the pressure. She'd be back on the front line soon enough.

They went to bed just after ten. It occurred to Mary that Don might have other reasons besides sleep for wanting an early night, and that the whole evening, the meal and the understanding hubby thing, might have been part of it. It wasn't a problem though; there'd been more than enough sincerity to make the evening real, and there was nothing wrong with wanting to sleep with your wife. She found the long satin nightdress that Don liked. It made her figure look good, even now. As he came out of the bathroom his eyes widened again, and he smiled.

In bed though things seemed awkward, and for a terrible moment Mary thought that intimacy had gone for them. When it came, Don's approach was so tentative - an arm lightly across her, a whispered "Mary, can we?" - that it almost broke her heart. He was one step away from begging her, and that would have been unbearable. The guilt kicked in now, with no defences against it. It was her fault, or at least the job's – the late hours, the stress, the perpetual tiredness. Her fault that there were still "just the two of you", as her mother put it; "career before family" as Don's mother had said at one terrible Sunday lunch. Her fear of ineffective contraception that made her treat love-making like Russian roulette, more so since her transfer to CID and her promotion to Detective Sergeant.

She thought of the old Don, the confident lover who'd take her in his arms and announce that he was going to transport her to heaven, and quite often did. She still loved him, tonight had taught her that, and she loved him the best she could now, through the tiredness and the memory of Katya Czwisnjowski lying dead on the table.

When it was over he stayed lying half on her, his weight pressing down. In the dim light of the alarm clock his eyes glistened as if there were tears in them.

"I do love you, Mary, you know that, don't you?"

"Yes, and I love you too." She pulled him down and kissed him softly. She was sure she felt a drop of moisture on her cheek.

The guilt receded. A female DCI had told her to play the system; get promotion, take maternity leave then let Don be the stay at home parent, an affordable option on a DI's pay. It wasn't a suggestion she'd considered putting to Don or his mother, but that wasn't her fault.

Soon Don was fast asleep. Mary went to the bathroom, then crept quietly out onto the landing and carefully down the steep stairs. She retrieved her phone from her bag and went back to the bedroom. Plugging it into its charger, she switched it on. No messages, no missed calls, the perfect end to the evening. She switched the silent option off, put the phone on the bedside table and got into bed.

In her dream Mary was on a beach, in her satin nightdress. From all around her she could hear the sound of a mobile phone ringing, but the phone was nowhere to be seen. It must be buried, but if it was, then how could she hear it, and why did it sound as if it was coming from everywhere? It was too big a problem to solve, and as she came awake she realised with relief that she didn't have to, but then that the sound was of her real phone, on the table next to the bed. The alarm clock read 06:57 – almost time to get up anyway. The phone's screen read 'DI Jones', which probably meant she'd be getting up in a hurry, although what for she couldn't guess.

Don seemed to be still asleep. She grabbed the phone, pulling the charger cable out as she did, and took it out onto the landing, closing the door behind her. She pressed the 'Answer' button and lifted the handset to speak, but the DI beat her to it.

"Sand Bay, south end car park by the pub. Quick as you can."

"What's up, Guv?"

"We've got another body."

Chapter 16

Sand Bay, two miles north of Weston, wasn't one of Mary's favourite places. Despite offering a mile-long beach with an unspoilt headland at its northern end, it had too many dogs, too many people in pastel leisurewear and too many drug and alcohol overdoses among the youngsters who drove out there for parties on summer nights. In Weston the grime from the Bristol Channel coated the sea walls; here it seemed to coat the sand. It was good for walkers and people interested in spotting rare seabirds, but neither of those was Mary's idea of a good day out.

Dawn was just breaking as she negotiated the hairpin turn into the road that led down to the south end of the beach. As she reached the bottom of the hill her headlights picked out a uniformed PC guarding the entrance to the car park. It was Durham, the probationer who'd found Katya Czwisnjowski's phone. She wound down her window and switched on the interior light so he could see her face.

"Morning, Detective Sergeant," said the young man, who appeared to be shivering slightly.

"Morning PC Durham," Mary replied, "you're getting all the best assignments, aren't you?"

"Something like that, ma'am, yes." Mary wasn't keen on being called "Ma'am", but Durham wasn't to know that.

"Is DI Jones here?"

"Just arrived Ma'am."

"OK, thanks. Try to stay warm – stamp your feet or something."

"Yes Ma'am."

Mary drove along the short access road and into the car park. Uniform hadn't wasted any time; they already had a mobile incident room parked up, lights blazing, and were erecting floodlights on the path to the beach. Mary pulled up next to the DI's Audi as he was getting out of it.

"Morning Guv."

"Morning."

"Tell me it's not like the other one."

"Not going to be your day, is it?"

The DI opened the boot of his car, rummaged inside and brought out two big torches, handing one to Mary. They walked to the edge of the car park, from where they could see a cluster of lanterns fifty yards or so away, down beyond the ridge that marked the end of the sandy scrubland at the top of the beach. The DI hesitated; the crime scene hadn't been secured yet, and blundering onto the sand might compromise it. As he stood there, a flashlight beam fell on him.

"Hang on Steve – that way's probably evidence."

The voice came from their right, by the wooden decking path which led north over rough ground to the main beach. Mary recognised it as belonging to Ted Deane, a uniformed inspector. Deane was the DI's contemporary, although he looked and acted older. Mary was glad to see him; if you needed someone to manage a difficult crime scene, you could do worse than Methodical Ted.

"Morning Ted," said the DI as Deane reached them, "What have we got?"

"Same basics as the pier," replied Deane, nodding to Mary, "just a lower arm visible, apparently attached to a body in the sand. This one looks male though, thick hair on the forearm."

"Who found him? Not a dog walker out here at this time, surely?"

"No, young revellers from an all-night party. Came for breakfast on the beach, got more than they bargained for."

"Breakfast on the beach, at six am in November?" said Mary incredulously.

"Come now, weren't you ever young and adventurous, Sergeant?"

"Not that adventurous, no, sir."

"Young and stoked up on Es, more likely," said the DI, "Where are they?"

"In the Incident van. They were still on the beach when we got here, in Stage One hypothermia. I thought we'd better thaw them out for you."

The DI allowed himself a smile. "Cheers. Can you keep 'em a bit longer? We'll take a look over there first."

"Sure. There are some tracks leading down that path to the body, probably evidence. This one definitely didn't come in by boat. I've marked out an alternative path, over to the right then back. Just follow the lanterns."

"Thanks Ted - see you back here."

Mary and the DI walked to the end of the line of big rocks which marked the edge of the car park, then used their torches to follow the path to a lantern, the first of a string which ran across the sand between tussocks of grass. In the first light the effect was oddly like that of a summer beach party at dusk, the way Mary imagined it would be in California, except that she didn't imagine California would be this cold. Ted Deane had done his job well; the SOCO team hadn't arrived yet, so there was no tent, but the area around the body had been cordoned off with tape and PCs to guard it. The lantern trail took them out to the side of the cordon then in again; as they turned towards it they could see the car park on their left ablaze with lights, now joined by dimmer house lights on the hill above it. Kewstoke was waking up; soon there'd be crowds, and reporters too.

As they reached the cordon tape the DI shone his torch beam up onto his face for the benefit of the PC guarding the entrance, receiving a "Morning, Sir" in response. PC Durham had, in fact, got the relatively easy posting, thought Mary – it was even colder here than at the car park entrance. The light was increasing rapidly now, but they still moved carefully towards the centre of the cordon, the DI in front, keeping their torches trained on the ground, looking for anything that the SOCOs might not want them treading on. Finally they reached the inner group of four lanterns, spaced 20 feet apart, which marked the zone that was off limits until the SOCOs had processed it. They trained their torches on the centre of the zone. Clearly visible in the beams, rising at an angle from a low mound of sand, was a human arm. Mary raised her torch beam until it found the hand, then stopped.

"Guv."

"Yes, I can see it."

The DI trained his beam on the hand too, bringing it into sharper detail. The thumb and three smaller fingers were curled inwards, leaving just the index finger extended straight in line with the palm. It might have been chance, but it didn't look like it; the finger was pointing, deliberately, away from them towards the thick woodland that marked the southern end of Sand Bay.

They both stood silent for a moment, then the DI spoke.

"We can't do anything here until the SOCOs open it up. Let's get back to the van and see those kids."

Still treading carefully, they made their way back along the lantern path. As they reached the car park they met the SOCO officers, already in white overalls, carrying their tools and folding tent.

"Another buried one, Inspector?" said the SOCO

leading the group.

"Yes – you'll need your hoist again. Make sure to get plenty of shots of the hand, close detail. You'll see why when you get out there."

"OK, will do." said the officer.

"Can you give me a ring when you're ready for us to come out? And hold off digging until we've had another look."

"Sure."

The incident van was warm and almost blindingly bright after the gloom outside. At one end, next to two catering-size vacuum flasks, PC Durham sat nursing a hot drink – Ted Deane doing his job again, thought Mary, rotating his officers through warm pit stops between sessions outside. At the other end of the van sat five teenagers, three boys and two girls, dressed in what Mary assumed was the current fashion for attending all-night parties in Weston. All were cradling paper cups of steaming liquid. One of the girls was quietly crying, and one of the boys looked like he might burst into tears at any moment. The others just sat silently, staring at the floor. To Mary they all looked about 15, although everyone seemed to look younger as she got older.

Filling paper cups of their own from the flasks, Mary and the DI approached the group.

"Hello, I'm Detective Inspector Steve Jones, and this is Detective Sergeant Mary Miller. We're from Weston CID."

The group looked up at them and nodded in acknowledgement. The girl went back to crying.

"The first thing I need to ask you is are any of you under 17?"

One of the floor-starers looked up again.

"Surely you're not worried about whether we've been drinking under age?" More incredulous than cheeky,

Mary thought. The DI seemed to see it that way too.

"No, no, nothing like that." he said, sitting down on a spare chair. "It's just that if any of you are under 17 then we have to get your parents or another suitable adult here before we can talk to you."

"Oh, right. No, we're all 18."

"I'm 19," said the young man next to him.

"Yeah, he's 19." said the first youth.

"Have you got any proof of your ages? It's not that we don't trust you, we just have to be very careful where young people are concerned."

"Of course we have." said the 19 year old, producing a student card from his wallet with the practised air of someone who was used to being ID'd. The others followed suit. Mary was slightly surprised to see the younger-looking of the two girls produce a full driving licence.

"OK, good. Well I expect you'll want to contact someone anyway, and we will need to take full statements from you, probably at the station in Weston, but do you all feel up to answering a few basic questions now? It would be a big help."

They all nodded.

"Good. Perhaps we can start with your names." Their names were on their ID cards and the witness forms that Ted Deane's officers had already filled out, but it was better coming from them.

The girl with the driving licence spoke.

"I'm Ellie, this is Tamzin," she said, then pointing at the young men "and that's Damian, Zac and Ewan."

Mary wondered whether anyone called their kids basic names like John or Jane any more. It seemed not.

"OK, and how did you all come to be here this morning?"

"We'd been at a party in Weston." Ellie seemed to be the spokesperson, or at least the person who spoke.

"An all-nighter?" asked Mary.

"Not really. Everyone crashed out around three, then we woke up and decided to come down here."

"Breakfast on the beach?"

"I suppose. There was food left over at the party so we took some."

"And what time did you get here?"

Now the 19 year old, Zac, joined in.

"About a quarter past six. I checked my messages when we got here."

"And what happened then?" asked the DI. "Can you tell us exactly what you did?"

"We got out of the car," said Ellie, "and we went onto the sand in front of the car park."

"You went straight onto the sand, you didn't go onto the boardwalk?"

"No, straight between the big stones. We were going to light a fire to keep warm, and we thought we wouldn't get seen so much if we stayed up this end."

"What happened then?"

"We couldn't see much, we only had our phones to light up the way." It was Zac again now, "But we could see tracks in the sand, well more like just one track, like something had been dragged along. We thought there might already be a barbie or something out there, and it might still be going, so we followed the track. Then we found it. Almost walked into it."

"Found what, Zac?" asked the DI.

"The fucking arm sticking out of the ground!" said Damian, so loudly that the reheating PCs at the other end of the room turned to look. This set Tamzin off crying again, while Ewan, who had yet to speak, looked closer to tears than ever.

"What happened then?"

Zac took charge now, as it became clear he'd done out on the sand.

"Ellie and Tamzin wanted to get out of there, but I said no, we should stay where we were and not disturb things any more. I saw that on CSI."

Thank goodness for American cop shows, thought Mary.

"Plus we didn't know who might be waiting for us in the car park."

Shrewd lad.

"So I rang 999. I thought they'd think we were messing about, but they took it pretty seriously. The police car came in about 10 minutes."

"Once we saw the blue flashing light we knew it would be safe to go back," Tamzin sniffled, "but Zac said no, so we waved our phones at them and they came out to us."

Mary had by now developed a new-found respect for the mobile phone, in the hands of these youngsters at least. Torch, emergency communications device, distress beacon – what else could they be used for?

"Now I have to ask you this," said the DI, "and nothing you say will get you in any trouble, so please be completely honest. Did any of you touch the body at all?"

Tamzin screwed her face up.

"Eeew! Gross!"

"Course we fucking didn't," said Damian.

"We moved back about ten feet away from it and stayed there," said Zac, "none of us touched it."

These were fairly unusual teenagers, Mary thought. She'd encountered some who would have filmed each other shaking hands with it (or worse) and posted the results on YouTube. Which was, of course, something else you could do with a mobile phone.

"Did any of you take any pictures or video of it?" she asked.

"No." said Damian. Angry seemed to be his only tone

of voice, but then he had just had a fairly traumatic experience.

"You're all sure about that?" said the DI, scanning their faces, "Any pictures you did take might contain vital evidence, something on the ground that was blown away later by the wind."

Tamzin seemed shocked by the suggestion. "You don't understand. We didn't see it properly at first, but when we got closer we could see the finger pointing, like something out of a horror film only for real. It was really scary, as if we were having a curse put on us or something. I can't stop thinking about it now. I just wanted to get away from it, but Zac said we should stay. None of us wanted that on our phones."

"None of us took pictures, Inspector." added Zac, gravely.

"Would you mind if we took a look at your phones anyway?" said the DI. Seeing their expressions change he held up his hands. "OK, OK, I know that doesn't sound very trusting, but we can't always take people's word for things. Sometimes we have to double-check the facts, especially in a serious case like this."

"I'm not sure I want you going through my phone," said Tamzin, "I mean, there's personal stuff on there."

"We can just impound them if we have to," said the DI, "but I'd much rather you gave them to us voluntarily. We've seen most things before and we're not interested in any minor transgressions you may have captured on your memory card. This is just about that body out there, nothing else."

And the possibility, however remote, that you filmed yourselves burying him there, thought Mary, although she didn't think there was any real chance of that.

"OK then," said Tamzin, and the others nodded in agreement.

"Thank you," said the DI, "one of our officers will

collect the phones from you now, and we'll let you have them back as soon as we possibly can. If you want to call anyone on them first, go ahead." That was taking a chance – quick sleight of hand could send an image into the social networking labyrinth or into oblivion - but it was probably worth it in the interests of good relations.

"Just one more thing for now – were there any other vehicles in the car park when you arrived?"

"No." said Ellie.

"You're sure about that? Nothing tucked up under the trees at the back?"

"No. I was driving. I drove round so my headlights showed up the whole car park. If there had been anyone there we wouldn't have stayed. You get some pervs here sometimes."

"Yes, quite. And did you see any other vehicles on your drive out from Weston? Especially anyone coming up the road from here?"

"Only in Weston. A couple of taxis. It was really quiet."

"There were some tail lights, just as we were turning to come down here." It was Ewan, speaking for the first time since they'd entered the Incident van. "They were heading away from us, towards Bristol. I was in the front, I saw them. I think it was a pickup truck, a Mitsubishi, you know, with a hard top on the back."

The DI turned his attention to him. "Any idea what colour?"

"Black, I think. I only caught a glimpse of it."

"I don't suppose you got any of the registration number?"

"No, it was just a glimpse, just for a second. Then we turned into the beach road."

Tamzin, who'd now stopped crying altogether, suddenly became animated.

"I'm not... Oh my God, this is the same as that girl

under the pier, isn't it?" she said, eyes staring, "If that was the murderers and we'd got here five minutes earlier..." She put her hand up to her mouth.

The shock was wearing off, thought Mary, and they were beginning to think about what they'd seen and perhaps come close to encountering. Time to get them to somewhere safe where their parents could comfort them, IDs or no IDs. The DI had evidently reached the same conclusion.

"I think that's enough for now. Let's get you back to the station and call your parents or whoever it is you want to call. We'll take you in our cars. Ellie, if you can let us have the keys to your car I'll get an officer to drive it back."

"I can drive it back."

"No, we'll need to examine it, I'm afraid. Until then it's best if none of you are in contact with it."

"Are we suspects then?" said Ewan, sounding shocked. It was clearly the first time the possibility had occurred to any of them.

"We have to eliminate you, it's the procedure. Nothing to worry about, I can assure you."

"Anyway, Ellie, it might not be a good idea for you drive right now." said Mary, as gently as she could.

"What, because of alcohol you mean? I haven't had any, or anything else."

"Not at the party?"

"No. I'm pregnant."

Full of surprises, our youthful-looking Miss Ellie, thought Mary. Full of confidence too, although in a year's time she'd be having a different type of all-night experience, and Mary wondered if she really understood what was coming. She'd seen enough young girls who hadn't.

"I meant because you're probably very tired and upset." Mary half-lied. "Congratulations though."

"Thank you." said Ellie, and her face suddenly broke into a smile of quite astonishing sweetness. Mary wondered which of the young men, if any, was the father. Ewan, perhaps, who'd sat in the front with her on the drive out from Weston. It was always the quiet ones. Or perhaps she didn't want the father involved; a lot of young women didn't these days. She could always change her mind later. A girl who could smile like that was never likely to be without a partner if she wanted one, even with a baby in tow.

Chapter 17

It was daylight outside as Mary and the DI watched the youngsters being driven off in two patrol cars. Ellie's car had been her final surprise – not the ten year old Vauxhall Corsa, unlikely to pass another MOT, which Mary associated with young motorists in Weston, but a shiny, late-registration Golf which she'd assumed was Inspector Deane's. Wealthy parents, unless young Ellie turned out to be a dotcom millionaire living incognito. Either way, it didn't look as if she'd be worrying about the price of disposable nappies.

There had been no need to call DCs Cox and Lane into the office; they were already booked in for what would quickly become known as the 'first' beach murder case. While the cars were being arranged for the youngsters Mary had called Cox and briefed him to handle their statements. She'd also told him to run a CCTV check on dark Mitsubishi pickups in the region since midnight, as well as getting details of all such vehicles registered within a 50 mile radius. Plus, she added, a quick background check on the teenagers and details of the party they said they'd been at.

As the Golf disappeared round the bend in the access road, Mary turned to the DI.

"Did you find them just a little bit strange, Guv?"

"No stranger than most," he replied, "They're Generation Y – tech savvy, brand disloyal, tightly focused on their interests via specialised media channels. We seem as strange to them as they do to us."

Mary looked at her boss with frank amazement.

"Know your customers, Detective Sergeant. You should know all that too, especially working in Weston. I might look into booking you on a demographics awareness course."

"I'll look forward to it."

"Pull the recording of the 999 call anyway though. Let's hear exactly what young Zac had to say."

"I've asked Cox to check them on CRO," Mary said uncertainly.

"No harm in being thorough. Right – get your boiler suit on. We've got a body to see."

It was warm in the tent, just as it had been under the pier three days earlier, the heat provided by the lamps and the bodies of two SOCOs plus a different pathologist this time, Dr Ravinder Singh, who'd arrived while Mary and the DI had been in the Incident van. As promised, the SOCOs had touched nothing; there was the coffin-shaped mound of sand, indicating an even shallower burial than the previous one, with just the right arm, in the backstroke position, rising at an angle from the ground with thumb and fingers arranged in the pointing gesture. Seen up close, it was even more unsettling than before.

"Ah, Inspector, we've been awaiting your arrival." said Dr Singh as the DI pushed his way through the tent flap.

"Doctor," replied the DI.

"For some time," added the doctor.

"My apologies for the delay," said the DI, "the body was found by a group of five young people, and it took us a while to speak to them all."

"Not a problem. It must have been traumatic for the young people. Good morning, Detective Sergeant. How are you today?"

"Very well thank you, Doctor Singh," said Mary. She liked him. He was old school, and unfailingly polite. He and the DI always found something to spar about, but he wasn't a grumbler like some of the pathologists. Having made his point about having to wait, he'd drop it and move on.

"This is a bad business," continued the doctor, "we already have one body from a beach at the Centre, now another. Who is doing this?"

"That's what we're here to find out," said the DI, crouching down and peering at the hand, "Doctor, is there any way the fingers could have set in this position naturally?"

"None whatsoever. The fist fully clenched, perhaps. With the forefinger alone extended like this, impossible. This has been staged, elaborately." The doctor came and crouched next to the DI, took a pen from his pocket and used it to point at the hand. "You see this deposit on the thumbnail? I think we will find that it is adhesive, from a tape of some kind used to hold the thumb and fingers folded into the palm. My guess is that they also used some kind of splint, or perhaps a tube, to keep the forefinger extended. They must have kept the hand like that until rigor mortis set in, then removed the tape."

"So he would have been dead before he was brought here?" said Mary, peering over the men's shoulders. Dr Singh turned round to face her.

"Most likely, Sergeant, unless they were willing to sit for six to eight hours on this spot waiting for him to stiffen up!"

"So he's been dead for at least that long?" Attempting to get premature time of death estimates from pathologists was a time-honoured CID tradition, to which the DI fully subscribed. Dr Singh, however, had served his time too.

"Inspector, competent though I like to think myself, I cannot guess at time of death based on a visual examination of one lower arm. If you were to allow me to see more of the body, perhaps, then I might be in a better position to speculate."

"Sorry."

"The margin of error will be fairly wide anyway," the doctor continued, "unless we can establish how long the body has been out here, and where it was before it came here. Ambient temperature affects the speed of the rigor mortis process – the colder the environment, the slower its progress. If he was kept in a warm room after death, then his fingers may have set in position in more like three to four hours."

"Either way though, it's likely that he was kept somewhere else for a long period?" asked Mary.

The doctor smiled, a kindly smile that a GP might give to a patient who didn't fully understand the meaning of the term "stool sample".

"Well that would depend on the definition of 'long', and whether there was any requirement to distinguish between, say, a fifteen hour period and one considerably shorter. Other indicators may help us to narrow it down somewhat. This is where the traditional approach of examining the whole body, rather than just half an arm, may pay dividends."

Mary saw the SOCO photographer suppress a smile. She was aware of having asked two stupid questions in a row. She put it down to the early start, or too much coffee, or not enough, or an infection of vague thinking caught from Generation Y. The response could have been a lot worse than Dr Singh's gentle irony, and she was grateful for that. The DI wasn't doing much better, either, although he seemed preoccupied with other things.

"The bottom line is that this must mean something," he said, pointing at the hand.

"It would seem unlikely that they went to all that trouble for mere decoration, yes," replied the Doctor, "To me it looks more like some kind of ritual or sign, but then I am neither an anthropologist nor a criminologist, so my view is uninformed."

"Quite frankly, Doc, your view is as well-informed as ours right now."

"Then I wish you good luck, Inspector."

The DI got up and gave a questioning look to the photographer, who nodded to indicate that he'd got the shots they needed of the hand.

"OK, Doc, he's all yours," he said, signalling to the senior SOCO officer to start digging.

Mary, looking on, had a sudden, unexpected feeling of something close to panic. She didn't know why, but starting to dig was wrong. Actually she did know why – it was the voice in her ear, as unwelcome now as it had been the previous night, then remembered on the drive to Sand Bay, and on the path between the lanterns.

"Stop!" she heard herself say, "I'm really sorry, Dr Singh, can you just give me a minute? Guv, can I see you outside?"

"What?" said the DI as they emerged into the cold morning.

It was the second time in three days that Mary had interrupted the investigation at a critical moment to haul her boss outside, and the second time she'd had just a few seconds to think of an explanation that wouldn't send him ballistic. This time she'd come up blank.

"I had a call from Michael Slade last night."

"Slade? I told you to tell him to stay well clear of us."

"I did, Guv."

"Well you obviously didn't tell him well enough."

"Actually he'd seen you on the news saying that we'd worked out the Polish angle on Katya Czwisnjowski's phone. He was ringing to complain about us stealing the credit for his breakthrough. He was talking about going to the papers with it."

The DI was silent for a moment as he digested the idea of Michael going to the papers with what would, all things considered, be a valid grievance. It gave her the minimal advantage she needed.

"I managed to persuade him out of that one, then I did what you said and told him to forget the case. In the end I put the phone down on him."

"So?" It seemed the DI's feeling of disadvantage was already coming to an end.

"Well just before I did, he was trying to tell me that he'd come up with a theory..."

"Yes well we don't need Mr Slade's theories.."

"... about the way in which Katya's arm was arranged when we found her. He asked me which direction her hand was pointing in."

"You didn't tell him, did you?"

"Of course not." Best to just come out with it. "But I think we should. And I think we should get him down here now and show him this one before we dig it up."

The DI looked at her as if she'd suggested they head out into the Bristol Channel in a child's inflatable.

"Are you mad?"

"I don't think so, Guv. His observational skills, well, they're weird but they work. He sussed out an entire crime scene from 200 metres away. He took one look at that phone and gave us the only breakthrough we've had so far. He tried to tell me that the position of Katya's arm was significant, and ten hours later we've got another body where the significance is beyond doubt."

"Well that could be because he already knew there was going to be a second body, couldn't it?"

"Yes, it could. But it probably isn't."

"Probably?"

"Very probably - almost certainly. I know he's made himself look bad, but at the end of the day the binoculars and the CCTV checked out, didn't they? I've spent more time with him than you have, Guv, seen him more relaxed, in his own place. My gut instinct is that he's on the level."

"Woman's intuition, eh?"

"Call it that if you like, although I'd prefer perceptive character assessment based on empathetic interaction."

The DI smiled at her skill in throwing his own occasional tendency towards management-speak back at him, but his response was serious. "Or 'a load of bollocks' if it turns out we invited a serial killer to view his own crime scene. That could end both our careers, you realise that, don't you?"

Mary thought for a split second, then took another plunge.

"My career, Guv, not yours. You go back to the Incident van, I'll bring him straight here, and you'll know nothing about it. Completely unauthorised, just like me showing him the phone."

The DI stared at her for an uncomfortable few seconds.

"That's not how I work, Sergeant, and I thought you knew that. Not to mention the fact that Professional Standards would see through a story like that before they'd had time to get their coats off. You may be a half-decent detective, but you're completely crap at gross misconduct - leave that to the officers who've got a talent for it."

"So we can get him here?"

"I didn't say that. I'm still watching my career flash before my eyes."

Mary hadn't for a second thought that he'd accept her offer of a cover-up, even though she'd meant it. Now he was inviting her to give him more reasons, besides her intuition, to risk his job bringing an almost-suspect to the scene of the crime.

"Look at it this way, Guv," she said, "This is either

gang warfare or a serial killer now. Unless we make instant progress on this they're going to have to get the Squad down, and we'll either be carrying their bags or back on car thefts. Michael Slade could be the killer, he could cost us our jobs. But it's far more likely that he'll stare at the body for half a minute then make some connection we'd never have thought of. I saw him do it with the phone – it's a bit spooky, to be honest, but I really think it's genuine. At the very least we should let him tell us his theory about Katya's arm, and see if this one fits with it."

It was all she had to offer. She stood there, the rising wind beginning to rustle through her paper suit, as the DI thought it over.

"He'll be in Bridgwater, won't he? Said he sees his family every weekend."

"It's only half past eight. He may not have left yet. I can ring him on his mobile, anyway – his number's on my phone from last night."

The DI gave a brief nod.

Mary unzipped her suit, reached inside and pulled her phone from the pocket of the knitted top she'd worn against the cold. Michael Slade's number was second in the recent callers list, behind the DI's; she found it and pressed Dial. She and the DI looked at each other as it rang.

"Hello?"

"Is that Michael?"

"Yes, who's this?"

"Mary Miller, Weston CID."

"Oh. What is it, Mary – I didn't think you wanted to talk to me?"

"Look, sorry about that Michael, it was just a bad time. The thing is, we've got another situation now."

"At Sand Bay, yes."

Mary paused, hoping the DI hadn't heard what

Michael had said.

"It's on the local news," Michael explained, seeming to have read Mary's reaction, "that's why I'm still here. Normally I'd have left for Bridgwater by now. I go to see my family there every Saturday, if you remember."

"Yes, I do remember. We – I – thought you might have gone." Mary was looking across to the main beach. The road that ran alongside it was hidden by flood defences, but she could see the top of a white van with a big satellite dish on it, and another manoeuvring into position. The car park, with its SOCOS and uniforms going about their business, had been an illusory oasis of calm; beyond the curving access road, guarded by PC Durham and his colleagues, the media would be working themselves into a frenzy. As if to emphasise the point, the sound of a helicopter, coming in from the Channel, began to fill the air.

"Another body, I assume?"

"I can't discuss that until I've spoken to you." She had to raise her voice above the noise of the helicopter, and pressed the phone closer to her ear.

"About what?"

"Pardon?"

"Spoken to me about what?"

"Confidentiality. I'd need you to understand that anything we tell or show you mustn't be passed on to anyone, not even your family, and least of all the media."

"Of course." There was a note of excitement in his voice; he wouldn't have missed the word 'show'. "Who were those teenagers who were being driven away in police cars? I thought I recognised one of them."

"I can't tell you that either. I need to talk to you face to face first."

"I can see you, Mary!"

"What?"

"Outside the tent, with it looks like your Detective

Inspector. On the TV."

Mary looked up and saw the helicopter hovering above them. Instinctively she turned away from it. The DI was also on the phone now, barking something about "impeding a police operation", and "Civil Aviation Authority" into his handset. She found the idea of Michael watching her unsettling; already he seemed to know more about this case than he should, although she quickly reminded herself that he only knew things because he spotted them, and that he was watching her now on public TV, like thousands of others. Too late to change her mind anyway, after persuading the DI to back her judgement.

"Are you at your flat, Michael?" She knew he was, but sillier mistakes had been made for want of double-checking.

"Yes."

"Good. I'll come and get you."

"To go to Sand Bay? No need, I can drive over myself."

"No, better to arrive in my car. It's turning into a circus here, you probably wouldn't make it off the Kewstoke Road. Have you got an anorak, any kind of jacket with a hood?"

"Yes, I've got two in fact, a blue and a green..."

"Wear one of them, whichever you prefer. I'll be with you in ten minutes." The helicopter's sound was becoming deafening, made louder by a sudden change in the wind. "I'll sound my horn. Be ready."

"OK."

Mary ended the call and turned to the DI.

"I'm going to fetch him, Guv," she shouted over the helicopter noise.

"Make sure you read the riot act to him," the DI shouted back, "I don't want him in that tent unless he's had the fear of God put into him about blabbing anything he sees."

"Will do. Last chance to change your mind, Guv," she said, but either he didn't hear her, or chose to ignore her.

"I'll go and tell the Doc he's got to wait before he can see the rest of his corpse," he said. "Don't be long."

Suddenly the helicopter's noise faded as it banked away out over the water. As Mary picked her way back across the sand, the DI called after her.

"What are your cooking skills like, Mary?"

"Cooking skills?" she replied over her shoulder, "I hate cooking."

"Good. Then remember this – if it all goes tits up the best I'll be able to afford on my early retirement is the lease on some grubby little backstreet cafe. You'll have to work as the cook."

"Yes Guv," she shouted, as she reached the first of the lanterns.

"Greasy breakfasts, all day long."

"Yes Guv." she shouted, as she reached the inner cordon tape.

"Minimum wage!" came the DI's voice.

"Yes, Guv," she said to herself as she headed for the big stones by the car park.

Chapter 18

The exit from the car park had, indeed, become a media circus, with three uniform PCs, Durham included, struggling to keep reporters and cameramen out of the access lane. Mary edged her car through them, turned right and accelerated sharply up the steep hill, then executed the near-360 degree turn onto the Kewstoke Road towards Weston-super-Mare.

The stretch from here to Weston was known locally as the Toll Road, and had been one until the mid 1990s. It ran through the foot of Weston Woods, the forest that blanketed the hill at the northern end of the town, rising and falling like a gentle roller coaster with constant glimpses of the sea through the trees. It was beautiful here, but the road had a bad safety record, with vehicles plunging over the unguarded edge and down onto the rocks below. Many had been driven by people of Generation Y's age, who saw the council's corrugated traffic-calming patches as a challenge to be negotiated at maximum possible speed, especially late at night. After one particularly bad crash – a teenage couple, neither wearing seatbelts, both dead, she two months pregnant - the local paper had named it "The Road of Death".

Mary had a sudden urge to go home and slip back into bed with Don, but knew she couldn't, partly because of the job and partly because he'd be downstairs by now watching European football on TV, his favourite Saturday morning relaxation. Last night had been lovely, but she was grown up enough to know that it hadn't marked a sea-change in their marriage. Her thoughts turned involuntarily to young Ellie, with her alcohol-free pregnancy and shiny new Golf. She was exactly half

Mary's age. Sometimes it didn't do to dwell on life's inequalities.

The Birnbeck district of Weston backed onto the Woods, and it was only a short distance from the end of the toll road to Michael Slade's flat. Mary saw him in his living room window as she drove up. She flashed her lights and briefly sounded her horn. He raised his hand, disappeared from the window and, shortly afterwards, appeared through the street door. He was wearing a blue waterproof jacket (more good quality clothing, she noted), underneath it the same shirt and trousers he'd worn both times she'd previously seen him. He could have passed for someone from Tech Services called out on their day off, which was ideal for where they were going.

"Morning, Mary," he said as she pushed the passenger door open for him, "This is quite exciting, I must say."

"Get in, Michael," she replied. In fact she'd almost panicked and driven off, as the enormity of what she was doing hit her. She knew next to nothing about him except that he remained just a hair's breadth away from being a person of interest if not a full-blown suspect, and she was about to take him to see a corpse still buried in the sand, where he'd be able to contaminate the scene at will, fatally compromising any evidence of his own involvement in the crime. Suddenly she saw it from the DI's point of view and was astonished that he'd agreed to it. He must be really desperate to have something to tell the Squad when they arrived.

"Before we go anywhere, I need you to understand that you mustn't talk about anything you see or hear today. Not in the pub, or on the checkout, nor to your family, and least of all to the media."

"You've already said that, Mary, and I've agreed."

"I just need to be sure you've taken it on board."

"Actually it's a bit unfair of you to be like this. I didn't say anything about you showing me that phone, did I? Not even when your Detective Inspector was doing his best to intimidate me."

"Yes, well, that was nothing compared to the way he'll be if he reads confidential information about this case in the Mercury next week."

"Well if he does it won't have come from me. I know how to keep confidences."

She'd just have to hope that he did.

Mary swung the car round and headed back down the hill towards the toll road. Michael sat hunched up in the passenger seat, leaning slightly forward, his knees almost up to his chest, like he'd done on his sofa a few days earlier.

"That seat will go back a bit if you need more legroom."

"No, I'm fine like this thanks."

She glanced at him again, and realised what he reminded her of in that pose – that famous sculpture, *The Thinker*. Perhaps people who thought a lot really did sit like that.

"So what are you going to show me, Mary?"

"A buried corpse, just an arm visible." She was committed now - might as well get straight to the point.

"I thought it might be."

"Why?"

"Because you'd hardly have got me out here for a completely unrelated case – a fatal dog bite or something." He seemed to find this funny, and half-chortled to himself in his strange way.

"Last night you said you had a theory about the position Katya Czwisnjowski's arm was found in?"

"I was trying to say that, Mary, but you cut me off."

"Sorry." Obviously still a sore point.

There was silence for a few seconds, then Michael

broke it. "The position of this new arm will make it much easier to see if there is any significance," he said, sounding surprisingly like a pathologist postponing speculation on cause of death until the test results were back.

"Good," said Mary. They'd obviously moved on, although in the silence she'd realised that there was another subject she needed to broach, one that hadn't occurred to her while she'd been persuading the DI to bet his career on her judgement.

"There is one other thing, Michael."

"What's that?"

"This one has all the signs of being a professional job, even more so than Katya's. Whoever did it, they're unlikely to be nice people. You could be putting yourself in the firing line by helping us."

Michael said nothing.

Mary's heart sank. "I'm sorry," she said, "I should have said that earlier. It's not too late for you to change your mind – I can turn round now and you won't be involved."

"But I am involved already, aren't I Mary?" Michael said, "I gave you the clue about the phone."

Her heart sank further. When she'd produced Katya's phone in his flat, she hadn't warned him what he might be getting into. "Duty of care" loomed in her thoughts and wouldn't go away. She'd blown it, possibly big-time.

"So I'm committed now. Anyway, it's no different to if I was, say, a metallurgist called in to give expert advice on a piece of evidence, is it?"

Mary found herself in what the more upmarket newspapers called an ethical dilemma. Michael was wrong. Expert witnesses were professionals, which earned them grudging recognition by the criminal fraternity as part of the protected circle of law enforcement, though even then not always. He was an amateur, which meant he was more likely to be seen as an informant – a grass. Should she tell him that, turn the car round, face the possibility that he'd cut up rough about the way she'd already got him involved? Or say nothing, let him help them solve this murder, in the overwhelming likelihood that nothing would actually happen to him anyway?

"Besides, it's my civic duty to assist. I feel very strongly that if we, as citizens, want a safe society then we should be prepared to contribute towards keeping it that way."

Mary kept the car on course.

"Perhaps it wasn't a bad thing that the DI kept your name out of it at the press conference, all the same," she said.

Michael turned to her, and for the first time his face showed signs of worry.

"No, perhaps it wasn't."

They were back on the toll road now, the water below them visible through the trees on the left. Michael turned away and peered out of the side window, seemingly intent on the view.

"The road of death – a grimly appropriate title this morning." he said, without turning his head.

"I suppose so, yes."

"Some people think that the Bristol Channel ends here and becomes the Severn Estuary, but in fact the line is taken from Sand Point, at the north end of the bay. Gives Weston a bit more buffer against having to change its name to Weston-super-Aestuario!" He chortled loudly to himself. Mary smiled, relieved that she wasn't the only one who was nervous.

Chapter 19

They found the end of the toll road in chaos. The road to the beach had been closed, and was guarded by two traffic officers. A car was stopped by the junction, its driver remonstrating with one of the officers, causing a four-car tailback. People were milling around, unsure whether they were allowed down the beach road on foot. Others stood on the far side of the road, their phones held up in camera mode, capturing the scene for posterity.

Mary thought of the DI, in the tent with an increasingly impatient pathologist.

"Put your hood up, Michael, and keep it up from now on," she said, then reached under the dashboard and pressed a switch. A two-tone siren burst into life, and the car in front showed the reflection of Mary's headlights flashing alternately on and off.

"Wow!" said Michael, and fell back into his seat as Mary pulled sharply out onto the right-hand side of the road. One of the traffic officers saw the car, stepped across to stop oncoming traffic, and beckoned her forward. As they reached her, Mary wound down her window.

"What's it like down there?"

"Better since we closed the road, Sarge. You should be OK."

"Thanks."

As they drove down the beach road, Michael turned his head, fully sideways, and stared at her.

"You really are a proper police officer, aren't you Mary?"

Mary laughed out loud, letting the tension go with it.

"What did you think I was, a social worker?

"You just don't seem like a police officer a lot of the time."

"Well I am one – and don't you forget it."

At the car park, Mary found two paper suits in the SOCO Land Rover and gave one to Michael.

"Keep the hood up and remember – don't touch anything. And keep your face turned towards the sea on the way out to the tent – there'll be photographers with long lenses all over the hillside. There were a couple on the toll road. I'm sure you won't want your supermarket colleagues asking what you were doing out here."

"No," replied Michael, then quickly afterwards "Shit!"

"Pardon?"

"Oh, I'm sorry Mary. I forgot to ring my wife. She'll be expecting me soon."

"Can you ring her now?"

Michael did, and a lengthy conversation took place in which Michael, at Mary's prompting, told his wife that he was assisting the police as a technical advisor on IT matters, and Mary was eventually required to take the phone and assure her that yes, this was true, and no, he wasn't in any trouble. Mrs Slade sounded worried by all this, but also as if worry was a pre-existing condition for her. Mary guessed that being married to Michael might have something to do with it.

Right now though Mary's main worry was the DI, cooling his heels in the tent alongside Dr Singh. The phone call had lasted no more than three or four minutes, but the DI would know to the nearest pound how much that had cost in the doctor's attendance fee, besides which he wasn't someone who liked waiting for people, least of all people like Michael Slade.

At the last moment she had an idea, went back to the

Land Rover and borrowed an aluminium equipment case from a reluctant SOCO officer.

"Carry this," she said, handing the case to Michael, "it'll make you look official. That way no-one will take any notice of you."

The direct route to the tent was still off limits, so she led Michael out across the sand and grass between the lanterns. Telling him to wait, she poked her head into the tent.

"Sorry, Guv, it's chaos up on Kewstoke Road."

"Have you got him?"

"Yes, he's outside. All suited up. I've read the riot act to him as well."

"I'll come and give him another reading."

She'd thought that might happen.

"Where's the Doc, Guv?"

"Back in the Incident van enjoying an extended coffee break at the taxpayer's expense. Says he's thinking of the Seychelles for his Spring holiday. Right, let's get Sherlock Holmes in here."

The DI came out and gave Michael the same warnings as Mary had on confidentiality, this time emphasising the punitive nature of the repercussions that would flow from any breach. Michael replied with the same reminders that he had, in fact, kept confidentiality even in the face of sustained pressure from the DI. The formalities over, the DI suddenly softened his tone.

"Have you seen a dead body before, Mr Slade?"

"No."

"It can be a very difficult experience. Don't be embarrassed if it gets the better of you – I hueyed up myself the first time I saw one."

"Have you already dug the body up then? I was hoping to see the arm in its original position."

"No. It's undisturbed in there, but even a small part of a corpse can have a powerful effect, believe me."

"The body bereft of its soul?"

"If that's how you see it, yes."

Mary was already opening the tent flap, and looking back saw Dr Singh coming along the path between the lanterns.

"They told me you were back." the doctor half-shouted from twenty feet away. Then, as he drew near, he looked at Michael and the case by his feet.

"You have brought us another Scenes of Crime officer, Detective Sergeant?" he said, then, tuning to Michael, "Good morning."

Mary didn't think for a second that the Doc thought Michael was a SOCO.

"Er, this gentleman's a technical advisor, Doctor."

"'Technical Advisor' covers a multitude of specialities," said the doctor, then turning to Michael again, "Forgive me for prying, but out of interest which is yours, sir?"

"General advice" said Mary, aware that the situation was slipping quickly away from her.

The doctor smiled. "Then I assume that this is the gentleman who advised the police that the phone found by the pier last week was used to send text messages in Polish?"

The DI fixed Michael with a "who have you been talking to?" look. Mary fought to keep the surprise from her face. Perhaps he had gone to the papers after all.

But the doctor's kindly GP smile was back now. "It is unfortunate," he said to Michael, " that our otherwise estimable police colleagues consider us humble pathologists, while capable of making rough guesses at time of death or type of weapon, to have no other deductive powers whatsoever. This is a mistake, as some of us have quite adequate levels of general intelligence." Seeing the DI look embarrassed, he continued. "Despite his sometimes rough-hewn manner, our Detective

Inspector here is an excellent officer and extremely cost-conscious, an important attribute in today's police force. He would not have kept a pathologist sitting idle on weekend rates for anyone less than the person who had unlocked the secret of the phone." He held out his hand to Michael. "Doctor Ravinder Singh, pleased to meet you sir."

"Michael Slade, very pleased to meet you, Doctor," said Michael, his smile broadening to match the Doc's.

"Excellent call about the phone," said the doctor, "we had been wondering who really worked it out."

"It was fairly obvious really," replied Michael happily, "the wear on the 'A' key was quite pronounced."

"You have a background in cryptography, I assume?"

"Just an interest. As I'm sure you know, letter frequency analysis is only relevant in very basic encryptions, and..."

The DI cleared his throat.

"Gentlemen, we have a body to examine, shall we...?"

"Oh yes, of course, Inspector," said Dr Singh, "my apologies for sidetracking your expert. Perhaps we can talk of this later, Mr Slade? Cryptography is an interest of mine too, but I have studied it only at the most superficial level."

"I'd be very glad to." said Michael. Then he turned to Mary and beamed her a smile, not as sweetly beautiful as Ellie's an hour earlier, but of such unalloyed happiness that for a second she believed there could be goodness in the world.

Inside the tent things were as they'd been when Mary had left. As she'd expected, Michael's demeanour changed as soon as he saw the body. If he felt queasy, he showed no sign of it. Instead he fell silent and stared intently at the arm, his face expressionless. The Doctor watched with evident fascination, the DI with what looked like a mixture of surprise and unease. Mary had seen it before; it was the way he'd stared at Katya's phone in its plastic evidence bag two days earlier.

Michael crouched down beside the arm, murmuring an unprompted "I won't touch anything" without taking his eyes off it. He stayed there for a minute, then shuffled sideways across the sand and peered at the hand from a different angle.

"They must have bound the fingers and thumb to keep them like that until rigor mortis set in," he said, looking up at the Doctor, "and used some kind of splint to keep the forefinger straight."

"Precisely," said Dr Singh, "or perhaps a tube for the finger."

"Yes, a large cigar tube might have done it. It would have to have been a tight fit though, or the finger wouldn't be as straight as this. A splint seems more likely."

"Michael, what about your theory on the direction the arm is pointing in?" said Mary, keen to move on from ground Dr Singh had already covered.

Michael looked up at her as if he'd forgotten all about it. Then he got up and stood alongside them, looking down on the arm.

"The young woman last week," he said to the Doctor, "was her arm extended like this?"

"I did not attend that scene," Dr Singh replied, "these officers did."

"It extended out of the sand, but the fingers weren't arranged like this," said the DI, "the hand was just open."

"And what direction was the arm pointing in?" asked Michael, keeping his gaze on the arm.

"It wasn't pointing anywhere, just sticking up."

"Leaning then," he said impatiently. "Was it sticking

up vertically, or did it lean, and if so in which direction?"

"It was leaning," said Mary, "but it's difficult to say in exactly which direction, because it was inside the tent and we didn't check it at the time." She remembered the photograph the DI had shown the Czwisnjowskis, of the arm before the SOCOS had erected the tent, with the pier legs behind it. "Towards the prom though."

"South or north of the Pier?"

"What? Er, I think..."

"To save time I think you might lead your witness a little more," said Dr Singh, smiling as if at some private joke.

"All right," said Michael, "was it leaning towards the Winter Gardens?"

Mary thought for a few seconds, trying to visualise the photograph.

"Yes, I think it was."

"Good choice," said the doctor.

"We can verify that by checking our pictures," added the DI, "but what's the significance of all this?"

Instead of answering, Michael moved around until he was standing behind the hand, in line with the direction of the pointing finger. Pulling down the zip of his paper suit, he reached inside and brought out his mobile phone. Quickly pulling the zip up again, he held the phone horizontally, just below chest height, pointing away from him.

"No photographs!" said the DI.

"I'm not going to take any photographs, Inspector," said Michael, "but I will need your help in a moment." He touched the phone's screen and it turned into a large compass display, the needle swinging backwards and forwards like a real instrument. Then he turned the phone round in his hand until the compass's 'N' was above the needle, and looked along the line of the hand.

"Just about exactly South East" he said, "Now

Inspector, if you could stand just there, you'll be my magnetic North reference." The DI, not entirely happily, did as he was asked. Michael touched the phone's screen a few more times, and the compass was replaced with a map, which he adjusted until it showed their location at Sand Bay. Then he pointed the phone at the DI, and made the map zoom out until it showed the whole of Europe.

"My theory about the direction of the arms, Mary," he said, "is that they're a sign or message, a sort of 'Yankee go home', perhaps, or 'we know where you came from'. If you draw a line from where Katya was found through the Winter Gardens, it goes to Gdansk, in northern Poland, which I understand is where she came from. I think that if we follow a line south-east from here, it will lead to wherever the owner of this hand came from."

"And I'll bet it won't be Cheddar," said the DI.

Michael began his strange chortling, evidently enjoying the DI's grim humour. "No, I'd be surprised if it was too," he said.

Mary peered at the phone, trying to see where a line following the direction of the hand would lead. "Italy?" she said.

"Not quite. In fact I think they initially pointed it there by mistake and had to adjust it after the body was buried. Rigor mortis held it in place once they'd moved it. If you look at the sand, it's compacted just under the inner arm where they pulled it over, with a corresponding depression by the forearm. That means they moved it slightly to the east of Italy. I think you'll find that this hand is pointing to Albania."

Mary and the DI exchanged glances. The DI and Dr Singh exchanged glances. Dr Singh and the SOCO, who peered over Mary's shoulder to see the map on Michael's phone, also exchanged glances. Michael looked at the phone, then at each of them in turn.

"Was it something I said?"

Chapter 20

"Right, listen up everyone!" the DI shouted across the crowded squad room. Voices fell silent, promises to call back were made and phones were put down.

"As you probably all know by now, we have a second body, found early this morning at the south end of Sand Bay. A male this time, currently unidentified, similar age to our female victim last week." He turned to the board and pointed at Katya Czwisnjowski's photograph. "MO looks similar too – the body is buried except for one lower arm - but there are differences. This one was not brought in by boat - the site is well above the high water mark and there are no tracks to indicate anyone approaching the scene from the seaward side, while there is a clear trail across the sand from the car park. And the victim's arm is arranged more precisely, with the fingers in a definite pointing gesture," he arranged his own fingers to show them, "which we're told must have taken some time and effort to achieve."

Indeed, thought Mary. Michael Slade had reiterated it as he left the tent. The DI had, unexpectedly, let him go back in to see the body once it had been uncovered, but he hadn't said much, just stared intently at one part of the corpse then another. Mary had been struck by how Michael and Dr Singh acted almost as if they were a team, Michael keeping carefully out of the Doc's way, the Doc drawing his attention to a birthmark on the victim's neck as if he were a colleague from the Path lab. The DI had seemed disappointed that Michael hadn't produced any more insights. "With a mind like Mr Slade's, Inspector, you must let it all percolate," had been the Doc's cryptic advice.

"This arm business, Guv – it's a bit weird, isn't it? What's it pointing at?" came a voice from the back of the room.

"Good question, and here we have some new information about Katya's case too. We missed it last week, but her arm was in fact pointing towards her home town of Gdansk in Poland. The hand wasn't formed into the pointing gesture, and of course it could be just coincidence, but given the obviously deliberate way that today's hand has been arranged, we don't think it is."

The body had come up just like Katya's – fully clothed (jeans, t-shirt, trainers), no sign of injury, all identification removed. The man looked roughly Katya's age, too – dark hair, the same olive skin, quite handsome. With no ID, however, he could be anyone from anywhere, and so far there was no mobile phone on the beach to help them.

"So it's some kind of sign, or message?"

"That's what we think, yes. 'Yankee go home', that kind of thing."

"Where is today's hand pointing at, Sir?" came a female voice from the centre of the room.

The DI hesitated for a moment. Might as well spit it out, thought Mary.

"It's pointing South East."

Everyone looked across at the map of Europe that had been fixed on the wall, a pin already marking Gdansk.

"Albania," said a voice from the back. Murmurs broke out all over the room. Looks were exchanged, as they'd been in the SOCO tent earlier. Someone had been bound to spot it.

"Let's not jump to any conclusions. It could equally well be Paris or Athens."

"Or Southampton," said another voice, and there was a smattering of laughter.

"Let's stay objective," said the DI, more firmly now, "we don't have an ID on the second victim yet, it may be something and nothing."

"Surely there must be a link, Guv! Too much of a coincidence!"

"Even if the victim does turn out to be from Albania, it doesn't automatically mean he's connected to anyone living in this area."

"Anyone such as the Troshanis, you mean, Guv?" This came from Sam Yewell, a burly DC from the evidence gathering team who'd been out grabbing CCTV footage all week.

Again the DI hesitated. He was losing the troops, the first time Mary had seen it happen to him. It was happening now because they thought he was about to put politics ahead of what everyone in the room knew; that if the hand pointed to Albania then it was, indeed, odds-on that there was some connection to the Troshanis, a family of general-purpose criminals from Tirana who were operating in the town. She was surprised at how little sympathy she felt for him.

"It would make sense to check with the Troshanis though wouldn't it Guv, see if he's one of theirs?" The female voice again; Penny Blake, DC on the admin team.

The Troshani family and their hangers-on – or the "Albanian Community", as they liked to style themselves - were already a political hot potato in Weston. Their arrival had been followed by a sharp increase in certain types of crime, including drug dealing, vehicle theft and muggings. The police had responded with a sharp increase in arrests, which had begun to get the problem under control. Mary had been involved in quite a few of them, and had felt glad to be doing her job.

Just as the situation was settling down, however, politics had entered the equation. After complaints of victimisation and some negative coverage in the national media, the order had come down from on high that community relations must take priority in the policing of Weston. In practice this had meant taking a hands-off approach to the Troshanis. Crime had gone up again, while members of the gang swaggered around town boasting that they were untouchable. Local people were angry about it, and they were blaming officers on the street for police inaction. This was causing increasingly bad feeling in the ranks, hence the reception the DI was getting now.

It had caused particularly bad feeling for Mary, who'd been accused outright of racism by a self-appointed "Community Spokesperson" because of her high arrest rate, despite the fact that nearly everyone she'd arrested had either pleaded guilty or been convicted in court. She'd been around too long to expect rock-solid backing from her superiors, but even so she'd been shocked by their almost total failure to support her. And this had been one occasion on which the DI hadn't gone out of his way to back his officers. It would have been career suicide for him to do it, but even so it remained a sore point which they both avoided.

"Unless we've got to avoid offending the Albanian Community, of course." Sam Yewell again, his tone not far enough away from insubordination.

It was the hijacking of the term "Albanian Community" by the Troshani gang, and its ready acceptance by the media and even the Force in its own press releases, that made Mary really angry, angry enough to stand up for Yewell now if the DI came down on him. This bunch of small-time villains weren't any more representative of Albanians in general than the old lags on the Costa del Crime were of the British. However she knew what effect a stereotype like that could have on other immigrant families, and especially their kids. It was one reason why she'd been so keen to stamp the gang out, although that motivation had proved too complex for her superiors to grasp; instead they'd taken the view that she simply didn't like Albanians.

Mary looked across at the DI. It was a difficult rank. As the lowest level of senior officer, you didn't have the luxury of handing policy down to other senior officers, who could generally be relied on to be onside; instead you had to impose it on the rank and file. DI Steve Jones, however, knew when to stop, which was short of insulting his officers' intelligence, or of allowing it to seem that he'd swapped his own for an Inspector's pay and pension.

"All right, if we assume, hypothetically, that the victim is Albanian, and that he does have links to a local Albanian family, then what's the story?" The DI still couldn't, it seemed, bring himself to say "Troshani" in public.

"He and the first victim are both connected to the murderers somehow?" came a female voice from the front of the room.

"So we're saying it was the same perpetrators both times? It looks that way, but don't forget the differences in the MOs – the more careful arrangement of the fingers."

"Perhaps they're getting better with practice, Guv!" A voice from the back, some laughter.

If fact neither the DI nor Mary thought both murders had been committed by the same people, for reasons that weren't just about modus operandi, but which were nowhere near substantial enough to float in front of the assembled squad. As they'd walked back between the lanterns to the Sand Bay car park, Michael Slade had suddenly said "This one feels different from Katya, doesn't it Mary, done by someone else?" Mary had nodded agreement before she'd even realised it, then questioned why it felt that way and decided that it just did, only later wondering how Michael could have sensed it too, when he hadn't been at Katya's crime scene.

"Copycat, sir?"

"It's a possibility, although very unlikely. Copycats tend to operate alone, and this would have taken a team, like the first one. Plus it hasn't been made public that Katya's arm was pointing to her home town, so they wouldn't have known to point the second victim's arm to his – assuming that is where it was pointing."

"Seems obvious then, doesn't it Guv?" It was Yewell again from the back of the room.

"OK then Sam, what is it?"

"Old man Czwisnjowski crossed the Troshani mob, they killed his daughter, now he's returned the compliment by killing one of theirs." Murmurs of agreement came from around the room.

It was what senior officers called a "seductive" theory, by which they meant one based largely on circumstantial evidence, which those in the ranks below them should avoid grabbing too quickly without at least considering the alternatives. But it was also what Michael had said to Mary as she'd driven him back to his flat. And it certainly made sense, especially to Mary, who'd seen Mr Czwisnjowski at close quarters. She had no difficulty imagining him giving the order from his suite in the Avon Gorge Hotel, minutes after seeing his daughter's body on the table. And he'd seen something else too; the pictures of Katya's arm sticking up out of the sand, pictures he'd manipulated the DI into showing him. Turning a bereaved parent into a suspect was always difficult though, and turning the Czwisnjowskis into suspects would be made far harder by the presence of their embassy minder. That left the DI in the middle of two political situations, while still needing to keep his troops onside. Now she did feel sympathy for him; sometimes she was glad to be a mere DS.

"Well that's quite a leap. On the face of it this is two murders by the same perpetrators. Even if we think it's not, we've got no evidence that Katya's murder was intended as an attack on her father, or that her father is connected in any way to the second murder. But it is a theory we'll consider."

"What if Czwisnjowski had his daughter murdered, then had the second one done to make it look like a serial killer?" From the back of the room the slightly nervous voice of a young man, perhaps feeling that he ought to make some contribution to the briefing he'd been unexpectedly invited to attend. Probationary PC Durham. Mary, who'd included him as a reward for his phone-holding efforts on the beach two days earlier, hoped the old hands wouldn't be too rough with him.

"You've been reading too many detective novels, son!" said Tony Lane drily.

"Bad ones!" added Sam Yewell.

"I'd keep polishing the buttons on that uniform if I were you – you're not going to be getting out of it any time soon."

The DI came to his rescue. "All right, that's enough. At this stage we're not ruling anything out, however imaginative, especially until we've got an ID on our new victim."

"Will Major Crime be taking this over, Guv?" Penny Blake again, the voice of restored reason.

"They're getting involved, but on a supervisory basis for now. As things stand it remains our case, with DCI Spence as SIO. I'll be seeing someone from the Unit later this afternoon."

"So can we start bringing the Troshanis in?"

"Yes, but just to show them pictures of the Sand Bay victim, see if we can get an ID. DS Flanagan will be in charge of that. DS Miller will be with me."

Swings and roundabouts, thought Mary. On the plus side she was still at the sharp end of the investigation, rather than lumbered with Tom Flanagan's job of treading on eggshells with uncooperative Troshanis. On the minus side, perhaps she was only at the sharp end because her superiors didn't trust her to deal with the Albanians. Putting the latter thought down to paranoia induced by stress, sleep deprivation and one cup too many from the Sand Bay coffee flask, she followed the DI from the room.

Chapter 21

"Well, what do you think?" asked the DI as he sat down behind his desk. Mary waited until she'd finished closing his office door before speaking.

"I'm not sure what I think, Guv." It wasn't the best thing for a DS to say to their DI, but it was the truth. "The only thing I do feel pretty sure about is that the Czwisnjowskis are more than just bereaved parents in all this, although that's only instinct based on what I've seen of them. Like you said, until we get an ID on the second victim it could be almost anything, even PC Durham's father-kills-daughter scenario."

"Yes, Durham – who let him in?"

"I did. I thought he deserved it after finding Katya's phone then standing on the beach half the morning holding it up for us to look at."

"Fair enough." The DI looked straight at her across the desk. "It got a bit rough out there, didn't it?"

Mary knew he wasn't talking about Lane and Yewell's ribbing of the probationary PC. She considered her response. Again the truth seemed best, put as diplomatically as possible.

"I think they were worried that they might be told to keep the Troshanis out of it."

"Is that what you thought?"

"I'm glad we're bringing them in." She wasn't going to lie about that, either.

"Yes, I'm sure you are."

They were on difficult ground. Mary had long ago decided, in the interests of her career, to put the business of her and the Albanians in the past, but only if everyone else did.

"To me a villain's a villain, whatever passport they're carrying – or not, as the case may be."

The DI looked at her for a couple of seconds, which seemed to her like a couple of minutes.

"Yes well, apparently that view's been gaining some currency in high places since we've had the new Commissioner. Amazing what a few voters bending your ear in the shopping precinct can do."

"I'm glad to hear that, Guv."

"Don't expect any apologies though – it doesn't work like that, as you know."

Mary said nothing. The DI broke the silence.

"You can have an apology from me if you want one, although it might irretrievably damage what is on the whole a positive and fruitful working relationship."

Mary smiled, just. The wave of political correctness that had swamped the station hadn't been his fault, even if he could perhaps have done more to defend her. This was as near to a *mea culpa* as she was going to get.

"I'll skip it then Guv."

"Good. And I meant what I said out there – let's not jump to conclusions, just because we've seen a finger pointing south-east from Sand Bay. It could still be nothing to do with the Troshanis or Katya Czwisnjowski's father. But we won't ignore it either. Hence Tom Flanagan stuck having afternoon tea with our Albanian friends, while you get on with the proper detective work. If I was him I'd be accusing me of giving you the best jobs because of some politically correct drive to advance the careers of women in the Force, so be grateful."

Mary smiled, more broadly now. He was mocking her, but gently. Time to move on.

"What time are we expecting the Squad, Guv?" she asked, looking out into the office as if checking where they were going to put the visiting detectives.

"We're not – they're expecting us. They're interviewing the Czwisnjowskis at 4.30, and we're invited."

"Where?"

"Bridewell Street."

"Great." It would mean hacking through Bristol's city centre traffic, which was bad even on a Saturday, and hunting for somewhere to park. The wardens didn't take prisoners up there, and had been known to slap tickets on cars that still had their blue lights flashing. Mary smiled briefly at the thought of a diplomatic standoff between a Bristol wheel clamper and Borowski's embassy driver. It was far from certain who'd win.

"Are the Squad treating the Czwisnjowskis as suspects?"

"No, still bereaved parents who might be able to give us some background on the first murder."

"Who'll be running the interview?"

"Stan Kopacz."

Mary paused for a second to digest the news.

"Do you think that's deliberate?"

"Could be, especially if the Chief Constable's had Borowski in his ear."

There was no traffic car escort for their journey to Bristol this time; they took the DI's Audi and stuck to the speed limits. Both were silent, and Mary guessed that the DI was turning the case over in his mind, as she was in hers. They had almost nothing except two dead bodies, one of them as yet unidentified, and a couple who probably knew more than they were letting on, but who might be just bereaved parents. Yet something must be happening, because one of the Force's most senior detectives had now been diverted from the pursuit of whoever was killing Bristol University's students to interview the bereaved couple.

Detective Superintendent Stanislav Kopacz, known universally (though not always to his face) as "Stan", was a legend throughout the Constabulary, a detective of the old school who had seen everything and arrested most of those responsible for it. He was a Bristolian born and bred, but his ancestry lay further east; his father had escaped from Poland in 1939 and, aged 19, flown a Hurricane in the Battle of Britain with 303 Squadron, scoring 18 kills. Of all the Polish war aces, Flying Officer Kopacz was reckoned to be the fiercest and most fearless; he was reputed to have said that his greatest pleasure was seeing the eyes of the German pilots as he shot them down.

He had passed some of that ferocity on to his son, whose own heyday had been the golden age of armed robbery in the 1970s and early 80s, before computerisation made wages in cash a thing of the past. He had fought the villains of Bristol hand to hand outside the factories of St Anne's and Bedminster, twice getting shot, and awarded commendations for bravery, in the process. These days the factories were gone and Stan, near retirement, played the wise sage on the Murder Team, but it was said he could still put fear in the heart of a suspect, even under strict PACE rules. Yet he was also known for his kindness, and tireless community work in Easton, the tough part of Bristol where he'd grown up. Stan was a complex man.

As they passed the Clevedon exit Mary's phone rang. Retrieving it from her bag she checked the display and this time recognised Michael Slade's number. She hesitated, then decided to take it. Michael was, after all, semi-official now.

"Hello?"

"Is that you, Mary?" The voice was unmistakeably Michael's but sounded as if he was talking from the inside of a washing machine on its spin cycle. Hands-free, she assumed, probably from a car.

"Yes."

"It's Michael here."

"Yes." No need to encourage him too much.

"Luan Redzepi." The words were so unfamiliar that she couldn't be sure it wasn't just the hands-free and background noise corrupting the sound.

"Pardon?"

"Luan Redzepi. He's the victim at Sand Bay."

"What?" She was all attention now. "Hang on Michael."

She reached into her bag again, scrambling around until she brought out her notebook.

"Can you spell that for me?" As Michael spelt it out she wrote it, in capitals, on a clean page of the notebook, then held it up to the DI, mouthing 'SAND BAY VICTIM' as she did so.

"Where did you get this name from, Michael?"

"I did some research."

"You did what? What kind of research?"

"I know someone who's friendly with the young Albanian men in Weston. I asked if she knew anyone with a birthmark on his neck, and she said yes, Luan Redzepi."

They were on the split-level section of the M5 now, sandwiched between a giant supermarket truck and the retaining wall that held up the southbound carriageway above them. The light was beginning to fade and there was a spattering of rain and spray on the windscreen, which the Audi's wipers intermittently swept away. Mary's head was swimming.

"Who is this woman, Michael?"

A strange chortling noise came over the airwaves.

"I'm not sure I can reveal that, Mary – got to protect my sources and all that."

The car lurched as the supermarket lorry swung

towards the outside lane and the DI avoided it. Trailer and wall seemed to be closing in on them. Mary wanted to reach out across the digital ether, grab Michael by the throat and throttle him, but instead had to settle for second best.

"Don't play games with me, Michael, I'm warning you," she said, with such venom that the DI turned and looked at her in surprise, though not necessarily disapproval. "Now who is this woman?"

The chortling had stopped. There was silence for a couple of seconds.

"Jolene Buller."

"Who?"

"Madge and Billy's daughter, from Between the Lines."

Mary tried to place the name, eventually coming up with an image of pink leather boots, cowboy hat and expansive cleavage. Jolene Buller, landlord's daughter and part-time Dolly Parton tribute act.

"Billy Buller's daughter? But she must be in her forties?"

"There's no law against it, Mary." The chortling was back now. "Jolene says she just offers them the hand of friendship. If she offers them more then that's her business, and I'm sure she checks their passports to make sure they're not under age – those that have passports, that is."

"And did this," Mary looked down at her notebook, "Luan Redzepi have a passport?"

"Don't know – I didn't ask her."

OK, they'd have to. In the meantime Mary had an urgent call to make.

"Where are you now, Michael?"

"On my way to Bridgwater. I called into Between the Lines on my way through, on the off chance. Lucky Jolene was there, wasn't it?"

Yes but for who? They were dealing with professional killers here, something which genius IQ Michael seemed to have overlooked, despite Mary's earlier warning.

"I have to go now, Michael. Keep that phone on and with you. Stay in Bridgwater until I speak to you again."

"Why?"

"Why what?"

"Why stay in Bridgwater, Mary?"

Mary hesitated.

"To spend some time with your family. Look, Michael, thanks for this, but don't do anything else like it. You can't go round acting like a private investigator – it's not safe. Stay in Bridgwater. I'll speak to you later."

"Oh, all right."

"Goodbye, Michael."

"What's Billy Buller's daughter got to do with this?" asked the DI, not taking his eyes off the road.

"Apparently she's friendly with young Albanian men," replied Mary, "and recognised this Luan Redzepi from Michael Slade's description of his birthmark."

"What, Slade asked her about it?"

"Yes, he went to see her at Between the Lines."

"Fucking prick!" said the DI, turning to face Mary now, "What the hell does he think he's doing?" It was unlike him to swear. "Did we know about Jolene Buller's links with the Albanians?"

It should have been a minor moment of triumph for Mary, but she was concerned that, in the circumstances, it might end with them in the crash barrier or under the wheels of a supermarket lorry. She said it as neutrally as she could.

"We were told not to keep tabs on the Troshanis or their associates, so no, we didn't."

The DI had told Mary this personally - "Lose interest in them, Sergeant" had been his exact words. Each knew that the other remembered it. There were a long few seconds of awkward silence.

"I'll get Cox onto this, Guv", said Mary, pointing to her notebook. The DI nodded. Mary found Cox's number and dialled it.

"Hello Sarge?" Thankfully Cox's voice was clearer than Michael Slade's had been. It sounded as if he was still in the office, which was even better.

"Pete, we may have an ID on the Sand Bay victim - Luan Redzepi." She spelt it out, hearing the clatter of keys as Cox typed it into his computer. "Believed to be Albanian, so if he's legal he'll be on the Border Agency system. If he isn't, get what you can from the Albanian authorities – they have a database of criminal records but we'll have to get authorisation via the DCI to access it. If that draws a blank, check the Home Office records for asylum seekers – his family may have been refugees from Kosovo in the 1990s, or at least pretending to be."

It was a display of expertise on Albanian migration that might have earned Mary an informal reprimand just a few weeks earlier. She was enjoying it now. The DI didn't cut it unduly short, but did eventually break in.

"Is Tom Flanagan there? If he is, I'd like a word."

"Is DS Flanagan there, Pete?"

"Yes Sarge."

"Put him on, will you? The DI wants to speak to him."

Technically it was possible, Mary knew, to connect her phone wirelessly to the DI's in-car audio system and built-in microphone, but such things were for the likes of DC Cox and, she imagined, Michael Slade. Instead she asked the DI if speakerphone was OK, and when he nodded, pressed the button and held her phone near his ear.

"Guv?" said Flanagan's tinny voice.

"Tom, we may have an ID for this morning's victim." He pointed to Mary's notebook, and she held it up. "Luan Redzepi, Albanian national, known in Weston before he was killed. Cox is chasing it. Tell him to keep you briefed, and to keep it just between you and him. Have you got the Troshanis in yet?"

"They're on their way. I had to send uniforms out to collect them."

"Good. Show them the victim's picture but don't tell them we've got any idea of who he is. Let's see if they admit to knowing him. Keep Agron Troshani till last, so he doesn't get a chance to brief his footsoldiers on what it's all about."

"Right, Guv."

"And tell Cox to let Mary know the minute he gets anything."

"Will do, Guv."

"Cheers."

The DI nodded to Mary, who said her own goodbye to Flanagan and ended the call. She had a question, but something had told her not to ask it while the speakerphone had been switched on.

"What about Jolene Buller, Guv? Shouldn't we get her in, find out what she can tell us about Redzepi? I can ring back and get Lane to fetch her."

"We'll go and see her ourselves. I don't want her blabbing to Lane or anyone else that it was the Michael Slade Detective Agency that tracked her down. And one of us needs to have a serious conversation with Mr Slade, too. If he's lucky it'll be you. But that can wait."

Chapter 22

They were on the Avonmouth bridge now, eight lanes of drizzle-soaked tarmac rising up over the river Avon next to its junction with the Severn Estuary. To the left was the water; Wales on the far side, the lights of Avonmouth's docks and chemical works beginning to show below them. To the right, five miles upriver, was Bristol, a city with a shameful past as a slave trade port, now rehabilitated by Concorde, Banksy and trendy urban regeneration. Plus a university, one of the best in the country, whose students currently feared to walk the streets after dark.

The DI took the next exit and drove down the Portway, along the Avon Gorge next to the river. Mary looked up at the Clifton Suspension bridge as they passed underneath it, glad that the DI hadn't chosen it as his route. The road deck, 200 feet above them, looked narrow and fragile, and she wasn't keen on heights. The city centre traffic was true to form, snarled up, crawling from one set of lights to the next, but they'd given themselves time. The multi-stories were beginning to empty now, and they soon found a space.

The old Bridewell police station had been a fearsome building in a dank street near what had become the Broadmead shopping centre. Its replacement, in a redeveloped area nearby, could not have been more different, a gleaming white office block with a glass-fronted stairwell running its entire height. The Constabulary shared the building with a firm of accountants, and it was the accountants who looked more at home coming and going from it. The Major Crime Investigation Unit was based at Constabulary HQ in Portishead, ten miles to the west, but its Murder team, still known in the Force as the "Bristol Murder Squad", had taken up residence on the seventh floor of One Bridewell Street after someone had started murdering Bristol University students on the city's streets. Thus had Stan Kopacz's career come to span both Bridewells.

The DI looked up at the building as they approached it.
"The Ivory Tower, eh? We're going up in the world."
"Looks like it, Guv." To Mary's disappointment, there was neither a black Mercedes nor a clamping crew in front of the entrance.

It was Kopacz himself who met them at the lift. He was a huge bear of a man, thinning silver hair, crumpled suit, hands like dinner plates, an unmistakeable sharpness in his eye. Mary wondered how his father had fitted into a World War II fighter plane; perhaps the size came from his mother's side of the family.

Kopacz shook hands with the DI, then turned to Mary.

"DS Miller – Mary, isn't it?" he said, in as strong a Bristol accent as she'd heard in 17 years of policing the region.

"Yes, Sir," Mary replied, shaking his offered hand with some concern for her own hand's bone structure. As it was, the grip was merely firm, although she was sure it could be a lot firmer.

Kopacz began to lead them along the corridor. "The Czwisnjowskis are already here, along with their embassy minder and a lawyer."

"A lawyer?" said the DI.

"Adrian Grey of Grey, Fuller and Partners. Merchant Venturer, his ancestors helped to fund Cabot's voyage to Newfoundland in 1497." Kopacz was evidently familiar with the solicitor's pedigree, and sounded less than overawed by it, "£500 an hour minimum to get him out of bed on a Saturday is my guess. Probably charging them extra for having to come down from Clifton as well."

"Fits with what we've seen of the Czwisnjowskis so far, sir."

"A-listers, eh?" The showbiz term sounded strange coming from the veteran detective, but surprise was part of Stan's armoury, and he had a lot of grandchildren.

Though fully equipped with computers, whiteboards and even a coffee machine, the Murder Squad's office still had an air of impermanence; nothing was fixed to the walls, everything looked like it could be packed up and shipped back to Portishead within a working day. The room was largely empty, just one or two faces Mary didn't recognise looking up as they came in. Stuck to one portable whiteboard were two large photographs, underneath them the names Amelia Foster and James Penhaligon: the Bristol University victims. A woman and a man, both young, like ours, thought Mary.

DSI Kopacz showed them into his office, a corner of the room partitioned off with snap-in walls. On the wall behind the desk was the exception to the apparent rule against fixtures; a framed print of a painting depicting a World War II RAF fighter plane in battle, its wing-mounted canons blazing. A Hurricane, Mary assumed.

"We may have an ID on the Sand Bay victim, sir," said the DI as they sat down, "Luan Redzepi, probably an Albanian national, seen around Weston before the murder. We're checking it out now."

"Good," replied Kopacz, easing himself into his chair, "Any link to the Czwisnjowski girl or her family?" The "Czwisnjowski girl" jarred in Mary's ear; in Weston they all called her 'Katya", as if she was a friend, her death a personal loss. No time for sentiment on the Murder Squad, it seemed.

"None we've found yet, sir, but we are working on

the assumption that the two cases are connected. The format of the burials is too unusual to be coincidence, and too complicated for the second one to be a typical lone copycat."

"Ah yes," said Kopacz, squinting at his computer screen, "this business of the arms sticking out, as if they were pointing at something. You don't see many of those on the off-chance, certainly not two in a week." He squinted at the screen again. "I see this morning's was pointing at Albania, and Wednesday's at Poland."

"Northern Poland, sir – Gdansk, where Katya Czwisnjowski came from," Mary chipped in, and felt instantly like PC Durham two hours earlier.

"Allowing a few hundred miles either way for the effects of rigor mortis, yes." said Kopacz, the hint of a smile on his lips. Mary's Durhamisation was complete. "Who put you on to this – the same bloke who spotted the phone keyboard? I heard you had him at the scene this morning."

Mary's heart sank. The whole Force seemed to know about Michael, DSI Kopacz probably through Doc Singh, whose work engendered a close relationship with the Murder Squad. Thankfully the DI saved her the trouble of wondering how to respond.

"Yes, sir. Michael Slade. He's been helpful on a couple of aspects of the case."

"Clever chap, spotting the way that keyboard had worn," said Kopacz, seemingly not too concerned about any breaches of procedure that might have occurred, "I've been speaking Polish for 60 years and I wouldn't have seen it."

"He does seem to have insights, sir."

"Or inside information. Should we be treating him as a suspect?"

So this was what it was like to face Stan under PACE rules. Impressively, the DI didn't flinch.

"He was informally a person of interest at one point, but we've ruled him out. We interviewed him twice, the second time after he turned up on CCTV walking along the seafront on the night Katya Czwisnjowski was buried. He said he hadn't been near the pier though, and a CCTV trail confirmed his story. DS Miller has had the most contact with him, and she's of the view that he's not involved. I back her judgement on this."

Backing the DI was the least Mary could do in return.

"I interviewed him at his flat, sir, and I showed him the phone," she said. No point in hiding it, especially as Kopacz almost certainly knew. "He's an odd character, but he has an extremely high IQ, beyond genius level, and from what I gather that goes with the territory. He has a habit of stating his theories as if they're established fact, which can make it seem as if he has inside knowledge, but he's been able to show the logic behind everything he's worked out so far, based on his own observations. It's just my view, sir, but I think he's a gifted amateur, not an insider on these murders." She thought for a second. "And Dr Singh seemed to take to him."

"Yes, so I gather. Well in my experience Doc Singh's a pretty good judge of character, so we'll take that as a plus point."

Throwing Dr Singh's social preferences into the mix could have been another Durham moment, but to Mary's relief the gamble had paid off.

"I don't suppose Michael Slade put you on to this Luan Redzepi as well, did he?"

Mary's relief was instantly replaced by dismay, which she fought to hide as she waited for the DI to respond. There was no way she'd even dream of trying to field this one.

"He told us about a local woman, Jolene Buller, who's friendly with young Albanian men in Weston." The DI's voice remained firm. "She recognised the description of our victim's birthmark."

It was a dangerous half-truth, and one the DI could come to regret if – when, more likely – Kopacz learnt the full version. Mary could understand why he'd done it; it must already look to Kopacz as if Michael was leading the investigation, and admitting that he was now interviewing his own witnesses might be the final straw. Misleading Kopacz was a huge risk, nevertheless; a word from an officer of his seniority could put a career on permanent hold. For now though, at least, Kopacz didn't seem to suspect there might be more to it.

"I see. Useful chap to have around, your Mr Slade."

"Yes, sir."

"Are you confident he can be managed? Amateurs, gifted or otherwise," Kopacz glanced briefly at Mary, "have a habit of blowing up in your face, either with the press or in court."

"I am confident, yes, sir. DS Miller has established a good rapport with him. He takes what she says seriously."

Not all that seriously, thought Mary, since Michael's response to her instruction not to tell anyone about what he'd seen at Sand Bay had been to rush straight out and describe the victim's birthmark to a Dolly Parton tribute act. No need to bring that up now though.

"All right," said Kopacz, "so what about the murders?" It seemed the discussion about Michael was over, although from recent experience Mary wasn't banking on it. "Assuming they are linked, what's the setup?"

"Well if Luan Redzepi is part of the Troshani family's gang," said the DI, "then either the Czwisnjowskis and the Troshanis are on the same side and someone else is hitting them, or they're against each other and Redzepi is Czwisnjowski's retaliation for the Troshanis killing his daughter."

"But either way, the Czwisnjowskis are in deeper than just being the victim's parents?"

"Specifically Mr Czwisnjowski, sir," said Mary, hoping she'd be able to keep the Durham factor low this time, "he's every inch the player – real man of steel type. Borowski, the consular official, seems scared stiff of him."

"And which do you think it is – is he with the Troshanis or against them?"

"We tend towards the latter, sir, but it's only a feeling," said the DI.

"Based on what?"

"The second crime scene, sir." Mary again, hoping she wasn't talking too much. She glanced at the DI, who seemed happy for her to carry on. "It was different. There were the specifics – the hand formed more precisely, body brought by land not sea – but it went beyond that. It just seemed like someone else's work. I can only call it intuition, based on my experience of crime scenes."

"There's nothing wrong with that, Sergeant. We used to call it copper's nose, and it nicked a lot of villains. What's your view, Inspector?"

"Again I agree with DS Miller, sir. Hard to pin it down, but the second one seemed more professional, done by a team who were used to working together. The first one was more like a gang of men who'd been given shovels and told to get on with it."

"A gang who left the victim's phone behind on the beach." said Kopacz.

"Exactly, sir. I'm not expecting us to find anything like that at Sand Bay."

Mary considered adding that Michael had thought the crime scenes seemed different too, then remembered the unresolved question of how he could have reached that judgement, having seen only one of them. Better not to bring it up.

"And what about Mr Slade? Did he have a view on it?"

Did Kopacz read minds or something?

"Er, yes, sir. He thought it was different perpetrators too."

"Is that what he said?"

"His exact words were 'This one's different, isn't it?'".

"How did he manage to work that out then, if he'd only seen one of the crime scenes?"

Mary said nothing, hoping it was a rhetorical question. Kopacz waited long enough to establish that an answer wasn't going to be forthcoming, then supplied one himself.

"My guess is that he watched you two, and gauged your responses to the scene. The man obviously has an instinctive grasp of senior management methodology. Sounds like he'd make a good DCI."

Mary thought of the DI, who made no secret of his own ambition to progress to Detective Chief Inspector and beyond. He'd find it hard not to take Kopacz's suggestion that a supermarket checkout operator, however gifted, had DCI potential as implying that he didn't. She looked up at the painting of the Hurricane and realised that its wing canons were, in fact, firing at them. All in all it had been an alarmingly difficult few minutes.

"Right," said Kopacz, closing up the file on his desk, "I think the Czwisnjowskis have had long enough to stew. Until we have any evidence linking them to the second murder this will have to remain a background-checking exercise, anything that might help us identify who'd want to kill their daughter, etcetera. What I actually want to know is how much Mr Czwisnjowski is willing to tell us about himself."

Kopacz got up, with some effort, from his chair, which creaked in response. The DI and Mary followed suit.

"This Borowski," said Kopacz as he moved around the desk, "bit of an awkward sod, is he?"

"More like a nervous one," replied the DI, "He seems desperate to show the Czwisnjowskis that he's on the ball. Czwisnjowski's slapped him down a couple of times, and he just takes it."

"Hmm. OK - this way," said Kopacz, and led them from the room. As they crossed the main office, Kopacz asked them to wait while he went over to check something with one of his officers. Mary turned and spoke, *sotto voce,* to the DI.

"Do you think there's going to be trouble over Michael Slade, Guv? It was like a disciplinary hearing in there."

"It was a rehearsal for one," replied the DI, "He was checking out how well we'd stand up if things do go wrong with Slade."

"Did we pass?"

"I don't know – let's hope we don't have to find out."

Chapter 23

Kopacz led Mary and the DI out of the Squad office and into the corridor, where he stopped.

"Mary," he said, "I'd like you to observe the interview from our monitoring room. Space is tight in the interview room, what with Czwisnjowski bringing his minder and a lawyer, and anyway three officers asking questions might seem like overkill. It'll also mean you can keep in touch with your office for any developments on the second victim ID. But I don't want you to think you're being sidelined, because you're not."

This was the kind side of Uncle Stan. Mary was disappointed, but hid it. She could see the logic of what he said.

"That's fine, sir. Where do I go?"

"In here – I'll show you how it works", said Kopacz, and opened the door next to them.

The room was a bit larger than Kopacz's office, its blinds pulled down. Against one wall was an enormous flat-screen display; near the other wall a long table with a small control box on it, and three chairs behind. On the screen was a high-definition video image of Mr and Mrs Czwisnjowski, plus Borowski and a man who Mary assumed was their lawyer, Adrian Grey. They weren't talking, but Mary could hear the sound of Borowski tapping a pencil on the table.

"Right, this is a live feed from the interview room," said Kopacz, pointing to the screen, "You'll be able to hear everything that's said. I'll be wearing an earpiece, so if you want to tell me something, or you want us to ask a question, press this button and speak. The others won't be able to hear you. If I tap my earpiece it means I didn't get the message, so repeat what you said. Please don't shout though – my hearing's bad enough already without getting deafened. The interview room is three doors down, so you can use your phone, eat a bag of crisps if you like, we won't hear you."

For someone who'd made her fear for her professional future a few minutes earlier, Kopacz was doing a pretty good job of putting her at her ease now.

"OK, got that sir. What about these other controls?"

"The joysticks pan and zoom the camera, but best to leave them alone. We don't want to draw their attention to it. The Volume knob controls the speakers in here. The other buttons are for recording and playback, but we're not recording this one – not unless we decide to caution them, anyway, and if we do that I'll send a DC in to operate it."

Caution the Czwisnjowskis? Something told Mary that Kopacz was a big step ahead of them, although she had no idea how he'd got there. She looked at the DI for any sign of surprise, but he had his best poker face on. Either that or he was a big step ahead of her too.

"You OK then?" said Kopacz, reaching for the door handle.

"Yes, sir."

"Good. I'll be interested to hear your observations afterwards, especially your view of where the mother stands in all this." He turned to the DI. "Right, let's go. See you later, Mary."

Mary chose the middle chair, sat down and scrutinised the figures on the screen. She'd seen plenty of taped interviews before, but not a live relay like this one. From their studied silence she had a feeling that the people in the room knew they were on camera, but even so it felt strangely intrusive. She hoped it would be different once the interview started.

As Kopacz had said, the room was too small for so many people. Borowski, at the left-hand corner of the table, was fidgeting like a nervous schoolboy in his very slightly too-small suit. Next to him Mrs Czwisnjowski sat impassively as always, immaculate in a cashmere jumper with a silk scarf draped over her shoulders. Mr Czwisnjowski, next to her, was like stone. At the right-hand corner of the table was Adrian Grey. Slim, fair hair, mid-40s perhaps, sitting back relaxed in his chair despite the cramped circumstances, his manner and appearance exuding centuries of good breeding. His suit had a lustre, as did the silk handkerchief in his top pocket, as did he. Mary had never seen a man look so impeccable - apart, that was, from the man sitting next to him.

Through the speakers either side of the screen Mary heard a door opening, and saw Kopacz and the DI enter the room. They stood with their backs to the camera, Kopacz's so big that he obscured Adrian Grey and Mr Czwisnjowski.

"I'm sorry to have kept you waiting," she heard Kopacz say, "I'm Detective Superintendent Kopacz, from the Major Crime Investigation Unit, and this is Detective Inspector Jones from Weston-super-Mare CID, who most of you already know. Thank you very much for coming in."

Mary saw Kopacz extend his arm to shake the hands of the visitors, then the DI doing the same with Grey, who murmured his name to confirm his identity. Mary noticed that Kopacz didn't ask who was who among the other three, just spoke directly to Mr Czwisnjowski as he sat down.

"I see you've chosen to have legal representation here this afternoon, sir. Any particular reason for that?"

Grey answered, in a comfortable drawl that didn't appear to require the movement of any part of his body.

"Mr and Mrs Czwisnjowski felt it might be useful to

have someone who could clarify any unfamiliar points of English law, Superintendent," he said, with a slight emphasis on "and Mrs".

Now Borowski joined in.

"Superintendent, are you part of the Murder Squad? I wish to assure my Ambassador that appropriate resources are being deployed."

"As I said, sir, I'm from the Major Crime Investigation Unit. There is no separate Murder Squad, but I am on the Unit's Murder Investigation Team."

"So you are now the Senior Investigating Officer?"

"No, sir, that remains DCI Spence at Weston-super-Mare. He's the most senior CID officer at the location where the crime was committed. Major Crime are involved on a supervisory basis."

"But I...." Borowski began building up to Diplomatic Protest mode, but Kopacz cut across him.

"Mr Borowski," Mary noticed that Kopacz pronounced the name differently from the way she and the DI did, the middle syllable rhyming more with 'cow' than 'off', "I believe your Ambassador has spoken with our Chief Constable, and has received the assurances you refer to. I suggest it would not be productive to go over that ground again now. Perhaps we can instead try to move forward towards the arrest of whoever murdered Miss Czwisnjowski."

Mr Czwisnjowski nodded, almost imperceptibly. Borowski sat back in his chair.

"Now," Kopacz continued, addressing the Czwisnjowskis, "Just so I'm clear on this, you last saw your daughter in Gdansk on the 24th of October, and reported her missing on the 26th?"

"I reported her missing, yes," said Mrs Czwisnjowski, her gaze fixed steadily on Kopacz.

"So you reported her missing what, less than 48 hours after you last saw her? Wasn't that rather soon? She was an adult, after all. Young people that age just head off for a few days, visiting friends and things."

"She was supposed to be at work. She would not have gone off like that without telling us. She was very conscientious." Mary, watching the screen, wrote "past tense" on the A4 pad she'd taken from the corner of the desk. Most mothers were in denial at this stage of the grieving process, referring to their children as if they were still alive. Katya's seemed to have adapted very quickly.

"I see. And Katya worked for your company?"

"Our main company, yes." Mr Czwisnjowski took over, his wife instantly reverting to her impassive pose. There was a silent magnificence to her, real film star quality. Mary felt sorry for the men crammed into the room with her.

"That's import-export, isn't it?"

"Trading, yes."

"And what exactly was your daughter's role at the firm?"

"She was learning the ropes, as you say here. We are a family business. One day she would have taken over from me."

"So she was a general management trainee?"

"If you like."

"But she must have been doing something specific? She wouldn't have just been roaming around your offices at random?"

Mary, fresh from her own grilling by Kopacz, sensed that he was after something.

"She was working in our Shipping department, arranging the transit of goods."

And that seemed to be it, if the hint of reluctance in Mr Czwisnjowski's voice was anything to go by. Plus the flick of Adrian Grey's eyes towards him, then quickly away. He'd heard it too.

"Import or export?"

"Both."

"And would that have involved ships docking at Avonmouth, down the river from here?"

"We ship to and from all the major ports in the United Kingdom, so yes."

"But Avonmouth, Portbury – Bristol Port. Is that somewhere you deal with regularly? Often?"

Czwisnjowski hesitated for half a second. Grey's eyes flicked again.

"Grain, yes. We handle the delivery side of futures trading."

"I see." Kopacz made a note in his pad. "Can you tell me where you originally come from, sir?"

Whoa, thought Mary. International shipping to Czwisnjowski's home town, just like that. She began to see that Kopacz's shakedown of them over Michael Slade had been just a warmup for the main event.

"Poland." No hesitation from Mr Czwisnjowski, but his eyes looked just a fraction colder.

"Yes, but whereabouts in Poland? Gdansk? Warsaw? Krakow, perhaps?"

"Is this necessary, Detective Superintendent?" Grey asked the question dispassionately, as if checking the admissibility of evidence in court.

"Yes, Mr Grey, it is. We believe that the nature of Miss Czwisnjowski's murder and burial was too complex to be the work of a random killer, jilted boyfriend or anything like that. We're treating it as a contract killing, with the possibility that it was ordered by someone with a grudge against the Czwisnjowski family or their business interests. In that context we need to know as much as possible about the family and their background, so we can try to work out who might have had a motive."

Grey nodded, his duty of care duly executed.

"Olsztyn."

"Olsztyn," Kopacz repeated, "And when were you born, sir?"

"1959."

"I see. Your family stayed on then?"

In two days Mary had seen Mr Czwisnjowski deal with the police, a press mob, his daughter's murder scene, her corpse on a trolley, all with barely a flicker of emotion. Now his eyes blazed, a moment of undisguised anger before he checked himself.

"My family are Polish," he said, unable to keep the emotion out of his voice.

Kopacz had clearly touched a nerve, big time, although Mary had no idea what it was. For some reason the suggestion that his family might have 'stayed on' in Olsztyn had been taken as a grievous accusation by Mr Czwisnjowski, one he'd felt it necessary to vehemently deny. The only thing Mary felt sure about was that Kopacz had known full well what Czwisnjowski's reaction would be.

Mary heard the sound of papers shuffling, probably Kopacz taking a moment to let the tension disperse, or sink in. Remembering her brief, she tried to gauge Mrs Czwisnjowski's reaction, but the woman seemed unmoved. The shuffling stopped, and she heard Kopacz take a breath before starting his next question. Then, suddenly, the sound from the speakers was drowned out by the loud warbling of her phone, coming from near her feet. Her initial reaction was panic, until she remembered that the people she was observing couldn't hear her. She retrieved the phone from her bag and checked the letters on the screen: "Dr Singh, Path". Hoping the Doc wouldn't keep her away from the interview for too long, she pressed the Accept button.

"DS Miller."

"Ah, Detective Sergeant, Dr Singh here, from the

Pathology Centre. I am glad to have reached you. DI Jones's phone appears to be switched off."

"Yes, he's in an interview at the moment with DSI Kopacz," said Mary, "Can I help?"

"I hope I can help you. I have been examining the body and clothing of the young man we saw at Sand Bay this morning, and I have found something – two things, actually - which I think will be of interest to you."

"Well spit it out then," would have been Mary's reply if this had been Cox, Lane or Durham. Dr Singh warranted a little more indulgence.

"I'm all ears, Doctor – what is it?"

"Sand between the toes. This young man should have learned to wash between them, or at least to change his socks."

An obvious question presented itself. Again, Mary phrased it in a different way than she'd have done with one of her Constables.

"Sorry, Doctor, I'm being a bit thick here. Wouldn't we expect him to have sand between his toes, from being buried in the beach?"

"Ah yes," replied the doctor, with audible relish. She'd supplied the setup, now he could deliver the punch line. "But not sand with flecks of paint and rust mixed in with it, matching the flecks we found in the sand retrieved from the burial site under Weston Pier last week, which in turn matches the paint from the supporting legs of the Pier itself."

"Are you sure about this, doctor?"

"Oh yes. Your forensic team established the match between the burial sand and the pier last week. At that time, it seemed to be merely confirming the obvious. Now the exercise appears to have borne greater fruit".

It was obvious where this was going, but Mary's professional caution made her stop short of assuming it would go the whole way.

"But that only indicates that he'd been on Weston beach near the Pier, doesn't it, Doctor? It's not enough to put him at Katya Czwisnjowski's burial."

Two things, he'd said.

"Not on its own, no." said the Doc. Mary sensed the imminent arrival of a second punch line. "But the human hair which we also found attached to the sock might add sufficient weight of evidence, once the results of the DNA test come back. On a purely visual check it is a good match for that of Miss Czwisnjowski."

Mary felt the goosebumps rise. Forensic evidence placing a suspect – even a dead one - at the crime scene was always worth its weight in gold. It felt like the first real, case-breaking step forward.

"That's brilliant, Doc!" Mary heard herself gush like a schoolgirl, then quickly corrected the over-familiarity. "Sorry, I mean Doctor."

"Doc is fine. It's what all my friends call me."

"Thank you. And thanks for this. When can we expect the DNA results?"

"I fast-tracked the test – I was sure your DI would consider the additional cost worthwhile. We should have it in the morning."

At that moment Mary heard two beeps in her ear. Lukewarm as she was about technology, the demands of the job had obliged her master call waiting; she held the phone away from her face and saw "DC Cox" on the screen.

"That's great – Doctor Singh, I've got another call waiting, it's one of my DCs from the office. I think he may have news on the ID of the victim from this morning. Do you mind if I take it?"

"Of course not, Detective Sergeant."

"It's Mary, please."

"Then good luck, Mary – keep me updated on the identity, if you will."

205

"I will – I'll get the DI to call you as soon as he's out. Goodbye."

The beeping was still coming, meaning Cox was still on the line. Mary pressed the button, and the display changed.

"Pete?"

"Yes, Sarge," Cox sounded excited, "ID on the Sand Bay victim is confirmed by the Albanian police as Luan Redzepi. Age 21, Albanian National, been in their youth system a couple of times, nothing as an adult. He's not on the Border Agency computer, so he was illegal here."

"Excellent - well done, Pete," replied Mary. It was well done – she'd still be trying to log into the Border Agency system. She was about to tell Cox about Dr Singh's call when he broke in again.

"There's something else, Sarge. The Albanian police were very helpful, gave me extra background on Redzepi. His mother's from a well-known family in Tirana, well-known here too. Her maiden name was Troshani."

Jackpot! Mary suppressed what would have been a very unseemly whoop, especially on the phone to a junior officer.

"Any relation?"

"Oh yes, Sarge. She's Agron Troshani's sister."

Chapter 24

Mary had missed a few minutes of the interview, but that didn't matter. She looked at the microphone on its flexible metal stand, and the red button next to it. She hadn't had training in this, and she didn't want to get it wrong, send a stream of gibberish into the DSI's ear just as he was asking a crucial question, or getting the answer to one. Wait for a pause and be concise seemed to be the obvious things to remember.

She waited, until Mr Czwisnjowski had finished answering a question about the extent of his futures-traded grain shipping enterprise, then pressed the button.

"Sir, developments. The ID on the Sand Bay victim is confirmed, and pathology have evidence placing him at Katya Czwisnjowski's burial. Also, he's the nephew of Agron Troshani, the top man in our local crime family."

Kopacz gave no sign of having heard her, but he didn't tap his earpiece either. As soon as she stopped speaking, however, she heard his voice through the speakers.

"Could you excuse us for just a minute? There's something the Detective Inspector and I need to check on."

The Czwisnjowski team looked surprised, but made no objection. Mary sat back, heart rate still slightly elevated, but pleased that it seemed to have gone OK. Thirty seconds later Kopacz and the DI came into the viewing room. Mary wasted no time, launching straight into the briefing.

"Albanian police have confirmed the Sand Bay victim as Luan Redzepi." she said, "He'd done youth custody there, and had no visa for the UK. His mother is Agron Troshani's sister."

She turned to Kopacz and began, "Sir, Troshani runs...", but Kopacz interrupted her.

"Yes, I know what Agron Troshani does."

"Oh – OK. Also, Dr Singh rang. He's found sand between Redzepi's toes containing paint flecks from Weston Pier, plus a hair he thinks is Katya Czwisnjowski's. He's fast-tracked the DNA test on the hair, said he thought you wouldn't mind the extra cost, Guv."

The DI didn't reply.

"Right," said Kopacz, "this makes the tit-for-tat theory odds-on favourite, doesn't it? Troshani's gang kill Czwisnjowski's daughter, he has Troshani's nephew killed in return. The questions are, what triggered the first killing, and who did Czwisnjowski get to do the boy in? I can't see him and his wife digging holes in Sand Bay."

"No, sir, and Consular Official Borowski will no doubt alibi them for last night too," said the DI.

"Yes, no doubt he will," replied Kopacz. "OK, you two had better come with me."

Kopacz led Mary and the DI back across the squad room to his office, gesturing to Mary to close the door behind them. He unlocked a desk drawer and pulled out a file, thicker than the one he'd taken into the interview room earlier. On the cover was a big red stamp: "RESTRICTED".

"This," he said, holding the file up, "is the other file on Mr Czwisnjowski. I'm afraid I can't let you read it, and I hope you won't take that personally. Some of it's from SOCA/NCA, some from Special Branch. Most of it's from other sources; here, Poland, all over Europe and beyond, police forces and other agencies."

Mary struggled to keep her jaw from dropping. This

time last week she'd been investigating a spate of gas bottle thefts from a caravan site in Brean.

"Czwisnjowski is a major player in just about everything illegal that crosses borders," Kopacz continued, "drugs, guns, good old fashioned contraband, you name it. He's got political connections too, as you'd expect for someone in that line of business – hence the restricted file. But his import-export firm in Gdansk is legit, and that's been the problem with him. He keeps firewalls between himself and the illegal operations, sometimes two or three layers deep, and so far no-one's managed to prove a connection. We wouldn't normally expect to see him within a hundred miles of a crime scene, but this time it's different."

"Because of his daughter?" asked the DI.

"Yes. She was his only child, and they were close. He was grooming her as the heir to the business. But we don't think he's just here to grieve. If that was all it was, he'd have stayed well clear and had the Polish embassy hassling us to release the body. We think he came here to fix things, hands-on, which is unknown for him. He's on foreign turf, and he's emotionally destabilised. If he ordered that Albanian boy's murder, then it's the best chance anyone will have had to nail him."

"How do we nail him though?" The DI again.

"The usual ways. Look for evidence, hope he's made a mistake, see if anyone will talk, see if we can make him give something away. There's people all over Europe who'd give their eye teeth to have him in an interview room, and we've got him. Let's see if we can rattle him a bit, push him into doing something stupid."

"Is that what that business about his home town was for, sir?" asked Mary, "What did you mean by his parents 'staying on'? You certainly rattled him with that."

"Yes, it got a response, didn't it? Olsztyn, where he

was born, is in Poland now, but until 1945 that part was called East Prussia, and it belonged to Germany. Most of the German population ran away from the Red Army in 1944. There'd always been a small minority of Poles in East Prussia, but they got branded as 'Germanised', and most of them left too after 1945. But, a few stayed on."

"Including the Czwisnjowskis?"

"Yes. It seems they were very good at reaching an accommodation with whoever was in power. Nazi Germany, Stalin's Russia, it was all the same to them. Even so, he wanted to make it clear that he isn't German. You'll find a lot of Poles are particular about that."

"So Czwisnjowski is Polish then?"

"Technically yes, although by the look of him a fair bit of German crept into the bloodline along the way. Legally he's certainly Polish – Uncle Joe Stalin very kindly gave the bulk of East Prussia to Poland in 1945, although as he was occupying Poland at the time it didn't make a lot of difference. If anything, our man Czwisnjowski is more Russian than German. As a young man he served in Polish Military Intelligence, but he was really Spetznatz – Russian special forces, trained in the Motherland then sent back to help Uncle Joe's successors keep a tight grip on the Poles. I imagine it's not something he likes to talk about much these days, like his family history."

Not something Flying Officer Kopacz would have had much time for either, thought Mary, looking up at the Hurricane's wing cannons. As for herself, she felt more out of her depth than she'd ever felt in her career. More than as a cadet, told to comfort an hysterical mother while the Fire Brigade tried to rescue her children. More than during CID training, surrounded by graduates fast-tracked for Inspector and beyond. More than when she'd had to start giving orders to DCs, most of them male and some of them older and more experienced than her. She knew little about Stalin and nothing about Spetznatz, but what she'd just heard had confirmed her feeling that she wouldn't want to be in an interview room with Czwisnjowski asking the questions.

"Right," said Kopacz, "Let's get back to them." He put the file back in his desk drawer, locked it, and began to rise from his chair, which creaked in recognition of its lightened load. "Oh yes, Mary - what did you make of the mother?"

Mary's throat felt dry. In the past ten minutes the game had changed; then it had been her local murder case, now she was being asked to make her contribution to an international organised crime investigation.

"I thought she adopted the past tense rather easily when talking about Katya, sir. Most mothers would still be in denial at this stage, referring to their children as if they were still alive."

"Even though she's seen the body?"

"Oh yes, sir. It's subconscious, a refusal to accept what's happened. The first of the five stages of grieving – or seven, depending on which model you use."

"And why would Mrs C be different?"

"It could just be that she's a tough character, like her husband, but it could also be that she knew it might happen, like mothers do when their sons are in the military – or the police. People in that situation tend not to experience the "it can't happen to me" reaction, or not so strongly, anyway. There was that business of her shouting at Katya's father at the Path centre, something about her not wanting Katya to come here because it was dangerous."

"Yes, I saw that. Can you remember exactly what she said?"

Mary desperately searched her memory. It was going well, and she didn't want it to end on a negative note.

"No, sorry, sir. It was in Polish, or at least it sounded

like it, and it didn't mean anything to me."

Kopacz looked at the DI, who shook his head.

"No matter. That's very interesting, thank you."

Shame about the end, but not too bad overall. That week of Family Liason training hadn't been wasted after all.

The DI was holding the Weston CID file, which suddenly seemed thin and rather tame by comparison with Kopacz's fat wad of major international crime. Kopacz nodded towards it, nevertheless.

"Have you got a picture of this morning's victim in there?"

"Yes, sir," said the DI, and took out a head and shoulders image of Luan Redzpei, photographed on a mortuary slab that lunchtime.

"Can I borrow it?"

"Of course, sir." There could only have been one answer to that question, but it was good of him to ask. Mary was beginning to get the hang of DSI Kopacz.

"Thanks – right, once more unto the breach then. See you later, Sergeant."

Mary settled into her chair just in time to see Kopacz and the DI appear on the screen. Kopacz wasted no time.

"Sorry about that – something we had to attend to," he said, placing the photo of Redzepi on the desk in front of Mr Czwisnjowski. "Do you recognise this man, sir?"

Mr Czwisnjowski looked at the picture for a few seconds.

"No, I'm afraid I don't," he said.

"Mrs Czwisnjowski?" said Kopacz, sliding the picture to his right.

"Surely it is inappropriate to ask Mrs Czwisnjowski to look at pictures of this..." began Borowski, but Mrs Czwisnjowski waved him away.

"I do not recognise this man either, Superintendent."

"I see. Well, he was found this morning buried in a similar manner to your daughter, in a beach two miles up the coast from Weston-super-Mare. You may have heard about it on the TV or radio this morning."

"Yes, we saw the news report at our hotel," said Mr Czwisnjowski.

"Are the police assuming that the two crimes are linked, Superintendent?" asked Borowski, this time without any apparent censure from the Czwisnjowskis.

"Yes sir, we are assuming that. All the evidence points to it."

"And do you know what nationality this man is?" A professional enquiry, no doubt, thought Mary. Borowski wondering if he'd have to deal with two sets of relatives.

"We believe he's Albanian, sir, from the Tirana area. His name's Luan Redzepi. Does that name mean anything to you, Mr Czwisnjowski? Mrs Czwisnjowski?"

Both shook their heads.

"Does the name Agron Troshani mean anything to either of you?"

Mary watched the screen closely for any sign of reaction, but if either of the Czwisnjowskis did know of him then they kept it well hidden.

"Is this Troshani someone you suspect of the murders, Superintendent?" Borowski again, seeming keen to speak while he was allowed to.

"One of the murders, yes sir."

"One of them? But you said that you are assuming the two murders are connected?"

"Connected, yes, but not committed by the same people. We have evidence that Luan Redzepi was involved in Miss Czwisnjowski's murder. That would make Redzepi's death more of a revenge killing. Mr Czwisnjowski, can you tell me where you were between six pm and midnight last night?"

Borowski went instantly from keen to diplomatically

outraged. "Superintendent, this is not what we agreed to...," he started, but Mr Czwisnjowski cut across him as if he wasn't there.

"At our hotel. We dined in the restaurant between eight and nine-thirty, with Mr Borowski, then we went to our suite."

"And did you communicate with anyone outside the hotel during that time, sir? We will be checking phone and internet records."

This time Borowski wasn't going to be silenced, or ignored. Mary saw him look straight at Kopacz, with surprising ferocity.

"To jest oburzaj¹ce - jesteœmy twoi rodacy!" The words were spat out, like fire from a wing cannon.

"Nie jesteœ!" Kopacz's reply came out as a growl, so deep that Mary could feel the vibration through the loudspeakers. "You're in the United Kingdom, Mr Borowski. Speak English please, so that our colleagues can understand."

But it was Grey who spoke next, his English as impeccable as his suit.

"Clearly a new line of questioning is emerging here, Superintendent. Before responding, my clients and I need to confer, off these premises. Perhaps we can reconvene in a day or so."

"Of course, sir." said Kopacz. Mary heard the file's cover flop over as he closed it. She was surprised that he was making no attempt to keep them there, but sure that he knew what he was doing. He hadn't quite finished yet though.

"We will need to speak to you and your wife again, Mr Czwisnjowski, so please don't leave the UK without informing us."

Borowski, temporarily quietened by Kopacz's growl, came back to life, but Kopacz pre-empted him.

"This is a double murder enquiry, sir. Like I said,

you're in the United Kingdom now. We don't like people using our seaside resorts for their gang warfare. If you want to make a diplomatic incident of it, go ahead. My Chief Constable will have your ambassador hauled in for a chat with the Foreign Office and we'll be all square, won't we?"

Borowski struggled, visibly, for an answer, but Mr Czwisnjowski saved him the trouble.

"We will not be leaving until we can take our daughter with us," he said quietly, "It is my wife's wish. So you have us at your disposal."

"Thank you, sir."

They were all getting up now, Kopacz and the DI's shoulders filling the video screen. From beyond them, Mary heard Mrs Czwisnjowski's voice.

"I need to use a bathroom," she said, apparently unembarrassed to disclose this to the group of men around her. Mary was sure now that the accent was Italian.

"Detective Sergeant Miller will show you the way, Madam," replied Kopacz, making no attempt to explain where Mary was or how she'd know her presence was required. Mary, for her part, was learning fast how these games worked. She pressed the microphone button.

"On my way, sir."

Kopacz gave no indication that he'd heard her, but didn't tap the earpiece either.

Mary picked up her bag and went into the corridor. She didn't know exactly where the interview room was, but a red light burning above a door near the end made it obvious. Kopacz, she guessed, would want her to continue the 'no explanations' routine, just appear as if by magic and whisk Mrs Czwisnjowski off. She knocked lightly on the door then opened it without waiting for a reply. The group all turned to look at her.

"Mrs Czwisnjowski, if you'll come with me." She

hoped she'd made it sound just enough as if she was leading her off to the cells. Disappointingly the visitors, even Borowski, showed no curiosity about her sudden appearance. They all seemed to know the game too. It suddenly occurred to Mary that she didn't know where the toilets were, but Kopacz was one step ahead of her. As she turned to him he said "Turn right, down to the end of the corridor, it's just on your left." Any hopes she'd had of appearing to be a seventh floor regular dashed, she led Mrs Czwisnjowski away.

They walked to the toilets in silence, Mary gesturing for Mrs Czwisnjowski to go first when they reached them. Mary was relieved to find the facilities clean and smelling of air freshener. In fact they seemed not only clean but unused, nothing disturbed since the cleaner's last visit. She wondered if that was due to there not being many women working up here in the elite squads of regional crime fighting. At least it was one less thing for Borowski to protest about.

As they stood in front of the washbasins, Mary caught Mrs Czwisnjowski's eye in the mirror.

"I'm sorry it was a bit rough in there."

Mrs Czwisnjowski looked back at her reflection.

"Do not worry. Police have to have theories. With two murders like this the police at home would be rougher."

"Home," said Mary, "do you mean Poland? I'm guessing you're not from there originally?"

"Torino."

That figures, thought Mary. Turin, in the rich North of Italy, known as a city of industry, culture, wealth, although Don knew it as the home of Juventus FC.

"And you are Italian also?" the face in the mirror said.

Mary turned and looked directly at Mrs Czwisnjowski.

"Just on my father's side. How did you know?"

"Your colouring, my dear." She reached across to Mary's hair, the faintest of touches. "Only an Italian woman has this raven hair - è così bella."

Mary's Italian didn't stretch to the exact meaning, but she knew it was a compliment.

"Thank you."

"Where did your father come from?"

"Napoli." Mary surprised herself with the Italian name. "But it was my grandfather who came. He was a prisoner of war here, and stayed." She just managed to stop the "on" before it came out. "My grandmother was Italian too, but my father married an English girl."

Naples, in the poor south. Home of the Camorra, Italy's most violent mafiosi. She was giving too much away - she should be asking the questions.

"How did you meet your husband?" she asked, via the mirror again now.

"By chance. I was a student in Milano. He was visiting on business. We met at a party." Not the kind of party where the guests brought bottles of £2 Riesling, Mary thought.

"What were you studying?"

"Fashion, of course! I study design."

Of course.

"And did you pursue your career? Sorry, I'm not very knowledgeable about the world of fashion."

Mrs Czwisnjowski gave a light laugh. Her teeth were perfect.

"My studies were a father's indulgence. Italy and Poland, both Catholic countries. Once a woman is married her place is with her husband and her..."

Still she kept her composure, even though the word wouldn't come out.

"I really am most sorry for your loss, Mrs Czwisnjowski."

"I know you are, my dear, and you are trying to catch

who did this. We are grateful. In places I have lived we would have to pay the police to investigate properly. It is not like that here."

"Definitely not. And we will catch whoever did it."

Mrs Czwisnjowski smiled again, but there was visible sadness now.

"I hope so."

Chapter 25

It was dark as they drove back onto the Portway. High above them the Clifton Bridge was illuminated, white bulbs picking out its shape like a giant float from a Somerset carnival. There were more lights as they went onto the motorway and crossed the Avon Bridge; ships in the docks, perhaps some of them carrying the Czwisnjowskis' futures-traded grain. The big Audi pulled smoothly up the side of the Gordano valley until it reached the crest of the hill and Mary's favourite view, the Somerset levels laid out below them with a glimpse of the Bristol Channel to the right. She didn't much like Bristol, or the things that went on there. People laughed when she said she preferred Weston, but she meant it. This view always felt to her like coming home.

Surprisingly little had been said after the Czwisnjowskis had left Bridewell Street, although DSI Kopacz had seemed satisfied with the outcome. Mary had reported what Mrs Czwisnjowski had told her in the toilets, though not what she'd told Mrs Czwisnjowski about her own background. Kopacz had shaken her hand and said "Good work, Sergeant, thank you", which she took to be a positive result. The DI hadn't said much at all, either at Bridewell Street or in the car. She decided that now was the time to broach the subject.

"Looks like we were out of our depth, doesn't it Guv?"

The DI gave a quiet snort.

"Just a bit, yes." Hearing the trace of bitterness in his voice made her think about what the session at Bridewell Street must have been like for him. He'd gone into it thinking that he was the lead investigator, only to find that Kopacz had been there on the seventh floor all the time, with his thick file from the NCA and 'other agencies', pursuing the real objective of nailing Czwisnjowski. Quite likely Weston CID had been allowed to keep the case in order not to scare the Czwisnjowskis away. Now, after the second murder, the gloves were off and the strategy had changed; it was "Big Stan is watching you", and don't leave the country. Weston were left as little more than bag-carriers.

"Do you think Major Crime have been using us as a smokescreen all along?"

"Doesn't matter if they have. We might not like it much, but at the end of the day what matters is that Czwisnjowski gets his comeuppance."

She was surprised at how quickly his bitterness gave way to equanimity, but at the same time she knew he meant it. Ultimately he believed in the command structure, even when it meant he was too junior to read a file on the main suspect in a murder case he was supposed to be investigating. He accepted the system and worked with it, which was why he'd probably end up as one of the people who were allowed to read the file. She couldn't give it such unconditional loyalty, which was one of the reasons why she probably wouldn't.

"And what about the Troshani gang?"

He turned to her, smiled briefly and looked back at the road.

"Don't worry – we'll nick them too. Major Crime will need their involvement in Katya's death as proof of motive for Czwisnjowski. They won't be forgotten."

Mary said nothing. The system would make those decisions.

They reached the Weston-super-Mare junction, went down the long sliproad, around the roundabout and onto the dual carriageway. As they passed the exit for the back road to Kewstoke and Sand Bay Mary thought of Luan Redzepi. Had Czwisnjowski's people taken him along that road last night in the back of a Mitsubishi pickup, his corpse already set rigid by rigor mortis? It occurred to her that it was the young people who were dying in this gang war, if that was what it was, and the old ones – Agron Troshani, Wiktor Czwisnjowski – who pulled the strings. Just like a real war, she supposed.

A couple of miles further brought them to the roundabout by the big out of town supermarket. They were within walking distance of Mary's house, but she'd left her car at the station and didn't fancy persuading Don to drive her in the next morning. Besides, there was still work to do.

"What about Jolene Buller, Guv? I can go round and see her on my way home if you like."

"No, I'll talk to Ms Buller. No need for you to come – pick your car up and get off home."

Mary was grateful, but also surprised. The DI wasn't an enthusiastic payer of house calls, preferring to have his interviewees brought to the station by a DC. Also, as the lead investigator (in Weston, at least) it wasn't his job to interview secondary witnesses. He had people like her to do that – or at least he was supposed to have.

The surprise turned to worry. Was there a black mark in her personnel file, a "do not deploy on anything connected with Albanians" flag? She'd seen enough that afternoon to know it was possible, and had enough experience of the Force to know that a rethink on dealing with the Troshanis didn't necessarily mean that previous assumptions about her would be automatically corrected. No – she wouldn't let paranoia get the better of her. He was just doing her a good turn, letting her be the one who got home with something like an evening left. Nevertheless...

"I'd prefer to come. Michael Slade's my contact, and I'd like to hear from the horse's mouth what he's been up to. Also it might be as well to have a female officer along, rather than seeing her on your own. No point in taking chances, especially if she's a friend of the Troshanis."

The DI let out an audible sigh.

"Please yourself then. But don't blame me if your husband complains about you getting home late."

"I won't, Guv." Not exactly encouraging, but not a refusal either.

The Audi glided down the last of the dual carriageway to the big roundabout by the railway station. The DI took the first exit, turned into the station car park, and pulled up outside a small door in the side of the station building. Above it was a wooden sign. In the middle, in large letters, was "BETWEEN THE LINES". Around the periphery smaller lettering announced "Real Ales", "Ciders", "Sandwiches" and "C&W Karaoke".

"Sure you want in on this?" asked the DI as he switched off the engine, "it's not a place I'd go to from choice."

It occurred to Mary that the DI was, in fact, doing exactly that, since she'd offered to do the interview. Her paranoia had subsided; she no longer thought the DI's uncharacteristic behaviour was anything to do with her, which left her intrigued to find out what it was to do with.

Inside, Between the Lines seemed little wider than a railway carriage. At the far end it was furnished as a cafe, complete with plastic tablecloths and sauce containers shaped like tomatoes. Halfway along the room the décor changed abruptly to red plush, one wall lined with seating and tables, the other accommodating a bar, with not much room to squeeze between the two.

The landlord, Billy Buller, was behind the bar,

polishing a glass with a cloth that looked as if it contravened all known environmental health regulations. He was short but sturdy, age somewhere north of 60 but still active, a man who'd change his own barrels. He was wearing a grey cardigan with suede patches on the elbows and shoulders, underneath it a tieless striped cotton shirt. His hair, also grey, was smoothed back with old-style hair cream; his chin had yet to see a razor that day, perhaps the day before too. He displayed the telltale fidgeting of someone who didn't know what to do with his hands now that smoking was banned indoors. The glass, Mary guessed, probably never made it to the shelves, which in all likelihood was a good thing.

Mary was used to getting a mixed response from pub licensees to the sight of police officers entering their premises, but she wasn't expecting the one they got now. On seeing the DI, Billy's eyes lit up and a broad smile spread across his face.

"Stevie - Stevie Jones! Haven't seen you for ages. How are you?"

"Hello Mr Buller. I'm very well thanks. How are you?"

"Fine 'n dandy, thanks. How's your mum and dad?"

"They're very well too."

On the one hand, Mary was aware that there were aspects of this situation with which she was not familiar, number one being why Mr Buller knew the DI as "Stevie". On the other, the mystery of why the DI hadn't wanted her to come in with him was quickly evaporating.

"You still playing?" The glass and bar towel lay discarded now, as Billy focussed on his guest.

"No, I gave that up ten years ago."

"Still in the police though?"

"Yes."

"Pity you gave up the rugby – you were good. You could've played for Exeter or Bristol, Bath even if you'd put your mind to it. They make some money, them top players these days. You could've been on millionaire's row!"

"I'm very happy where I am, thanks," said the DI, "Risky career, rugby."

"I suppose it is," Billy replied, considering the point for a moment. "What's your dad doing now? They still in Weston?"

"Draycott, got a bungalow out there. Dad's retired, spends most of his time in the garden."

"Yeah, your dad always was keen on his garden. Draycott, eh? Done well for themselves."

"Dad did twenty years in the warehouse, built up a decent pension."

"Yeah, I remember him going to the warehouse. Better than those coal wagons, I can tell you, 'specially in winter. We was both glad to get off 'em!"

The DI smiled. "Yeah, that's what dad says."

"Oh well, give him my regards, won't you, and your mum. Now what'll you have to drink? On the house." Billy turned his attention to Mary, his landlord's eye running swiftly over her left hand and wedding ring. "This your Missus? Done well for yourself here. Pleased to meet you, love. I'm Billy, used to work with your husband's father on the coal lorries." He looked more closely at her face. "Don't I know you from somewhere?"

You should, thought Mary – I arrested three car thieves here in January. She suppressed an urge to burst out laughing, but said nothing. This was the DI's situation – he could sort it out.

"This is my colleague, Detective Sergeant Miller. And I'm a Detective Inspector these days, Weston CID. We're here on official business – nothing serious, but official all the same. Is Jolene around?"

Billy's face fell, so suddenly that Mary almost wanted to continue the illusion that this was a social call and she was the DI's wife, just so he'd cheer up.

"Detective Inspector? Yeah, she's upstairs I think," said Billy quietly, "She's not in trouble, is she?"

"No, she's not in any trouble. We just want to ask her about something."

"Oh," said Billy, still looking dejected, "You better go on up then." He pointed to the door marked "Private".

"Thanks, Mr Buller – there's no trouble, really, don't worry."

Behind the door marked 'Private' was a steep, twisting staircase that led to an old-style plank door. The DI knocked, and a woman's voice said "Come in."

The upstairs room was a loft space that had been furnished to provide the Bullers and their staff with somewhere to relax during breaks. There were no windows, and headroom was limited. Jolene Buller was sitting with her legs over the arms of a chair that had seen better days. She was wearing a suede skirt with a long fringe at the hem, a cowgirl shirt with rhinestone detailing, and pink leather boots with stiletto heels. It was hard to tell whether she was in costume for her Dolly Parton tribute act, or if this was just her normal outfit.

"Stevie Jones!" she said, turning her attention from the talent show that flickered on the old TV, "What a surprise!"

"Hello Jolene, it's been a long time."

"Yeah it has, hasn't it? What you doing here? Dad send you up, did he?"

"Yes, he did. I'm here on official business. Nothing to worry about."

"What sort of official business, Stevie? You with the council now, Environmental Health or something? Don't usually see you lot out on a Saturday night."

"I'm a police officer, Jolene – Detective Inspector."

"Oh yes, so you are. I forgot. Who's this then?" She nodded towards Mary.

"This is my colleague, Detective Sergeant Miller."

"Oh. Pleased to meet you, love." She turned back to the DI. "Seems strange you ending up a copper."

"I don't know why – it's what I always said I was going to do."

"Yeah, but we didn't take any notice of you. Thought it was like saying you wanted to be an engine driver. How many boys end up engine drivers, eh? But here you are, a real policeman."

"Indeed I am. And like I said, I'm here on official business."

"Are you? What, am I in trouble? What for?"

"You're not in any trouble, Jolene. We just want to ask you about something. Can we sit down?"

"Sure, course."

Mary and the DI sat on the small sofa opposite the chair, crammed uncomfortably close together.

"I believe you know a man called Michael Slade," said the DI, "is that right?"

"Michael? Yes, course I do. Works at the supermarket, comes in here regular." She was suddenly serious. "Why, is he in trouble?"

"No he's not, Jolene." Not altogether true – not if the DI had his way, anyway.

"That's good," she said, brightening, "He's a nice bloke, very clever. Knows about all sorts of things. He's wasted over there if you ask me."

"Yes, quite likely. Now Mr Slade tells us that you identified a young Albanian man from a description of his birthmark, is that right?"

"That's right, yes. Why did he tell you about it though? I thought you said he wasn't in trouble?"

"He isn't." The DI was beginning to sound exasperated, as if dealing with a difficult child. "What was the young man's name, Jolene?"

"Luan." She pronounced it almost as 'Loon'.

"Luan Redzepi?"

"Yes, that's right. He's not in trouble, is he?"

"No, he's not."

If the DI had hoped Jolene wouldn't twig the real purpose of his questions, he was in for a disappointment.

"Then why are you here asking about him?" she said suspiciously, "And how is Michael mixed up in it? Is Michael working for you or something?"

The DI and Mary remained silent. The serious expression came back to Jolene's face, like a big dark cloud sweeping over it.

"Is Luan OK? He isn't, is he?"

Still no reply.

"It was him found dead at Sand Bay this morning, wasn't it?"

Never judge a book by its cover, thought Mary. For someone who gave the impression of being none too bright, that was quite a leap of perception.

"Did Mr Slade tell you that?" asked the DI.

"No, but it was, wasn't it?"

"Why did Mr Slade say he was asking about him?" If the DI and Jolene went back a long way, it didn't show in his line of questioning. Tears were beginning well up in Jolene's eyes.

"He said someone had told him there was a young Albanian lad who could get cheap iPhones, and you could tell him by the birthmark on his neck. Asked if I knew him. But it is him, isn't it?"

Good cover story, Michael, thought Mary – well done. Except they'd just blown it.

"We're pretty sure it is, yes," said the DI quietly, "We're just waiting for formal identification."

"I don't want to identify him. Anyway, I don't know him that well."

"Just arrived in Weston, had he?"

"No – he's been here six months at least. Back in April, May I first saw him."

Great, thought Mary. Albanian illegals drinking in the local pubs for six months and they didn't even know about it. She decided it was time to ask a few questions of her own.

"When did you last see Luan, Jolene?"

Jolene looked at her in surprise, as if she'd forgotten she was in the room.

"Last Wednesday. Day that girl got found under the pier."

"Was he with anyone?"

"Ardi Troshani and his gang – the usual lot. Early evening it was, about seven. They said they were going up Bristol. Ardi was already half cut but it was his brother driving. I made sure of that, otherwise I'd have nicked his keys and told him to ring his uncle for a lift."

"What, Luan's uncle?"

"No." Jolene looked at Mary as if she'd failed to grasp a very obvious point. "Ardi's uncle, the big man, Agron. Ardi likes to act tough but he's scared shitless of his uncle, they all are. Agron doesn't like the youngsters getting pissed and causing trouble round town. He's trying to go all respectable, isn't he? Doesn't go with the image."

"Did Luan like to get drunk?"

"No, he didn't. He was a really nice boy. He'd just have a half of cider and that was it for him, all he wanted. He dodged out of going up Bristol with them that night, said he had gut rot. Had his half then went off home."

"You say you didn't know him all that well," said the DI, "What exactly was your relationship with him?"

Jolene looked genuinely hurt. She reached into her bag, took out her cigarettes and lit one.

"That's what you all think, isn't it – that I sleep with those Albanian boys? Well I did with one or two, but that was ages ago and I'm not proud of it. I'm just friends with them now, and more like a mother to the young 'uns. Poor little buggers, they get dragged over here through Portbury or whatever, then he works them half to death doing up those so-called hotels of his..."

"Agron Troshani's hotels?" asked Mary.

"of course Agron Troshani's – who else do you think I'm talking about? Doss-houses more like. Anyway, some of them get really homesick and they come to me. I give 'em a drink and someone to talk to, not that some of 'em can manage much English. But I don't go shagging 'em."

"Sounds like you're the only friendly face they get to see." said Mary. Jolene seemed genuine to her – either that or an outstandingly good actress.

"That's right, love, I think I am."

"And Luan was one of the homesick ones?"

"More pissed off really. He said he had to work twelve hours most days, sometimes fourteen, on a place up near Grove Park. That's why I didn't see much of him."

"And you didn't...?"

"No I didn't, nor with most of 'em, whatever some people might be saying."

"Jolene," said Mary, "has anyone come in looking for Luan recently, or asking about him?"

"No, not that I remember. Except Michael, of course. I don't know where he got that idea about Luan selling iPhones. He didn't do anything like that."

No comment, thought Mary.

"And did Luan have any enemies that you knew of, anyone he'd fallen out with?"

"No, he just stuck with Ardi's lot, and they all seemed to get on all right. Ardi can be a little bastard when he's pissed, but it's all over the next day and he doesn't bear grudges, not even when I've nicked his keys."

"Is that something you have to do often?" asked the DI.

"Now and then. Like I said, his brother does the driving most times, and he doesn't drink anything."

"What sort of car does Ardi drive?" Another reason why he was a good DI – not too grand to collect a bit of local intelligence to give to Traffic.

"Mostly his uncle's crew bus when he's got his mates with him, blue Transit 10-seater. He's given me and the band a lift in it a couple of times. Don't half stink in there though."

"Of what?"

"Sweat. Chips. Beer. Usual stuff. He should open the windows more, or get an air freshener."

"Yes, I imagine he should," the DI sympathised. It wouldn't be sweat, or chips, that the Traffic car officers would be sniffing for when they pulled the van over sometime soon.

"Is there anything else you can tell us about Luan? Other friends, places he went to, that sort of thing. Anything like that might help us catch whoever - well, you know." Mary couldn't bring herself to say "murdered"; she could see Jolene's tears beginning to well up again.

"Not really," Jolene sniffled, "like I said, I just saw him when he came in here with Ardi and the others. He did say he missed his mum though."

"Did he tell you who his mum was?"

Jolene looked at Mary as if she'd missed another very obvious point.

"Well she was his mum, wasn't she? I don't know what you mean otherwise."

"She's Agron Troshani's sister," the DI broke in. "Luan was Agron's nephew, same as Ardi. He never mentioned that?"

"No, he didn't." Jolene seemed genuinely surprised. "I thought he was just one of the boys they brought in....." She stopped, as if suddenly remembering again that the DI was a police officer. "Well, you know."

"Yes," the DI said gently, "Well I think that's enough for now. Thanks for your help, Jolene. If you remember anything else about Luan, let us know, won't you? Here's my card."

Jolene took the card and stared at it.

"Detective Inspector. I never thought you'd get high up in the police like that, Stevie. Didn't think you'd even make it to Constable, to be honest. You've done well, haven't you? Dad always said you would."

"Yes, well, it's what I always planned to do."

"Yeah, you did, didn't you?"

"Goodbye then, Jolene."

"Yeah, goodbye Stevie." She looked up at Mary, "Goodbye love."

"Goodbye." Mary resisted the urge to bend down and give her a hug.

Downstairs, Billy Buller had reverted to polishing the glass. He put it down as the DI emerged from the Private door.

"All done then?" he asked warily.

"Yes thanks, Mr Buller," the DI replied.

"Is our Jolene OK?"

"She's a bit upset. We had to bring her some bad news, I'm afraid, about one of her friends. She'll tell you about it."

"All right. Want that drink now?"

"We'd better not, we're on duty. Thanks for the offer though - appreciate it."

"Any time. Don't forget to give my regards to your mum and dad, will you?"

"I won't forget."

"We used to think you and Jolene might, you know..."

"You can never tell how things are going to work out, can you?"

Outside it had begun to rain, hard and very cold. Mary's coat was in the car; she was glad the DI had opted for the double yellow lines directly outside the building rather than the parking bays on the other side of the station forecourt. As they settled in, she did an impromptu assessment of the risk involved in making some discreet background enquiries. The DI, however, got there first.

"I know what you're thinking, Sergeant, but there are no skeletons in that cupboard, so don't bother looking for any."

"I wasn't going to, Guv."

The DI put the lever into 'Drive' and swung the Audi round towards the exit.

"Yeah, right. Billy Buller may have had ideas about me and the lovely Jolene, but he's the only one who did, I can assure you. I didn't even know her that well. She's a year older than me, and that's half a generation when you're in your teens, especially when the girl's the older one. She was off on the back of motorbikes once she was sixteen, and that was pretty much the last I saw of her."

"She seems nice though. Not what I was expecting."

"Simple, you mean. The Buller family have never been the brightest bulbs on the Christmas Tree, none of them. They were decent people though. My dad had a lot of time for Billy when they were on the coal waggons together. In the winter the cold would get to dad's chest, and Billy would make him stay in the cab for half the round, carry his sacks for him. Dad never forgot it."

"So how come they lost touch?"

"Everyone moved on. When they closed the coal yard Dad got a job in the warehouse at Locking, Billy and Madge went off to Devon to work in her uncle's pub. That's where they learnt the licensed trade, I guess. I didn't even know they'd come back until recently."

"Perhaps they'll get back in touch now?" This was the most the DI had ever talked about his background.

"Yes, they might." And now it was over. Mary thought of the DI's actual wife, Karen, the perfect slender blonde, a child psychologist by profession. About as much the opposite of Jolene Buller as it was possible to be. Everyone had moved on.

"One more thing."

"Yes, Guv?"

"If I hear the name 'Stevie' uttered in any part of the station, or over a Traffic car radio, then I will find a reason to make you spend a very long time in Ardi Troshani's stinky crew bus with the doors and windows shut."

"Understood." Business as usual.

It was a short drive to the police station; already they were approaching the mini-roundabout that led onto Walliscote Road.

"You can tell anyone you like about my dad being on the coal waggons though. And my mum – she was a school dinner lady for 36 years. Honest working people, put a lot in, didn't expect much back. Put every penny they had into sending me to university. I'm proud of both of them."

The DI took the first left.

"You helped them buy their bungalow in Draycott, didn't you?"

"No comment." said the DI, as the Audi approached the second mini-roundabout. "You might make a detective yet," he added, as he kept straight ahead towards the station.

The DI drove to the car park entrance and waited for the security gate to open. Above them the windows of the CID office were dark. It was 7.30pm on a Saturday night. Not even the reappearance of Jack the Ripper would have got detectives into the office at that time.

"You're not going home, Guv?"

"I'll check HOLMES, update my diary. Make sure you do yours, and your notes on what you saw in that viewing room. Oh, and another thing – have that chat with our friend Mr Slade, tell him any more freelance detective work and I'll have uniforms hauling him off his till in front of his workmates every day from now till Christmas."

"Yes, Guv – do you want me to get him back from Bridgwater in the morning?"

"No, it'll wait. See if he's coming back tomorrow evening. And make sure you impress on him that it's not safe poking around the Troshani gang – leave that to us. Apart from that take tomorrow off. I'll need you fully refreshed and recuperated, 8am Monday in the office. I've got a feeling it's going to be a busy week."

"OK, thanks Guv." The old-fashioned detective in Mary said that taking the day off just 24 hours after a murder discovery wasn't how it should be done either, but she was getting used to the DI's modern ways.

The rain was even heavier now, a storm blown in from the Channel. The DI slid the Audi into a parking space, and switched off the engine. Mary grabbed her coat and bag from the back seat, pushed open the Audi's door and prepared to make a run for it through the downpour.

"See you Monday."

"Yes, see you."

Mary sat in her car, rain-soaked after only a few seconds in the open. Water had splashed into her shoes and soaked through her tights; her feet felt cold and wet. She gave an involuntary shiver, then started the engine to get the heater going. She watched the DI run to the back entrance of the station, punch in the access code and disappear into the building. She pressed the clutch pedal, reached for the gear lever, then let the clutch out again, leaving the lever undisturbed. The night's work wasn't over for her; she had some more questioning to do, and she wasn't looking forward to it. Still, she couldn't avoid it. She pressed the pedal again, put the lever into first, and drove slowly towards the gate.

Chapter 26

Don's van was in its usual space outside their house. There had been hardly any traffic; the drive home had taken barely ten minutes, but the heater had done its job, and Mary's feet felt warm, if not dry. 19:48. She could hardly believe that just over 24 hours ago she'd pulled up here at the start of their romantic evening in. Since then there'd been another murder, those strange kids at Sand Bay, Michael Slade in the forensics tent, Kopacz, the viewing room, secret files, the case turning into a whole different ball game, none of which she'd had any idea was coming when she'd switched out the light last night. Last night seemed more like a month ago.

She wasn't expecting another romantic evening, any more than she'd thought that a romantic morning might have been possible earlier that day. She was, however, pleasantly surprised when she got into the house. Yes, Don was on the sofa watching football (Juventus, at it happened, versus Inter Milan, a real regional derby), but the place was as tidy as it had been the previous night, and he jumped up straight away as she came in.

"Hello Love, long day, eh?"

"Very long. I'm done in." Suddenly the tiredness had hit her.

"Been on that Sand Bay business, I suppose? It's been all over the news, on the main six o'clock bulletin."

"Yes, they were filming us from a helicopter."

Don's face lit up. "Helicopter? I'll bet Jones didn't like that! Not too keen on having his picture taken, if I remember rightly. I wouldn't be if I looked like him."

Mary smiled along with him. The mild insult, she knew, was Don's substitute for what he really wanted to say about the DI, and the amount of time his wife spent with him. She sometimes wondered how she'd feel if it was the other way round.

"Have we got any food in, Don? Sorry, I just haven't had a chance to..." It was ridiculous, apologising for not having taken time out of a murder enquiry to pop into the supermarket, but she felt the need to do it anyway.

"Chicken Tikka Masala OK? I've got some naan too, and some salad to go with it."

"Oh, that sounds perfect!" she sighed. It did. Two days in a row, and not a word of complaint. Who was this imposter pretending to be her husband, and what had they done with the real Don?

"You go and have a shower, wash the sand off. I'll heat it up. Glass of wine?"

"I'll have it when I come down." She reached out and touched his arm. "Thanks, love. Really."

"No problem, sweetheart. Ready in about 15 minutes, all right?"

She nodded. She wanted to lean forward and kiss him, but didn't.

Mary went to their bedroom, switched on the light and turned on the shower in the en suite. Don's overalls were on his side of the bed, where he'd taken them off. Normality partly resumed then. As she undressed, she thought about what she had to do, either later or tomorrow morning. The sooner the better, according to the procedure manuals. She wondered whether the DI had held back from mentioning it, to allow her to pick her own time.

The shower was a pumped unit, top of the range, installed by Don himself. She set it to cool, the jets to thin and fast so they made her skin tingle as they hit her. Once he would have followed her in there, his clothes left strewn over the bed and floor. Had that been why she hadn't kissed him? She adjusted the jets to soft and aerated; they flowed over her like a warm breeze. Then she turned the dial to 'off'. As the noise of the shower subsided, she heard the clink of plates from the kitchen downstairs.

Back in the bedroom she found her jersey dress and black cardigan, unwrapped the towel from her head and brushed her hair back into shape. She looked at herself in the full-length mirror, transformed again from detective to wife. For a sudden, unexpected moment she wished that Don had come into the shower. The moment decayed into hope that that he had, at least, wanted to, then worry that she'd made him feel he couldn't.

And, wife though she was, she still had to be a detective that night. "Interview potential witnesses as soon as possible." That's what the manual said. She knew someone who might have known Luan Redzepi, someone the manual would say they ought to talk to. She knew the exact location of the Troshani building project that Redzepi had been working on near Grove Park, that it was the conversion of two big Edwardian terraced houses into an eighteen-bed hotel. She knew that it had a new gas-fired central heating system, with separate balanced-flue condensing boilers on each floor. She knew this because the system had been installed by Don Miller Heating.

It had been the cause of the worst row they'd ever had, from which they'd yet to fully recover. Mary's initial line had been that it was difficult having the husband of a police officer doing work for a family of known criminals, however legitimate the work, but when Don had refused to accept it, she'd blurted out, in her anger and frustration, what she really thought - "they're only giving you the job to compromise me!"

That had triggered an eruption of what seemed like fifteen years' worth of bitter resentment from Don; how it always had to be about her and her precious career, and couldn't she see that it might just once be about him being good at what he did and other people respecting that, even if he was only a glorified plumber not a hotshot detective. And it hadn't stopped there. Perhaps if she spent less time being a detective she could spend more on pulling her weight around the house, because he was sick of having to do the shopping on his own, then eat on his own, then load the dishwasher on his own the next morning because she'd forgotten to do it when she'd finally come in the previous night. And then the big one. Perhaps if she spent less time being a fucking detective she'd have time to be a mother, because giving birth was one thing she couldn't dump onto him, Equal Opportunities or no fucking Equal Opportunities.

Mary's reaction had been astonishment – astonishment that she hadn't noticed it building up, that she'd gone on thinking that everything was OK. The problem was that they were both right. She hadn't been doing her share of the shopping or cooking. She didn't remember to empty the washing machine when she'd left her clothes in it, but she never forgot to take her contraceptive pill. Deep down inside, though she'd managed never to say it, she did think that keeping the streets safe was more important than fitting gas boilers; she'd seen the victims of crime. Whether that was more important than having a child was something she simply didn't think about, except involuntarily on birthdays.

She was also right about the reason the Troshanis gave Don the work, she was certain of it. Not because she didn't think Don was good at his job – he was, everyone said so – but because it just wasn't the Troshanis' style to employ a proper tradesman, even for something as potentially dangerous as a gas installation. As it was, they hadn't even tried to bargain him down. It had been a well-paid job (and those, as Don pointed out, weren't exactly thick on the ground just then), but of course that would only make his relationship with them look more suspect.

And she had no doubt that the Troshanis knew exactly who Don was, and who she was. It had been 'local businessman' Agron Troshani who'd sat at the press conference while his lawyer denounced the 'persecution of this disadvantaged minority group' by the police, including 'vendettas by individual officers'. It had resulted in her being given something close to a reprimand, and told to leave the Albanians alone.

That had been four months ago; the job had been finished a month later, after weeks during which, at all costs, no mention was made between them of where Don had been working that day. Since then it had been allowed to fade into history, along with the spike in the revenues of Don Miller Heating (the Troshanis had paid promptly, to Mary's relief not in cash). Now she had to bring it up again, mention the unmentionable. If she didn't then someone from the station – Lane, Tom Flanagan, worst of all the DI - would have to, and that might drive a whole new kind of wedge between them, turn a casual enquiry into an official police action in which she and Don were on opposite sides.

She waited until after the Chicken Tikka Masala, microwaved this time but served with the salad in bowls and the Balsamic dressing they both liked drizzled over it. A glass of cold Chauvignon Blanc gave her confidence.

"Don, there's something I have to ask you about. Nothing big, just whether you might remember someone. I have to ask because I know you might." Not too bad, although she might have overdone the explanation.

"Official?" So far his expression was unchanged – no anger, but no smile either.

"Yes."

"Fair enough – fire away."

"You don't mind?"

"Why should I? I'm not a suspect am I?"

"No, of course not." This could be heading off the rails, big time. Mary quelled her panic, or at least tried to stop it from showing. Don, however, seemed to have seen it.

"Look, love," he said, "it's OK. You're on a murder enquiry – double murder now. Serious business. If you think I can help then ask away, whatever it is."

"OK, when you were working at Grove Park," she looked for a hostile response in his eyes, but saw none, "do you remember a young Albanian man, around 20?"

Don gave a short laugh. "You'll have to be a bit more specific, love, there were lots of Albanian lads on that job."

Of course there were. Nerves were making her fluff it, like a probationer interviewing her first street theft victim.

"Sorry. He had a birthmark, just here." She pointed to her neck.

Don's face lit up in recognition.

"You mean Lennie? Yes, I do remember him – quite well, in fact."

"His name was Lennie?"

"Not really, no, but we couldn't pronounce his real name properly, so we just called him Len at first, then it became Lennie."

"Luan? Luan Redzepi? Does that ring a bell?"

"Yeah, that's it. Only he didn't pronounce it like you do either."

"And you say you knew him quite well?"

"Well, only to talk to in the breaks. He was a football fan, mad on Serie A, said they got it live on satellite where he came from. Mad keen Lazio fan – each to their own, I suppose. I thought about inviting him round to watch it here, but...." His voice tailed off. Time to move quickly on.

"When did you first see him?"

"He was there when we started the job, still there when we finished."

"And you haven't seen him since?"

"No."

"What work did he do?"

"A bit of everything, like most of those lads. I don't think he had a trade. Used to do a fair bit of painting though – doors, skirting, the trickier stuff. He was a good worker."

Like Don then, thought Mary, although perhaps she didn't say it often enough. She decided to make an error that could get a probationer into serious trouble. She owed it to him.

"Don, I shouldn't tell you this because it's not official yet, but it was Luan Redzepi we found at Sand Bay this morning. I'm sorry."

She wasn't expecting Don's response, the look of overwhelming shock that came over his face.

"Lennie? Oh shit. Are you sure?"

"Yes. He hasn't been formally identified yet but the birthmark makes it pretty much a certainty."

Don had downed his glass of wine in the time it took to her to say it. She'd never seen him this shaken by anything.

"He was a nice lad. Intelligent. Not one of the tearaways. You could have a conversation with him. And he's been murdered?" Don looked at her as if hoping she might say it had all been a mistake.

"I'm really sorry, Love, yes." She put her hand over his and squeezed it, felt his fingers grasp hers as she did. He wasn't used to people being murdered, even to the small extent that she was. Unexpectedly she found herself forcing back a tear. This was becoming difficult in a way she hadn't anticipated. Perhaps she should have got Tom Flanagan to talk to him after all.

No - pull yourself together, Detective Sergeant, even if it is your husband on the other side of the table.

"Is there anything else you can tell me about Luan, Don? Was he friends with Ardit Troshani - Ardi?"

"What, Zamir Troshani's boy? Now he is a tearaway. Never saw him do a proper day's work, always going off somewhere then turning up again a couple of hours later. Lennie seemed to be part of his crew but not part of it, if you see what I mean. He came to work with them in that bus of theirs, and they included him in whatever it was they talked about in Albanian - I didn't want to know - but Lennie sort of kept a distance from them too. Like I said, he was a nice lad."

"But he was definitely part of their group?"

"Well they all were, love. I think all the Albanian lads lived together somewhere, another one of Troshani's hotels, probably."

"Did Luan ever mention any links he had to the Troshani family?"

"No. He only talked to us about football. Like I said, I didn't want to know about the Albanian side of things." He looked suddenly shamefaced. He knew, Mary realised, that he'd done the wrong thing in getting involved with the Troshanis, had known it probably since soon after starting the job. He was almost too honest for his own good, and she loved him for it. But he'd been too proud to admit his mistake and pull out of the job, and in a way she loved him for that too. Or perhaps she just hadn't wanted to be the only one of them left in the wrong.

She knew she should leave it there; any good wife, or husband, would. Sometimes, though, she let being a good detective take priority.

"He was actually Zamir and Agron Troshani's nephew," she said, "their sister's son. So he was Ardit's cousin. But they never gave any indication of that, didn't treat him differently because he was family?" In court a barrister would have been admonished for attempting to influence the witness's memory by now, but they weren't in court, and they needed evidence that Redzepi was an integral member of the Troshani family, to support motive for Katya's father having him killed.

"Well I suppose Ardi did treat him a bit differently from the others. He'd kick and punch at them, and swear at them in Albanian, but he did seem to leave off that with Lennie."

Thank you, Mr Miller, you can leave the witness box now.

"Thanks, love, really. I'm sorry I had to tell you the bad news about Luan."

"It's OK."

"We might need a formal statement from you, just to confirm what you've told me. It'll have to be someone else taking it - I can ask Tom Flanagan to do it."

"Yes, that'd be fine." It was a good choice - DS Flanagan was one of the few of Mary's colleagues Don actually liked.

The wine bottle was still half-full. Don topped up their glasses.

"Do you think it was the same people as killed the Polish girl?"

The wine was still cold, its effects seeming to reach Mary's brain as soon as it hit her throat. She wanted to relax, but then talking about the case with someone who wasn't a fellow officer was relaxing, helped by what was still the novelty of having Don show any interest in her work.

"We did at first – the MO's the same, buried fully clothed, all ID removed, hand sticking out, but now we think it may be a revenge killing, tit for tat."

"By the Polish girl's family?"

"Yes, specifically her father. It turns out he's a real hard case, ex Russian military." She checked herself, remembering the file in Kopacz's office with its big red 'Restricted' stamp.

"So if Lennie had no ID on him," continued Don, "how did you find out who he was? The birthmark, I suppose?"

"That's a bit of a sore point." Sore with the DI, she thought – Don would enjoy this. "It wasn't us who traced him, it was... Shit!"

"What's up?"

"I've got to make a phone call. Sorry, Love."

"No problem."

"My bag's in the hall." She looked at the wine bottle, nearly empty now like Don's glass. "Do you want me to bring you a lager from the fridge on the way back?"

"Don't worry, love, I can fetch my own lager," Don chuckled, recognising her clumsy attempt at mood management. "Go and make your call, go on!"

In the hallway Mary found her phone and checked the display. 9:18pm, still a reasonable time to be calling someone in the bosom of their family, even one they only enjoyed two days a week. The number was in her phone's address book now, another feat of technology she'd mastered. She found 'M Slade' and pressed Dial.

"Hello?" It was Michael's voice. In the background Mary could hear a TV, announcing the results of the Lottery draw.

"Hello Michael? It's Mary Miller here, from Weston CID."

"Ah yes, hello Mary."

"Where are you?"

"In Bridgwater – where did you think I'd be?" He

sounded as if he'd fetched himself a lager or two from the family fridge.

"Michael, I need to have a chat with you."

"Fire away then. Will it take long?"

"No, not on the phone – in person."

"What, now? I can't drive, I'm afraid, I've had some alcohol. You'll have to come here, although it's a bit inconvenient..."

"No, I mean tomorrow." The conversation was already becoming hard work. "When are you coming back to Weston?"

"Ah, you're in luck, Mary." He sounded quite drunk now. "I don't normally come back until Monday, because as you know I work Tuesdays, Wednesdays and Fridays. But this week they want me in on Monday as well, to cover for staff sickness – terrible bug going round, half the checkout team down with it, but I seem to be immune, probably thanks to my judicious consumption of alcohol." She heard him give his strange chortle. "So I'll be coming back tomorrow night. That's lucky, isn't it?"

Lucky for you, she thought, because if you hadn't then the DI would have taken pleasure in sending a marked car round, complete with sound and lighting effects, to bring you in.

"Yes, it is. What time will you be back, Michael?"

"Quite early, I think, because I have a 7am start on Monday. Then I've got to revert to my usual three to eleven shift on Tuesday, which is going to throw my sleep patterns out badly. I think that's asking a bit much, don't you Mary? Still, it's an emergency. All hands to the pumps and that."

Mary thought of the perpetually worried Mrs Slade, sitting in front of the TV. Perhaps their part-time family life was as much for her benefit as his.

"Would 7pm be OK then? It'll only take twenty

minutes, half an hour at most. That will leave you plenty of time to get an early night." And plenty of time for her to get back and switch off in front of some Sunday night TV.

"Yes, I suppose so." he sounded doubtful, as if Mrs Slade might not approve. "I wouldn't normally leave here quite that early..."

"7.30 then?" She'd still be back in time for the 9pm drama.

"OK, that's better for me."

"Good. Shall I come to your flat?"

"I'd rather meet you somewhere. I like to go out on my first night back in Weston each week."

And your second, and third, thought Mary. Still, it would save her having to explain to the DI why she'd been to his flat a second time and still not snooped around the rest of it. She had no desire to examine Michael Slade's bedroom, even less his bathroom.

"OK, where?"

"How about the Brit? Do you know it?"

A pub – not ideal, if his present state was anything to go by. But he was hardly likely to drive drunk to meet a police officer, so she'd probably get enough sober minutes to deliver the message from the DI.

"Yes, I do."

"I like to sit on the sofas around the far side of the bar, where they have the books on 1960s music. They take a chance just leaving them on the shelves like that - some of them are valuable, you know. Still, they'll be safe enough while you're there, won't they Mary? Under police guard, as it were!" The chortling came back, louder this time. Mary hoped that Mrs Slade wasn't trying to check her lottery score.

"Yes, I suppose so. OK Michael, I'll see you in the Brit at 7:30. In the meantime, please remember what I said about not telling anyone about anything you saw at Sand

Bay this morning, not even your family. My DI is annoyed enough about that already, and believe me you don't want to annoy him any more."

"Oh yes," said Michael, as if remembering something for the first time, "I assume my information proved correct? Was it indeed Luan Redzepi?"

"Michael!" she barked down the phone at him, as she'd done the previous night. "I assume your family are there with you. Please don't go blurting things like that out in front of them. We could all end up in trouble."

"OK, sorry." he sounded contrite, although she had a feeling it wouldn't last. "Was I right though?"

"We can discuss that tomorrow evening. 7.30 at the Brit – I'll see you there. Bye, Michael."

"Bye Mary." He sounded like a tipsy lost child. Still, he was Mrs Slade's problem again now.

As Mary put her phone back in her bag, she heard a bump and a low curse from the part-open kitchen door, followed by the click and hiss of a ring-pull. Shame – she'd have liked to have fetched Don's lager for him, for all sorts of reasons, although she'd probably get another chance. Back in the living room he'd settled on the sofa. On the TV the lottery show was just ending. She collected her wine and went to join him.

"Who was that you were phoning then, Love?" he said over his shoulder as she came in.

"Michael Slade, that man I told you about last night. I need to meet him for half an hour or so tomorrow evening." It suddenly occurred to her that she hadn't asked Don whether he had any plans for them, which in the spirit of rapprochement would have been a good idea. "I hope you don't..."

But Don was quick to smooth away any potential upset.

"No problem, it'll give me a chance to catch up with the footie. This Slade chap still helping you then?"

"Yes and no. He's a bit of a loose cannon." She hesitated, then decided to say what came next. "He got hold of Luan Redzepi's name for us, but stepped over the line doing it. I've got to read the riot act to him tomorrow, or the DI will do it at the station on Monday."

Don's face was brightening.

"Got up Jones's nose again, has he?"

"Just a bit, yes."

"Buy him a pint from me then!" Don beamed, "Sounds like my kind of bloke!"

Mary gave him her best shot at a pretend-cross smile. It had been a good evening; time to gently change the subject.

"Are we millionaires?" she asked cheerfully as she sat down.

"Fifteen lines and not even a tenner," Don said in mock disgruntlement, "Syndicate's a waste of time. A tax on stupidity, someone called that lottery. I reckon they were right."

Once, in the lunch break of a joint police/pathology crime scene workshop, Doc Singh had given Mary a primer on the comparative odds against a lottery jackpot and other life-changing events. Statistically they'd all be dead from an asteroid strike before their numbers came up, but she didn't want to rob Don of his enjoyment.

"You never know, love – this time next week..."

"You'd still be a copper though, wouldn't you?" She could tell he didn't mean it to sound as harsh as she could have taken it.

"A rich one though. The only Ferrari in Britain with a siren and flashing headlamps."

They both laughed. She'd sat down close to him on the sofa, and felt comfortably close to him now. The football had magically reappeared on the TV screen and she smiled again as she remembered how he'd cultivated his knowledge of the Italian league in order to impress her father, only to find that he had no interest in the game. It had worked out well though – her father had appreciated the effort, and they'd found common ground in Formula One motor racing, while Don had developed a genuine appreciation of what he considered the superior playing style of Serie A. Once he started something, he stuck at it and finished it properly.

In bed she lay in her silk nightdress hoping that he'd reach out for her, and do it with confidence. Instead he was quickly asleep. After most of the wine and two cans of lager, not to mention the previous night's exertions, that wasn't surprising, and she wasn't too upset. They'd come to bed happy and relaxed, she could see a way forward for them. She welcomed the drowsiness, and was soon asleep too.

Chapter 27

The clock on Mary's dashboard read 19:22 as she turned into West Street and drove towards the Brit. It had been a good day, exactly what she'd needed – up late, lazy breakfast, Sunday lunch at the Harvester, where they'd managed to get a table away from the loud group of kids whose parents didn't seem to care much what they did. Now Don was settled happily in front of last night's Match of the Day, already comparing the playing style in the English Premier League unfavourably with that of its European counterparts. A brief pep talk with Michael Slade and she'd be home in time to relieve her husband of the remote control by the 9pm watershed.

She found a parking space just a few yards from the Brit entrance, unsurprisingly as the streets were virtually empty. The rain had stopped, but it was even colder now, a dry wind coming from the north east - from Moscow via Gdansk, the weather forecaster had said on the local news. She took her coat from the back seat and carried it, in case the rain came back while she was inside.

The Brit was approached by a lane which turned into the pub's courtyard, covered by a glass roof. A few die-hard smokers were shivering at the tables, talking quietly under the music piped out from inside. Mary didn't recognise any of them, and none of them took any notice of her, even though her on-duty outfit of dark blue skirt and jacket didn't exactly blend in. If they noticed her at all, they probably thought she was the landlord's accountant arriving for an emergency VAT meeting.

Inside it became clear that the courtyard smokers

represented the large majority of the Brit's current customers – all of them except one, in fact. She was sitting on one of the high stools at one of the even higher tables that filled that side of the horseshoe-shaped bar, nursing a glass of clear, fizzy liquid which could have been a gin and tonic but probably wasn't, as Mary guessed when she recognised who it was.

"Hello, Ellie isn't it?" said Mary. She didn't particularly want to approach her, but with no-one else in the room except the barman it would have been awkward not to. "Mary Miller, I was there yesterday morning."

She instantly worried that she might be referring to something which the pregnant teenager was trying to forget, but Ellie's response didn't show any sign of it.

"Yeah, Sand Bay. How are you?" It seemed a friendly enough question, although one which Mary should really have been asking.

"Fine thanks – how are you? It must have been a difficult experience for you all."

"Yeah, you read about these things but you don't think it's going to happen to you. Tamzin's still pretty cut up about it, won't come out."

"Are you meeting your friends here?" Mary meant it as a casual enquiry, nothing more than something to say, but worried that it sounded like questioning. Something about this girl unsettled her.

"Just my boyfriend. He should be here by now. Supposed to work till seven, but they always seem to keep him hanging on."

"Is that your baby's father?" She'd meant it as a woman-to-woman enquiry, but to her it sounded wrong, horribly intrusive. Perhaps it was a mother-to-mother subject. Still, however, Ellie didn't seem put out.

"Yeah – what about you?"

"Me?"

"Are you meeting someone?"

"Oh – yes. He's not here yet either, at least I don't think he is." She looked towards the other side of the bar, hoping that Michael might be lurking there, his nose buried in a book about 1960s rock music.

"No, it's just me and Charlie at the moment." She looked towards the barman, a lad her own age, who glanced up briefly from his paper then quickly returned to it. "Do you want a drink?"

The offer took Mary by surprise. It seemed genuine, and on reflection she couldn't think why she'd assume it wasn't. Perhaps the DI was right – she was misreading Generation Y's attitude as hostility when it was really just self-containment.

"Don't worry, I can get my own." Now she sounded hostile. She wasn't good at dealing with younger people.

"Oh – sorry. Aren't you allowed to let people buy you..."

"No, no – nothing like that." Put it right, Mary, just relax. "Dry white wine, please, that would be nice."

"You're telling me it would!" said Ellie ruefully, looking down at her stomach. She called out to the barman, "Charlie – can we have a dry white wine please?" The effect was instant; Charlie's paper dropped onto the bar, he retrieved a bottle from a cold cabinet, found a glass, filled it and brought it over to their table. Perhaps he valued the business on such a dead evening. But there was also something in Ellie's voice that said she was used to having people do her bidding. It reminded Mary of someone; at first she couldn't think who, then was surprised to realise that it was DSI Kopacz and, less benignly, Wiktor Czwisnjowski. An eighteen year old with natural authority; no wonder she found her unsettling.

The wine wasn't bad. In fact for a pub wine it was pretty good. It occurred to Mary that if she, rather than

Ellie, had asked for a 'dry white wine' she might have got something less palatable, dispensed from the optics above the bar. Best not to go down that road. Instead she opted for another stab at woman-to-woman conversation.

"When are you due?" Her mother had said it to an old school friend of hers they'd met in the street, with a sidelong glance of disappointment at her own daughter.

"End of May. I'm just coming to the end of my first trimester."

"Everything going well?"

"Yeah, strong as an ox, this one." Ellie patted her stomach and smiled that sweet smile of hers, the one that had lit up Sand Bay the morning before.

"You seem really happy."

"I am." There was no trace of qualification in Ellie's voice or expression. "Yeah I know, a lot of people think eighteen, pregnant, your life's over, but I see it the opposite way. My mum was 19 when she had me, she's still young now with all her child-rearing behind her, and we're like friends."

"Your family are being supportive?"

"Hundred percent. Dad too. You should see the nursery room he's done up. Mum and I both told him it was bad luck so early on, but he did it anyway."

"So you'll be staying with your parents after the baby's born?"

"They've got a big place, plenty of room. It wouldn't make sense to be crammed into a flat somewhere in Weston, although they did offer. Besides, Mum can't wait to be a hands-on granny – 'motherhood without the cracked nipples' she calls it – eugh!" She grimaced in mock disgust.

No mention of the baby's father in any of this, Mary noted, although if she was meeting him here then he obviously hadn't done a runner.

"What about your boyfriend?" Mary realised that she still didn't know exactly who that was. "How does he feel about it all?"

"He panicked at first, of course," Ellie replied, "but once he realised that Dad wasn't going to kill him, and I wasn't going to be asking for any maintenance, he was OK."

Just "OK" – not exactly the committed father then, although it sounded as if the family had it all planned without him anyway. For a brief, painful moment Mary thought of how committed a father Don would be. Baby talk wasn't really safe ground for her.

"Have you got kids?" Right on cue, Ellie. For a split second Mary thought that a tear was going to well up.

"No, it's not easy in my job." she heard herself say, her voice commendably steady.

"They should provide proper crèches for women at work, especially in jobs like yours," said Ellie, sounding suddenly political. "What does your husband do?" she asked, glancing at Mary's wedding ring as Billy Buller had done 24 hours earlier. The question sounded political too, and Mary found herself jumping to Don's defence.

"He's a heating engineer, gas boilers. He gets called out on emergencies, especially in winter. Neither of us have jobs that allow a fixed routine, I'm afraid." Mary didn't want to pursue the subject. It was easy to talk about crèche facilities when you knew you'd never have to use them, and about the husband's role when you knew you didn't have to rely on one of those either.

"What about your career - university, that sort of thing?" she continued, firmly turning the subject back to Ellie, "Won't you regret not going?"

"Who says I won't be going?" Ellie replied, looking genuinely surprised at the question, "Lots of universities have childcare facilities these days, good ones too. They have to accommodate us, not the other way round. I've had a couple of offers - I'll defer for a year or two then go when I think we're ready."

Mary was taken aback by Ellie's confidence that the university system would bend to accommodate her and her child, although she had no doubt that it was based on fact rather than wishful thinking - Ellie didn't seem the wishful thinking type. Had things really changed that much though since she'd been Ellie's age? Or had it just changed for young women whose parents made sure they didn't have to worry about maintenance, or a place to live, and would do the same with tuition and childcare fees? Not that it affected her personally, as a student or parent.

"That sounds really good – I hope it all goes well for you," she said, and meant it. Give the girl the benefit of the doubt – even with Mummy and Daddy behind her, being a mother at eighteen and going to university took some guts.

"Thanks," she said, and the smile lit the room again, "I'm just going to take things one step at a time, learn to be a good mum first."

Lucky baby, thought Mary, who'd met a few children whose mothers hadn't taken the trouble, while their fathers' presence was at best part-time (although that was sometimes a blessing). This one seemed genuine though.

She was thinking of something to say next when there was a loud banging on the door in the back wall of the room. The door opened into the narrow street behind the pub, but wasn't marked as an entrance. It seemed, however, that it was used as one by customers who gained entry by knocking speakeasy-style. Either that or it was Trading Standards doing a snap inspection on overtime.

At first nothing happened, then the knocking came

again. This time, when it was clear that the barman wasn't going to remove himself from his paper, Ellie intervened.

"Charlie! Can you get the door?"

The paper dropped again, as instantly as it had done when Ellie had ordered the wine, with Charlie seeming keen to make up for not having opened the door on the first knock. It was as if Ellie was the pub's owner rather than merely a customer, and for a second Mary wondered whether she, or at least her parents, might actually be. Or perhaps Charlie was passionately in love with her. He almost certainly wouldn't be the first or only one.

As Charlie pulled the door back, Mary saw why Ellie had shown an interest in having it opened. It was Ewan, the quiet one who'd ridden in the front of Ellie's car out to Sand Bay the previous morning, and whom Mary had thought – correctly, it now turned out – might be the father of her child. He and Charlie seemed to know each other but exchanged no greetings, Charlie merely shutting the door behind him and pushing the big chrome latch handle home. Ewan's greeting to Ellie wasn't much more effusive, just a mumbled "Hi" which she reciprocated with a quiet "Hi" of her own.

"You remember Mary, from yesterday?" she said.

"Police, yeah," said Ewan. A night's sleep obviously hadn't made him any more communicative, or friendly.

"Ewan, isn't it?" said Mary. She fought a rising tide of dislike for the youth, his ill-fitting fleece, with its company logo, reminding her that he'd just finished a shift in a supermarket on a cold Sunday evening.

"Yeah," he said and instantly turned to Ellie. "Zac and Damian are in the Dragon. I said we'd meet them there."

"Do you want a drink here first?" Ellie replied. For the first time, Mary thought, her composure seemed less than solid.

"No, let's go. Where's your car?"

"Just outside."

"Good."

Ellie slipped down from her high stool, it struck Mary in much the same automatic way that Charlie had stood up from his paper a few moments earlier.

"Nice to talk to you." she said to Mary, slipping the strap of her bag over her shoulder.

"Yes, nice talking to you too," Mary replied, still struggling to take in the transformation from super-confident young woman to obedient arm-candy.

There was no goodbye from Ewan, and Mary had no plans to offer him one. Instead, from over her shoulder, she heard a greeting.

"Hello Ewan, this is a coincidence. Have you just come off shift?" It was Michael Slade, coming in from the courtyard entrance, bringing a draught of cold air with him. In their short acquaintance Mary hadn't been more glad to hear his voice than she was now. She turned to face him.

"Ah, hello Mary," he said, pre-empting her own greeting, "I didn't know you knew Ewan?"

"She doesn't." the youth interjected, "Come on Ellie, I said we'd meet them at quarter to."

For a moment Mary thought Ewan was going to grab Ellie by the arm and drag her to the door, and for a moment she thought of grabbing him by the arm, twisting it behind his back and arresting him for assault. Luckily for her the opportunity, and the can of worms it would have opened, didn't arise, and instead Ellie followed him as he walked off, leaving them with an openly apologetic smile, not the one that had lit the room and beach.

"Is he always like that?" she said to Michael, who by comparison suddenly seemed like a model of friendly rationality.

"Ewan? Most of the time, yes. He's got issues, as they say. Would you like another drink, Mary – dry white wine, is it?"

They settled into the leather sofas on the other side of the bar, Mary making sure to sit where she could see who else was in the room. The alcove shelf next to them was packed with books about music she remembered her father liking, some of them big, original-looking hardback volumes which probably would be quite valuable. In the few steps from the till Michael had already downed a quarter of the pint he'd bought. She'd need to get their business done fairly quickly, although she had some curiosity to satisfy first.

"How do you know Ewan?" she said, sipping at her wine. It was still the one Ellie had bought her; she wasn't taking any chances with her driving licence or the above-bar optics.

"He works with me at the supermarket," said Michael, taking another large gulp from his pint, "Well, not actually with me – he's on shelves most of the time, I just talk to him in the breaks now and then. He isn't till-trained, which is strange really, as he's a bright lad. Just got four A*s."

"Perhaps they think he'd frighten the customers."

Michael gave a short chortle, then gulped again. "Yes, you could be right about that, although I think it's mainly that he doesn't do many shifts these days. He cut them back last spring to concentrate on his exams and never put them up again."

"You said he's got issues – what about?" She knew she shouldn't be wasting valuable time on this, but in mitigation it was Ellie's welfare she was really checking up on.

"Ellie, his girlfriend, mainly. I assume that was her?"

"Yes it was - don't you know her then?"

The chortle was back, enough of it now to delay his next visit to his glass. "I don't socialise with Ewan outside work, Mary, I'm more than twice his age. You'd probably arrest me if I did!"

Mary smiled back. Not arrest, although he might well end up on a watch list.

"I can see why he's like he is about her though," Michael continued, reaching for his glass, "she's a rather lovely young woman, isn't she?"

"How is he about her?"

"Mad." Michael saw the look on Mary's face and quickly put his glass down, mid-gulp. "As in madly in love, head over heels, that sort of thing. He worships her."

"It didn't look like it just now. More as if he treats her like dirt."

"Ah, you don't understand the psychology of the situation, Mary," he said. Mary sensed him warming to a subject, not something she necessarily welcomed, especially with beer on tap. "He's covering up his crippling insecurity by pretending to treat her like dirt. In fact he's terrified that she's out of his league and will dump him for a rock star or merchant banker at any minute."

"How do you know that?"

"He told me – it's surprising what people tell you on evening shift. My theory is it's something to do with circadian rhythms. I think they..."

"What did he tell you, Michael?" His glass was nearly empty now, and she had no doubt that he'd be refilling it.

"She's from a wealthy family. They've got a big farm out near Congresbury and they've built up a haulage business there too, lots of lorries. He's just a poor boy from a terraced house in Worlebury. He hates it when she pays for everything, even though she can afford it and he can't. He thinks she'll revert to type and go off with someone rich and glamorous like herself. Having seen her now I can understand why."

Mary could understand why too.

"The funny thing is," Michael continued, pausing to quickly drain his glass, "by all accounts she's mad about him too. His mate Zac works at our place sometimes, when he can be bothered to turn up, and he told me that she's been like it since she was 16 – eyes for Ewan only, that sort of thing."

"What does she see in him?"

"Ah, there we have it. You see a sullen teenager, Mary, but Ellie sees a tortured genius, and worships him for it. He's deep, you see. He knows the fundamentals of the universe."

"Pardon?"

"Particle physics. He's a scientist, of outstanding potential by all accounts. He can name five types of hypothetical hadrons, and describe the theories postulating their existence."

"Really?" Particle physics wasn't Mary's strong point. She'd thought the Large Hadron Collider was named after a person, like the Hubble Space Telescope.

"Oh yes – like I said, clever lad is our Ewan." Michael was rising from his sofa, empty glass in hand, "Tipped for Cambridge, although for some reason he hasn't started applying yet. Ready for another?"

"No thanks, I'm driving." Mary looked at him pointedly. "Are you, Michael?"

"No, I parked my car outside my flat and walked back down," he said, then seeing the trace of doubt on her face, "You can always check the CCTV along the seafront if you don't believe me."

Fair cop.

"No sorry, of course I believe you," she said, starting

to raise herself from the depths of the sofa, "I'll get this."

"Oh, thank you," he beamed, sitting back down, "Betty Stogs, please."

"Who?"

"Betty Stogs, a fine Cornish ale, four percent alcohol by volume. Ideal when you've got an early shift the next day." He chortled happily to himself.

"I see," said Mary, already imagining having to say "Betty Stogs" to Charlie the barman, "Any crisps?"

"Excellent idea – cheese and onion please."

Mary returned from the bar with Michael's drink and crisps, to find him reading one of the books from the shelf. He held up the spine for her to see.

"Bob Dylan - The Acoustic Years," he said, "some of his early material really was spine-tingling stuff, you know. I do 'Masters of War' in my karaoke set." Mary wasn't familiar with Masters of War, but had an idea of how it would go down at Between the Lines. As she sank back into the sofa, Michael placed the book back on the shelf, then turned to her.

"How come you know Ellie, Mary?" The lack of preamble took her by surprise and left her struggling for the optimum answer. For the second time that evening, she was reminded of DSI Kopacz.

"I don't really."

"But you were having a drink with her." He looked down at her glass, still holding some of the wine Ellie had bought her. "Ewan seemed to be dragging her away from you."

She thought back to her basic training - "Assessing the dynamics of a scene in progress, as quickly as possible on arrival". Michael would get a gold star for it, just as he would have done for spotting the phone from 200 metres. But she was supposed to be asking the questions.

"I met her once in the line of duty – that makes it Police business, I'm afraid, so I can't say any more."

"She and Ewan found the body at Sand Bay, didn't they? Luan Redzepi."

"What? I can't talk to you about that, Michael – in fact what I've come to talk to you about is..."

"The hoodie Ewan was wearing under his fleece – I saw it in the TV pictures of the car being driven away from there yesterday morning. There was someone with blonde hair too. That must have been Ellie."

"Like I said, I can't talk to you about that," she said firmly.

Michael looked angry, modifying it quickly to disappointment.

"But I thought I was helping you on a semi-official basis now. Your DI let me into the crime scene."

It could have been taken as a threat, of the "Your DI won't like reading about that in the Mercury" variety, but Mary decided to give him the benefit of the doubt. He had helped them, after all. She saw that the Betty Stogs was already a quarter gone; she hadn't even noticed him drinking it.

"You're an outside adviser, Michael, not a police officer. You only get to see and know what we think is appropriate – that's how it works, I'm afraid. And what we think is appropriate isn't much at the moment, after your bit of private enterprise with Jolene Buller. That's what I've been sent here to talk to you about. You promised you wouldn't repeat anything you saw at Sand Bay, not to anyone – then you go and do that."

"But I didn't say anything about Sand Bay to Jolene," he protested, "I used a cover story – a pretty good one, though I say it myself. I said that someone had told me there was a young Albanian man with a birthmark who could get me a cheap iPhone, and asked if she knew him. You can ask her yourself, if you like."

"We have asked her, and she confirmed what you say," said Mary, then, seeing Michael's face brighten, "but that's not the point, as I'm sure you know. You can't go round playing Sherlock Holmes on your own, and you definitely can't do it using information that's been disclosed to you under strict confidentiality at a crime scene."

"But what was I supposed to do, Mary? If I hadn't asked Jolene about it, you probably still wouldn't know the victim's name."

"Don't pretend to be stupid, Michael, it really doesn't suit you. You know perfectly well that you should have told us about Jolene, and let us talk to her."

"Yes, well, she might not have been as helpful with you as she was with me. Some people don't like the police, you know. Having seen your DI in action I can understand why."

He had a point, but it was a weak one and his expression said that he knew it. Mary went for a conclusion, before Betty Stogs got any lower in the glass.

"It still doesn't matter, Michael. Going out on your own like that is dangerous. We're virtually certain now that both murders are gang-related. That means people you really don't want hearing that you've been asking questions about them."

"The Troshanis, you mean?" He was a little quieter now.

"No comment. Just promise me that you won't do anything like it again, because if not then my DI will do it his way. Believe me, he'll arrest you for obstructing an enquiry if he has to, and keep you on remand until this case is over. Magistrates in North Somerset tend to give the police what they ask for."

Now he was deflated. His glass remained half-full, untouched for the previous few minutes.

"We do seem to have a strange sort of working

relationship, Mary," he said quietly, "I keep giving you breakthroughs in your murder cases, and you keep threatening me. It doesn't quite seem fair."

Nice spin - he'd make a good journalist, as well as a good DCI. She had the answer ready though.

"Come on, Michael, it's about sticking to the rules, you know that. Those banks you write computer programs for - I'm sure the programs are great, but if you broke the bank's security rules, left your laptop on a bus with their passwords on it or something, they'd sack you all the same, wouldn't they?"

"I suppose so, yes." Sheepish now, and a long sip of Betty Stogs. Stage Two of the Five Stages of Admitting You Were Wrong.

"So do we have a deal - a real one this time? You keep whatever you learn from us to yourself, don't talk about it or use it in any way?"

"Deal."

"How do I know I can trust you, Michael?"

"Because you can, Mary." A hint of indignation now - Stage Three. "I got it wrong about Jolene, but I've kept every other confidence. I wasn't going to drop you in it about you showing me that phone, was I? Even with your DI threatening to lock me up."

"OK, that's true," she agreed, although it didn't seem to reassure him.

"You aren't going to trust me though, are you?" he said, staring despondently at his remaining drink, "You won't tell me anything else now. One mistake and that's it with the police."

Stage Four, and a danger of reversion to Stage One. Basic training: "Sometimes it is necessary to make decisions quickly and act on them, even if this involves an element of risk."

Mary checked that there was no-one within earshot at the centre section of the bar. Charlie was presumably with his paper by the main door, on the other side.

"Ellie and Ewan found the body yesterday," she said, her voice lowered, "along with three other friends, including Zac. They'd been at a party in Weston all night and decided to go for breakfast on the beach. You were right – the victim is Luan Redzepi, recently of Tirana, Albania." She hoped she was right to be telling him this.

A big smile spread across Michael's face. Stage Five. "Thanks Mary," he said, consigning the last of the Betty Stogs to his digestive tract, "I won't let you down. Fancy another?"

They left the Brit together, after Michael had made short work of another pint of fine Cornish ale, slurring slightly now as he wished Charlie good night. There were one or two more smokers in the courtyard, but the street beyond the lane was still quiet, just a couple of young men examining the posters outside the Playhouse Theatre. Mary was secretly glad when Michael declined her offer of a lift home, saying he'd enjoy the walk on this crisp night; cold air and exercise would probably do him good, as well as keeping the beer fumes out of her car.

To her surprise he didn't head down West Street towards the seafront, but along the old High Street, past the Playhouse. For a moment she wondered just how drunk he was, and whether she should persuade him to accept her offer of a lift, then decided that, being Michael, he probably knew what he was doing, and might well be planning to end up not a million miles from the pubs on Upper Church Road. By the time she'd got to her car and driven back round the corner, the street was empty. As she slowed for the junction at the end, she looked across at the darkness of Grove Park, and the big terraced houses that climbed the hill alongside it. She turned right, drove across town to the roundabout by the station, and reached home at 20:34.

Chapter 28

Agron Troshani sat behind the table in the Weston CID interview room. He was older than the DI, late forties but still with a thick head of hair, wearing jeans and a check shirt left open to reveal an equally dense forest of chest hair. His stubble, jet-black and two or three millimetres long, looked as if it could be used as an offensive weapon, capable of removing a layer of skin at a single pass. He leaned back in his chair, looking relaxed. Next to him, looking less relaxed, was his solicitor, Hugh Jenkins, a wiry man with grey hair and surprisingly cheap-looking clothes given the amount of business he did at the police station and courts.

The DI sat down and placed a folder on the table in front of him.

"Thank you for coming in, Mr Troshani. Hopefully we won't need to take up too much of your time. So that we're all clear, I'm Detective Inspector Jones and this is Detective Sergeant Miller."

"What is she doing here?" Troshani spat out the words, with a brief, hostile glance at Mary.

"Mr Troshani..."

"I don't want her here – get her out."

"I think what my client means, Inspector," said Jenkins, nerves audible in his voice, "is that it might be more conducive to good relations if..."

"Good relations," said the DI, addressing Jenkins but flicking a glance at Troshani too, "will be best served by your client cooperating with us, which includes leaving it to us to decide who conducts interviews. We have a new Police Commissioner and a new Chief Constable. Solving crimes takes top priority now, and when our beaches are being used as graveyards for murder victims I do mean top. Is that understood?"

Way to go for 9.30am on a Monday morning, Boss, thought Mary. Karen must have given him two helpings of high-energy cereal. Troshani remained impassive, like a massively less elegant, more threatening version of the woman who'd sat in that chair a few days earlier. Jenkins, meanwhile, didn't immediately give in. In fact his voice, with its mixture of native Welsh and acquired North Somerset, seemed more confident as he moved onto legal territory.

"Understood, Inspector, and I'm sure you understand that my client is here on a purely voluntary basis, to give whatever help he can in solving these crimes. His time is extremely valuable, so I hope you have reasonable grounds for thinking that he may have relevant information."

"Highly reasonable, Mr Jenkins," said the DI with more than a faint hint of relish. He took an A4 photograph from the folder and put it on the table in front of Agron Troshani. "Do you recognise this man, sir?"

Troshani gave the picture the briefest of glances before turning away.

"No."

"Are you sure? Look at it again, please."

Another glance, longer this time.

"No."

"I'm extremely surprised by that, since he is, in fact, your nephew."

Not a flicker from Troshani, although Jenkins had the expression of a lawyer who'd just heard something he'd rather his client had told him earlier.

"Big family."

"You're telling me you don't recognise your own sister's son?"

"I have many sisters, they have many sons."

"Well I'm still very surprised, because we have witnesses who say he was working on one of your building sites, here in Weston, until last week."

"My brother runs the building work. He doesn't tell me names of everyone who works for him."

"What, he had your nephew working for him and he didn't mention it to you?" Mary hoped her voice didn't sound too aggressive. She'd waited a long time to question Agron Troshani, and she didn't want to blow it.

Troshani turned to look at her. Being questioned by a woman unsettled him; she knew that was one reason why she was here, and why he'd singled her out for his complaints about police persecution of his 'community'. He seemed to realise, however, that this wasn't a game to be played today. His eyes seemed dead, just a blackness with nothing human behind them.

"You say he was working for my brother. I don't say that. Perhaps you are mistaken."

"Well either way I regret to inform you, sir" said the DI, "that this young man is dead. We dug him out of Sand Bay beach on Saturday morning. I'm sorry for your loss."

Troshani said nothing, just gave the smallest of shrugs.

"You don't seem very upset by this news, Mr Troshani?" said Mary.

"You don't know how we deal with death. Where I come from it is not so unusual. We must face it."

"Still, what about your poor sister?" the DI joined in, "Mothers grieve for their children, whatever the culture."

"I will ring her, offer sympathy."

"Which sister will that be, sir?" Mary again. It wasn't just about her chromosomes; she and the DI were a good double act when they got going.

"What do you mean?"

"You've told us you have many sisters," said the DI, smoothly taking up the thread, "and that you don't recognise the man in the picture, so how will you know which sister to ring?"

"Because you will tell me."

"Not necessarily, " the DI replied, tapping his finger on the photograph, "We might go looking for witnesses who saw you with this young man, and when we find one, we'll start asking you why you lied to us about not knowing he was here. Only then you won't be here on a voluntary basis. Obstructing an investigation - not the kind of thing our new Commissioner takes a kindly view of."

Agron Troshani, pinned to the interview room table by a two-pronged attack, 9.38 on a Monday morning. It was only a small triumph, but all the same weeks didn't start much better than this, and Mary stored it away for later, when she'd no doubt need it. Troshani was still for a moment, then leaned over to Jenkins, put his hand up to shield his mouth, and whispered something in his ear. Mary strained to hear what it was, but both men were too practised at this mode of communication to give anything away. The interview room at Bridewell Street probably had ultra-sensitive microphones in the ceiling for just this purpose. This, however, was Weston.

Jenkins was whispering in Troshani's ear now. When he finished, Troshani turned his attention to the DI.

"I was mistaken – this picture is not good. I see now it is Luan, my sister Arta's son, from Tirana."

"And were you also mistaken when you told us that your brother – Zamir, I assume that is – hadn't mentioned that Luan was here in England and working for him?"

"He may have mentioned it – I cannot remember." A shrug that said 'My lawyer says you can't prove he did.'

"What can you tell us about Luan, Mr Troshani?" asked Mary.

"He was a good boy, gave his mother no trouble."

That instant use of the past tense again, like the bereaved mother who'd sat there last week. Still, with Agron Troshani it was less unexpected.

"What about his father?" asked the DI, "How well do you know him?"

"He is dead, seven years ago. Motor accident."

Never ask a question you don't know the answer to, as the lawyers said. The DI was going somewhere with this, although Mary wasn't sure where.

"I see." said the DI, "That must have been terrible for the boy. How did his mother manage after that?"

"I send her money. In Albania we help our family."

"Young Luan must have been very grateful to you for helping out like that." The DI sounded impressed by Troshani's family spirit. Mary got it now.

"I guess so. Like I said, he was a good boy."

"And how far would he go to repay your generosity?" Her turn. She made it sound as innocent as she could.

"I don't know what you mean." Job done. Troshani looked genuinely puzzled.

"Would he have murdered someone for you?" Back to the DI for the big one, the accusation let out into the open air for the first time. Normally best done under caution, so that the response was admissible in court, although that didn't matter so much when you knew what the response was going to be. It was the DI's call, as it had been for DSI Kopacz on Saturday.

In fact the response came from Jenkins, his confidence growing again as he saw them moving onto questionable legal ground.

"Inspector I must protest," he interjected, "My client is a bereaved relative, here on a voluntary basis, but you're treating him like a suspect. Have you got any justification for this?"

"Two minutes ago your client didn't recognise the relative he'd just lost, Mr Jenkins, but we'll let that pass." The DI opened the folder again, pulled out another photograph, and placed it on top of Luan's.

"Do you recognise this woman?"

"No."

The DI didn't bother to express surprise at Troshani's denial.

"Her name is Katya Czwisnjowski, and she was found dead under the Grand Pier last Wednesday morning."

"What does this have to do with me?" asked Troshani, Jenkins' expression asking the same question.

"We have evidence placing Luan Redzepi – your nephew – at Ms Czwisnjowski's burial."

"So?"

The DI pulled another photograph from the folder. "Do you recognise this man?"

Another quick glance. Mary thought she saw just a flicker of response before the face set.

"No. Who is he?"

"Wiktor Czwisnjowski, Katya's father. But I think you know that, Mr Troshani. I think you had his daughter killed and buried under the pier, and that Luan Redzepi was one of the gang who did it for you – not excluding, of course, the possibility that you took part in it yourself."

Troshani was no longer sitting back relaxed. He leaned forward, elbows on the table, dead eyes fixed on the DI.

"Prove it!"

"Do you have any proof for this theory, Inspector?" said Jenkins, emphasising the "Do". The DI ignored him.

"Where were you last Tuesday between eight pm and midnight?" he asked Troshani, meeting his stare. To

Mary's surprise, Troshani's response was to lean back again and break out into a broad smile.

"Family party, my wife's birthday. We took over Marco's restaurant, left at one am. My wife, my brother, his wife, our kids – everyone there. Ask Marco."

Perfect alibi, but also perfect cover if you wanted some of the guests to slip out for an hour. Still, they'd never thought this one was going to be easy.

"We will be asking him. And was Luan there?"

"I don't remember."

"It would have been a bit strange if he wasn't, wouldn't it? You said everyone was there, the whole family, and he was as much your family as young Ardit is."

"Family here in England. Me, my brother, our families."

"I think that's enough for now, don't you Inspector?" Jenkins again, still confident. "If you're going to continue this line of questioning it'll have to be under caution, with my client and I given time to confer in private first."

"If your client is innocent, he has nothing to fear by answering my questions, does he?" The DI clearly wanted another round or two before the bell.

"Best to end it now, Inspector, for your own good. Judges take a strict line on PACE these days, as I'm sure you know. Your Commissioner certainly does. You're already compromising the admissibility of anything my client might say later, and it is being noted."

Ouch, thought Mary. The DI's wife clearly wasn't the only one who'd been dishing out the extra energy bars this morning. That was the thing with Jenkins though – the shabby suit camouflaged a sharp legal mind. It fooled her every time.

"Very well." said the DI, putting the photographs back in the folder. It was strictly professional between them, no animosity. Jenkins was known to drink with the senior officers after meetings at the Masonic Lodge. "I will want to speak to you again, Mr Troshani, and next time it will be under caution, so I'd have a good long consultation with your solicitor first if I were you."

"Thank you for your advice, Inspector" said Troshani, making a good job of the mock gratitude, "I will bear it in mind."

"You do that, Mr Troshani," the DI replied, picking up the folder, "I'll have an officer show you out."

"Well, that's both sets of suspects lawyered up now," said the DI, as he and Mary made their way back to the office, "although I think we did as well as could be expected with both of them."

"Why do you think Troshani tried to deny knowing his nephew, Guv?" asked Mary, "He must have known it wouldn't stand up."

"Knee-jerk reaction is my guess," the DI replied, pushing open the door of the squad room, "The boy was illegal, as are probably most of the lads they've got working on their sites. Deny everything, we probably couldn't make it stick."

"Especially if he already knew Luan was dead, so wasn't going to be telling us anything."

"It certainly looked that way, didn't it? He'd probably worked it out, or someone had told him. Either that or he really is the coldest-hearted so-and-so ever to walk the planet."

They'd reached the DI's office now. He sat down behind his desk, motioning Mary to take a chair.

"How did you get on with Mr Slade yesterday - marked his card in big red felt tip, I hope?"

"Yes, I made sure he understood, Guv. I don't think he'll be doing any more private investigating. "

"Let's hope not." The DI put the Troshani file in his desk drawer, and took another one out. "How did he seem?"

"He was sinking the pints a bit quickly, but otherwise OK."

"Great – so now we've got a high-IQ piss-artist on the loose with privileged crime scene information."

"He'll be OK, Guv," said Mary reassuringly, "I think it was just being off the leash after a weekend in the sober bosom of his family." Not entirely sober, since Michael had sounded drunk when she'd spoken to him on Saturday night, but no need to mention that. "He wouldn't be the first man to react that way."

"Huh – an expert on men now, are you Sergeant?" The DI did mock indignation as well as Agron Troshani had mock gratitude.

"I've had to deal with them on occasions, sir, yes."

"Hmm. Anything else?" The DI was multi-tasking now, reading the new file as he asked Mary the question.

"I bumped into one of the teenagers who found Redzepi's body. Ellie, the pregnant one."

"Where was that then?" asked the DI, turning a page.

"In the pub where I was meeting Michael Slade."

"Pregnant in a pub eh?" He looked up from the file. "Not a great image of young motherhood."

Mary suppressed the urge to deliver a lecture on a woman's right to visit pubs during all three trimesters if she felt like it.

"Strictly mineral water, Guv. She seems to have motherhood all planned out, down to the last disposable nappy."

"Good for her. Karen was like that – it was like a military operation."

Mary would have expected nothing less from Mrs Jones. It was obviously the cool blonde approach to pregnancy.

"Oh, and the baby's father turned up too – turns out it's Ewan. I thought it was him."

"The silent brooding one?" said the DI, still reading his papers, "How was he?"

"Still fairly silent, with a side order of hostility. He wasn't much friendlier to Ellie than he was to me."

The DI looked up.

"Any suspicion of violence towards her?"

"No, nothing like that," said Mary, "Just moaning - 'I want to go and meet our other friends' stuff. It turns out Michael Slade knows him from the supermarket."

The DI closed his file. "Well at least the lad does a bit of work. More than some of his age do. Anything else I should know?"

"Only that Tamzin, the other girl from Saturday, is taking the experience hard and won't go out socialising, Guv," said Mary. "Apparently refusal to socialise amounts to serious cause for concern," she added, making no attempt to hide her sarcasm.

"At that age it does, yes," he replied. It occurred to Mary that he could have added "As you'd know if you had kids of your own", and she was grateful that he hadn't. Her expertise on men, good or not, was still better than her knowledge of her own sex at that age.

"Get family liason to check up on her," the DI added, "offer her counselling again. She may decide to take it this time."

"Will do, Guv." She felt slightly chastened. Thankfully the DI moved the conversation straight on.

"Right, we'd better start checking the Troshanis' alibis," he said, "Tony Lane dealt with Marco over that credit card business last year, didn't he?" Then without waiting for a reply, "Send him round there – Marco should still be eager to please. Tell Lane no free lunches though, and to keep away from the bar. I expect to see him back here eating a sandwich by 1.30."

"OK, Guv," said Mary, adding it to her mental list. She'd tell Lane to bring her a sandwich too, so he'd have to come back.

"And your friend Michael Slade – ask him again what he knows about Jolene Buller's relations with the Troshani boys. She might not have been telling us the whole story when she said she was like a mother to them, in which case she might not have told us a few other things."

No special treatment for old non-flame Jolene then. The DI caught her expression.

"It isn't easy policing your home town, Sergeant. The only way is to treat everyone the same, including the ones you went to school with."

"Fair enough, Guv. Michael Slade's at work until three today. Will after that do?"

"Yes, no great rush. Try to make it today though. Now there's something I need to talk to you about...."

The DI was interrupted by the warble of his desk phone. He looked at the display, then picked up the handset.

"Doctor Singh, good morning," he said.

"Good morning, Inspector." Mary heard a thin version of Doc Singh's voice leaking out from the earpiece. The Doc always spoke loudly on the phone, even from his office.

"I have an interesting development concerning our deceased male at Sand Bay. The preliminary tox report is back, and..."

"Hang on Doctor," the DI interrupted him, "can I put you on speakerphone? I've got DS Miller with me."

"Of course," came the thin voice, then, suddenly amplified, "Good morning, Detective Sergeant, how are you today?"

"Good morning, Doctor Singh, very well thank you. How are you?" said Mary, realising that she was shouting herself.

"Just fine, thank you. Anyway, the preliminary tox

report on our unfortunate friend has just this minute come back, and it appears that I was mistaken as to the cause of death on Saturday."

"What, you mean he wasn't poisoned?" said the DI, looking puzzled.

"Oh no, he was poisoned all right, but not with barbiturates as I thought at the time. The tox report indicates that he was killed with a far more sophisticated substance, a synthesised alkaloid compound which mimicked some of the effects of strychnine, but not others."

"And does this have any effect on the case?" asked Mary. It was a blunt question which she hoped hadn't sounded too much that way, but they had busy days ahead of them.

"I would say it does, yes. You see the effect which it doesn't mimic is that of severe, muscle-twisting convulsions, which leave the victim coiled up in agony. The effect it does mimic is that of almost instant rigor mortis. So your victim would not have had to be killed six to eight hours earlier in order to fix his hand in the pointing position. The fatal dose could have been administered there on the beach, just minutes before he was buried."

The Doc had both their attentions now. "So what is the revised time of death?" asked the DI.

"I need to read more on this poison before I can make an estimate, but it could be quite soon before the body was discovered. One other thing, Inspector."

"Yes, Doctor?"

"This substance is not something you can buy in shops, or make in your kitchen. Nor, to my knowledge, is it readily available on illegal markets, although your own intelligence sources may have a better idea of that than me. Synthesising it requires sophisticated laboratory equipment and no small degree of skill. It is likely that whoever killed this young man had access to the resources of an industrial-grade pharmaceutical operation, run by professionals."

And probably not a legal one. The thought of whose it might be seemed to occur to Mary and the DI at the same moment. What hadn't occurred to Mary was what the DI said next.

"Doctor, this is very valuable information," he said, cutting across the Doc slightly, "and I appreciate you ringing me so quickly with it, but I think it would be better if you spoke directly to DSI Kopacz about it. Our current theory is that Katya Czwisnjowski's father ordered the boy's murder, and access to an industrial lab fits in with intelligence we have about his activities. However the Major Crime Unit have taken over that end of the investigation, so they'll be chasing anything like that up."

"Oh!" The Doc sounded gratifyingly disappointed. "I'm sorry, Inspector, I did not realise that. There has clearly been a failure in communications, not unknown in dealings between our organisations as I'm sure you know."

"I'm sure Major Crime were planning to inform you this morning," said the DI. The speed and smoothness with which he switched to corporate message mode was impressive, if not always welcome.

"But you are still involved with the case? The victims were found on your patch, surely?" Again, Mary appreciated the Doc's loyalty, although of course things didn't always work as they "surely" should. It was more than possible for Major Crime to take over the whole investigation, while they were sent back to chasing car thieves.

"Yes, we're still involved," said the DI, looking at Mary as he spoke, "The Troshani family here in Weston are prime suspects for Katya Czwisnjowski's murder, and we're concentrating on them."

It made sense. Katya's father was in Bristol, previously unknown to Weston CID and with a trail stretching across the globe, documented in a file they weren't even allowed to read. The Troshanis were on their doorstep, with their own drawer in the CID filing cabinet. It could have been an entire cabinet and a good few more convictions, but it was best not to dwell on that now, just make the most of their new-found freedom to investigate them.

Dr Singh evidently agreed. "Ah, that is good to hear, Inspector," came his voice from the phone, "Well I had better get on to Detective Superintendent Kopacz then. Nice to talk to you, and to you, Detective Sergeant. Incidentally, I had a most entertaining discussion on cryptography with your friend Mr Slade last night, at the Criterion pub in Weston. I think he had already visited another such establishment before meeting me, but even through a certain degree of haziness he was still most informative. A remarkable intellect, although it seems a shame to punish it with quite so much alcohol. I may invite him to see some of our brain specimens at the Path Centre, it may encourage him to moderate his intake."

Mary was still taking in the fact that Michael hadn't said anything about going to meet Dr Singh when he'd left her the previous night. She wondered whether to tell the Doc about her own meeting with him, but decided against it. Michael clearly liked to keep his social arrangements compartmentalised, and there was no reason to go against his wishes.

"He certainly is remarkable," she said, "I'll say that for him."

"He speaks very highly of you too, Mary. He said you are not like the stereotypically adversarial police officer but instead much more empathetic, and thus much more likely to obtain cooperation from the community."

Despite the compliment, Mary felt uncomfortable. Had Michael told the Doc that he'd met her first, so that the Doc would now be wondering why she hadn't mentioned it? She wasn't cut out for subterfuge. Still, she was committed now - too late to mention her meeting with Michael without it appearing forced.

"That was very nice of him," she said.

"I am afraid he didn't pass any comment on you, Inspector."

"I'm sure I'll survive the disappointment," said the DI drily, "Perhaps Mr Slade can recommend some empathy training I can book myself on."

"I'm sure such training would be entirely unnecessary. You are both extremely fine officers", the Doc said, then added "in your own respective ways. Goodbye!"

"Slade didn't tell you he had a date with the Doc, did he?" said the DI, an undisguised trace of satisfaction in his voice.

"No he didn't," replied Mary, "but I can understand why. It was private, and he was probably worried I'd want to tag along." Behind her rationalisation of Michael's reasons for not telling her, she was busy suppressing an irrational feeling of having been left out. She conjured up a mental image of sitting in the Criterion, a small, often crowded pub, listening to the Doc and a half-drunk Michael Slade discuss cryptography. It helped, but not entirely.

"You're probably right," said the DI, "but all the same, next time you're thinking what an innocent soul he is, remember that he doesn't always tell you everything."

Just like he hadn't told them he'd been walking along the seafront the night Katya Czwisnjowski was buried. The DI did have a point.

"Fair enough, Guv."

The DI seemed pleased by her acceptance of his advice, so offered some more.

"And here's a tip – when you speak to him about Jolene Buller, make sure you drop into the conversation that you've found out about his little tête-à-tête with the Doc."

"I'm not sure there was anything to be 'found out'."

"Let him know anyway." he replied, a hint of exasperation entering his voice, "Use this opportunity to put him in the wrong, so he feels he owes you. I thought you women were supposed to be good at that."

In different circumstances, between different officers, the remark could have been the start of a disciplinary process. Mary took it as a compliment, albeit an odd one, that the DI assumed it wouldn't. It did, however, give her a chance to practice what he preached.

"Well in that case, Guv, how come you hadn't told me that we'd lost the Czwisnjowski end of the investigation to Major Crime?"

The DI smiled at her with something approaching pity. "That's how you see it, is it, that we've lost the Czwisnjowskis? You see the way I see it, we've held on to the Troshani end of things when we could be back chasing gas bottles. And it's you who knows the Troshanis better than anyone else, which is one reason why we've held on to them. But you're not getting another apology, so don't hold your breath waiting for one. I've got enough dead bodies to deal with as it is."

She hadn't actually got a first apology, but being told that they'd held on to the Troshani investigation because she had the knowledge to nick them was good enough. It put her treatment over them behind her at last – or at least she hoped it did.

"Cheers, Guv, I'll do my best," she said, trying not to sound too grateful.

"Good." said the DI, making it sound as if she should

be. "Now this business of Major Crime taking over the Czwisnjowskis. That's what I was going to talk to you about when Doc Singh rang. I'll brief the troops at the squad meeting, so let's get our story sorted out. And remember, Sergeant – glass half full!"

Chapter 29

By 3.15pm the euphoria at being given free rein to chase the Troshanis was beginning to wear off. The DI had explained their new focus in his 11am briefing, the team appearing to buy enthusiastically into his view that they were lucky to keep the Troshanis rather than unlucky to lose the Czwisnjowskis. Such had been their enthusiasm, in fact, that he'd had to warn them not to give Agron Troshani's family genuine grounds for a complaint of victimisation; their job was to collect admissible evidence for a murder trial, not to settle old scores. That, however, was proving hard to do.

When Lane hadn't returned from Marco's by 1.45pm Mary had sent Cox to fetch him, but that had only meant two DCs instead of one telling her how insistent Marco had been that the entire Troshani clan had occupied his restaurant from 8pm until nearly 1am the previous Tuesday, producing the bill, totalling more than £1,000, to prove it. Other members of Marco's family had confirmed it, his daughter saying that the Troshani boys, under the eagle eyes of their fathers, had behaved in a more civilised way than many of the drunken businessmen she had to deal with while waiting tables. As for Luan Redzepi though, none of them could say whether he'd been there or not – there had been many Troshanis they hadn't recognised, including some who looked a bit like the photograph Lane showed them. No-one could remember the birthmark, but no-one could be certain there wasn't one either.

That left them with one solid alibi (Mary could just imagine Marco's family, a transparently honest and hard-working bunch, trooping through the witness box) and so far nothing to counter it. One possibility was evidence similar to that which had linked Redzepi to Katya's crime scene; the wrong kind of sand in the socks, a hair or DNA on the clothing. The DI was applying for a search warrant for the Troshanis' properties, which DS Flanagan, his DCs and a team of uniforms were on standby to execute as soon as it came. The way things stood, their chances of making a case against the Troshanis rested, as the DI put it, on whether Redzepi's cousins were any better than he'd been at washing between their toes.

At 3.30pm Mary remembered to ring Michael Slade for their chat about Jolene Buller, also remembering the DI's advice to drop in a casual reference to Michael's meeting with the Doc, but wondering how she was going to do it without sounding forced. To her relief his phone went straight to voicemail ("Your call is undoubtedly important and I respect that, so please leave a message but be quick, as I have to pay to listen to it", complete with a trace of his trademark chortle), giving her time to work on the casual reference. She left a message for him to call her back, although in her experience such messages seldom yielded results from members of the public.

At 3.45 the DI arrived back from the magistrates, warrant safely locked in his briefcase. They held a pre-raid briefing, during which Mary ran through her catalogue, albeit a slightly outdated one, of the key Troshani family members and what they could expect to find in their homes, with various offensive weapons, large bunches of car keys and, if they were lucky, some Class B drugs figuring prominently. A week earlier she'd have worried about why she wasn't going on the actual raid, but now she was fine; going through Agron Troshani's underwear drawer wasn't her thing, and even she recognised that sending her in to do it might have been construed as provocative.

At 5pm she tried Michael's phone again, got his voicemail again, and left a message again, slightly more tetchy in tone than the first one. For a man who could turn his expensive-looking smartphone into a compass or world atlas at the drop of a hat, he seemed remarkably unskilled at turning it into a phone and answering his messages. She'd have no choice but to keep chasing him; once the DI told you to do something, however small, he expected it to be done, and got quite serious about it if you didn't finish the job. He'd explained to her that this zero-tolerance approach was deliberate; you could only delegate, he said, if you could be sure the person you delegated to would see the job through. As with many other aspects of police work, she could see his point.

As she was thinking this the DI turned up at her desk, to pass on a not very encouraging report from DS Flanagan's search team. The Troshani family, it seemed, had exceptionally high standards of domestic hygiene. Every single item of male clothing in both Agron and Zamir Troshani's houses appeared to have been freshly laundered, while the houses themselves were spotless and smelt overpoweringly of cleaning materials. It looked like that most frustrating of things – evidence that evidence had been there, but had been removed. Unfortunately that tended to have little or no value in court.

True to form, the DI hadn't forgotten about Michael Slade.

"Have you spoken to Slade about Jolene Buller yet?" he said, for all the world as if it was the line of enquiry that was going to crack both murder cases wide open. Sometimes, of course, it was enquiries like it that did.

"I've tried his mobile a couple of times, Guv, but it's going straight to voicemail. I've left messages, but he may not be getting them. If there's still no answer I'll drive round to his flat on my way home, that way I can leave him a note if he's not in." It sounded a credible, well-considered plan for achieving her delegated task; in fact she'd thought of it as she'd been speaking.

"Good – and don't forget, let him know that you know about his social arrangements with Doc Singh. We know everything, that's the message."

"Will do, Guv." she said, relieved that her commitment had passed scrutiny.

"Everything except how to prove that the Troshanis killed Katya Czwisnjowski, that is," the DI continued, half to himself as he walked away.

At 6pm Mary tried Michael's phone again, and got the same answering message. Resigning herself to a detour, she switched off her computer, grabbed her coat and bag, said her goodbyes and headed for the car park. There was hardly any traffic on the seafront, and in less than ten minutes she was turning right by the Clarendon, up Madeira Road towards Michael's flat.

As she drove up the steep slope she reflected, as she often did, on what a strange area Birnbeck was. On the hill with views out over Weston and the Bristol Channel, it should have been the most well-kept, prestigious part of the town. Yet in reality it had a derelict pier and a derelict hotel that had burnt to the ground second time round, plus another semi-derelict hotel which many said was a burn-out waiting to happen. It should have been like Clifton, high up above Bristol, but this was Weston, so it wasn't. Yet she still loved the town, Birnbeck perhaps most of all. Perhaps she'd find a psychiatrist who could explain that to her some time.

Pulling up outside Michael's flat, she saw that the windows were dark. Switching on her car's interior light, she found her notebook, wrote "Michael, please ring me when you have a moment, Mary Miller" and her mobile number. She got out, locked her car, went to the front door and pressed the entryphone button for Flat 16. As expected, there was no reply. She took the note from her pocket but thought better of posting it through the letterbox, which emptied into the shared hallway for the modern extension. From previous visits to flats in the main part of the building she knew that there was an entrance at the far end, with individual mail boxes for all the tenants. She set out for it, squeezing through the gap between the corner of the building and the wall that separated the tenants' car parking area from the street.

The main building, like the extension, was largely dark, just a couple of lights showing dimly though curtains. Mary wondered where all the other occupants were; still working perhaps, or gone off to work in pubs and hotels, although employment wasn't, from her recollection, high among the residents of 118 Birnbeck Drive. Car ownership didn't seem to be high either, if the three vehicles parked on the forecourt were anything to go by. One of them might be Michael's, but she didn't know which.

Something she hadn't remembered about the block, however, was that its parking spaces were marked with the numbers of the flats. She found number 16, occupied by an old grey Renault Megane. Taking out the small torch Don had given her ("could be a life-saver one day, Love, believe me"), she peered into the car. A copy of the Weston Mercury on the back seat, some old-style cassettes on the passenger seat; a single-occupant vehicle, on its latest trip at least, though without anything to confirm that it was Michael Slade's.

Mary took her phone from her bag, found the number she wanted and pressed the button. It was answered on the second ring.

"Support team."

"DS Mary Miller here, Weston-super-Mare CID. Can

you run a vehicle index check for me please?"

"Yes, Detective Sergeant. Go ahead with the index please." Their computer system would already have recognised her phone number, logged its location as being on her patch, checked that she hadn't reported it stolen. Holding the phone against her shoulder, she stepped away from the back of the car, shone the torch on it and read out its registration number using the phonetic alphabet.

"Thank you, hold on please."

Mary looked around her as she waited for the response. All the buildings seemed dark, the streets were empty; the place had what she thought of as the "Birnbeck atmosphere". At the bottom of Madeira Road she could see the lights of the Clarendon through the tree branches that hung out from the coach park.

"DS Miller?" The voice from the phone made her jump.

"Yes."

"Vehicle details grey Renault Megane 1.4 petrol, registered keeper Michael John Slade, Flat 16, 118 Birnbeck Drive, Weston. Licence, insurance and MOT are all current, not reported stolen. No outstanding actions on the vehicle or keeper. Anything else I can help with?"

"No, that's all. Thanks." said Mary, and pressed the 'End' button. Proper documentation and his parking tickets all paid up – she'd have expected nothing less from Michael. Nor was it particularly odd that his car was here but he wasn't, since he liked to walk and liked to drink too. He might well, in fact, be in the Criterion right now, just a few streets away, his phone switched off, discussing his theories on something or other with someone.

And yet... Mary went round the side of the building, into the dark passageway whose light came from a single bulb, dulled by dirt and low wattage, over the main entrance. The outer door was unlocked to allow postal deliveries, but held shut by a powerful spring mechanism which she struggled to overcome. Inside it was barely lighter than outside, and she had to use her torch to read the flat numbers on the bank of mailboxes that lined the wall. But as she followed the sequence across she knew which one would be Michaels. One door sat wide open, the box empty. As she pushed it shut with her torch she saw the number: 16.

Woman's intuition? Copper's instinct? Either, or a mix of the two, sent her back out onto the street and into her car. Her first call was to the supermarket, its manager's number still in her phone from the previous week. The call diverted to the evening duty manager, who told her that no, Michael Slade hadn't turned up for work that morning, and that they were not at all pleased about it as he was supposed to be covering for two sick colleagues. Without actually saying it, she managed to imply that his absence might be due to over-consumption of alcohol the previous night, and that it wouldn't be the first time such a thing had happened, all without breaking any rules of confidentiality – a skill which Mary imagined was finely honed among managers these days.

She thought next of calling Michael's wife, but realised that with his car in Weston he was unlikely to be in Bridgwater, and that giving an already worried woman more cause for worry was to be avoided unless absolutely necessary. She thought of calling the Criterion, but realised that she could easily end up spending the next hour calling all the pubs he might be in, and that it would be quicker to drive round them anyway. He was almost certainly fine, having slept it off all day and now settling happily into his second or third hair of the dog somewhere among those lights down in the town.

And yet...

She looked up at the dark windows of Michael's flat. What instinct was it that told you that a place was empty when it shouldn't be? Whatever it was, it was telling her now. She clicked through her phone's address book until she found the one she wanted, "Wston Genl", and pressed the button.

"Weston General Hospital, how can I help?"

"Hello, it's Weston police here, can you put me through to A&E please?" Check them off the list, then perhaps try a couple of the pubs.

"Hello, A&E?" A nurse by the sound of it, none too pleased at finding herself on evening duty.

"Hello, Detective Sergeant Miller here, Weston CID. Have you had a Michael John Slade admitted? White male, aged 42, five ten, slim build, fair hair?"

"Yes, but he's gone up to ICU. Do you want me to transfer you?"

Intensive Care. Mary felt a cold chill in her stomach.

"What was wrong with him?" Perhaps it was a heart attack.

"Assault, quite nasty, he's under obs for internal bleeding. But the police already know about this – your officers called the ambulance in last night."

Last night?

"Who's speaking please?" came the voice from the phone, sounding suspicious now, "Are you actually the police? We're not allowed to give details to..."

"Yes, yes, Detective Sergeant Mary Miller, Weston CID. You say our officers called it in last night? Do you know when?"

"Yes, hang on," the line went quiet, with just a faint click of computer keys in the background. "He was admitted at 10:51pm, brought in by an emergency ambulance who'd attended at 10:26 just off Highbury Road. Initial call received by ambulance control at 10:13."

On his way home from the Criterion.

"OK, thanks. There's obviously been a breakdown in communications at our end, sorry to have bothered you."

"No problem." The nurse seemed more friendly now, but still slightly cautious. "You are a police officer though, aren't you? It's just that we can get into trouble if we give patient details to the press."

"I'm really a police officer. My boss is DI Steve Jones – he's probably still at the station if you want to ring him and check."

"No, that's OK," she said, seeming to finally make her mind up on the matter, then continued, "Mr Slade was lucky. One of his ribs almost punctured his lung." The words hit Mary like a hard kick to her own ribcage. She struggled to keep her voice steady.

"OK, well thanks, and sorry about the mixup. Goodbye."

"Goodbye."

She sat there for a few moments, eyes fixed down on the car's dashboard, her breathing shallow. Then she chose the DI's mobile number from her phonebook and pressed the button.

"Mary? I thought you'd gone home?"

"Are you still in the office, Guv?"

"Where do you think I am?"

"Something's come up. I'll be there in ten minutes."

Chapter 30

Mary sat opposite the DI in his office. The door was closed. The DI had dialled a number on speakerphone and they were waiting for it to be answered.

"Deane." The voice of Ted Deane, the uniformed inspector who'd managed the Sand Bay crime scene, filled the small room.

"Ted. Steve Jones. I've got DS Miller with me."

"Hello Steve, Mary. What can I do for you?" Deane sounded relaxed, the sound of an officer who'd had worse days and whose shift was nearing its end. Neither of those things could confidently be said about his two colleagues.

"I understand uniform attended an assault last night in the Highbury Road area," said the DI, "white male early 40s. Is that right?"

"Hang on, I wasn't on last night…" There was a clunk as the phone handset was placed on the desk, then a a rustling of papers, then Deane picked up the phone again. "Yes, in an alleyway off Highbury Road. Resident called it in, said he went into his garden to put some rubbish out, saw two men running away, found the victim outside his back gate. It was a nasty one by the look of it – the victim's still in Weston General."

"Victim's name?"

"Michael John Slade. Address in Birnbeck Drive, so he wasn't far from home. They had no problem ID-ing him because he still had his wallet – cash, cards, everything. Nothing taken, in fact."

"So it wasn't a mugging?"

"Could be the chap from the house disturbed them before they'd got anything," said Deane, sounding distracted, "but from this report it looks more like a pure assault. What's your interest, Steve?"

It was an innocent enough question, but once Methodical Ted had asked it, he'd make sure he got an answer.

"We've had some contact with Mr Slade on the beach murders." Mary listened with dismay. It was the kind of limited disclosure police officers made to reporters, not to each other.

"Have you?" Deane sounded a little less relaxed now. Mary heard computer keys being clicked. "Nothing came up on the system when we booked him in - if it had, we'd have let you know. What is he, PoI?"

"No, he's just helped us with a couple of technical things. Is there anyone with him at the hospital?"

"No – should there be?" A hint of suspicion had appeared in Deane's voice.

"It might be an idea, at least until we've looked into it."

Mary wouldn't have expected Ted Deane to settle for that. He didn't.

"So what's the story on this Michael Slade, Steve? I'll need to know if I'm going to send someone out to babysit him. The hospital will want to know too, for their own risk assessment."

Of course they would. And of course this was going to unravel, just as the DI had said it would when she'd told him about the assault ten minutes earlier.

"It could just be unprovoked assault, Ted." The DI paused, at the point of no return, "We know that Mr Slade was drinking in the Criterion yesterday evening, so he could have just picked up a couple of nasties who followed him out. It wouldn't a first for Weston, would it? But," another pause, "do you remember that handling case we had against the Troshani family last year, the main witness ended up in an alleyway with a broken cheekbone, lost his memory after that? Well, the MO sounds similar, and we have an indirect link between Slade and the Troshanis."

"Hang on Steve," there was genuine concern in Deane's voice now as he interrupted the DI, "let me get this right. You had this Slade character under surveillance as a known associate of the Troshanis, he's ended up in hospital and there's nothing about him on HOLMES?"

"Not under surveillance, no. We were told he'd been in the Criterion by the person he was drinking with."

"And who was that?"

"Doc Singh."

"Doc Singh?" Deane repeated the words back, a brief pause between them, as if testing them to see just how far beyond the bounds of reality they would land.

"And I'd met Slade in the Brit earlier, Sir, before he went off to meet Dr Singh, although I wasn't aware at the time that he was going to meet him." Mary didn't know why she'd said it – it was almost as if she wanted to outdo the DI in career-threatening revelations.

There was silence at the end of the phone, then Deane's voice.

"I'm coming up. Two minutes."

"Do you want me to leave?" asked Mary as the DI pressed the button to end the call.

"You're joking, aren't you?" he replied, "You can stay here and face Ted Deane along with me. He won't let this drop, you know."

"I thought you and he went back a long way?"

"We do, but that's not going to make any difference. They don't call him Methodical Ted for nothing – by the book, every time, that way nothing goes wrong later, that's his motto. Looks like he's got a point, doesn't it?"

"Yes, Guv."

The DI looked over Mary's shoulder into the squad office.

"Here he is now. Just tell the truth – no point in anything else, because he'll find out anyway. It beats me why they don't just make him the detective around here."

Mary turned just as the door opened and Inspector Deane came into the room. Like the DI he was a trim figure, slightly above average height with sandy hair that was thinning visibly on top. His face was the sort that elicited responses such as "dependable" and "trustworthy" in psychometric tests, although from experience Mary knew that "sharp" would be accurate too. He was in shirt sleeves despite the time of year, black epaulettes across his shoulders with the two pips that denoted his rank. Mary suppressed the irrational mixture of reassurance and fear she'd felt when first encountering an officer of the law as a little girl. As he came in she got up to give him her chair, the more comfortable of the two on that side of the desk, but he waved her back into it.

"Stay where you are, Sergeant, I'll be OK here," he said, sitting on the smaller chair. Then it was straight down to business. "Steve, who is this Michael Slade, and what exactly has he got to do with the beach murders?"

In fact it was Mary who told the story, at the DI's request. Inspector Deane's jaw dropped open as he learned that Michael Slade had twice been on the edge of being a formal suspect for the murder of Katya Czwisnjowski, but had nevertheless been shown her phone (in the living room of his flat), and had been allowed into the crime scene tent at Sand Bay, but hadn't been recorded in the log of people attending the scene (a genuine oversight on Mary and the DI's part, although it was unlikely to be seen that way now) and had used information acquired there to go off and do his own private investigations, and that after all that he was in hospital but still not on HOLMES.

At the end of it Deane sat silent for a moment, then uttered a single word.

"Why?"

"My responsibility, sir" said Mary, as firmly as she could manage, "the DI was going to put him on the system as a suspect or person of interest, but I persuaded him not to."

"And why on earth did you do that?" Ted Deane asked it as a genuine question. He was starting to take on the look of a man who'd found himself in a strange parallel universe where conventional logic didn't apply.

"Because I thought he could be of real value to us as an advisor. I took a risk showing him Katya's phone, but it paid off. If he'd gone onto the system as a suspect or PoI there'd have been no way we could have let him see anything else, including the Sand Bay scene."

"So why not log him as an expert advisor?"

"Expert in what, sir? He's a computer expert but this isn't computer crime. Other than that his only regular employment is as a checkout operator. Basically he's an amateur sleuth. He happens to be a brilliant one with a superhuman IQ, but we can't write that on a registration form."

Deane's expression was one of helplessness now, although Mary had a nasty feeling that this meant helpless to prevent the wrath of senior management coming down on them like the proverbial tonne of bricks. He turned to the DI.

"And you went along with this, Steve?"

"Yes I did. I had my reservations about Slade but Mary knows him a lot better than I do. I backed her judgement on this, and still do. I'll take full responsibility."

Deane was silent for a few long seconds.

"Was he warned about the possible dangers of what he was getting into?"

Mary was quick with the answer. "Yes, sir, I specifically advised him that the case looked as if it involved violent professional criminals, and that he may prefer not to get involved."

"And when was that?" No pulling the wool over Ted's eyes.

"When I picked him up to take him to Sand Bay on Saturday morning."

"So after he'd already been involved in examining Ms Czwisnjowski's phone?"

"Yes, sir." No point in lying, either. Mary wondered whether she should mention Michael's belief that he'd enjoy the same protected status as forensic experts, and her failure to make it clear that he probably wouldn't.

"It's worth pointing out," said the DI, breaking in before she could decide, "that what brought Slade to the Troshanis' attention – if that is what happened here – was most likely him breaking the strict agreement he'd made not to divulge anything he saw at Sand Bay to a third party."

"You think Jolene Buller tipped the Troshanis off about him?" asked Deane.

"Well it's the obvious explanation." Mary was struck by how dispassionately the DI spoke about his childhood friend. "He goes in there on Saturday lunchtime asking her about birthmarks, we go in there on Saturday evening asking her about him, he gets assaulted on Sunday night." His tone softened slightly. "Not so much tipped off as mentioned in passing, probably, but the same effect."

"Pillow talk, you mean?" said Deane. He's obviously heard the rumours too.

"She denies it, says she's more like a mother to them," said the DI, sounding inclined to give her the benefit of the doubt, "We were hoping to get a view from Mr Slade on how true that is, but it looks like we'll have to ask her directly now."

"It does, doesn't it?" Deane's expression had gone from helpless to pensive. "And he was definitely told that whatever he saw at Sand Bay was confidential, and he agreed to that?"

Mary jumped in again. "Absolutely, sir. The DI told me to read the riot act to him before bringing him there, which I did, and then the DI read it to him again before we let him in the tent. He agreed both times."

"Hmm." Deane nodded in approval. The relief, however, was short lived. "Nothing in writing though, I assume? Not that it'll make much difference if Slade decides to sue us for putting him at risk."

"I don't think he will, sir. That really wouldn't be like him."

"It's not him we've got to worry about, Sergeant," said Deane, "it's the lawyers who'll sniff a nice fat payday pushing his case. Married, is he?"

"Yes sir, two children." Mary knew, as she spoke, where this was going.

"Add his wife to that then. Husband off work, two mouths to feed, lawyer promises a six-figure settlement, next thing you know she's on the regional news and the case is with the IPCC. And we all know that even a half-awake brief could make a convincing argument that we endangered him by letting him see the birthmark in the first place."

Mary noted how Deane, like the DI, tended to say "we" rather than "you" in circumstances like these. It was a minor comfort, although the only one she could see just then.

"So what do we do, Ted?" asked the DI, who clearly saw about as many positives in the situation as Mary did.

"There's not much you can do about Mr Slade except hope that he's got no permanent injuries and doesn't like lawyers."

"But we're still up the creek about not putting him on HOLMES, aren't we?" said the DI, "If the lawyers get their hands on that then we really are stuffed."

Inspector Deane folded one arm across his chest and cupped his chin in his other hand. He was silent again for a few seconds, and when he spoke it seemed to Mary that his voice was a notch or two lower than before.

"I'm going to go out to the Hospital," he said, as if their previous topic of conversation hadn't existed, "check out the lie of the land, perhaps have a word with the duty ward manager. That's going to take me about an hour. When I get back I'll assign an officer to watch over Mr Slade, assuming it seems necessary. If by the time I do that Mr Slade was on HOLMES as a civilian advisor in the beach murder cases, then the sequence of events, at least, would be correct."

Mary had read a magazine article once about cognitive dissonance, the loss of mental equilibrium that occurs when reality differs from expectation. She experienced it now as she heard Methodical Ted coaching them on how to bury their failure to register Michael Slade on the police computer system.

"But what kind of advisor should we register him as, Sir?" asked Mary, reviving the practical problem she'd raised earlier. One way people dealt with cognitive dissonance, apparently, was to act as if the discrepancy didn't exist.

Deane thought for a moment.

"You said he spotted the make and model of Ms Czwisnjowski's phone from 200 metres away when my probationer was holding it up?"

"He did, sir, yes."

"Well that makes him a telecommunications expert in

my book, as borne out by his later insights when examining the phone at close quarters. And since the second murder was clearly linked to the first, I assume you got him out to Sand Bay so that he could give you his expert opinion on any similar device that might be found there?"

"I think you assume right, Ted." said the DI steadily. There was no smile, no wink, no secret handshake, but no way now of avoiding the dissonance. Mary knew that this had become a Lodge conversation, and they were letting her witness it. She didn't know whether to swell with pride or run a mile.

"Telecomms expert it is then," said Deane, matching the DI's matter-of-fact tone, "And as it happens, I'm a bit late writing up the Scene Attendance Log on Sand Bay – I didn't get away from there until five in the afternoon and I was already way over my shift. So if you've got any attendees you forgot to give me at the time, then get the details on my desk within the next hour and they'll go in as original entries. A slip of paper will do – no need for emails."

"I think we can manage that, don't you Sergeant?" said the DI. Mary, unable to find words, just nodded.

"One other thing", said Deane, "my advice is to leave Mr Slade to us from now on. We'll take good care of him, I can promise you that. But it would be best if CID had no contact with him of any kind. That way we won't have a lawyer claiming that you tried to put pressure on him not to make a complaint."

"Understood, Ted. Thanks."

"No problem. This conversation is best forgotten by all of us – agreed?"

The DI and Mary both nodded.

"Good – I'll be off then. Bye Steve – Mary." And with that Inspector Deane got up, left the DI's office and made his way across the now empty CID room.

Mary watched him go, still struggling to take in what she'd just seen and heard. Despite being done for her benefit, it was still shocking, like finding your favourite maiden aunt with her hand in the till.

"Cheer up," said the DI, who'd seen the look on her face, "I know what you're thinking, but it's not exactly planting evidence, is it? Welcome to the world of grown-up policing – you're one of us now."

True, thought Mary – she did, indeed, feel as if she'd grown up a bit in the past fifteen minutes, been shown things that the adults had previously shielded her from. It wasn't altogether a good feeling.

"I'm as surprised as you are at Ted coming across for us," the DI continued, opening a desk drawer, "I think he just doesn't want to see some smart-suited lawyer taking us to the cleaners when we haven't actually done anything unethical."

"No, Guv." Nothing unethical except failing to correct Michael's assumption that criminals would see him as being within the fold, like pathologists and forensics officers. Would Ted Deane have been so willing to help if he'd known about that? She felt a familiar wave of guilt wash over her.

"Anyway," said the DI, putting a file into the drawer and pushing it closed, "if we get out of this alive we're going to owe him the mother of all drinks, and you're paying."

"Yes, Guv." said Mary.

"And what he said about us having no contact with Slade – that's an order. Not in person, by phone, email or anything else. And don't talk about Slade to anyone, not even at home. Understood?"

"I was hoping to go and see him once, just to make sure he's all right."

"Absolutely not. No flowers either. No leeway,

Detective Sergeant." He was suddenly deadly serious. "I've backed you so far, but if you go against my orders on this then I'll start looking after number one. Is that clear?"

"Yes, Guv." It certainly was.

"Good. Don't forget it." The fangs were withdrawn but she wouldn't forget them, just as he didn't intend her to.

"You and Inspector Deane really do go back a long way, don't you?"

The DI shrugged. "Well I did save his life once."

Mary remembered the wing canons on Kopacz's Hurricane.

"What, operational?"

"No, training course in Hertfordshire. We had to cross a lake – the usual nonsense – Ted wasn't a great swimmer and he fell in. I went in after him and fished him out."

Mary had been on a course like that. It had been hell, although the water exercise, at least, hadn't held any fears for her, since she was a competent swimmer. She hadn't known that the DI was one too.

"I didn't have you down as the aquatic type, Guv?"

The DI pointed at his chest.

"Avon and Somerset Schools Under 13 Freestyle Champion," he said, in mock indignation. "There's a lot you don't know about me."

"Yes, Guv." That was certainly true.

Chapter 31

Jolene Buller sat at the interview room table, in the chair that Agron Troshani had occupied twenty four hours earlier. Her fringed skirt and pink boots had been replaced by a tired-looking tracksuit and trainers, and although the blonde hair was still piled high, its dark roots seemed to have grown longer since Saturday night, while the makeup around her eyes looked as if it might have been applied the previous day. It was 9.22 am; she evidently wasn't a morning person. Mary had taken pity on her and found her a cup of tea, but it hadn't done much to improve her mood.

The DI put a thin grey file on the table.

"OK, Ms Buller," he said briskly, "You're here voluntarily but you have been cautioned and this interview is being recorded. Anything you say may be used in evidence. Present are Ms Jolene Buller, Detective Inspector Jones and Detective Sergeant Miller."

"What's this 'Ms Buller' stuff about, Stevie?" said Jolene resentfully, "You know my name well enough, have done since you were five."

"This is official, Ms Buller, and in this room it's Detective Inspector Jones. Let's keep it that way, shall we?" There was a coldness in the DI's voice that surprised even Mary, who'd been with him in plenty of interviews, often with people suspected of serious, violent crimes.

"Please yourself then." Jolene spat the words back at him, but her eyes glistened with something that looked more like pain than defiance.

"Good," said the DI, "Now I understand that you know Ardit Troshani, and other members of the

Troshani family and their friends?"

"Going on about that again, are you?" Jolene looked indignant, "I told you, I'm more like a mother to them. Saying I have sex with them all, it's disgusting. I don't."

"No-one's saying that," said the DI, with the patient air of someone practised in dealing with attempts to change the subject, "I'm merely asking whether you know them or not. Do you?"

Jolene nodded.

"For the recording please, Ms Buller – yes or no?"

"Yes." Mary realised that Jolene had nodded because she found it difficult to speak, her voice almost breaking now as she pronounced the single short word. Being treated so formally by someone she thought of as an old friend would be disorienting for anyone, but for Jolene, who wasn't far from needing an appropriate adult in the interview with her, it would be too much to cope with. This didn't seem right. Breaking in now risked the wrath of her boss, but Mary did it anyway.

"Jolene," she said, in a tone very different from the DI's, "I'm sorry we have to ask you this, but we're investigating a murder and we have to know all the relevant details. Are you having a sexual relationship with any of the Troshani family or their friends, or have you had such a relationship recently?"

It was actually quite a brutal question, but put in a less confrontational way it didn't seem to upset Jolene so much. In fact she seemed glad to unburden herself with the answer.

"I did have – all right? Like I told you on Saturday. About a year ago, a bit longer perhaps, Ardi and me, well, a couple of times, but his uncle stopped it, told him he should show me more respect. Same with a couple of his cousins who were over here then. I was stupid, made myself look a right slag, embarrassed my mum and dad. If truth's known I was grateful when Agron put a stop to

it."

Mary found it hard to believe that she was listening to a 43 year old woman, talking like a teenage girl about embarrassing her parents. Nevertheless she was talking, and Mary needed to keep her that way.

"So now you and the Troshanis are just mates?"

"That's right, only I wouldn't exactly call it mates. I wasn't mates with them even when I was..." she faltered, the embarrassment momentarily returning, "... you know. Like I said, I'm more like a mother to 'em now, especially the young lads who've just come over. Terrible homesick, some of 'em."

It occurred to Mary that Jolene had probably done more practical good than all the county's migrant community outreach workers put together, even if her clients had been mostly illegal migrants. For Mary at least, Jolene's account of her sexual entanglements with the Troshanis rang true; she waited a moment to give the DI chance to pursue it further, and when he didn't, moved on to the other reason Jolene was there.

"OK Jolene, that's clear now. Thanks for being open with us about it. Now you also know Michael Slade, don't you?"

Jolene tensed again. "You know I do," she said, "I told you that on Saturday too. You don't think I've been with him as well, do you? Well I haven't. He's just a customer, that's all."

"No, we don't think that, Jolene," said Mary, trying to keep her voice as calm as possible, "Saturday was just an informal chat, but this is a formal interview, so I'm afraid we do have to go over some of the ground. Do you get on well with Michael – just as a customer?"

Jolene brightened. "Course I do – he's a nice bloke," she replied, "Dad's had to chuck him off the karaoke a couple of times for trying to sing that folk rubbish, but apart from that he's as good as gold, never any trouble even when he's had a few. And he knows lots of things – very clever man, Dad reckons."

"Yes, he is. And he came to see you at Between The Lines last Saturday afternoon, to ask if you knew a young Albanian man with a birthmark on his neck, is that right?"

"Yeah, that's right. He said he'd heard he could get him a cheap iPhone. I don't know where he'd got that from, 'cos Luan never had anything to do with that sort of thing. That was more..." Jolene stopped, as if suddenly remembering where she was. Mary began to wonder, seriously, whether they should be interviewing her without someone else there, and whether anything she said in these circumstances would stand up as evidence. She was also beginning to realise why she hadn't yet heard a sharp "Thank you, Sergeant" cutting across her, as the DI took back control of the interview.

"And you remember DI Jones and myself coming to see you on Saturday evening and asking you about Michael?" She kept to her best Good Cop voice, resigning herself to the role she'd been manoeuvred into yet again.

"Yeah, 'course I do. Only he didn't mind me calling him Stevie on Saturday, like I've done since we was at junior school together." Jolene glared at the DI with such a comical expression of resentment that Mary had to look away and cough, while trying desperately to excise the grin from her face. Seeing that his Good Cop was temporarily indisposed, the DI took up the questioning.

"Who did you talk to about Michael Slade and us coming to see you, Jolene?" he asked, his manner gentler now.

"No one," she replied, her manner towards him still frosty.

"Not Ardi, or any of his mates?"

"No." She sounded irritated, as if he was ignoring a

very obvious point. "They haven't been in, have they? Not since last Wednesday."

"You're sure about that?"

"Yes – ask Mum and Dad if you like. Dad'd know if they had - he can't stand 'em, starts going on at me to get rid of 'em as soon as they arrive."

"And you haven't spoken to any of them on the phone?" asked Mary, earning herself a look from Jolene that said she'd just beaten the DI to the "most stupid question asked this week" award.

"I don't phone Ardi or his mates, it's not like that," she said scornfully, "If they come in, I see them. Otherwise I don't."

"What about if you want Ardi to give you a lift to a gig?" asked the DI.

"Then I asks him when they come in. They're in some time most weekends."

"But not this weekend?" asked Mary.

"No, I already said that, didn't I?" replied Jolene, who seemed convinced now that she was being interviewed by two idiots with serious short-term memory problems, "You're getting as bad as him."

"And when did you last see Michael Slade, Jolene?" The DI said it quietly, but Mary noticed his fingers moving on to the thin file that lay closed on the table in front of him, the contents of which he'd yet to share with her. Jolene took the question as final proof of her interrogator's memory issues.

"Saturday afternoon, like I told you," she said, as if explaining the date of her next house call to an ageing relative, "I ain't seen him since – nor talked to him on the phone neither, before you ask. I don't even know his number, do I?"

"And have you got any idea where he is now?" The DI's finger reached for the file again, lifting the corner of its cover a millimetre or two from the table's surface.

"Having his breakfast probably," said Jolene, "He works lates on Tuesdays, comes in the pub after if they let him bunk off early. Why, has he done a runner or something? Is that what this is about? What's he in trouble for?"

The DI flipped the cover of the file open. For a second Mary caught sight of the A4 photograph that sat on top of the thin stack of papers, and thought she was going to be involuntarily sick. Then the DI spun the photograph round, and Mary saw Jolene's face whiten as she recognised who it was.

"Michael Slade's in Weston General, Jolene," he said in a matter-of-fact tone, "Intensive Care, with one of our officers guarding him. He was assaulted on Sunday night, on his way home from the Criterion. As you can see, they did a thorough job on him."

Even from the wrong way round, Mary could see that they had, indeed, been thorough. The picture was of Michael's face, although he was recognisable mainly by his fair hair and the wisp of beard on his chin. Both eyes were blackened and almost closed, there was heavy bruising on both cheeks, and his mouth was swollen up in a way that Mary knew resulted from a kick rather than a punch. No-one policed the streets of Weston for long without becoming something of an expert on assault, and the differences between, say, a glassing in a pub over a girl and the settling of a drug-related debt in a dark alleyway. Irrespective of what had been done to other parts of Michael's body, these facial injuries represented violence expertly applied for maximum visibility, a warning to others not to cooperate with the police as he'd done. She felt guilt and nausea, in equal proportions, flood over her.

Jolene, meanwhile, was quietly crying, rivers of tears cutting through the thick foundation under her eyes. Most people, men or women, would have looked away, but she kept her gaze on the photograph, as if she didn't want to show Michael disrespect by turning away from him.

"Is he going to be OK?" she asked, her voice little more than a whisper.

"He'll pull through," said the DI, "in fact they say he was lucky. Lots of superficial injuries – painful ones too - but not as many broken bones as they thought at first."

In other words the work of pros, who knew how to make it hurt and look bad without risking a murder charge.

Jolene was still looking at the photograph, the shock that had written itself across her face turning to sadness now.

"You think Ardi and his mates did this to him, don't you?"

"We think it's a possibility, yes." The DI's voice was calm but no longer cold, his tough-guy persona gone completely now.

"And you think I told them about him, said he'd been in asking about Luan?"

"Not necessarily on purpose, Jolene. Perhaps you said something to someone else, that might have got back to them?"

Jolene looked up from the photograph and fixed the DI with a look that seemed to combine anguish for herself with scorn for him. "I know you think I'm stupid, Stevie, but I'm not that stupid. I know what Ardi and his mates are, and I know better than to go letting on to anyone that you'd been asking me about Michael and Luan. I didn't even tell Dad about Michael, not that it would have made any difference if I had. None of us would do anything to drop him in it. Like I said, he's a nice chap." She looked back down at the photograph, then pushed it away from her, tears welling up in her eyes again. "He didn't deserve to have that done to him".

"No, he didn't."

"It don't make sense though, does it?" Jolene said, sounding genuinely puzzled. "You're trying to find out who murdered Luan, you'd think they'd want people to help you with that, not go beating them up for it."

"We think Luan was involved in something," said Mary, choosing her words carefully, "and that other members of his family were too. We think he was killed because of it. The Troshanis are probably worried what we'll find out about them if we dig too deep into why Luan was murdered."

Mary thought how quickly Michael would have worked out that the "something" was the murder of Katya Czwisnjowski. In fact he wouldn't even have needed to ask the question. From Jolene, however, there was just a nod. Mystery explained, case closed, no curiosity beyond that. Jolene certainly wasn't the brightest bulb on the Christmas tree. But she wasn't the one lying in Weston General either.

Chapter 32

The DI sat down behind his desk, unlocked the drawers and put the file away.

"Good work in there," he said to Mary, as she settled into her chair.

"Thanks, Guv," she replied quietly.

"So what do you think of Jolene's story then?"

"I think she's on the level. I'll get Cox and Lane to check whether anyone else saw the Troshanis at Between The Lines over the weekend, but I'd be very surprised if they did."

"Yes, same here. I've known Jolene a long time and she hasn't got the wits to lie about something as complicated as that, even if the Troshanis were threatening her. She'd probably have told them to take a jump anyway. Not the sort to give in to threats, our Jolene."

"No," said Mary.

"Shame though. I was banking on her to give us the link. Now we've got to go looking for someone else who knows the Troshanis and knew that Mr Slade was helping us, and there aren't going to be many of those."

Mary made no reply. Like the DI, she'd assumed that Jolene would be the link between Michael Slade and the Troshanis. But unlike the DI she knew of another candidate who fitted the bill, someone she hadn't even thought of at the start of the interview, but whose name had begun to nag at her as it had become clear that Jolene hadn't told the Troshanis anything. It wasn't a name she was prepared to say out loud until she'd had time to think.

At the first opportunity she made her excuses, left the

CID office and headed for the toilets. She checked that the cubicles were all empty, went into the last one, bolted the door and sat down. She stared at the coat hook on the door back, trying to suppress a rising feeling of panic and accompanying nausea. Once she'd regained some control she went over the facts that had come, unwelcome, into her mind as she'd sat in the interview room. Someone who knows the Troshanis. Plenty of those, from Marco the restaurateur to half the tearaways who hung out in the pubs and clubs at weekends. Someone who also knew that Michael Slade was helping the police. Far fewer. Not even their own officers, especially before Michael had been added to HOLMES, and that had been after the assault. But one person, who'd worked for the Troshanis and knew in detail Michael's involvement with the beach murders case – knew more about it, in fact, than anyone except herself and the DI. Who'd been behind the kitchen door when she'd arranged to meet Michael in the Brit on Sunday evening. Her husband, Don.

Bile rose up in her throat, and for a moment she thought she was going to be sick, crazily thinking that at least it wouldn't be hard to wipe it off the sealed cubicle surfaces. Her mother would be proud that she'd given proper consideration to hygiene at such a difficult time, more proud than she was of her being a detective, which was what she needed to be right now. All police officers knew that one day they might have to deal with something like this. The procedure was straightforward: examine the information you have, and if there is any possibility that you'd think it warranted investigation if the person was unconnected to you, then take it to a senior officer, who'll use "appropriate discretion" in dealing with it. The unspoken rule was to err heavily on the side of "possibility", take the information to your boss if there was even the slightest chance of it being relevant. Better that than having to explain yourself to Professional Standards later.

The information in this case would warrant investigation by any standards. Don had banked thousands of pounds from what had been a notably well-paid contract with the Troshanis. She'd given him chapter and verse on Michael's involvement in their enquiries. He had almost certainly overheard her arranging to meet Michael, so knew exactly where Michael would be on Sunday night. And he'd had ample time to contact the Troshanis after she'd left the house.

And yet it couldn't be him, because he was her husband, the man she'd shared her life with since she was nineteen. How many wives had she heard saying that though, about men they'd shared their lives with? The "evidence" against Don was purely circumstantial; it proved only that he had the knowledge and opportunity to tip the Troshanis off about Michael, not that he had done. But the DI had dragged Jolene Buller in on the basis of less, and Mary had done the same in her time on other cases. Circumstantial evidence was often all the police had in the early stages of an investigation, and if enough of it pointed at the same person they started looking for direct evidence to back it up. Enough pointed at Don in this case, even perhaps at her for telling him so much about Michael. Suddenly she saw them both on the receiving end of the cold, mechanical logic that drove much of the detective work in cases like these. Once it targeted you, it never completely let you go. Once a suspect always a suspect.

Mary looked at the unblemished door panel a few inches from her face. She felt calmer now, as she always did when the chips were really down. There were options. Her superiors already knew about Don's work for the Troshanis – it had been discussed higher up the command structure, with input from her Federation rep, and formally agreed to have no bearing on her position within Weston CID. She'd logged Saturday's conversation with Don about Redzepi and Grove Park on HOLMES the previous day. That side of things was all in order.

No-one knew that she'd told Don about Michael's involvement with the beach murders investigation. It was this second piece of circumstantial evidence that would tip the probability meter over the line, and she could choose not to mention it. Except that it would put her over the line, into withholding information; actual corruption that would mean the end of her career, and worse, if it came out. She might have taken that risk if she could have been 100 percent certain that Don was innocent, but the awful truth was that all her years of training and experience told her she couldn't, however well she thought she knew him. She closed her eyes, and saw the image of Michael Slade, his face beaten to a pulp. There was only one option.

"Can I have a word, sir?"

The DI looked up from his desk.

"This sounds serious. I hope you haven't come to resign – I need you on this case."

"Can I sit down?"

The DI looked serious now. "Yes of course," he said, closing the file he'd been reading, "Shut the door."

"Guv, there is someone else besides Jolene Buller who knows the Troshanis and knew that Michael Slade was helping us," she said, trying to keep her voice level, "In fact he knew exactly what Michael had been doing, and where he was going to be on Sunday night."

"Yeah?" The DI's interest had clearly been aroused. "Who's that?"

She paused. Once said, it couldn't be taken back.

"Don."

"Your husband?" The DI's tone managed to convey both surprise and the question of whether she might want to reconsider having said it. Mary could see that his mind was already racing through the implications.

"Yes, Sir." Keeping it formal was the only way she'd be able to cope. An informal chat would probably end with her breaking down completely.

"How did he know about Slade?" asked the DI. It had taken him no time to home in on the important part of what Mary had just told him. The answer was obvious, but he'd want to know the full details.

"He was there when Michael Slade rang me on Friday night," said Mary, "We were at home, about to have dinner. He asked me what it was about, and I told him. Then I think he overheard me ringing Slade on Saturday to arrange to meet him the following night. I can't be sure, but I think he did."

"Why did you tell him about Slade?" The DI was slipping into formal mode himself now. It wasn't comfortable, but it could have been worse; Mary was glad it wasn't DSI Kopacz in the chair opposite.

"As I said, Guv, he asked me." She paused, not wanting to delve into her personal life but knowing that she had to, "We've had some problems about my work – the hours and things, me not being around to help out." She wondered for a second whether the always-cool Karen ever gave the DI grief for not being around to help out; somehow she didn't think so. "Friday was like a fresh start for us," she continued, "Don had made a real effort with the meal and everything, said he understood that with a murder case it was different, I had to be on it 24/7. When he was OK about the phone call interrupting the evening, and showed some interest in what I was doing, I didn't want to knock him back."

She realised, even as she was saying it, that it could be read as Don softening her up with a nice meal then pumping her for information about the case. Probably would be, in fact; it was how they were trained to think. She couldn't completely stop thinking that way herself.

The DI gave no indication of how he'd read it, only that he understood her unhappiness at having to talk about her marriage.

"All right," he said, then quickly moved on. "And when you say Don knows the Troshanis, you're talking about that heating job he did for them at Grove Park?"

"Yes."

"He finished that a while back, didn't he? Has he done anything for them since?"

"No. I don't think he wanted any more work from them."

"Did he have any other contact with them, apart from working at Grove Park?"

"No – at least I don't think so." The truth was that she had no idea. He could have been meeting them every day for a lunchtime pint – or an evening one, while she'd been out catching car thieves.

"And have you found any evidence of him being in contact with them since Friday night?"

"No, but he has had opportunity. I was on duty all day Saturday, or he could have rung them after I went out on Sunday evening. You'll have to check the phone records." Mary heard herself talking about her husband like any other suspect, adding up the points against him. Anything less would seem like covering up for him, especially if Professional Standards got hold of it, but it still felt like betrayal. The Troshanis had known what they were doing when they paid Don generously for the Grove Park job.

A stab of panic hit her. "Guv, what if the Troshanis are out to frame Don? What if they transfer money into his bank account to make it look as if they're paying him off?"

"Whoa," said the DI, raising his hand like an old-style PC stopping a motorist for a defective headlamp, "let's not get carried away. We don't even know for certain that the Troshanis are behind the assault on Michael Slade, or that he didn't advertise himself to them by blabbing in some other pub. And if the Troshanis did want to frame your husband, I expect they'd choose something a bit less obvious than shoving cash into his account."

"You'd better check the account anyway, Guv." Her panic was under control; now resignation was taking over.

The DI stared at her for a few seconds, long enough for it to become disconcerting.

"Let's not go round the houses on this," he said, breaking his silence at last. "Mary, you know your husband better than anyone. Do you think he tipped off the Troshanis, or anyone else, about Michael Slade?"

"No, Guv." She meant it, but even so she couldn't keep the doubt out of her voice.

"But you're not certain?"

"It's just that it's what every wife or husband would say, isn't it?"

"Every wife or husband isn't a police officer with 17 years experience. Or one who'd come to their senior officer with this instead of trying to keep it buried."

"I could be trying to double-bluff you by drawing attention to it." One day she'd get this tendency to play Devil's Advocate against herself under control.

"Or treble-bluff me by drawing attention to the double-bluff," said the DI, welcoming the chance to lighten things. "You need to stop watching cop shows on TV, the scriptwriters have got far too vivid imaginations. Anyway, do you think you could bluff me for long?"

"No Guv."

"Exactly. I can read you like a book, and don't forget

it."

"So what happens now?"

"I'm going to take this away and deal with it in an appropriate manner. Leave it with me. Have you got Don's mobile number?"

Mary nodded and reached into her bag. She brought out her phone, found Don's number and passed it to the DI. He reached for the pad, in an RNLI-branded holder, that he used for taking notes and messages. She noticed that he tore a page from it and put it on the desk before writing the number down.

"Am I off the case, Guv?"

The DI looked up in surprise.

"Think you're getting a holiday out of this? No chance. Like I said, I need you here. Just stick to placing the Troshanis with Redzepi at the Pier last week. I'll get Tom Flanagan to look into the Slade assault."

"Yes, Guv. I told Don that I might ask Tom to take a formal statement from him about Grove Park, so he'll be expecting him." Won't have his suspicions raised by him, she meant. Colluding to catch her husband off guard – what would she be doing next, luring him into bedroom confessions?

"Good," replied the DI, then added, "Does Don know about the assault on Slade?"

"Not as far as I know. I didn't say anything to him about it last night."

"Keep it that way then. Let Tom break the news to him, unless he hears it from somewhere else first."

"OK." One more bit of collusion wouldn't make much difference.

The DI looked at her like a doctor examining a patient. She could see from his expression that what he saw wasn't good. She felt as if she'd had some terrible electro-convulsive therapy.

"Take a couple of hours off," he said, "Get out of here

– go to the pictures, go for a drive in the beautiful Somerset countryside, whatever. Forget about all this, especially this business with Don. That's an order. I'll see you later."

"Yes, Guv. Thanks."

Mary didn't go to the pictures, or tour the Somerset countryside. Instead she bought coffee and a filled ciabatta, propped the bag carefully on the floor of her car and drove along the seafront, past the Grand Pier, the Winter Gardens and the College, on past Knightstone and the Marine Lake, up the hill past the Clarendon and the Somerset Royal Legion, stopping just beyond the flattened ruins of the Royal Pier Hotel. It was overcast but dry, and although it was cold there was little wind. Taking her things from the car, she walked across the old hotel car park and down the few steps to the terrace that looked out over Birnbeck Pier.

The Pier looked almost in ruins itself, its ironwork rusting badly, the boards that ran its length like death traps waiting to give way under the slightest weight, the old jetty for the steamers from Cardiff seemingly in the process of slow-motion collapse. The buildings on Birnbeck Island looked little better, their doors and windows missing, roofs dotted with holes, debris surrounding them. In the middle of all this sat the canvas marquee that covered the Weston lifeboat, looking incongruously like something from a summer fete, reached by a narrow strip of new footway laid along the pier.

Mary would have liked to have gone out there; she had a thing about ruins, in their proper, ruined state before they were restored to pristine condition and the echoes of the past erased. Duty, mostly searching for drug stashes, had taken her inside the Royal Pier Hotel a few times before it had finally burnt down. It had been like the Marie Celeste, menus still pinned to notice boards outside the dining room, bar towels still on the bar. The Beatles had famously stayed there in the 1960s, and she could hear their accents echoing down the corridors, see them out on the sun terrace.

There'd be no visit to Birnbeck Island for her today though. As always, she wasn't dressed for it, and even if she had been, the pier and island were strictly no access, even to police officers on two hours compassionate leave. Instead she walked back to the circular shelter in the middle of the terrace. As she'd expected, she had the shelter – the whole terrace, in fact – to herself. She chose a bench facing the sea and sat in the middle, placing her bag to her left and her lunch to her right. A slight wind was beginning to blow, and she pulled her coat around her; her legs were cold but there was nothing she could do about it. She'd often taken a professional interest in the people who came to this terrace to sit in the strange little shelter, that looked like a child's roundabout but wasn't. Now she was one of them.

She took out her coffee, sipped from it and placed it carefully on the bench, then unwrapped the ciabatta and took a bite. Pastrami, soft cheese and salad, the bread still warm from the toaster - a disaster for her diet, but sufficiently comforting, along with the hot, strong coffee, for her not to care. For a good ten minutes, surrounded by the sea and the ruins of Birnbeck, she forgot about the Troshanis and Don and the Czwisnjowskis. If she focussed on Steep Holm, out there in the Channel, she could forget them for a few minutes more. She sipped more coffee, turned and took the last of the ciabatta from its bag.

From behind her she heard her phone ring. Her first impulse was to ignore it, but this was quickly displaced by the idea that it might be the DI. She twisted round in her seat, reached into her bag, pulled out the phone and read the display.

"M Slade"

It couldn't be. Michael was lying in intensive care with a mouth so badly kicked in that it was unlikely he'd be speaking again this month. Perhaps, though, someone had taken his phone – she didn't remember Ted Deane mentioning it among the possessions they'd found with him – and was working through the address book. Without speculating further, Mary pressed the Answer button and put the phone to her ear.

"Mwe?" The voice sounded like someone talking through layers of bandages, which she realised it probably was.

"Mary Miller here, yes – is that you, Michael?"

"Yef. Mwe I'f goh sm ideas bow the mwdrs."

"Michael!" She was lost for anything else to say. He sounded terrible, as if every syllable was causing him pain.

"Ca you com an see me? Wan to tal to you."

"Oh Michael," she said, a lump growing in her throat, "I'm not allowed to see you, or have any communication with you. You're in danger."

"But Mwe.."

"No Michael, I'm not even supposed to have this phone call. I'm going to have to hang up. I'm really sorry. I don't want to but I have to."

"OK." Even through the bandages she could hear his dejection, like a boy who'd been told he couldn't go on a trip to the seaside.

"Our uniform officers will protect you now, Michael. I really am sorry. I hope it all works out for you." Her voice was beginning to break. "Goodbye".

"By Mwe." The phone went dead.

Mary held the phone in front her, stared at it for a few seconds, then burst into tears, uncontrolled sobbing that shook her as she sat there. Michael was in hospital because of her, because she'd used him to do the detective work she didn't have the brains to do herself, let him see things that made him a threat to the Troshanis. And perhaps it was her own husband who'd told the Troshanis all this, got Michael kicked half to death. The guilt flooded into her, impossible to resist.

She felt a hand touch her lightly on the shoulder, and a female voice say "Are you all right, my love?" She looked up and saw an elderly couple, wrapped up against the cold, standing with concerned expressions. The woman held a paper handkerchief out in a gloved hand.

"Thank you," Mary said, taking the tissue, "I'm OK, I've just had some sad news, that's all."

"Family?" asked the woman, "That can be very hard, I know."

"No, a friend. He's been badly injured. He's in hospital."

"Oh dear, that's very sad. I do hope he'll be all right."

"So do I."

"Is there anything we can do for you?" asked the man, "We've got a car, we could take you to the hospital if you like. Is your friend in Weston General, or have they taken him to Frenchay or something?"

"No, it's all right, I've got a car. It's very kind of you though, I really appreciate it."

"That's all right, my love," said the woman. She reached into her handbag and brought out some more tissues. "Here, have these. Sure there's nothing we can do for you?"

"No, nothing – but thank you. You've been really kind."

"You're welcome, my love. Goodbye then."

"Goodbye."

In bed that night Mary thought about the strange,

unexpected normality that had surrounded her since her return from Birnbeck Pier. No-one had stared at her then turned quickly away as she'd entered the CID office. The DI had spoken to her only about establishing Luan Redzepi's movements in the 72 hours before Katya Czwisnjowski's body had been discovered, with no mention of phone records or bank statements. Don had seemed at peace with the world, expressing his appreciation of the mince and bottled pasta sauce she'd put together then settling on the sofa with a can of lager and Tuesday night's long-running TV hospital drama. Perhaps it could be like this; everything as before, just her doing her job with no complications. But then she remembered Michael's mumbling voice on the phone, and the click and hiss as Don had opened his lager, and realised that it couldn't.

Beside her, Don turned over. She felt his arm across her stomach, his hand below her breast.

"Mary" he said, in a voice that was half-asleep but also half-way back to the old, confident Don she'd thought had gone.

"I'm sorry, love. I'm a bit tired." She said, and turned away from him.

"All right," came the reply, less confident now, as he turned away.

The numbers on the alarm clock display became blurred as her eyes filled with tears.

Chapter 33

"Police Clueless In West Country Beach Murders"

It wasn't a headline anyone in the Constabulary wanted to see splashed across a double page spread of a national newspaper, although the officers closest to the case conceded privately that it wasn't all that far from the truth. The professional way in which both Katya Czwisnjowski and Luan Redzepi had been killed and buried had indeed left almost no clues, while the pursuit of the favoured theory – that these were tit-for-tat murders, first Katya by the Troshanis then Redzepi by the Czwisnjowskis – had yielded no proof.

Another tabloid had picked up on the fact that both victims were foreign nationals, showing great skill in conjuring up images of armies of immigrants slaughtering each other on Britain's beaches without actually saying anything that could leave them open to a charge of stirring up racial tensions. Another had dug deeper locally and unearthed tales of "community tensions" between the Troshanis and Weston's indigenous population, translating this into a broad hint that pitchfork-wielding North Somerset vigilantes might have been responsible for Luan Redzepi's death. Their reporter was no longer welcome in the town's bars. Thankfully no-one had made any connection between the beach murders and a violent assault on a local supermarket worker making his way home from the pub. There was no reason why they should; that kind of thing went on in Weston all the time.

It was now almost two weeks since Katya's body had been found, and although the national media were still trying to maintain interest in the story, nearer to home it was already becoming old news. The local view, not discouraged by the authorities, was increasingly that the murders were "nothing to do with Weston", that it was the town's misfortune to have been chosen as the burial ground for the casualties of someone else's war, and that the time to move on would be sooner rather than later. After a decent (but brief) period of respect, the council had removed the flowers that had accumulated at both burial sites, the ones at Katya's tied to the legs of the Pier to escape the tides. It was the second half of November, and peoples' thoughts were turning to the Festive Season. The main story in the local paper that week was the naming of the celebrity who would turn on this year's Christmas lights.

It was impossible to maintain the intensity of a major police investigation far beyond the second week, however committed the team, unless there was a red hot trail to be followed. Fatigue set in, lines of enquiry were exhausted, witnesses' memories began to fade, people who might have said something when the sense of communal shock and outrage was still strong reverted to the default position of not wanting to get involved. The CID team were beginning to see the case as old news too, although none of them would admit it and they were all determined to stay focussed on it.

For Mary, though, it was particularly hard. She felt responsible for the assault on Michael Slade, a situation made worse by her being forbidden to have any contact with him, so unable to offer him any apology or support. Having to report Don as a possible accessory to the attack had undermined the resilience that normally saw her through tough times at work, making her question, for the first time, whether she really wanted to be a police officer, or at least this kind of police officer. She hadn't needed to be Sigmund Freud to work out why it had affected her like this; Don was her rock, relied on to be there after every long day, even if he was complaining about her not doing her share around the house. If she had to see him as a suspect then she was on her own, for the first time in 17 years.

Her defence mechanism (more Freud) was an involuntary sense of moving on, of life after the beach murders, getting back to the normality of gas bottle thefts and hotel pilfering. She'd resisted it, but it hadn't helped that they'd actually solved a normal case, a spate of burglaries in the South Ward which had opened up after one of the victims had spotted their valuables for sale on the internet. The DI had sent her to make the arrest, two brothers with form going back to their early teens, a classic bit of local policing that made the community measurably safer; what she'd signed up to do.

Meanwhile the business with Don was, as far as she knew, unresolved. She'd asked no questions, just handed over phone numbers and business bank account details, the latter obtained in abject misery from Don's filing cabinet while he was out working. DS Flanagan had been out to see Don, for an interview disguised as the formal taking of a statement covering what he'd already told Mary. Either Flanagan had disguised it well, or he hadn't asked very much, since Don had seemed unperturbed by it.

Mary had a feeling that the investigation was being done unofficially; certainly HOLMES still recorded only that Don had done some contract work for the Troshanis, not that he knew about Michael Slade's involvement in the beach murders case. It was unthinkable that the outcome would be that Don had, in fact, tipped the Troshanis off about Michael, and Mary had no idea how she'd deal with it if it was. Even so, she was reaching the point where she'd rather have that than much more waiting, of going home every night to the man she loved but could no longer be 100 percent sure of.

True to his principles, the DI was taking a determinedly glass-half-full view of the overall situation. They'd failed (so far) to get the Troshanis for Katya's murder, but as he said, the Major Crime Unit had failed to nail the Czwisnjowskis, so they were in good company. In fact Kopacz's team had a double failure on their hands, having made no serious progress in the Bristol student murders either. The only bright spot was that no more students had been killed, which the Force's PR team were quietly attributing to effective policing of the city's streets.

Mary had started taking her lunch breaks out of the office, with the DI's tacit approval. When the weather permitted, she took a coffee and panini to the terrace overlooking Birnbeck Pier; when it didn't, she walked on down the steps, past the ruins of the Royal Pier Hotel, to the café in the cove at Anchor Head, which stayed open with a skeleton staff in winter. The food there was more bacon butty than toasted ciabatta, but she was fine with that. The cafe was warm, and being able to sit there quietly for half an hour looking out over the tiny cove and the Channel beyond it satisfied a need that was deeper than she'd have liked to admit.

She ordered soup and a roll today. The woman behind the counter recognised her, called her 'Love' and said they'd bring it over to her. Going into the small inner room she saw that the table next to the window was free, and sat at it. A flurry of wind blew rain spattering against the glass. She'd made the right choice coming indoors.

After a few minutes a young woman came into the room carrying a tray. She was slim and quite tall, with dark hair cut in a short bob that hovered on the edge of being spiky, and makeup that, with heavier application, would have qualified her as a Goth. Police officers are trained to remember faces, but even so Mary struggled for a moment to place this one, until it clicked into place – it was Tamzin, the quieter of the two girls from Sand Bay, who'd been refusing to go out in the aftermath of finding Luan Redzepi's body. Evidently she'd got over it, in the daytime at least.

"There you go," said Tamzin, putting the tray on the table and placing its contents one by one in front of Mary, "the soup's nice today – hope you enjoy it." She didn't seem to recognise Mary, or if she did, she wasn't letting on. Mary toyed for a second with the idea of pretending not to recognise her either, but then reminded herself that she was still a representative of the Constabulary, lunch break or not.

"It's Tamzin, isn't it?" she said, hoping not to sound too much as if she was stopping her on suss, "Mary Miller, I was one of the police officers at Sand Bay." As she'd done with Ellie in the Brit, she hoped that she wasn't dragging up something the girl wanted to put behind her, especially as this time she knew she'd had a bad reaction to the experience. As with Ellie though, there didn't seem to be a problem.

"Oh yes," said Tamzin, breaking into a slight smile, "I remember. Seems ages ago now."

Still not sure she'd done the right thing in talking to her, Mary scrutinised Tamzin's face, looking for signs of post-trauma nerves. In fact she seemed quite relaxed.

"I saw Ellie," Mary said, "she said you'd found it tough after that Saturday. I was sorry to hear that."

"Yeah," replied Tamzin, "I had nightmares at first and things, but it got better. One of your people came round – Family Liason or something – and she was really good. Talked me through a few things."

"Oh, that's good," said Mary, "I'm glad they were able to help." Shame it had been the DI, not her, who'd thought of sending them round to check on Tamzin. Checking herself, she decided that her lunch break did allow her absolve herself of guilt for that, if only for the next half hour.

Mary looked at Tamzin again. She was pretty; prettier than Ellie, in fact, but without quite the same degree of self-assurance and casual-chic grooming. Even so, she had enough of both to set her aside from the average 18 year old who hung around the centre of Weston.

"So do you work here? I've been coming in recently, but I haven't seen you before."

"No – not full time, anyway," Tamzin said. She'd picked up the empty tray, but now she put it back on the table. "I worked here in the summer, weekends and that. They've got someone off sick, asked if I could cover for them. The money's useful, to be honest."

"Aren't you off to university?" asked Mary, realising that again she might be touching on a subject the girl might prefer to avoid. Again she was let off the hook.

"Gap year. Well, it was supposed to be," said Tamzin, sitting down, "We were all going to go off together – VSO in Africa. Then Ellie got pregnant, Ewan said he wasn't going either in that case, and it all sort of fell apart. So here we all are." She waved her hand to indicate the extent of her domain; the small inner room of the cafe, the rain-lashed terrace outside overlooking the tiny cove. It was clear that it wasn't what she'd been hoping for.

Interest, personal more than professional, drove Mary to find out more.

"You seem quite a tight-knit group, you and Ellie and the others. Were you all at the College together?"

For a second Tamzin's expression became a strange mixture of condescension and regret.

"Not Weston College, no – Compton School." The last two words were enough to tell Mary everything she needed to know about Ellie's self-assurance and the whole group's oddly measured reaction to finding a body buried in the sand. She could have kicked herself for not working it out earlier. Compton School, ten miles outside Weston, co-educational, mixed boarding and day pupils, its own theatre, video production studio and dressage ring. The place where the successful sent their offspring to be taught how to be like them, how to get into the top universities, how to make a barman jump to attention on a slow Sunday night in November.

Tamzin was smiling again now. "I know what you're thinking, but I'm not one of the posh ones. Scholarship girl, me," she said, in an exaggerated Somerset accent, "common as muck but got something between the ears." She leaned forward conspiratorially, "Beats only having it between somewhere else, doesn't it?"

It took Mary a moment to work out the allusion; when she did she found herself slightly shocked but also laughing reflexively. She decided that she liked Tamzin.

"In my job you get to meet people who really are common as muck, and believe me, you're not one of them," she said, smiling. It was meant as a compliment, and she was pleased to see that it was taken as one.

"Well they must have done a proper job on me then, mustn't they?" said Tamzin, smiling back.

"Are you all scholarship students in your group? You all seem pretty bright to me."

"No, only me and Ewan. The others are bright and rich – well, rich parents, anyway – but they do their best not to go on about it. At Compton it's simply not the done thing to boast about Daddy's millions, you know!" Tamzin adopted a mock-aristocratic accent for the last sentence. She was a good actress, Mary thought. They both laughed.

"So are you still working on the Sand Bay case then?" Tamzin continued, "The papers seem to think the police haven't got very far." She said it sympathetically, rather than as an accusation. Mary noted that she avoided using the word "murder"; perhaps there were still things she didn't want to think about.

"No, we've split it with the Major Crime Unit in Bristol," she replied, "They're investigating the Sand Bay case, we're concentrating on Katya Czwisnjowski, the week before." If Tamzin didn't want murder spoken of, she was happy to oblige. She was also, she realised, happy to let Tamzin know that she was no longer working on the Sand Bay case, so she wouldn't think she had ulterior motives for talking to her. No harm in a bit of Force PR though, to help reassure the community. "We're making progress on both fronts," she added, "the press don't always know everything." Actually in this instance they pretty much did, but it was a lie in a good cause.

A voice came, loudly, from the next room.

"Tamzin!"

"Oops - that's me. I'm wanted!" Tamzin said, rising from her chair. Mary noticed that she did it gracefully, with a straight back, like a dancer. She'd clearly made good use of Compton School's performing arts facilities. "Nice talking to you."

"Nice talking to you too." said Mary. It had been.

"Might see you again if you come in regularly now. Amy - the girl I'm covering for - she's broken her leg, so she'll be off for a while."

"I'll look forward to it," replied Mary. She would.

"Me too - bye."

The soup was indeed good, and Mary did, indeed, enjoy it. Just as she was finishing she heard a beep from her bag; an incoming text. She was still on her lunch break, and would be, technically at least, until she got back to the office. She'd deal with it then; if it had been urgent they would have called her. Leaving the bag undisturbed, she picked up her knife and spread the last of the butter onto her roll.

Chapter 34

Back at the station Mary went to the DI's office, knocked and was beckoned in.

"You look cheerful," he said, glancing up at her, "I'll have to start having my lunch wherever it is you've been going."

"Anchor Head Cafe, Guv," she replied, "I can recommend the soup." She didn't mind telling him; there wasn't an earthly chance of him invading her solitude there. She pushed the door gently closed behind her, and sat down. The DI, recognising that this was something more substantial than a quick hello, put his pen down and gave her his attention.

"I wondered if there were any developments about Don," she said. If she'd looked cheerful a few seconds ago, it was fading quickly now. "It's, well, you know – difficult at home."

"I'm sure it is," replied the DI, sounding genuinely sympathetic. "This is off the record, right?"

"Of course, Guv."

The DI looked over Mary's shoulder, as if making sure his office door was fully closed.

"Tom Flanagan went out to see Don, as you know, and he got the impression that he wasn't hiding anything. He mentioned Slade to him, and apparently there was no reaction, apart from saying that he'd heard of him through you, and he was sorry to hear about him getting done over. We've checked the bank records, and they're all clean. Don hasn't received a payment from the Troshanis since September."

Not through his business account, anyway. It remained unsaid, but they both knew it.

"What about the phone records?"

The DI reached into his desk drawer and pulled out a thin file. Mary stared at it, unable to stop herself. She'd read hundreds, thousands of files like it in her career, written in them too. Except that this one was about her husband.

The DI saw her look, checked something in the file and quickly put it away.

"After you left the house on that Sunday there was no activity on Don's mobile," he said, "and he received one call on the landline, from another landline registered to a David and Christina Gaddely. Ring any bells?"

"Don's sister Tina," said Mary, glad to be able to clear at least one question up, "He said she'd rung. Apparently they've put her foot operation back again."

"Should have gone private, shouldn't she?"

"It would have saved a lot of upset, yes." Mary didn't resent the DI's flippancy; she knew he was just trying to lighten the mood.

"Look, Mary," he said, "The situation is we've looked for proof and there isn't any. It's all circumstantial, like saying Don could have done the High Street Bank job two years ago because he knew where it was and that there'd be money there."

"Not really, Guv," she countered, "Everyone knows where the bank is. Not many people knew about Michael Slade." Why was she doing this, arguing against the assumption of her husband's innocence? In fact she knew why – it was because she wanted him proved innocent beyond doubt, not just guilt unproven with suspicion, including her own, left lingering. At least she was certain of that.

The DI had his counter argument ready.

"Yes well, don't forget that there's no proof the Troshanis are even involved. Take them out of the picture and Don's completely in the clear, unless you think he's feeding information to some other gang of villains. Do you?"

"No Guv."

"No, I didn't think so," he said. Clever psychology, thought Mary, making her say she didn't suspect her husband, even if it was of something too far-fetched to be considered.

"Look," he continued, "I know what you want here, but you may not get it. You can't prove a negative, we've all been there often enough to know that. You may have to settle for there being no positives."

Unfortunately Mary couldn't quite settle for that. She took a deep breath.

"Do you think Don's involved, Guv? Straight answer, please." It was a lot to ask; she wasn't sure they'd worked together long enough for her to ask it.

The DI made eye contact and held it, as firmly as if he'd got an offender in an arm lock.

"No, I do not," he said slowly, "I don't think Don's got anything to do with the assault on Michael Slade. I know you think you're the empathy specialist round here, but Tom Flanagan's a pretty shrewd judge of people too, and he said that Don's reaction when he told him about Slade was 100 percent genuine, surprise and concern for Slade. And for you, as it happens. Your husband knows you better than you think; he had you sussed straight off, said you'd be blaming yourself for Slade's misfortune and loading yourself with guilt over it. Something to do with a Catholic upbringing, apparently."

Mary smiled. It was as good as she could have hoped for.

"Thanks, Guv."

"And when you do have something to feel guilty about I'll be the first to let you know. That's a promise."

"I'll rely on it."

The discussion was over. Mary got up and opened the door. Then, deciding to end on something more positive than the possible guilt of her husband, she turned back to the DI.

"By the way, I met another of the Sand Bay teenagers in the Anchor Cafe – Tamzin, the dark-haired one. She's working there for a while."

"Another one? They're following you around town, aren't they?"

"More like me invading their usual haunts. Did you know they were all at Compton School together?"

The DI chuckled to himself.

"No, but it makes sense. All that stiff upper lip business from the boys when they found the body. Plus the flash motor."

"I should have spotted it," said Mary.

"There goes that guilt thing again," replied the DI, "Don't be too hard on yourself. First, we saw them when they were half-frozen and still in shock, so not exactly their usual selves, and second it's not relevant anyway."

"No, I suppose not." In truth they should both have spotted it, since it was almost certainly in the background checks she'd had done on the teenagers, documents which had been pushed to the bottom of the pile by other priorities and remained there, still unread, more than a week later. Still, you couldn't read absolutely everything.

"Did Tamzin have anything new for us?"

"No, but she said Family Liason had been round and they'd been very helpful. Good spot, Guv."

The DI leaned back.

"Oh yes, she's the one who wouldn't go out, isn't she? Well I'm glad they did her some good. Are you likely to bump into her again?"

"Probably. She's covering for a girl who's broken her leg. If she does remember anything new I'll report straight back."

"Yes, well, just remember that Sand Bay is no longer our case. If by any chance young Tamzin, or anyone else, comes up with something, make sure it goes straight to Major Crime."

"Yes, Guv."

"With a copy to me."

"Yes, Guv." Mary smiled and closed the door behind her.

It was more than an hour later when Mary remembered the text that had arrived on her phone at lunchtime. It was unprofessional of her to have let it go that long, although in mitigation the person who sent her texts most often was Don, and she'd had various reasons for wanting to put off reading one from him. This one, it turned out, wasn't from him – not unless he'd moved to France since breakfast, as the sender's number began '+33'. The only French contact she had was a detective in Lyon who'd rung chasing a missing persons lead the previous year, and her phone didn't recognise it as her number.

When she opened the message she found something so strange that she had to do a double take. It began:

"U'd be surprised who Katya knew. If u want to find out, go to internet cafe in Orchard Place, visit this site:"

followed by a website address that began "http://bit.ly". After that came some stern warnings:

"Don't visit site from office or home, only cafe. Tell no-one, not even your boss. If you do, I'll know and u'll get no help."

The sender didn't leave a name.

Mary read the message through a third time. It could easily be a hoax – the police got dozens of them on every big case, and the teaser, "U'd be surprised who Katya knew", contained no proof that the sender had any real information. Her mobile number wasn't exactly a state secret either – she'd given it to plenty of people in the past couple of years, some of whom would no doubt enjoy winding her up now that the tabloids had branded the police 'clueless'. And yet you never knew. Plenty of major crimes had been solved through anonymous tipoffs over the years, and the French phone number and odd-looking website address might just be the modern equivalent of letters cut from newspapers and the postmark of a distant town.

Mary asked herself whether forty-five minutes spent chasing this up at the internet cafe off Alexandra Parade would be a worthwhile use of resources for the Czwisnjowski investigation. She looked down at the pile of reports awaiting her signature, all of them dead ends, and decided that it was. She turned and glanced at the DI's office. It was empty. She remembered that he was in a case review meeting with DCI Spence, probably not an enjoyable experience for either officer. She dropped the phone into her bag, grabbed her coat from the stand and headed out into the darkening November afternoon.

Chapter 35

In the centre of Weston-super-Mare, behind the Winter Gardens and the High Street shopping precinct, there was a warren of narrow streets, bounded by Alexandra Parade to the south and the Boulevard to the north. The buildings dated from the early 20th century, when development in Weston was booming. To the east, furthest from the sea, they were mainly terraces of small, flat-fronted houses, now sprouting satellite TV dishes fixed at tight angles to seek out the southern sky. Nearer the seafront the streets became filled with shops, of a kind fast disappearing from Britain's town centres: independents, these days increasingly nail bars, tattoo parlours and restaurants, but still including outlets for everything from home hardware to dog grooming supplies, model aircraft kits and computers. It was a land where the big coffee chains and mobile phone shops neither wanted nor needed to be, although with brown heritage signs already pointing visitors to the 'Orchard Meadows Shopping District', that might not be true for long.

In the daytime Mary enjoyed walking these streets, but there was another side to them, which she knew only too well. The clue was above the shop windows. This was a district where roll-down steel shutters adorned not only the off licences and convenience stores, but also the hairdressers and artist's supplies shops – most of the shops, in fact, in the streets nearest the seafront. On summer nights, when the pubs and clubs were full, it could get "lively", as one councillor had euphemistically put it. Mary's enduring recollection was of standing in a stab vest, beer glasses flying past her ear, looking out for a group of violent offenders on holiday from the North-West while two teams of uniformed officers, one bussed in from Bristol, loaded paralytic, bare-chested young men into custody vans on an industrial scale. Since then she'd avoided walking there alone after dark.

Orchard Place was a narrow lane on the southern edge of the central district, the nearest part to the police station but still further than Mary felt like walking on a damp November day, especially in heels and thin tights. She drove instead, banking on finding a parking place and getting one almost directly outside the internet café. The café was a small, dark place, previously a travel agents. Only a modest amount of conversion work had been done, with a counter serving coffee and muffins and the rest of the space given over to banks of computer screens and keyboards. To Mary's surprise it was almost full, mostly of people whom she guessed were from outside the UK, wearing microphone headsets and talking to video images of other people on their computer screens. It seemed that this was where the town's migrant hotel workers went to phone home.

The man behind the counter was in his 20s, slim build, around five foot nine with metal-framed glasses, brown hair in a pony tail and a sweatshirt advertising a rock band Mary had never heard of. He was using a computer himself, guiding an animated warrior through a gauntlet of medieval-looking (but laser-equipped) attackers on a laptop perched on the side of the counter. As Mary approached him, he hit a key and the screen froze.

"Hi," he said. His voice was soft, and Mary strained to hear it over the sounds of keyboards and voices into microphones. She was glad to find that she didn't recognise him professionally.

"Hello," she replied, "I want to use the internet, but I haven't been to an internet café before." That wasn't strictly true; she'd assisted in an obscene publications raid on another establishment, now closed, but hadn't hired a machine on that occasion. "How does it work?"

"Simple. You pay me, I switch the machine on. Two pounds for half an hour, three-fifty for an hour. You'll see a clock on screen telling you how long you've got left."

"OK, I'll just have half an hour please." She had no intention of staying any longer than that.

"No problem," he said, changing the screen display on his laptop to something more businesslike, "if you think you'll need the hour, let me know and I'll just charge you the three-fifty. Special winter offer."

"Thanks," said Mary, fishing for her purse. She found a two-pound coin and handed it to him.

"OK," he said, pressing some more keys, "those two by the window are free. The one on the left be OK? They're all pretty much the same."

"Yes, fine thanks." She'd have preferred something more secluded, nearer the back of the shop, but hopefully it wouldn't take long.

The man pressed some more keys. "Are you OK with Windows 7? If you want to use Skype we've got headsets but it's 50p extra to cover the bandwidth."

Mary didn't know what Skype was, but guessed it was what the other customers were doing.

"No, I just want to browse the Internet."

For some reason he seemed to find this faintly amusing, but quickly recovered his professionalism. "OK then, for browsing you've got IE9, FireFox and Chrome, we reboot with a quick scan after every session, histories are deleted too, so it's safe if you want to log on to something. " He looked suddenly embarrassed. "We have porn filters and they can't be switched off."

Mary smiled, to put him at his ease. She didn't particularly want him to remember her, although he almost certainly would. "That's all fine. The one on the left, yes?"

Mary sat down at the computer, which had burst into life as she'd approached it. Its location was less than ideal, right against the window, where anyone walking along the street could see her. She turned, saw the CCTV camera mounted high in the corner of the room, and had a sudden flush of anxiety. What if this was all a setup, designed to put her in a compromising position? She imagined the photographs of her guiltily typing away in a backstreet internet café, days before a large sum of money arrived in her – or Don's – account, or child pornography flooding onto her screen from the website she'd been told to log on to. Stranger things had happened, and there was no doubt that they were up against serious people now, where the Czwisnjowskis were concerned at least.

She told herself to calm down, in an inner voice that sounded disturbingly like the DI's. She was an experienced police officer following an anonymous tipoff, legitimate practice in any police force around the world. There was nothing illegal or unethical about using an internet café, and if an attempt was made to frame her, it would be seen as such by her senior officers. She hoped.

She double-clicked on the web browser icon, waited for it to load, then typed the website address in from the text message on her phone, getting it wrong twice before she finally hit the Enter key. There was a brief delay, then the screen display changed to a web page which even she could tell was crudely designed by modern standards, just some white text on a dark blue background. The message was clear enough, however:

PRINT THIS PAGE NOW. YOU WILL NOT BE ABLE TO VISIT IT AGAIN. DO NOT PRESS THE REFRESH

BUTTON, OR VISIT ANY OTHER PAGE, UNTIL YOU HAVE PRINTED THIS ONE.

Mary couldn't see the point of printing the web page, since it contained only the warning text, but she decided to keep going. She wasn't completely computer-illiterate, and knew how to find Print on the browser program's menus. When she clicked it, however, a message popped up: "Want to print? Please ask our staff for assistance." Thankfully this didn't turn out to be a major problem; a few minutes, and 30p, later, she'd collected two A4 sheets from the laser printer by the counter, and was studying it at her place by the window.

The printout didn't contain the text that was on the screen; instead there were details of how to log on to a different website, using a username ("BayWatcher") and password that had already been set up for her. There was also another username, that of the person who would, it said, contact her when she logged on: "TuringShroud".

Mary stared at the printout, her inner DI again telling her not to panic. It was hard to resist though. The whole situation – mystery texts, the internet café, strange usernames - was a disorienting mixture of fantasy adventure and real-life crime, the latter, she reminded herself, the professionally-executed murders of two young people. It could be anyone hiding behind the name "TuringShroud" – and anyone who'd set up the username "BayWatcher" for her, and would subsequently be able to use it to do things that would incriminate her. She was computer-literate enough to know that too.

And that name, "TuringShroud". It was obviously a reference to the Turin Shroud, the religious relic claimed by some to bear the image of Jesus Christ after the crucifixion. What, if anything, was the significance of that? An oblique reference to her own Catholic upbringing, by someone who knew her background? It was ringing bells for her, which frustratingly she couldn't quite get clear in her mind. Then it came: Mrs Czwisnjowski, from Torino – Turin.

The Czwisnjowskis would undoubtedly have IT people who could set something like this up. Would they go to this much trouble though, just to compromise a middle-ranking detective who wasn't even on the case any more (although they might not know that)? Perhaps they were hoping to get information from her. Or perhaps it was Mrs Czwisnjowski on her own, wanting to tell the truth about her husband's activities. She wouldn't be the first wife in that position, and she and Mary had sort-of bonded in the washroom at Bridewell Street that day. Or perhaps the bonding had been a ploy, to soften her up for this approach. But why had she spelt "Turin" wrongly, with a 'g' on the end? Just a bad typist? And why not "Torino", like she'd said in the washroom?

Mary stared at the printout some more. In her upper field of vision she could see the clock display at the bottom of the computer screen, counting down her remaining time; 18 minutes left. She had to make a decision now, then face whatever consequences came from it.

She was startled by a loud tapping on the window glass, a few inches beyond the computer screen. Her first thought was that she'd been spotted, but then again, perhaps not. More likely the tapping was for one of the hotel workers at the computers along the side wall of the cafe, a passing colleague reminding them they were due on shift soon.

She raised her head, and found herself looking at the smiling face of Doc Singh.

Chapter 36

"Detective Sergeant, what a pleasant surprise!" said the Doc as he came in through the shop door, "I called in to your office to say hello, but you were not there. Now my disappointment has been reversed!"

"Mary, please," Mary replied, doing her best to smile, "How are you, Doc?"

The Doc looked around the cafe, and on seeing the other occupants lowered his voice. "I am well, although I am in Weston on dispiriting business." His cheerful demeanour faded into regret as he spoke. "I have been giving my formal statement concerning the terrible attack on our friend Michael Slade. I confess to you that I feel guilty about it. As you know, Mr Slade was with me in the Criterion pub beforehand, and had consumed a significant quantity of alcohol. I feel that I should have delivered him safely home instead of leaving him to make his own way. But he was so insistent, you see, that he wished to walk. I could not persuade him to accept a lift."

"Don't blame yourself," said Mary, "I warned Michael not to tell anyone what he'd seen at Sand Bay, but he didn't take any notice of me either. That's probably why he was attacked."

"But you still blame yourself for it, do you not, Mary?"

"Is it that obvious?" She felt as if a big red 'Guilty' sign had appeared on her forehead.

"Your Detective Inspector told me. He is concerned for your welfare, says you should not feel responsible for other peoples' reckless behaviour, unless they are your DCs, in which case you are totally responsible." said the

Doc. They both smiled at the DI's uncomplicated approach to the chain of command, before the Doc added, "He was also wondering where you might be at this moment."

Now the 'Guilty' sign would be there, even if it hadn't been before.

"I'm just following a lead, a tipoff I was sent in a text message." She made it sound as commonplace as she could. "We get a lot of them on a big case like this. It's probably nothing, but we have to check every one."

"And this is a lead that cannot be followed from the CID office?" said the Doc. Suddenly she was reminded of DSI Kopacz, albeit in a much friendlier, less intimidating package.

"The text message said to do it from this café, and not to tell anyone," she said, realising as she spoke that she sounded as if she was reading from the pages of an adventure comic, not a CID officer's diary. She did her best to put it right. "I thought I should do as it said in the first instance, then hand it over to the Intelligence team if there looks to be anything in it."

"I'm sure that is the best approach", said the Doc encouragingly, "So how is it progressing – if it is not an intrusion to ask?"

Mary looked at the Doc's kindly face. He wasn't DSI Kopacz. He wasn't even a police employee. If she couldn't tell him, then short of rediscovering her faith and going to Confession she really was on her own.

"Actually I'm worried that it may be some kind of trap. I've been given the address of a website and a username to log in with, then I've got to wait to be contacted by someone." She was aware of being back in comic book territory, and that she was about to go deeper in. "This other person's username makes me think they may be connected with one of the suspects in the beach murders."

"So what is this username?"

Mary held up the printout and pointed to the name "TuringShroud".

"Katya Czwisnjowski's mother comes from Turin. She told me that. The only thing is, why the 'g' on the end? I think it may just be a typing error."

Mary had been looking at the printout, where her finger lay. As she turned back to the Doc, she saw that he was beaming from ear to ear.

"You need have no fear of this person, Mary, and in a moment I will explain why. First though, let me get us both a coffee from the gentleman behind the counter who, it seems, is so underemployed that he is obliged to engage in role playing games in order to relieve the monotony. It will do him immense good to interact with a living human being. White no sugar?"

The Doc returned with two surprisingly wholesome-looking cups of coffee, complete with saucers and small biscuits wrapped in cellophane.

"£1.50 each," he said, as he placed the saucers on the desk, "It would be £2.50 or more on the seafront, and of no better quality I'm sure. I shall come here again!" His cheerfulness seemed to have been entirely restored.

Mary sipped her coffee and found herself agreeing on its quality. However the clock on her screen now read 10 minutes; she needed to get going.

"So what about this username, Doc? You say it's safe? How do you know?"

"The username? Ah yes!" said the Doc, as if his mind had been on something else, "It has nothing to do with Turin, or any other European city. It is a reference to Alan Turing, mathematical genius and brilliant cryptographer, who led the team at Bletchley Park which broke the German Enigma codes in World War Two."

Of course. Mary recognised the name now, although

she knew virtually nothing about the person. She wondered if the breaking of an Enigma code had somehow led to her grandfather being captured and brought to Britain as a prisoner of war.

The Doc's smile faded. "After the war Turing should have been ennobled as a great national hero, like Viscount Montgomery of Alamein," he continued, "Instead he was chemically castrated and hounded to suicide because of his homosexuality. It is one of the more shameful episodes in this country's recent history, not to mention a tragic waste of one of its most brilliant minds."

"That's terrible," said Mary. It was, although thinking about the attitudes that bubbled just below the surface in one or two of her fellow officers, she wasn't sure how much things had changed.

"It has, at least, been officially recognised as such now," said the Doc, then, his face brightening again, "and now Turing has been recognised here too – the man who broke the Enigma an enigma himself, shrouded in the mystery of an online username. It is poetic! And just what I would expect from a brilliant mind of today."

Neither of them needed to say which brilliant mind the Doc was thinking of. Both, it seemed, sensed that it would be better not to.

"But why the secrecy?" asked Mary instead, "Is he trying to protect himself?"

"No, he is protecting you, Mary. My son is very high-powered in IT, and from what he tells me I have no doubt that TuringShroud would know exactly where you have logged on from, could prevent anyone from tracing anything back to him, and would know if they tried. By forcing you to do things his way, he is making sure you can honestly say you had no choice but to keep this contact a secret, even from your superiors."

It sounded a good plan, but as Mary quickly realised,

it had developed a flaw.

"But what about you, Doc? You know now, don't you?"

The Doc put his coffee cup down. "We doctors are accustomed to maintaining confidentiality. You are an experienced officer, for whose judgement I have the greatest respect. If you feel it is in the interests of justice for your contact with TuringShroud to remain privileged information then I shall keep it as such until you personally tell me otherwise. You can depend on that."

She didn't doubt for a second that she could.

"Thanks, Doc."

"You are very welcome, Mary," said the Doc, sipping quickly from his coffee then putting it down again, "and now I must leave even this excellent coffee as I have an appointment that I must not fail to keep." He picked up his oversized briefcase. "Good luck with TuringShroud – I would say give him my regards, but best to keep your conversations strictly to business, I think. Goodbye!"

"Bye Doc – and thanks again," said Mary as she watched the Doc make his way to the door.

Mary typed in the web address from her printout, and logged in as BayWatcher. She found herself at what she recognised as a control panel screen; as before, the design was curiously old-fashioned, like the online intelligence systems that had preceded HOLMES. At the top it said "Welcome, Baywatcher"; below, to the left, was a panel headed "Your friends". There was only one entry: TuringShroud.

She'd barely had time to take it all in when a message popped up in the middle of the screen.

"TuringShroud wants to chat. Allow?"

Mary clicked the OK button. The central area of the screen became marked off by a white border, while in the friends panel TuringShroud's name was now displayed in bold text with an asterisk next to it. At the bottom of the screen was an area with a flashing cursor, for her to type into. Before she'd had a chance to start typing, however, a message appeared in the central area.

"TuringShroud: Where have you been? I txtd you ages ago."

As greetings went it was on the blunt side, although it meant that TuringShroud was getting back to his normal self, which was good news.

"BayWatcher: Working on a murder case. Two actually." Mary shot the message back at him as quickly as it came into her head. She might not have been comfortable with computers, but she could type, the legacy of an evening course her parents had forced on her in the belief that it was her only chance of obtaining gainful employment while waiting for a husband. It would have been an old-fashioned attitude in the late 1970s; in fact it had happened in the early 1990s.

"TuringShroud: Oh. Fair enough, I suppose."

Thank you, Mrs Gardener of the Whitestone Secretarial College (and sorry I didn't do the exam). The prospect of life as a typist had been one reason why she'd joined the police; now she was grateful to her typing tutor once again. She'd need quick keyboard skills to hold her own with TuringShroud.

"BayWatcher: How are you?"

"TuringShroud: Physically functional. How are you?"

"BayWatcher: OK."

There was no immediate reply, but "TuringShroud is writing a message" began flashing below the message box. After a few seconds a new message appeared.

"TuringShroud: Good. Here are the rules. You have no idea who I am and it stays that way. If you tell your Detective Inspector or anyone else about me, I will know – believe me – and our contact will stop. Is that understood?"

"BayWatcher: Yes." This was TuringShroud in his natural habitat, 100 percent confident.

"TuringShroud: You can trust Dr Singh though, since it seems he already knows."

He was watching her! She turned and saw the CCTV camera in the corner panning guiltily away.

"TuringShroud: LOL! Sorry, but I had to be sure you weren't bringing reinforcements. And please don't go arresting Phil behind the counter – he doesn't know anything about it. They remote their camera to the alarm company, and once it's on the Net it's in my territory."

Mary didn't doubt that. Time to get back onto her territory though.

"BayWatcher: Who did Katya know then?" No point in beating about the bush.

"TuringShroud: Look at this, and see if you recognise her:"

A web address appeared under TuringShroud's message. Mary was about to click on it when the clock at the bottom of the screen turned red, and a message popped up.

"You have two minutes left. Please ask for assistance if you wish to remain online."

Mary delved frantically into her bag and found her purse.

"BayWatcher: Time running out – have to pay for more. Please wait."

"TuringShroud: OK."

Mary rushed to the counter, disturbing a couple of customers as she brushed past their backs. Phil was still engrossed in his game but large headphones now covered his ears. She reached over the counter and tapped him lightly on the arm. He turned and lifted one headphone away from his ear. She grabbed a £10 note from her purse and put it on the counter.

"More time please – take it out of that."

"Half hour, hour?" he asked, pressing keys on his laptop.

"An hour – and keep it coming," said Mary, already on her way back to her computer.

"BayWatcher: Sorry about that – I've booked another hour, so we should be OK."

"TuringShroud: Try the link."

Mary clicked the web address, and another web browser window appeared on the computer screen, overlapping the first. The page was the same plain design, but instead of text panels it contained just a single photograph, of three young women sitting on a sofa in what looked like a bar or club. After a few seconds the first web browser window came to the forefront again, overlapping the photograph.

"TuringShroud: Ignore the one on the left (although the photo comes from her Flickr account). Do you recognise the one in the middle?"

Mary clicked back onto the photograph. She had seen the face before, but she just couldn't place her. The woman – more a girl, really - looked as if she was having a good time; heavily made up, hair untidy, face shiny, eyes slightly glazed from alcohol and perhaps something else. She reminded Mary of someone she'd seen in a different context, but she couldn't remember that either.

"TuringShroud: Got it yet?"

"BayWatcher: No – tell me."

"TuringShroud: Amelia Jane Foster."

Mary had mouthed the words to herself even as "TuringShroud is writing a message" had stopped flashing. Amelia Foster, the second Bristol student murder victim. She'd only seen the photo of her that had been released to the press and stuck to the whiteboard at Bridewell Street; a very different young woman, neat, clear-eyed and studious. She was annoyed with herself for not making the connection more quickly, especially in front of TuringShroud.

"BayWatcher: What's this got to do with Katya though?"

"TuringShroud: Look at the one on the right."

Mary clicked on the photo again. The face of the woman on the right wasn't visible, just long tresses of dark hair where she'd turned towards her two friends.

"BayWatcher: You can't see her face."

"TuringShroud: Look at what she's wearing then."

When Mary clicked back to the photo she found, to her surprise, that it was now accompanied by a second photograph, underneath it on the screen. She recognised the new image straight away; it was the picture of Katya's clothes they'd released to the press when they were trying to establish her identity. Mary's perusal was cut short as the chat window forced itself to the front again.

"TuringShroud: Same skirt, different top, same shoes. That's a 66 percent match before we get on to the jewellery."

Which would no doubt move the percentage even higher up the scale. Mary wasn't going to waste time underestimating TuringShroud's observational skills. Looking at the photograph again she could see now that it was Katya – perhaps not clearly enough for evidence, but enough to use as a lead. And a lead was what it was.

"TuringShroud: The question is, what were Amelia and Katya doing drinking together, when Katya left Bristol university in the summer, and Amelia didn't start there until the autumn?"

Mary pulse had quickened. A link between the beach murders and the student killings! They hadn't even considered the possibility. Quickly, however, her professional training began to dampen down the excitement. Katya had stayed in Bristol until the start of October, well after Amelia had begun her first term.

Bristol wasn't that big a city, and students tended to gravitate to a few 'in' places. They could easily have ended up sitting next to each other in a bar by pure coincidence.

"BayWatcher: Any idea where and when the picture was taken?"

"TuringShroud: The Green Room Tavern, Old Market, Bristol, October 15th, according to Flickr."

Mary felt her pulse rate rise again. If the date on the picture was correct, then it had been taken after Katya had supposedly gone back to live in Poland. If it was pure coincidence, and purely innocent, then why hadn't Katya shown up on passport records re-entering the country? Even so, they'd need something else to make a strong case for anything more than faulty immigration records.

"TuringShroud: There's something else. Why was Katya in disguise, here and when she was buried?"

"BayWatcher: What?"

"TuringShroud: Look at this."

Another web address appeared under the message. Mary clicked on it. Another web browser window opened, this time showing three separate photographs. The first two were of the same, extremely well-groomed young woman. In the first she was power-dressed in a way that Mary had only seen in person while on holiday once in Rome; what looked like a Chanel suit, expensive but tasteful jewellery, real Jimmy Choo shoes. In the second she was dressed casually, but in clothes that probably cost almost as much as her first outfit; Ralph Lauren sweatshirt, figure-hugging designer jeans, gold toe-post sandals that looked as if they cost a few hundred Euros. In both pictures her blonde hair fell perfectly to her shoulders, while her skin had the perma-tan of the seriously rich. The third photograph was an edited version of the one from Bristol, showing just the girl on the right with her face obscured by her dark hair; the cheap cotton skirt and the worn canvas pumps. While there might still be some doubt about who this woman was, there could be none about the glamorous one in the first two pictures – it was Katya Czwisnjowski.

"BayWatcher: Where did the pictures on the left come from?"

"TuringShroud: A Polish social networking site. It's private, for bright young things to swap party invites, that sort of thing."

"BayWatcher: And Katya was a member?"

"TuringShroud: Yes. Interesting contrast, don't you think? She might just have done the power-dressing thing for work, then liked to go heavily downmarket (and dye her hair) when she was relaxing. But she's much less likely to have two types of leisure image, especially ones as different as the second and third pictures. I'd say that would leave the poor girl with serious identity confusion issues, wouldn't you?

Mary could almost hear a strange chortling sound coming across the Internet.

"TuringShroud: Unless one of them wasn't her real identity, but a fake one she was putting on. What do you think?"

Mary was getting used to the online chat system now. It gave her time to think like a police officer, and remember her CID training; don't jump straight to conclusions.

"BayWatcher: I think she adopted a different persona when she was in Bristol, one that made her look poorer than she really was. That doesn't necessarily mean anything though. Quite a lot of students from rich backgrounds do it, so they'll fit in."

"TuringShroud: At Bristol Uni? LOL!"

"BayWatcher: OK, perhaps not there." He had a point.

At Bristol they were more likely to put iPad 3 stickers on their iPad 2s, as a local DS had once put it.

"TuringShroud: Also, she's a bit off piste in Old Market, isn't she? Amelia too, for that matter."

TuringShroud's habit of spotting things just before she did could quickly become annoying. Mary's Bristol geography wasn't great, but she knew that the Old Market district, sandwiched between St Paul's and the redeveloped wasteland of St Phillips, wasn't the kind of place that cafe-bar loving Uni students tended to frequent.

"TuringShroud: If you ask me, she's working."

He really should be a DCI (sorry, Guv).

"BayWatcher: What, as a prostitute?"

"TuringShroud: Could be, although I don't think she'd be able to afford Versace jeans on the money she'd make turning tricks in Old Market, do you?"

The strange chortling noise seemed to come across the Internet again. This time though, Mary was ahead of the game.

"BayWatcher: No, you're right. I'd say it was more likely retail management."

"TuringShroud: Eh?"

"BayWatcher: Never mind."

It was ungenerous of her not to share the explanation with him, but she sensed that the advantage would only rarely be hers in their conversations, and wanted to savour it. Also, she still wasn't sure where anything she said might end up.

"TuringShroud: Ah, I see what you mean."

Of course he did. But she hadn't spelt it out for him, and she hadn't disclosed any of the intelligence Kopacz had mentioned about the Czwisnjowskis' drug trafficking. Her conscience could, at least, be clear on that. Now, however, came the difficult bit.

"BayWatcher: This is brilliant, but I can't present it to

my superiors as my own work. They'd never believe I went out and found it on the Internet." She remembered the DI describing what he'd do if she had any contact with Michael. "They'd know I'd got it from you, and I'd be in serious trouble."

No reply. No "TuringShroud is writing a message" either.

"BayWatcher: Could you send it directly to them? DSI Kopacz at the Major Crime Investigation Unit, I can give you his email address."

"TuringShroud: Yes, I can do that. But I wanted you to have the credit, Mary."

"BayWatcher: I know, and I really appreciate it."

"TuringShroud: I think we work well together, don't you?"

"BayWatcher: Yes, I do." Don't you dare let a lump come to your throat, Detective Sergeant.

"TuringShroud: I'll send it by anonymous email, shall I?"

"BayWatcher: Will that mean they can't tell where it came from?"

"TuringShroud: Not even GCHQ will be able to tell. Seriously."

She didn't doubt it.

"TuringShroud: I'm not going to sue the police, you know."

Mary checked that the CCTV camera was still pointing at the other side of the room. If she was going to fight back tears then she didn't want him to see her doing it.

"BayWatcher: They're worried your wife might."

"TuringShroud: She won't. She's had lawyers telling her to, but I said I'd move away altogether if she did. My mistakes, my decision."

"BayWatcher: We don't think Jolene Buller had anything to do with it." Well into instant suspension territory now, but she owed it to him, and to Jolene.

"TuringShroud: Of course not. She's a good soul is Jolene, and not half as daft as people think she is. Too strict about what counts as Country and Western on Karaoke nights, but that's her father's doing. Brilliant singer, BTW – you should see her."

"BayWatcher: I'll try to."

"TuringShroud: Perhaps we could all go, when this has all been sorted out."

"BayWatcher: I'd really like that."

"TuringShroud: Bye then Mary. Best not to spend too long logged in – wires have ears, you know!" The chortling sound seemed to come again, although it might have been just in Mary's imagination.

"BayWatcher: Bye TuringShroud."

Mary sat on the sofa with Don, watching a reality TV show about people in Essex who were too obese to clean their houses, or something like that. That afternoon she'd got back to the office, told the DI that she'd been re-checking the central area for missed CCTV cameras, and then had to say nothing to anyone about the biggest breakthrough so far in the four recent murders – two of the victims, in what had previously been assumed to be unconnected cases, sitting in a bar together, ten days after one of them was supposed to have left the country, wearing the clothes she'd been killed in, which now appeared to have been an alter ego disguise. It had been a tough few hours.

She desperately wanted to talk about it now, to let it out, give voice to her ideas on what it might all mean. She wouldn't be able to talk about it to her fellow officers until it became common knowledge, following TuringShroud's email. And yet it was important to do it while the information was still new, while the connections it triggered were still there in her subconscious, waiting to be snatched and hauled to the surface.

She turned to Don. Catching her in his peripheral vision, he turned to her.

"Don," she said, "can I...".

"Oh yeah - there's something you'd better know, Love," he interrupted her, without quite turning his full attention away from a large couple whose kitchen was stacked high with old newspapers, "I've got to go to the Troshani place on Friday, up at Grove Park. Post-installation safety check – tightening up the jubilee clips, old Tommy used to call it." He smiled at the recollection of his first boss, who'd taken him on as an apprentice. "That's not a problem, is it?"

It wasn't a challenge, as it might have been a few months – weeks – earlier. Instead he seemed genuinely concerned that it might cause her embarrassment.

"No, not at all," she replied.

"They didn't seem keen on it. Wanted to know if it was absolutely necessary, asked if I could put it off until a more convenient time. I told them they'd lose their fire certificate if it wasn't done. That seemed to change their minds."

"I should hope so."

"Any news on that Michael Slade chap? Has he left hospital yet?"

Mary looked at her husband; running slightly to fat now, the shirt over his stomach rising and falling as he breathed, his face lined, but still Don, smelling slightly of his day's work, the heavy masculine smell that had attracted her so much when she'd first met him. The man she knew so well; the one with the file in the DI's desk drawer.

"No, nothing," she said, "It's all gone a bit quiet, to be honest."

"Don't worry," Don replied, resting his hand briefly

on hers, "Something'll turn up." On the screen the large woman was showing the presenter her bathroom. Don screwed his face up. "That's disgusting!" he said, and pressed the button for the on-screen TV guide.

Chapter 37

The CID squad room was already buzzing when Mary arrived the following morning. Seeing her, the DI called her into his office.

"Have you heard?"

"Heard what, Guv?"

"Major Crime got a tipoff by email, a real game-changer. It turns out that Katya Czwisnjowski was drinking buddies with one of the student murder victims, Amelia Foster. Photograph of them together in a pub in Old Market, dated 15th October."

"Just before they were both killed."

"Indeed. Tech Services are checking the image file now to see if it's been faked, but if it has then it's been done very well." The DI took a sheet of paper from the pile on his desk and gave it to her. It was a printout of the first picture that TuringShroud had shown her the previous day.

"I assume it's Katya on the right," said Mary, "but how do we know? Her face is covered." She realised that she was actively faking a lack of prior knowledge, and to her DI. It felt wrong. She tried to console herself with the fact that the secrecy was at TuringShroud's insistence, but she wasn't entirely convinced.

"The clothes are the same as the ones we found her in," said the DI, "jewellery too. Build, height, hair all match. We're 99 percent certain."

"And who's the girl on the left?" This one she didn't know; it hadn't come up in the online conversation.

"Nyesha Rose. She's from Barton Hill, apparently, so unlike the others she wasn't far from home. The picture was originally posted on her Flickr account, although it seems she'd taken it off the system. Major Crime are picking her up."

Mary began to see other reasons, besides her welfare, why TuringShroud wanted his existence kept secret. On the other hand, if the picture had been removed from public display then that would at least save the Force the embarrassment of explaining why they hadn't found it earlier.

"She's quite a looker, Guv." She was, indeed. Even sitting down, she was clearly taller than the other women, slender limbs extending from a dress that clung tightly to her figure and seemed to radiate its own bright Caribbean light. Her hair was cropped short; underneath it her face looked like a work of art carved in dark, polished stone, beautiful curves to her cheeks and lips, long-lashed eyes in perfect symmetry. She'd have given the young Sophia Czwisnjowski a run for her money in the glamour stakes.

"Yes, she certainly is, quite beautiful," said the DI. It was unlike him to comment on the attractiveness or otherwise of members of the opposite sex, but Nyesha was an exceptional case.

"Do we know who sent the picture in?" asked Mary. More deceit, but at least she was protecting her source now, leaving the door open to further assistance from him.

"No – anonymous email, and in this case that means properly anonymous. The message came from Slovenia, but that wasn't where it started out, and Tech haven't been able to trace it any further back. They're talking about asking the spook squad in Cheltenham for help."

They needn't bother, thought Mary.

"So what does it all mean?"

"Quite a lot, it seems," said the DI, "The lovely Ms Rose is a known associate of the gang that runs most of the drugs in central Bristol. Very nasty bunch, by all accounts. She's even got her own slot on the NCA filing system."

Mary took a moment to digest the possibilities.

"So it could be the Czwisnjowskis and this Bristol gang joining up to muscle in on the Troshanis' patch? That sounds a bit one-sided."

"It would be. Perhaps enough to make the Troshanis top Czwisnjowski's daughter out of desperation. Bridewell Street are refining their theories on that as we speak. Then of course there's the Foster girl – her being there is too much to be a coincidence, especially as Katya Czwisnjowski was supposed to be living back in Gdansk when that picture was taken. Major Crime are treating it as a link between the beach and student murders, although exactly what kind of link remains to be seen."

"They don't think the Troshanis killed Amelia Foster, do they?"

"All theories given due consideration at the moment. They're hoping Ms Rose will be able to help them with some of it, but she wasn't at home when they called round yesterday evening. Neighbours said they'd seen her the day before though, so hopefully she isn't buried in the sand somewhere between here and Portishead."

"No, hopefully not, Guv." Mary was beginning to find discussing the photograph and its implications hard work, even when they weren't on aspects of it which required her to conceal prior knowledge. To her relief, the DI rose from his chair and began to collect the papers from the file together.

"Right, well Bridewell Street is where I'm off to now. Strategy meeting, including the head of the Drug Squad. Apparently she wasn't best pleased to discover that the daughter of one of Europe's biggest traffickers had been on her patch and no-one had told her. I imagine sparks may fly."

Mary smiled. The head of the Drugs Squad, the

Force's most senior female officer, wasn't known for suffering such things gladly.

The DI looked suddenly awkward.

"It's just me going to this meeting, I'm afraid. I'm only there because I've been effectively hands-on SIO, otherwise it'd be DCI Spence. Other than that it's Top Brass only – I'm the token pavement-pounder." The self-deprecation was his way of letting her down gently over not being included. In fact, while she did feel a slight, reflexive irritation, it was heavily outweighed by relief at not having to face being grilled by the Force's biggest heavyweights while trying to avoid any slip-ups about her conversation with TuringShroud. In particular she didn't want to face DSI Kopacz yet. There was something she wanted to find out before the DI left though.

"That's fine, Guv – rather you than me." She paused, looking at the file as he put it in his briefcase. "Did the anonymous emailer send any other pictures?"

The DI looked surprised by the question.

"No – should they have?" His expression changed to one of dawning comprehension. "I'm not keeping anything from you, if that's what you're thinking. One picture, that's all that came through, along with details of the date and place it was taken, and the names of the three women. You want to get that paranoia looked at – it's getting worse."

"No, I didn't think that," said Mary, aware that she'd probably given him precisely the impression that she had, "I just wondered, that's all."

"Well, not unless Major Crime are keeping them from me," he said, snapping his briefcase closed, "and I'm not going to dwell on that possibility because O, that way madness lies."

"Pardon?"

"King Lear, Act 3, Scene 4. GCSE English, Grade B, one of my finer achievements." He took his coat from its hook. "I'll be back this afternoon, not sure when, I expect it'll depend on how long DCS Palmer takes to express her dissatisfaction at the ineffectiveness of intelligence sharing between operational units. See you later."

"Have a good time, Guv," she said as he disappeared across the office.

Mary went to her desk, fired up her computer and sat thinking while it went through its startup routine. Why hadn't TuringShroud sent Major Crime the pictures of Katya in her designer outfits? It left her in an impossible position. The pictures were evidence that Katya had been leading a double life and, crucially, that her parents were complicit in it. Yet no-one in the Force besides her had seen them, and she couldn't say anything about them without exposing the whole TuringShroud business.

She could have cursed TuringShroud for the stupid secrecy thing, except that it wasn't his fault, except that it was, for blabbing about what he'd seen at Sand Bay, except that it still might be hers for blabbing to Don, and was anyway for getting him involved in the first place. That way, as the DI said, madness lies. She thought of going straight back to the Internet Café, but then thought better of it. TuringShroud was no fool; he probably had his reasons for not sending the other pictures, possibly technical ones connected with avoiding the scrutiny of the 'spook squad'. He might send them later. Time to show some trust in his judgement.

She typed her password into the computer. The more she thought about it, the less disappointed she was at not being in the strategy meeting with the DI. Major Crime would take over the whole thing now, treating the beach and student murders as one big case, probably running it from Bridewell Street. That was if the National Crime Agency didn't muscle in and run it from somewhere else. The DI's role at the meeting would be to say "Yes, sir" and "Of course, Ma'am" to instructions for handing over the material, such as it was, that Weston CID had on Katya's murder. Not much fun, or professional fulfilment, in that.

Again she found herself looking forward to a time beyond the beach murders, when things were back to normal and they could concentrate on the small-scale crime that bubbled below the surface of a seaside town; "ABC', as the DI called it - Assault, Break-ins and Car theft. This time she found herself resisting it less. She remembered a song her father had liked, by a British pop group from the 1960s: "Gasoline Alley Bred". It was about someone giving up on their attempt to get away from their roots, instead going back where they belonged, on the wrong side of the tracks. It seemed to her that Weston was full of people who'd made that choice; she just hadn't, until now, thought that she might be one of them.

The Constabulary logo filled her computer screen. A few mouse clicks later she was in HOLMES, tidying up the loose ends of their investigation into the beach murders.

Mary felt like spending her lunch break in the open air, but the weather dictated otherwise. So she drove to Birnbeck Pier, pulled her coat tightly round her and made her way down the steps towards the Anchor Head cafe. As the cove came into view she found herself hoping not just that they'd have more of yesterday's soup, but that Tamzin would be there too. Talking to her, and to Ellie, had taught her a lot about Generation Y, not least that they were actually quite normal human beings, and that it wasn't impossible for her to communicate, and even empathise, with them. She was keen to have another go.

Her luck was in; as she entered the cafe Tamzin

appeared from the inner room, carrying some empty plates, smiling as she saw her.

"Hello again," Tamzin said, "can't keep away, eh? Must be the soup."

"It's very good. Is it still on?"

"Winter vegetable today, but just as good. Pauline's mum makes it – genuine Old Somerset recipe, apparently." She said the last bit in a convincing stage Yokel accent, causing them both to smile. Their mirth, however, was interrupted by an even more authentic-sounding regional accent coming loudly from the kitchen.

"Hey – don't you go taking the Mickey out of my mother, young lady, or her soup. You're not too old to go over my knee, you know!"

Tamzin and Mary both put their hands over their mouths to suppress their laughter, Mary recovering her composure first.

"Sounds great - I'll have that then."

"Coming up," said Tamzin through a fit of giggles, "I'll bring it through."

Mary got the window table again, although with the rain beginning to beat more insistently against the glass, and the mist in the channel developing into fog, there wasn't much to see. After a few minutes Tamzin came in with her soup, placing everything carefully on the table as she'd done the day before. Mary watched the precision of each operation, as Tamzin's slender fingers placed a knife by her side plate, the spoon by her bowl. It reminded her of the way they laid the instruments out before an autopsy.

"Terrible weather, isn't it?" Tamzin said, looking briefly at the rain-spattered glass.

"Yes," said Mary, putting down her spoon, "I was hoping to get some fresh air up by the old pier, but it's a bit too fresh – well, more cold and wet really."

"It's been dead in here all morning," said Tamzin, looking around at the empty room, "Pauline's talking about closing up until the new year if it doesn't pick up." She slid into the chair next to Mary's, that dancer's movement again, her back bolt upright, her legs folding like the mechanism of a precision-engineered machine. "That wouldn't exactly be helpful, with the state of my finances. I'm well skint."

"That bad, eh?" said Mary sympathetically. She realised that what her generation would count as sharing private concerns was just the teenagers' habit – principally among girls, it had to be said – of talking about themselves in extraordinary detail to anyone who'd listen. Even so, she was pleased that Tamzin had shared this; it was a nice change from people being cagey with her.

"No worse than most of us who haven't got trust funds," Tamzin said, not entirely without bitterness, "That's the downside of being a scholarship student – you see your friends all going off to winter in Barbados, or work as an unpaid intern in Daddy's firm with a £2,000 a month allowance from Mummy, and you're left behind."

Mary could see her point – having your face rubbed in other peoples' ultra-privileged lifestyles couldn't be much fun. Unfortunately she couldn't think of much to say except to offer more sympathy.

"You were going to go off with Ellie and the others on VSO, weren't you? It's a shame that fell through."

"Yeah, it is. Still, no point in crying over spilt juice drink with added vitamins, as my mum always says." Tamzin did a theatrical shrug of her shoulders. "Just got to make it through to September, then I'll be off to uni where I can dig myself into debt for the next thirty years."

Mary found herself quite keen to move the

conversation on. Much as she liked Tamzin, there was, it turned out, a limit to her powers of empathy with Generation Y.

"So what are you going to do at university? Drama, dance?"

Tamzin looked surprised, though not upset. "What makes you think I'd do Drama?" she asked, as if genuinely interested in why anyone would reach such a conclusion.

"Well you're very good at accents," said Mary, instantly realising how much she sounded like an encouraging aunt, but committed now, "and you move very gracefully, like a dancer."

Mary was relieved to see that Tamzin seemed pleased by her explanation. Even so, she'd clearly had beginner's luck with her first couple of Generation Y conversations; this was proving trickier.

"I did Drama GCSE," Tamzin said, "it was pretty much compulsory at Compton – you should see the Performing Arts Centre they've got, it's incredible. Not A Level though. I'm a chemist, me, like Ewan - only not as good as him, of course."

"Ewan? I thought he was a physicist?"

"He's that too, and a biologist and a mathematician," replied Tamzin, as if weary of listing Ewan's achievements. "Brilliant at all of them, four A*s which is why he can push the limits and still go sailing into Cambridge. I got a mere three As, so I'm off to Sussex. I'm happy with that though. It's still in the top 10 for Chemistry, and I'll still be by the sea. It's in the blood, you see - my great-granddad worked on the steamers between here and Cardiff, the White Funnel Fleet. I've got pictures of him..."

"How do you mean 'push the limits'?" Mary interrupted her, more sharply than she'd meant to. She didn't want to be rude to Tamzin, didn't want to end the brief interlude when she'd been just a civilian having lunch and a chat. A corner of her brain marked 'Police Officer', operating autonomously, had done it for her.

"Sorry?" Tamzin looked confused by the interruption. To keep the interlude going, and perhaps their developing friendship with it, all Mary had to say was "Oh nothing. The White Funnel Fleet? I've heard of them."

"You said Ewan pushed the limits. At school? What did he do?"

For a second Tamzin gave her a cool, appraising look, the chatty, self-absorbed schoolgirl replaced by the privately-educated science undergraduate. Mary felt a pang of loss, then told herself to grow up. She was a professional too.

"He got in with the wrong people for a while, but he got away with it. Wayward genius and all that."

"Do they have the wrong people at places like Compton?"

Tamzin smiled. "Of course they do – where do you think their parents get the money from to pay the fees? In a fairer world your lot would have half of them under arrest for fraud or insider trading. It's in the blood!"

Mary smiled back, not quite the smile they'd shared about Pauline's mum's soup a few minutes earlier. Before she could say anything, however, the voice of Pauline herself came bellowing in from the kitchen.

"Tamzin? I've got a job for you!"

Tamzin rose from her chair, back straight, legs propelling her upright.

"Sorry, I'd better go." she said, embarrassment blended with relief.

"Of course."

Mary finished her soup in silence, then checked her phone for messages, collected her things together and left the room. Pauline was at the counter, Tamzin behind her in the kitchen area, scrubbing away at what looked like a large soup pot. She looked up as Pauline said goodbye to Mary, waved a goodbye herself.

Outside the rain had lessened to a chilling drizzle. It would be dark by 5pm, and the light already seemed to be fading. As Mary reached the first flight of steps up to the Birnbeck terrace, she heard a voice behind her.

"Mary!" It was Tamzin, still wearing her apron, running awkwardly in her indoor shoes.

Mary turned and waited for her, expecting her to announce that there'd been a mistake at the till, or that she'd left something behind.

"There was something else," Tamzin said breathlessly as she reached her, "That night at Sand Bay, Ewan said he saw a black pickup truck ahead of us, going round the bend in the Kewstoke Road. I think he got that wrong. He'd had quite a lot to drink, and some other things - well, you know." She looked awkwardly down at the path, then up again to Mary, "I was sitting behind him and I saw something too, but it wasn't a pickup truck. It was more like a van, you know, with doors in the back. And it wasn't black - it was dark, blue or grey, I couldn't tell because of the yellow street light, but not black."

Mary gave herself a moment to take in what Tamzin had said. She was glad of the cold air forcing her awake. Even so, she proceeded on autopilot.

"Did you get any of the registration number?"

"Not really - I think there may have been an 'A' in it."

"How sure are you about this, Tamzin?"

"Completely - well, pretty much. I know, I should have said something earlier, but Ewan seemed so sure of himself and he can get - you know - uptight if people contradict him, especially me. We were at primary school together. I think I remind him of his roots too much."

"Well you've told me now, and that's what matters. We'll probably have to ask you to come in and change your statement though – will that be OK?"

"Yes, of course."

"OK, leave it with me. And thanks, Tamzin."

"All right, bye," said Tamzin, then turned and walked back towards the café.

Chapter 38

Mary sat in her car, facing up the hill towards the toll road and Sand Bay. The rain had become harder again, just as she'd got inside; the windows were already misting up, and she could barely make out the old ruined pier through the glass on her left. Still she sat though, with the engine off, mulling over what she'd just learned.

Ewan the all-round scientific genius, who got in with the wrong people but got out again with his prospects intact, who got too drunk (or stoned) to tell a black pickup truck from a dark-coloured van. Suddenly it was it all about him, or was it just Tamzin making it seem that way, bringing everything round to him? Something, or nothing? It was the question a detective faced over and over again on every case. She could do with a second opinion, and she knew where she might be able to get one, perhaps solving another mystery at the same time. She started the engine, allowed the air conditioning to begin clearing the glass, and pulled out into the road.

Her drive took her from one café to another, back across the seafront, through the narrow central streets to Orchard Place. Phil, behind the counter, removed his headphones as she came in.

"Hi," he said, "More time?"

"Yes please," said Mary, putting her bag on the counter and rummaging in it for her purse.

"The same machine's free from yesterday if you want that one," he said, nodding towards the PC in the window.

"I'd prefer one of these, if that's OK," Mary replied,

gesturing towards the three empty seats on the side wall, facing away from the street. Clearly it was work time in the hotels.

"Sure. How long? We've got a special offer on today – buy an hour, get a free coffee."

"An hour then. Your coffee's very good."

"Thanks. We like to create a positive user experience here. That's three-fifty then – number one, in the corner, same config as yesterday. I'll bring your coffee over if you like."

"Thanks." It seemed she was getting the regular customer treatment. Shame she wasn't planning on making this a regular thing.

Mary sat at the table as the screen came to life. Looking up, she saw the CCTV camera panning until it was at full stretch, looking along and down the side wall onto her. She hoped the movement wasn't just random. Behind her, she heard a 'clink' as Phil put a spoon in her saucer. She double-clicked on the web browser icon, saw it launch into its home page screen, and left it there; she didn't want him remembering any usernames or web addresses from his coffee delivery run.

Phil arrived and placed her coffee on the desk, appearing quite scrupulous about not looking at her screen. She waited until he was back behind the counter, then typed in the web address from the slip of paper she'd retrieved from her bag.

Mary quickly realised that her new location had its own drawbacks; she felt exposed sitting there, her back to the room, unable to see who was watching her through the window. Even more than yesterday, she was keen to get out again as quickly as she could. Thankfully she didn't have to wait long. "TuringShroud wants to chat. Allow?" flashed up, just seconds after she'd logged in. She clicked 'OK' and immediately began typing.

"BayWatcher: Why didn't you send them the other

pictures?" First things first, get it out of the way.

"TuringShroud: Good afternoon to you, too. Nice weather and all that! I wanted to keep something back so you could have the credit, if you must know. I thought we could work out a plausible story for how you found them. Shall we do that now?"

He was a fool after all.

"BayWatcher: No – just send them! They're crucial evidence, they prove she was operating under disguise here."

"TuringShroud: Just trying to be helpful."

"BayWatcher: It doesn't work like that. Just send them, and any others you've got. We're off the case anyway – my DI is up in Bristol handing it over to Major Crime right now."

"TuringShroud: Ah, now I see why you're a bit crotchety :-)"

"BayWatcher: I'm not crotchety, I'm just fed up with you thinking you can do things your own way all the time. This is a murder investigation! You do know that withholding evidence is a criminal offence, don't you?"

"TuringShroud: Here we go again – I try to help you, you tell me off then threaten to arrest me! It's not really fair, is it?"

"BayWatcher: Life isn't fair. But OK, I know you're trying to help. You really can't play games with Major Crime though. If you ever meet DSI Kopacz you'll know why."

"TuringShroud: I'll bear that in mind. I'll send the pics now then, same method. Have they tried to trace the first lot?"

"BayWatcher: Yes, but no success. They're thinking of calling in Cheltenham."

"TuringShroud: I wouldn't bother if I was them."

"BayWatcher: That's what I thought."

"TuringShroud: If it got out how I did it, it could

cause a catastrophic loss of confidence in the Internet's fundamental security mechanisms, bringing the world economy to its knees. It's not just a Tor network, if that's what you're thinking."

That wasn't what she was thinking. She couldn't work out if he was being serious or not about the catastrophic loss of confidence. If he was, she didn't want to know.

"BayWatcher: Don't worry, I won't tell anyone."

"TuringShroud: Is there anything else? BTW the coffee there's good, isn't it?"

"BayWatcher: Yes."

"TuringShroud: Yes what? Something else, or good coffee?"

"BayWatcher: Both. Did you know that Ewan did chemistry as well as physics?"

"TuringShroud: Of course I did. He wouldn't get into Cambridge otherwise, would he? They don't let you in there with Physics, Media Studies and Travel & Tourism, you know! :-)"

Mary was sure she could hear chortling coming from the CCTV camera, although it might have been the fan heater mounted near to it.

"BayWatcher: How good a chemist is he? As good as he is at physics – all that hadron stuff you mentioned?"

"TuringShroud: Easily as good. To Ewan, chemistry is just a sub-branch of physics anyway. He specialises in quantum effects at the molecular level. To him everything is QED."

Mary knew this one.

"BayWatcher: Quod Erat Demonstrandum?"

"TuringShroud: Quantum Electrodynamics."

Oh. She had a sudden, strangely chilling vision of Michael and Ewan having evening-shift conversations, like two half-human, half-supercomputer mutants from a science fiction novel.

"BayWatcher: Would he be able to make synthetic

alkaloid compounds?" She wasn't completely sure what a synthetic alkaloid compound was, but TuringShroud probably would be.

"TuringShroud: Not with his bare hands, no, but with suitable equipment yes. It would be literally child's play to him – he was spotted for his scholarship at a primary schools science fair, where he knew more than the PhD students doing the experiments. It would still depend on the compound though – the complex ones need equipment that even Compton School wouldn't have. Why, what have you got in mind?"

Mary sensed TuringShroud's interest rising. That was the last thing she needed – him on the loose chasing synthetic compounds.

"BayWatcher: Nothing – I'm just amazed by Ewan's abilities. He must have been a real child prodigy."

"TuringShroud: That's not always an enjoyable experience, believe me."

"BayWatcher: No, I'm sure it isn't. Why didn't you tell me all this before?"

"TuringShroud: You didn't ask! Is this going to turn unfair again now?"

He definitely had a point.

"BayWatcher: Sorry – no. Thanks again for your help. How are you feeling now?"

"TuringShroud: A lot better. I don't think it was as bad as they thought in the first place."

"BayWatcher: I'm glad. You won't forget to send the pictures, will you? Can I get back to you from here if I need to?"

"TuringShroud: I won't forget. Yes, from there – I'll be here."

Mary heard a faint whirring, and looked up to see the CCTV camera doing a wiggle on its motorised mounting.

"TuringShroud: :-)"

"BayWatcher: You can get arrested for that too, you

know."

"TuringShroud: They'd have to trace it to me first. Anyway, hopefully we'll be able converse in a more conventional manner soon."

"BayWatcher: We'll see. Right, I must get on – things to do. Thanks again for everything. Bye."

"TuringShroud: Bye Mary."

Mary logged out, then did a web search, found a phone number and wrote it in her diary. She drank the last of her coffee and took the cup to the counter.

"All done?" asked Phil.

"Yes thanks. Excellent coffee – thanks for that too."

"You're welcome – tell your friends about this place!"

"I will." She wouldn't.

"See you again then."

"Yes." Hopefully she wouldn't be doing that either.

In the car, Mary made a phone call, noting a name in her diary next to the number she'd dialled. Then she rang the office.

"CID – DC Cox speaking."

"Pete – anything happening there?"

"Hello Sarge, no, nothing special. The DI's still away, we're still trying to get hold of the owner of the boat that was tied up at Knightstone on the Tuesday evening." He sounded listless, with perhaps a hint of knowing that the investigation would soon be out of their hands anyway.

"OK, book me out on enquiries, will you? I'll be back in about an hour, hour and a half. My phone may be off for a while. I've got an appointment with a school secretary."

It was a big night in the Champions League, and an even bigger one in the Miller household; Juventus v Chelsea in the group stage, a fixture which left Don's loyalties torn to shreds, but his excitement at fever pitch. So far he'd disagreed with the referee, both managers, the commentators and the pundits who'd given a brief summary before the broadcaster went into a lengthy half-time ad break. Now he was taking a break too.

Mary took her chance to speak to him. It was about something she really didn't want to raise, but the memory of Michael Slade's face in the photo gave her no option.

"Are you still going to Grove Park tomorrow, Don?" It was still difficult for her to say 'Grove Park' in an even tone, but she did her best. It was evidently not good enough, because she felt him tense beside her.

"I haven't got any choice, Love," he said, as if explaining why he had to pull down their conservatory and plough up the garden, "it's a safety requirement and I'm the contractor. If I ask someone else it'll look bad, like I don't trust my own judgement. It could lose me work."

"No, no – sorry, I didn't mean it like that. I just wanted to say to be careful."

He turned his attention from an ad for half price leather sofas.

"Of course I will. Anyway, I know how to inspect a boiler." He smiled indulgently at her, "I won't get myself blown up, I promise."

"I don't mean that," she said, the seriousness in her voice making Don's smile disappear, "I mean be careful around the Troshanis. They know we're after them for the Czwisnjowski murder, and they know you're my husband."

"What, you think they're going to take me hostage or something?" The indulgent smile was back, perhaps a little weaker this time.

"I don't know," she said, the seriousness in her voice giving way to anxiety, "I'm just thinking of what they did to Michael Slade."

"Yeah," said Don, serious himself now, "Tom

Flanagan told me about that when he came round for my statement. Shocking, wasn't it?"

Mary realised that this was the first time she and Don had spoken directly about the attack on Michael. She found herself wishing that she hadn't raised the subject.

"Tom's a good bloke, you know," Don continued, taking a sip from his lager, "Hides his light under a bushel though, not like some of the flash characters in that office of yours."

Mary had a good idea which flash characters Don was referring to. She was less sure about where this was going.

"When he told me about Slade, I got the feeling that he was checking how I'd react to hearing about him getting done over. He was subtle about it though, not like some I could think of."

This was it then. It had to be faced some time.

"Don, I..."

He put his hand over hers.

"It's all right, Love. You didn't have any choice. I know how your system works – it would have looked worse if it had come out later."

Mary felt tears welling in her eyes.

"I knew I was marrying a police officer," he continued, squeezing her hand gently, "It's like marrying someone in the military, different rules apply. It's my fault anyway for getting mixed up with the Troshanis. I took that job out of stupid pride, even though I knew the trouble they'd caused you. I haven't been able to forgive myself. I don't know how you forgave me – if you have, that is." Now his eyes were glistening too.

"Course I have, Love," said Mary, "only there's nothing to forgive. I'm the one who needs forgiving." It had all come out too suddenly, leaving her unprepared. The tears began to flow down her cheeks in little mascara-stained rivers.

"No you're not," Don said firmly, a flash of the old Don, mature beyond his years, who'd swept her off her feet as a teenager. He picked a tissue from the box on the table and dabbed at her face. There was silence for a few moments, then he spoke again.

"Did you think I'd done it – told the Troshanis about Slade?"

"Of course not! Don..."

"But you couldn't be certain." A guilty silence was all she could manage. For a second she'd thought it was going to be OK, but now...

"Like I said, it's all right," Don said gently, squeezing her hand again, "I know how your system works. I knew the Troshanis, I knew about Michael Slade helping you, there can't have been many people ticking both those boxes. It had to be checked out. I'm just glad your DI didn't have anything to do with it. Thanks for that, Love."

Now wasn't the time to put Don straight on how involved the DI had actually been, and particularly how he'd kept Don's name out of the official investigation into the assault on Michael. Better to move on. Mary took another tissue from the box and began making a rather better job than her husband had done of removing the run mascara.

"That's why I'm worried," she said, "The Troshanis know you, and they know who I am. If they think you're some kind of police spy there's no telling what they might do."

Don took another sip of lager, and put the can down on the coffee table in front of them. He took Mary's hand again, his palm still cold from the chilled tin.

"You're forgetting, Love," he said quietly, "that they asked me into Grove Park, I didn't go knocking on their door like some undercover policeman trying to infiltrate them. And I'm not Michael Slade either. The Troshanis aren't stupid. They know better than to start a war with the Miller family, because there wouldn't be anywhere in North Somerset safe for them to go if they did. Tomorrow will be the last time I have anything to do with them, and it will be OK, I promise."

It was a lovely speech, and Don was probably right about it being OK, even if his reasoning was seriously mistaken. The Troshanis would have no hesitation about starting a war with Don's extended family, or of using methods and weapons that the Millers, solid farming stock whose experience of violence ran to the occasional cider-fuelled brawl, would blanch at. But what they wouldn't do was attack the family of a police officer, because that would bring the might of the Force crashing down on them as surely as if they'd attacked a PC in uniform. No need to tell Don that though; his faith in the strength of the Miller clan was part of who he was. She just had to hope that her faith in the might of the Force, and its effect on the Troshanis, was well-founded.

"If you're sure then, Love. You will be careful though, won't you?" She squeezed his hand.

"I'll be careful, I promise," he said, as if promising not to get tomato sauce down his best shirt, "and I'll ring you as soon as I'm away from the place, to let you know I'm OK."

"OK, thanks – and if you change your mind about going there...."

"I won't," he said, taking the lager can from the table, "Anyway, if there's any trouble I'll send our Tina in. They've just put her op back again. The Troshanis'll soon wish they were back in Albania – I reckon that's where Dave wishes he was right now. Still, I did tell him not to marry her..."

Chapter 39

The next morning DCI Spence told the CID team that there'd be a 10am briefing, at which DI Jones would have "something to announce". The DI hadn't returned from Bristol the previous afternoon, which Mary took as a sign that the Czwisnjowski case had been taken from them, and that he was less than happy about it. It was virtually unknown for him not to call into the office on his way home, however far away he'd been.

He didn't arrive until 9.20 am, although his appearance, immaculate as ever, told Mary that this was more likely the result of catching up on phone calls at home than a night drowning his sorrows. He went straight up to DCI Spence's office, pausing only to tell her that she probably wouldn't be too surprised by what he was going to say. Perhaps he'd been at home briefing Special Branch, the NCA or whoever else was going to be involved with Katya's case, and was now on his way to put Spence in the picture.

The mood in the CID room was resigned acceptance of what they all knew was coming. Mary felt strangely at odds with it; while everyone else was on the point of giving up, her instinct told her that she might be on the verge of breaking through. At the moment it was still only instinct; she needed just a couple more facts, a couple more connections, and there'd be a case to make. Not that it would make any difference to the takeover by Major Crime. That, it seemed, was a done deal, and nothing she said would undo it now. She had to accept that if she did have a case then she'd probably end up making it to one of Kopacz's DIs, not her own.

At 10am the DCI appeared, spoke a few words and

handed over to the DI. He came straight to the point.

"As you all know, Major Crime received an anonymous tipoff yesterday, including a photograph which our Tech team have confirmed as genuine. This links Katya Czwisnjowski with Amelia Foster, the second Bristol student murder victim, and with Nyesha Rose, a known associate of the major drug dealing operation in Bristol. Since then there's been another development – more photographs, this time from a Polish social networking site, sent anonymously again but we believe from the same source. These pictures show Katya with different colour hair and a very different, more expensive style of dress from the clothes she was wearing in the first picture, which were also the ones she was found murdered in. The implication is that she was leading two different lives, one at home in Poland, the other here in the UK. Crucially, her parents were either unaware of her Polish identity, which seems unlikely as she worked for them, or they conspired to hide it from us, since they gave us pictures of her with her UK appearance."

The DI paused and took a sip of water from a thin plastic cup. No-one spoke.

"The upshot of all this," he continued, "is that the murders of Katya Czwisnjowski, Amelia Foster and James Penhaligon are now being treated as a single case, along with that of Luan Redzepi, which is still considered to be closely related to the death of Ms Czwisnjowski in particular." He paused again; no water this time, just a delay before he said the words.

"And since Major Crime are already investigating all those murders except Ms Czwisnjowski's, and since they have the resources to handle such a big investigation, it has been decided that they will take over the Czwisnjowski case too, and that Weston CID's involvement will cease as of now, except for whatever local assistance Major Crime may ask us to provide, which of course we will do."

It made sense, but that didn't make the blow less bitter. It had, in fact, made sense from the first time the Czwisnjowskis' Embassy Mercedes had rolled its tyres onto the pavement outside the station. If they'd handed it over then it would have gone down as normal procedure, the big guns from Bristol taking control as usual. But instead they'd hung on to it for too long; long enough to fail. Mary was no expert on football, but she could see the analogy that applied here: they'd been out of their league, minnows who'd gained accidental promotion to the big time and ended up relegated again without scoring a single goal. Unless...

Q&A took a predicable course. Were the Troshanis still prime suspects in the Czwisnjowski murder (yes)? Would Major Crime be running it from Bristol, Portishead or Weston (Bristol at present)? Did it mean no more overtime (what do you think, Sam)? The DI had moved on to the details of the handover when Mary heard a noise from her bag, quiet at first but growing quickly louder. She reached into the bag as the DI gave her a critical look, pulled out her phone and read the display: "Don". Miming that she was sorry but had to take this, she rushed to the door and out into the corridor, then pressed the Accept button.

"Don?"

"Hello Love, I've just left Grove Park."

"That was quick."

"We start early in the building trade, Love."

"Yes, I remember. And you're OK?"

"Right as rain, no problem."

"Great – look, thanks for letting me know, but there's a briefing on and I'd better get back…"

"Hang on, that's not the only reason I rang." Don stopped speaking as the sound of a siren swept past at his end, "I thought you might want to know, they've done something funny with the gas supply there."

Mary felt the slightest of shivers. Perhaps it was just cold in the corridor.

"What's that?"

"They've diverted it, put in a spur that takes gas off to somewhere else. It's their side of the meter, so they're not nicking the gas, but they have tried to hide it by boxing the pipework in. Of course that could just be because they've used an unlicensed installer and didn't want me to see it. That would explain why they weren't keen about me inspecting the system."

"But you're pretty sure there is a – spur, you call it – in there?"

"Oh yes, and something using the gas. I switched all the boilers and appliances off and the meter was still turning over, at a fair rate too. Something quite big, I'd say."

A bigger shiver now.

"And where does this spur pipe go?"

Mary heard her husband chuckle.

"Well that's it – it doesn't seem to go anywhere. The boxing runs floor to ceiling on the ground floor, there's nothing above it on the first floor, and down in the basement it runs floor to ceiling again. So the spur pipe appears to just run into solid rock."

"You went into the basement?" Her shocked tone made it sound more as if he'd jumped off the Pier, "Don, you promised me you'd be careful..."

"It's all right – the mains water supply comes in there. I had to inspect that, didn't I? Can't have the boilers running dry."

"No, I suppose not. Did you see anything else?"

"No. I didn't get a chance to go outside at the back and look for flues, but there'd have to be one if they've got something using gas at that rate, otherwise they'd all be dead from carbon monoxide poisoning."

"Don, you're a star. Where are you now?"

Another chuckle.

"Oldmixon, Love, just about to go in and finish that boiler swap for the old couple. I may not be experienced at this undercover business, but I'm not daft enough to sit outside the Troshanis' place talking to you about their pipework either!"

"No, of course not." The DI was right – Don did know her better than she thought he did. "Thanks again love, that's brilliant. I've got to go now – see you later."

"OK, bye Love." The connection went dead.

Mary stood in the corridor, her chest rising and falling as she took deep breaths to calm herself. This was it. It was still only her intuition that connected the dots, but there were enough dots now to make it probable that investigation would fill in the gaps. No-one else, not even TuringShroud, knew it, and she had her husband to thank for the final dot.

For a few seconds she savoured it. This was why she was a detective. No role-playing games for her; when she made the connections real villains were arrested, real crimes punished. It was like a drug, she knew that – a drug that could leave her with bitter regrets when it was too late to be other things besides a police officer, made her regret the things she denied Don and her parents now. Still, not one she wanted to give up yet.

Back in the office the briefing had ended. Frustratingly the DI had left with DCI Spence, presumably for yet another handover management session. Mary considered interrupting them, but thought better of it; barging in on them with what was still a theoretical, and fairly speculative, case could make them dismiss it altogether out of sheer irritation. She needed to float the idea via the proverbial 'quiet word'.

It was a day now since she and the DI had spoken properly; that seemed strange, but it also occurred to her that it was, in fact, how things would normally be. They'd worked closely together for the past two weeks because they'd been on a major investigation. Whichever way things worked out she'd eventually go back to running her own, much smaller cases, reporting to the DI every day or so alongside Tom Flanagan. The DI would go back to his budgets and management briefings. Normality didn't seem quite so attractive now that it was returning.

The DI was away for another hour. When he returned Mary got up quickly from her desk, determined to be at the head of the queue to see him.

"Sorry I haven't been able to talk to you before," he said, looking up from some papers as she tapped on his office door, "I don't expect there were any big surprises back there though."

"No Guv." She went in, sat down and pushed the door closed. He looked up again, acknowledging her presence.

"Don't let it get to you," he said, evidently assuming that she'd come to bemoan the loss of their big case, "It's been on the cards all along, we both knew that. You've done good work, and it hasn't gone unnoticed, here or in Bridewell Street."

"Thanks," she replied, temporarily thrown off course by the compliment.

"What was that call you got in the briefing? Anything useful?"

"That's what I wanted to talk to you about." Back on course. Mary knew that, even in a quiet-word context, the theory she was about to put to her boss might sound a little over-imaginative. She needed to choose her words, and her running order, carefully.

"You remember I said I'd met Tamzin, the Sand Bay

witness, in the café at Anchor Head? Well I met her there again yesterday, and she said a couple of things that got me thinking. It seems that..."

"Mary," the DI interrupted her, "Sand Bay isn't our case – wasn't ours even yesterday. If you've got new information stick it on HOLMES and ring Bridewell Street to give them a nudge." He sounded weary, despite the fact that it was still only late morning. Mary saw, suddenly, that he'd changed since the previous day. The spark had gone; he was back to being what his position made him, a middle manager preoccupied with budgets and policy.

"We've got a mountain of paperwork to deal with here, believe me," he continued, "Did you know Sam Yewell had been claiming overtime for drinking in the Cabot 'to facilitate meetings with information sources'. He's even been claiming for the drinks. It wouldn't be so bad if he'd actually sourced any information. I'll have his backside for this, Federation Rep or no Federation Rep."

"No, I didn't know about that," said Mary. The considerate thing would have been to leave him to tackle the complexities of Sam Yewell's expenses undisturbed. Instead she tried one last trick to get his attention.

"Look, Guv, could I just run this past you before I ring Bridewell Street with it? I don't want to look stupid to them."

"Perhaps later," he said, gesturing towards the thick pile of papers on his desk, "I've got to get through this lot first."

She knew better than to push him further, especially in the current circumstances. Everyone was entitled to some consideration.

"Fair enough, Guv. I'll see you later." She got up, pulled the door open and was almost knocked over by Tony Lane, who came half-tumbling in.

"Guv, Sarge," he said breathlessly, "I've just had a call

from uniform. It's all kicking off at Between the Lines. The Troshani boys are there mob-handed saying they want the landlord's daughter – Jolene, the one you interviewed on the Sand Bay case. Sounds like it's turning ugly."

Chapter 40

The DI had played rugby at right wing in the days when wingers were still lean and fast, and had kept up his fitness. He could probably have run to Between the Lines in less time than it took to get his Audi out of the car park and down Neva Road to the railway station; however that wasn't an option for Mary, so they drove, missing the big steel security gate by inches as it slid open. As the Audi lurched into the station car park they were greeted by a scene straight out of the Wild West. Five youths stood in a line, like gunslingers. Facing them was Billy Buller, standing square in the door of Between the Lines in the classic landlord's pose of no entry. Two uniformed officers stood at the side; one of them, Mary saw, was PC Durham.

The DI stopped his car in the middle of the car park and jumped out, Mary following. They could hear now what was being said.

"You're not coming in here, you're banned, the lot of you. Get away!" Billy Buller wasn't a large man, but he could be a fierce one. Odds of five to one didn't seem to worry him at all, or perhaps he was just putting on a brave front.

"Fuck your poxy joint," the evident leader of the youths shouted back, "I wouldn't go piss in there." The youth had his back to Mary but she knew the voice, the accent a blend of urban patois and what she assumed was Albanian. Ardi Troshani.

"Just send Jolene out, right?" he continued, "we just want take her for a ride. Got tings to discuss wit her."

The next voice Mary heard was the DI's, booming away a few feet to her right.

"What's going on here?" he shouted, causing all five of the youths to turn and face him.

"Hey – Detective Inspector Jones," said Ardi, pronouncing each syllable as a separate word, "and you brought your hot Detective Sergeant wit you. How are you, Detective Sergeant?"

Mary could see Ardi's eyes now. As always they had a merciless, empty blackness at their centre, but now they were glazed too, as if he wasn't fully there in mind. He was clearly on something, as were his friends.

"Move away from here, all of you," said the DI, "or I'll arrest you for breach of the peace."

Ardi ignored him, staring instead at Mary. He looked her up and down appraisingly.

"Tell me, Detective Sergeant," he said, pronouncing the syllables of her rank in his separate-word style, "Is your Inspector gonna fuck you when he gets you back to the police station? If you was my bitch I'd fuck you every day. You're juicy."

Female officers had training in this kind of thing, and Mary knew what to expect from Ardi Troshani. She also knew that sometimes it was the male officers who were affected by it, finding it hard not to react in defence of their colleagues. When the DI spoke, however, his voice was still calm.

"Move away. Last chance, Mr Troshani, or we'll take you in."

Mary noticed Durham talking into his radio, heard him say "backup". Ardi looked at the DI as if seeing him for the first time.

"Hey, Inspector. We just come to see our friend Jolene. You know her? Very friendly, Jolene. Buy her a drink and you can fuck her long as you like. She's a dirty bitch."

Mary saw Billy Buller stiffen in the doorway. His face was red with anger.

"What are you saying about my daughter? Come here and say it, you little shit."

Ardi turned round to face Billy. Mary saw one of the gang, a new face to her, reach into his pocket.

"Leave this to us, Mr Buller," shouted the DI. The sound of sirens came from the direction of Neva Road. Mary estimated their arrival at around 15 seconds.

Ardi turned back to the DI.

"Yeah, leave it to you, Mr. Inspector. You know Jolene, don't you, 'cos she been talking to you. You fucked her? You made her suck you? I have. Desperate ho like that, brother, she just do whatever you want."

Mary saw the DI's colour changing, to match that of Billy Buller.

"Backup's almost here," she said quietly, but there was no response.

"Troshani, don't push your luck." It was the DI's voice, but not the one she knew. Not the one that always stayed in control.

"It's not worth it, Guv, let uniform handle it."

"Hey Mr Inspector, am I embarrassing you? You had a little taste of Jolene pussy and now you ashamed? I can understand that, man. I ashamed too, of fucking a ho like it. Between the Lines – Between the Legs more like, and it got lots of customers, yeah?" He grinned at his joke, his gang grinning along with him.

"Troshani!" the DI growled now, like an animal ready to pounce.

"Sir!"

Mary saw a figure appear in the doorway, behind Billy. It was Jolene. From 15 yards away she could see tears rolling down her cheeks.

"Hey Inspector I hope you washed your dick good afterwards, 'cos she a real health hazard. Ain't you, Jolene?" He said it over his shoulder, somehow sensing that she was there. "You so filthy I won't touch your pussy now. Put you on your knees make you suck my dick, all you good for, bitch like you."

Mary saw the DI begin to move towards Ardi, heard the sirens and the squeal of tyres behind her. She wasn't ready for this, but sometimes you had to react in defence of your colleagues. She took a deep breath, and lunged forward between the DI and his target.

"Ardit Troshani, I'm arresting you for the murder of Luan Redzepi. You do not have to say anything, but it may harm your defence if you fail to mention, when questioned, something which you may later rely on in court. Anything you do say may be given in evidence. Do you understand?"

As a way of neutralising the situation, it was extremely effective. Ardi and his friends all stared at her as if she'd just announced that she was Xena the Warrior Princess. The DI stared at her as if she'd just arrested the Chief Constable. PC Durham and the other uniforms just stared, uncertain of what to do next.

Expertly, she grabbed Ardi's arm and twisted it hard up behind his back. "Do you understand, Mr Troshani?"

"Yeah," he gasped as his arm was pushed higher.

Mary pushed Ardi towards Durham. "Take him in," she said, breathless now, then turned to another PC. "That one may have a weapon in his pocket. Book them all for breach of the peace and threatening behaviour, plus anything else you find."

She was in trouble, but with luck she could get out again. She waited until Ardi had been pushed down into a squad car, then reached into her bag, took out her phone and speed-dialled the office.

"Pete? I want you and Tony to bring Ewan Taylor in, one of the Sand Bay witnesses. Caution him, and if he won't come, arrest him for conspiracy in the Redzepi case. Yes, that's what I said. Do it now please, and if he isn't at home then find him. Try the supermarket or his girlfriend, Ellie – she's on HOLMES too. Right, see you back there."

She was aware of the DI still standing there, looking at her now as if she'd added the Police Commissioner to her list of arrestees.

"Trust me, Guv."

"Looks like I'm going to have to, doesn't it?"

Chapter 41

Act in haste, repent at leisure. It was one of Mary's mother's favourite sayings. Mary fought to put it from her mind now as they drove back to the station, and the implications of what she'd just done began to sink in.

Arresting someone was the easy part. PACE, and subsequent SOCPA, legislation had made it possible for a police officer to arrest anyone, without a warrant, for any offence, and then to search the arrested suspect's property and possessions without a warrant too. But with this power came responsibility. The officer had to state, at the time of the arrest, their grounds for suspecting that the person was guilty of a crime, and their reasons for using arrest (or "deprivation of liberty contrary to the European Convention on Human Rights", as defence lawyers liked to call it) rather than issuing bail or a summons.

"At the time of the arrest" was the key phrase, designed to stop arrest from being used as a form of arbitrary short-term imprisonment, or a way of avoiding the need to apply for search warrants. These days "rounding up the usual suspects", without any evidence against them, was against the law. Whole cases could collapse if the initial arrest was judged to have had insufficient grounds. Judgements in various wrongful arrest cases had made it clear that the threshold of "grounds for reasonable suspicion" was low, but as her adrenaline level dropped, Mary was left facing the fact that her grounds, as things stood, were very low indeed.

The DI had been silent on the short drive back from Between the Lines, and remained so as he swung the Audi into the station car park. Mary guessed that he was considering the implications of what had just happened too.

The custody suite was in chaos when they walked in, the Troshani crew shouting, pulling, pushing and generally trying to make the process as dysfunctional as possible. The custody officer was a young sergeant, Coral Blakestone, not long in the job. She looked perplexed.

"Four from uniform, one CID – right?" she said to the room in general, apparently hoping that someone would respond, "Which one is CID?"

"This one," said Mary, "Ardit Troshani. I'm the arresting officer, DS Miller."

"OK," said Sergeant Blakestone, pressing some keys on her computer keyboard, "what's he been arrested for?"

"Murder," said Mary. Blakestone looked up from her computer screen.

"I ain't murdered no one, bitch!" Ardi shouted, "This is a fit-up. Police persecution, my whole family they got it in for." His gang started shouting back, requiring the officers to quieten them down.

"Who is he suspected of murdering?" Blakestone kept her cool, asking the question as if checking the details of a minor traffic offence.

"Luan Redzepi, found dead at Sand Bay, Kewstoke on November 7th."

"You talking shit, bitch!" Ardi screamed, "He was my fucking cousin! You a lyin piece of shit!" He pulled at PC Durham, who was still handcuffed to him.

"That's enough, Mr Troshani," said Blakestone firmly, "Any more and I'll have you restrained." Ardi was suddenly quiet. Mary was impressed – there was clearly more to Sergeant Blakestone than had met her eye.

"Grounds for suspicion?"

"Information received." Don't ask me what

information, for goodness sake.

"Reason for arrest?"

"To allow investigation and prevent the suspect from disappearing. He has an Albanian passport and extensive family in Albania, and I believe there would be a risk of him going there." At least she was on firmer ground here.

"And have you cautioned the suspect?"

"Yes, at the time of arrest."

"OK," said Blakestone, then turning to Ardi, "Mr Troshani, you've been arrested on suspicion of murdering Luan Redzepi, that suspicion being based on information which the police have received. You've been detained in order for the police to be able to conduct their enquiries, and because the arresting officer believes you may leave the country if you are not detained. Do you understand all that?"

"Fuckin bitch! You ain't received no information! It's all lies, big time fit-up!"

"Do you understand, Mr Troshani?" While barely raising her voice, the Sergeant managed to give the impression that if Ardi didn't behave she'd jump over the desk and deal with him personally. Again Ardi quietened down.

"Yeah," he said sullenly. Whatever Blakestone had, Mary wanted some of it.

"Right then," said Blakestone, "Now I'm going to advise you of your rights and ask you about any special needs you may have while in custody. DS Miller, do you have any further comments to make at this stage?"

"Better get the medical officer to have a look at him," said Mary. She found herself mimicking Blakestone's mixture of informal and formal language. "From my observations he seems to have taken one or more substances."

"OK, will do that. Thank you, DS Miller, that's all I

need for now."

Upstairs, after a lift ride that matched the silence of their recent car journey, the DI motioned for Mary to close his office door.

"So you think Ardi Troshani killed his cousin?" He sounded mildly astonished at the suggestion, although at least open to the possibility that she might have good reasons for making it.

"Yes Guv, in concert with other members of the Troshani family."

"Why did they do it?"

"I'm not sure. Perhaps they were scared he was going to blab to us about the Czwisnjowski murder. Or family rivalry - Ardi might have thought Luan was a threat to his position as top boy in the Troshani clan here."

The DI seemed impressed, or perhaps it was just relieved, that she at least had some credible ideas on motive.

"Right," he said, "you'd better tell me about this information we've received. And please don't say it's based mainly on what that girl in the cafe's been telling you."

He was going to be less impressed now.

Preparing the ground with double helpings of "Hear me out, Guv" and "there is more", Mary told him what she knew. During the part about her talks with Tamzin, the DI's face became a mask of despair, as if he could see his prospects of promotion, or even a full pension, disappearing before his eyes. But he perked up slightly when she mentioned the dark van Tamzin had seen, a bit more when she described her interview with the school secretary the previous afternoon, a bit more again when she told him what Don had said about Grove Park an hour earlier. What Mary couldn't talk about openly was her online conversation with TuringShroud, so she attributed his comments about Ewan's chemistry skills to Tamzin, who was, after all, an A-grade chemistry student herself. She didn't like the subterfuge, but she was well past the point of being committed to it now.

The DI sat back in his chair and blew air out from his puffed cheeks. It looked to Mary as if he was wishing he'd stopped her after the good bit about possible motives.

"What this adds up to," he said, "is some circumstantial pointing to Ewan's involvement in something, but nothing tying Ardi to the Redzepi murder except a glimpse of a dark van, seen by a nervous teenager who'd be torn to shreds in the witness box."

He sounded distinctly more in sorrow than anger, although that didn't make it any more encouraging. It was the moment when Mary should have experienced a crisis of confidence, wondered whether she'd seen dots that weren't there. Instead she thought about what she'd just told him, and knew she was right.

"I know it needs a lot more, Guv, but I'm certain." She was surprised to hear how confident she sounded. "Ewan's the key to all this. If we can get him to crack, we'll have the Troshanis."

"Big if," said the DI, "and if we don't, then we'll have the Troshanis after us for wrongful arrest, you know that, don't you?"

"After me, Guv – my collar." This was becoming familiar ground.

"Don't talk bollocks, Sergeant. We both know why you made that arrest."

There was silence for a couple of seconds.

"And if you are right," the DI continued, "that puts the Czwisnjowskis in the clear for Redzepi's murder. So either we've got to explain why we arrested an innocent young Troshani, or we've got to tell Major Crime that their hopes of nailing the Al Capone of Eastern Europe have been scuppered. I'm not sure which of those two I'd rather take."

"No, Guv." The prospect of telling DSI Kopacz that they'd muscled in on his case and put his prime suspect out of contention didn't appeal to her either. Nevertheless, her career might depend on them having to do it.

A few minutes later DC Lane tapped on the DI's door.

"Guv, Sarge, we've got Ewan Taylor in Interview One. He's cautioned and ready to go."

"Did he come voluntarily?" asked the DI.

"Yes, but he's brought a lawyer with him. Hugh Jenkins."

The DI gave a grim smile. "The Troshani family solicitor. Now why doesn't that surprise me? Still, it means we're on to something. Thanks, Tony." He waited until Lane had gone before continuing. "Right, let's go," he said, "You'll have to lead, because I'm still not 100 percent on why we've got him here in the first place."

Mary hesitated. "There's something I've got to do first – a quick phone call."

"Is it absolutely necessary?" said the DI sharply. Clearly he wasn't in the mood for any more surprises.

"Yes, Guv – but it won't take long, I promise."

"Make sure it doesn't then."

Mary went to her computer, searched for "Anchor Head Cafe Weston" and dialled the number that appeared on screen. It rang a couple of times.

"Hello?" It was Pauline, the owner. Not who Mary had hoped for.

"Hello, is Tamzin there please?"

"Who's calling?" Pauline didn't sound overjoyed at the interruption.

"Mary Miller."

"She's not allowed to take personal calls here. Call her mobile after 5.30. She's off then."

Normally Mary would have gone a bit further to save a youngster the embarrassment of being called by the police. Now there was no time.

"Detective Sergeant Mary Miller, Weston CID. I need to speak to Tamzin urgently."

"Tamzin! You're wanted on the phone!" Mary heard the words shouted through to the next room, then an unceremonious 'clunk' as the receiver was put down. Thanks for your help, Pauline.

She heard footsteps, then the phone being picked up.

"Hello?"

"Tamzin? It's Mary Miller from Weston CID. I'm really sorry to ring you at work like this, but there's something I need to ask you and it can't wait."

"OK." She sounded guarded, or perhaps it was just tired.

"That night, at the party, whose idea was it to go to Sand Bay?"

There was silence at the other end of the line.

"Tamzin? Are you there?"

"It was Ewan's. All right, I know you're going to think I'm just obsessing about him all the time, but it was him. I wasn't as drunk as the boys – I was keeping Ellie company on the fruit juices – and I remember it."

"What exactly happened?"

"We'd all crashed out, then about five o'clock Ewan woke us up and said we should go to Sand Bay, get out there among the elements. I thought he was on something, he was so manic. None of us wanted to go but he kept on about it. Then he started on just at Ellie, saying he wanted her to take him there now, he had to go now. He and Zac almost started fighting over it – Zac's, well, he's a bit protective about Ellie, he likes her. In the end we all said we'd go just to quieten Ewan down. We couldn't let Ellie go on her own with him. He was strange."

"Thanks, Tamzin. That's really helpful."

"Is that it then?" She sounded tired again.

"Yes, that's all. Thanks again for being so open with me."

"It's all right. Bye then."

"Bye."

Now Mary was ready – as ready as she was going to be – to tackle the troubled young genius of Compton School.

Chapter 42

Ewan Taylor sat at the table in the interview room. The formalities had been worked through, Hugh Jenkins making notes at each stage. It was the first time Mary had really looked at Ewan properly. He could almost have passed for Tamzin's brother – tall, thin, the same dark hair, cut in what was almost the same tousled style. But while Tamzin could cover any skin blemishes with makeup, Ewan's were visible all over his face and neck, red blotches standing out from his unhealthily pale complexion. And while Tamzin's default expression was a slight, shy smile, Ewan's was a scowl. He seemed to radiate dislike and contempt for everyone and everything he saw.

"Why am I here?" he asked, directing the scowl at Mary.

"To help us with our enquiries, Ewan," she replied calmly, "We're very grateful."

"Enquiries into what?"

"The murder at Sand Bay, of course. You were one of the group who found the body."

"Oh. Yeah."

Mary wondered what else he might think they wanted him for. She noticed the DI glance at Jenkins, and guessed that, like her, he was surprised that the solicitor hadn't interrupted with "Why is my client being interviewed under caution when he's merely a witness?" Holding his fire, presumably.

"The group – the five of you – seem quite tightly-knit," she continued, "You were all at Compton School together, is that right?"

"Yeah."

"And you've stayed close since you left school in the summer?"

"We've kept in contact, yeah. We all live around here. Most people at Compton don't."

"And of course you and Ellie are together, and expecting a baby, I understand. Congratulations."

"Yeah, thanks." Ewan's gratitude seemed less than profound.

"Is that all going well?"

"What?"

"Preparations for parenthood. Ante natal classes, that sort of thing."

"Ellie handles all that. And her mother." He sounded less than profoundly grateful for Ellie's mum's input too.

"Keeping you out of it, are they?"

"Ellie doesn't want to distract me from my academic work."

"That's very considerate of her."

"Yeah."

"What about other people from Weston who were at Compton with you? There must be some. Have you kept in touch with them?"

"Not so much, no."

"Really? What about, say, Ardi Troshani?"

Out of the corner of her eye Mary saw the faintest twitch of reaction from Hugh Jenkins.

"I don't know him."

Bingo. She could hardly believe that he was trying to lie his way out of it, but she was glad nevertheless. It wouldn't take long now.

"Ah, but you do," she said encouragingly, as if reminding her grandmother of a long-forgotten acquaintance, "He was your classmate at Compton School last Autumn term." She lifted up the cover of her file and glanced at the paper underneath, as if checking the details. "In fact you were in the same Chemistry and

Biology sets. By all accounts he was quite bright – not as bright as you, of course, but then very few people are."

"Oh yeah. I didn't really have anything to do with him. He was just in the same science sets, that's all."

Brain the size of a planet and he tries to bullshit two detectives who are bound to have checked the facts first. What do they teach these kids? And what kind of advice did Hugh Jenkins give him before the interview?

The DI joined in. "That's strange, because we've been told that you and Ardi hit it off, became quite good mates in fact. His dad used to give you a lift to school in his minibus, didn't he?"

"Yeah." No comment without actually saying "no comment". Ewan wasn't entirely without interview skills then.

"Ardi only stayed at Compton for one term, didn't he?" asked Mary, "Why did he leave?"

"He was chucked out. I'm sure you know that." Ewan smiled, a nasty smile that said he was going to play them around until it was hard to tell from the recording what he'd known at which stage of the interview.

"What for?"

"Something to do with drugs, I think. They're very tight on that kind of thing at Compton – can't have Mummy and Daddy's little darlings leaving with a crack habit, can we?" He sniggered at them.

"Something to do with you as well though, eh Ewan?" said Mary, flicking a glance at Jenkins, who looked up from his notes. "You were involved in the drugs business too but Ardi kept your name out of it."

For the first time Ewan's composure slipped.

"Who told you that shit?" he demanded, "That bitch Tamzin? She's just got it in for me because I won't fuck her. A woman scorned, and all that," he added, directing a sneer at Mary.

This was one woman, scorned or otherwise, who

wasn't going to be wound up by a small boy with a big mouth, however enormous the brain behind it.

"Tamzin's a bit common for you, is she?" Mary said empathetically, "Not like the landed gentry out in Congresbury. Let's stick to Ardi for now though. He's not the type to do people favours, and he must have wanted a pretty big payback for keeping quiet about you. What was it, Ewan? Did he make you work as his delivery boy, or were you in a more technical role?"

A crack in the composure again.

"I don't know what you're on about," he said, "He didn't make me do anything." The sneer returned as the crack was repaired. "Anyway, even if I had been mixed up with it Compton wouldn't have got rid of me. I was their star student. They'd have covered it up."

Now it was Mary's turn to sneer, almost.

"Oh, I wouldn't have banked on it. You said it yourself, Ewan – they couldn't have Mummy and Daddy's little darlings leaving with crack habits. When push comes to shove you scholarship boys are expendable. Mummy and Daddy's fees aren't. I'd say you'd have made a pretty good scapegoat, perhaps even for Ardi himself. After all, his family were paying, weren't they?"

She saw the jibe sting him, the little twitch of his eyes as he shrank from it. Tough luck, sonny.

The DI joined in again.

"Where would that have left you, Ewan? Back in Worlebury, begging Weston College to let you in to do your A levels. Cambridge out of the window – A* or no A*s, with 'Expelled for selling drugs' on your record you'd have been lucky to get into a third-rate ex-Poly. No well-placed family to get you a job somewhere either, not like the rich kids. Unfair, isn't it?"

"And what about Ellie?" said Mary, deciding that it could be laid on just a little bit thicker, "I doubt if her parents would have wanted her hanging around with a drug dealer. Mind you, she might have lost interest anyway once your brilliant academic career was gone."

"No she wouldn't," Ewan spat back angrily, "she's not like that. This is that fucking bitch Tamzin, isn't it? She can't stand me being with Ellie – she'd do anything to break us up. Well she wants to be careful what she says."

"Why's that, Ewan?" Mary kept her voice calm. The boy surely couldn't be stupid, or stoked, enough to make threats in a police interview with the recorders on.

Ewan turned his gaze to Mary, looked her straight in the face.

"You know," he said, and the sneering smile reappeared.

She did now.

It occurred to Mary, again, that Hugh Jenkins hadn't seemed his usual ever-vigilant self during the interview. She'd have expected him to challenge the validity of their line of questioning by now, and certainly to have prevented his client from making a second comment about Tamzin's need to be careful. But instead he sat silent, head down, focused on his notes, more like an observer than an active participant. It occurred to her, suddenly, why that might be. There is a certain spirit of fair play, laced with awareness of possible later defence strategies, that sometimes moves police officers to warn suspects if their solicitors are making a spectacularly bad job of representing their interests. In other circumstances Mary might have told this suspect that his lawyer really should be giving him better advice on what to say. She looked at the sneering smile and decided to say nothing.

"You do seem to have a high estimation of your effect on women, Ewan," said the DI, leaning back in his chair, "All this stuff about Tamzin trying to do you in because she can't have you. It's clouding your judgement, making you look in the wrong place."

Ewan made no reply, just shrugged.

"Do you know where Ardi Troshani is right now?" The DI leaned forward again.

"No. Why should I?" Ewan's sneer was still there but the eyes weren't quite backing it up.

"He's in a cell, downstairs in the custody suite. After we've finished with you we'll be bringing him up here, and my guess is that he's going to drop you even further in it than he already has."

"He hasn't dropped me in anything," said Ewan defiantly, "Ardi doesn't grass people up." The cop-show terminology, and the eyes, showed that he wasn't entirely sure what Ardi did.

"Then why do you think you're here under caution?"

No reply to that one. Top marks to the DI, thought Mary, turning their lack of grounds for dragging Ewan in into a tool to crack the boy's confidence. That was class.

"You see we're not a school, Ewan," the DI continued, pressing home the advantage, "We don't do 'leave quietly and we'll consider the matter closed'. We do arrest, conviction and imprisonment. I can't see Ardi relishing the prospect of being some sweaty con's bitch for the next fourteen years, can you? Not his style. He'll tell us whatever we want to know if it'll keep him out, and he'll paint you as the mastermind. And the funny thing is, there are people in Weston – respectable people, influential ones – who'd be happy to hear that version of things. The Troshanis are going legit, Ardi's uncle is mixing with the right people. You'll be expendable, just like you would have been at Compton School. Unfair, isn't it?"

"Fourteen years?" said Ewan, "For dealing a few drugs at a fucking school?" The sneer had gone completely, and he looked even paler than he'd done a few minutes earlier.

"Not for drugs," said Mary, "We've arrested Ardi for the murder of Luan Redzepi. He's looking at life imprisonment – if he and his family can't dump it onto you, that is."

"Just as well you've got this chance to put your side of the story first, isn't it?" added the DI.

The idea that the Troshanis would be able to frame Ewan for masterminding Redzepi's killing was a ludicrous one, but Mary and the DI knew the effect that words like "arrest", "murder" and "life imprisonment" could have on youngsters in trouble for the first time, even ones with superhuman intellects. Their job now was to use that effect ruthlessly. As it turned out, they didn't need to try very hard.

"It was nothing to do with me," Ewan blurted, "I just made…". He stopped mid-sentence as Jenkins grabbed him by the arm and started whispering furiously in his ear.

"I wouldn't rely too heavily on advice from Mr Jenkins, Ewan," said the DI, "he works for the Troshanis. If I were you I'd get another lawyer."

Jenkins' face turned red. He pulled away from Ewan and stared angrily at the DI.

"That is outrageous," he said, his Welsh accent seeming to get stronger with each syllable, "How dare you impugn my professional integrity in this manner. I shall lodge a formal complaint with your superintendent."

"I'm simply stating the truth, Mr Jenkins," said the DI, seeming completely unruffled by the lawyer's outburst, "You work for the Troshanis – in fact you're working for them now, unless Ewan's suddenly found the wherewithal to pay your fees. Is that what happened, Ewan? Ardi told you to ring his uncle if you were ever in bother with the police, said they'd sort out a good lawyer for you?"

Neither Ewan nor Jenkins made any reply.

"Shall I tell you what I think?" continued the DI, "I think that if Mr Jenkins stays in this room then he'll go straight from here to a private conference with Ardi, in which he'll tell him everything you've told us, so that Ardi can rig his story to contradict yours. And we won't be able to stop him."

Mary could barely believe what she was hearing. It was one thing to point out the facts about who paid Jenkins, another entirely to openly accuse him of acting corruptly. With Jenkins there they'd stand little chance of getting Ewan to incriminate the Troshanis, but she wasn't sure that getting rid of him was worth the personal cost to the DI of making the lawyer, and influential Lodge member, his enemy. Except, of course, that Ewan was their only real chance of making her arrest of Ardi stick. She wondered if this was payback for the way she'd stepped in at Between the Lines, and didn't like the idea that it might be.

"I'm warning you, Inspector" said Jenkins gravely, his face redder than ever.

"And I'm warning you, Mr Jenkins," the DI replied, in a voice that suddenly reminded Mary of DSI Kopacz's, "There is a clear conflict of interest here – two defendants who are likely to tell conflicting stories, and you're taking money from one to represent the other. From where I'm sitting you're one step away from conspiracy to pervert the course of justice, and don't think I wouldn't nick you for it, because I would."

Jenkins was literally speechless. Mary couldn't think of a constructive thing to say. The silence was eventually broken by Ewan's voice.

"I want a different lawyer."

"Ewan, don't listen to them," said Jenkins. There was desperation in his voice now. "They're trying to..."

"I want a different fucking lawyer, all right?" Ewan

said, with surprising authority. For a brief moment he reminded Mary of Ellie. "You can get me one, can't you? Duty solicitor, or whatever you call them."

"Yes we can," said Mary, "Interview suspended at 13:54".

Ninety minutes later Ewan sat in the interview room again, the chair next to him now occupied by Frances Holland, a young solicitor from a firm in the South Ward. She looked solemn, almost like a priest there to deliver the sacrament as he went to his fate. She'd had her own private conference with him, and presumably knew what he was going to say.

"Interview resumed at 15.28," said Mary, "Present are DI Jones, DS Miller, Ewan Taylor and Ms Frances Holland. Mr Jenkins has left the room. Just to remind you, Ewan, that you're still under caution and this interview is being recorded. Is that all OK?"

"Yeah." Not so hostile now. Resigned, fearful instead.

As they'd made their way back to the interview room the DI had reminded Mary that she'd have to lead the questioning, since he was still getting to grips with her theories on what had happened. He'd taken Jenkins out of the game; now it was up to her to get them over the line.

"Tell us about your involvement with Ardit Troshani and drugs at Compton School," she asked Ewan, as casually as if she was enquiring about his involvement in an after-school physics club.

"I was just running some dope for him, that's all. Nothing stronger, I told him I wouldn't touch it."

"Why were you doing that?"

Ewan looked at her as if she'd tripped over the bleeding obvious.

"For money – what do you think? I was always skint and I was sick of it."

"But you had your job at the supermarket, didn't you?"

"Those bastards pay peanuts and think they own you," he said, a flash of his previous anger returning. He paused. "Plus I had to give my mum something after my dad got made redundant then started drinking away his Jobseekers."

Mary caught herself hoping it wasn't true. If it was, then Ewan wasn't quite the over-cosseted egomaniac he'd seemed.

"And what about Ardi, did he sell stronger drugs?"

"I don't know – honest. I just took the dope from him and paid him when I'd sold it."

"So how come Ardi got caught and you didn't?"

"Just luck. A girl he'd sold to in one of the boarding houses went home for the weekend and her mother found the stuff in her bag. They raised hell – discretely, of course. I'd never dealt with her, so she didn't say anything about me."

"And Ardi didn't either?"

"No."

"They must have put pressure on him to tell them if anyone else was dealing at the school, surely?"

"I don't know. If they did, he didn't tell them anything."

"So after Ardi was expelled," said Mary, "is that when you started working for the Troshanis as a chemist, in the sub-basement at Grove Park?"

Ewan looked momentarily startled, as if he hadn't expected Mary to know about the Grove Park setup. It had evidently been a good guess.

"Not there at first. The lab was out at their place, in a garage. Then they moved it to Grove Park, got much better equipment."

"Did you spend much time there?"

"Quite a bit, yeah. They were moving a lot of stuff

through there."

"And where did you tell people you were when you were doing this?"

"What?" Ewan seemed puzzled by the question.

"What did you say to your parents, to Ellie?" the DI interjected, "Was it 'Bye Mum, I'm off to work in the drugs lab', or did you make something up?"

"Oh, yeah. I told them I was working in the supermarket." He seemed pleased with his subterfuge. "I kept a couple of shifts so I was still technically an employee."

"Didn't your friends notice you weren't coming to work much any more?"

"My friends from Compton don't work in supermarkets, Inspector," Ewan said, sounding like Tamzin had when she'd spoken about the Compton "done thing" in the café, "Zac used to, but he cut his hours right back so he could revise. The people at the shop all thought I'd done the same."

All except, perhaps, one highly observant supermarket employee you hadn't expected to find in Weston on a Sunday night when you were pretending to have just come off shift. That, however, would have to wait for later.

"This better equipment in the new lab," Mary asked, "was it good enough to make synthesized alkaloid compounds?"

Ewan hesitated for a long time. Frances Holland looked at him intently, but said nothing. Eventually he gave her a questioning look, to which she returned the slightest of nods.

"Yeah. But I didn't know what they were going to use it for."

"It", not "them". He knew they were talking about a specific compound.

"But you knew it was a poison?"

"Yes, but I didn't think that was what they wanted it for. They told me they were going to supply it to another lab, for use in another process – making a new kind of rock, that kind of thing."

The DI, who'd been leaning back in his chair, sat upright and began to put his papers together. The others all looked at him as if they'd forgotten he was there.

"All right then, Ewan, I think that's probably it for now," he said briskly, "We'll come and get you when we need you again. Interview terminated at 15:37." He hit the stop button on the recorder.

Mary tried to hide her shock. She hoped, dearly, that this was a trick.

"What, that's it?" said Ewan, looking bewildered.

"I think it is, yes." He leaned forward and looked Ewan in the eyes. "Because if you're going to waste our time with that kind of nonsense then we might as well get Ardi up here and let him start telling us his version of things, which will no doubt feature you in a starring role. At least that way we get to charge someone. One chance to put your side of the story, Mr Taylor, and do not try to play clever with us. Now which is it going to be?"

Ewan's shoulders slumped.

"All right."

The DI hit the start button; the red lights on the recorder glowed.

"Interview resumed at 15:40. Those present as before. Right, Mr Taylor, let's try again. How did you come to make this," he glanced down at his notes, "synthesized alkaloid compound?"

"Ardi had read about it somewhere – he's got a thing about poisons, the Borgias and all that. He asked me if I could make it, and I said yes."

"And you knew what he wanted it for?" Mary asked.

"As far as I knew he just wanted to see if I could do

it."

"I've warned you, Mr Taylor..." the DI said darkly.

"No, that's the truth," said Ewan, so emphatically that Mary, at least, was inclined to believe him, "It was like a challenge – 'bet you couldn't make that' sort of thing."

"And you could?"

"With some trial and error, yes. Took me ages though – over a week. There's a six-step process that goes through a tryptamine-derived Zincke aldehyde, but I couldn't get that to work, so I had to switch to the fifteen-step process based on the Diels-Alder cycloaddition reaction, and even that kept going wrong. I got there in the end though."

From most people "Tryptamine-derived Zincke aldehyde" would have sounded like a childish attempt to blind them with science, but from Ewan it sounded like everyday conversation, the words spoken at full speed without hesitation, no more alien to him than "M5 to Avonmouth". His eyes had come alive while he was saying it, like Michael Slade's had when he'd talked about letter frequency and its relevance to cryptography. He was the real deal, the kind of person who just might, one day, unlock the secrets of the universe. For a moment Mary could see why Ellie was in such awe of him. Her job, however, was not to be.

"You say it took you over a week to make this stuff?" she asked.

"Yeah – more like ten days actually."

"Why go to all that trouble for something that no-one had any use for?"

"Like I said, the challenge, and the chance to use some of the fancy equipment they'd installed. It made Compton's lab look like my mum's kitchen."

Ah, that was OK then. Boy genius relieves the boredom of his gap year by manufacturing a deadly poison for a gang of drug dealers. Any awe Mary might have felt evaporated as the police officer's responses took over. Why couldn't he have had a games console like everyone else?

"So when did you finish making it?"

"Ages ago. A month, something like that. It's stable if you keep it reasonably cool. I kept it in the fridge."

If it was made a month ago then that was well before the first, let alone the second, murder, meaning he'd most likely made it not knowing it would be used to kill Luan Redzepi. If he was telling the truth then he might just have saved himself from a conspiracy to murder charge, even if he would still be an accessory.

"And our expert witnesses will confirm that it takes this long to make, will they?" said the DI. He was obviously thinking the same thing.

"They'll probably be surprised I was able to make it at all," Ewan replied, "I was, to be honest." There was a matter-of-factness to the way he said it which was almost likeable. This wasn't, however, a likeable business.

"Did you know that Ardi had decided to use the poison to kill Luan Redzepi?" asked the DI.

There was another long pause, a rather sad look from Ms Holland, then that slightest of nods again.

"Yes."

"How did you know?"

"Because he told me they were going to do it."

"Who's 'they'?"

"The Troshani family – Ardi, his dad, Agron, the whole gang."

"What exactly did they tell you they were going to do?"

"Kill Luan then bury him in Sand Bay, the same way the Polish woman had been buried."

"Did you make any attempt to stop them?"

Ewan laughed. "What, me against the Troshanis? They'd have buried me along with Luan."

"But you did try though, didn't you?" said Mary, "that's why you made your friends go to Sand Bay from the party – in the hope that you'd be in time to stop it. Did you suddenly have second thoughts?"

"Something like that, yeah."

"Did you know Luan Redzepi personally, Ewan?" The DI came in again now.

"Yeah, we talked a bit. The Grove Park lab was a big secret, but he was allowed in because he was family. He was a smart guy. A bit too smart really."

"Did you know he was involved in the murder of Katya Czwisnjowski – the Polish woman, as you call her?"

"Yeah."

"How did you know?"

"He told me."

"And do you know why the Troshanis killed him? Was it because they were afraid he'd tell us about them murdering Katya?"

All of a sudden Ewan's face broke into a broad smile. It wasn't a sneer, or a snigger, just pure, almost innocent amusement. It was the nearest to happy that Mary had seen him, and probably the nearest she ever would.

"You don't know, do you?" he said, still smiling.

"Know what, Ewan?" said Mary, mystified as to what had suddenly made him so cheerful.

"Luan helped to kill the Polish woman, lured her to her death in fact," Ewan said, "But he wasn't helping the Troshanis. They didn't have anything to do with it."

Chapter 43

The DI approached the interview room table and placed two plastic cups on it. Mary was already seated with hers; Ms Holland had declined the offer of a drink from the machine. Neither the lawyer nor her client were aware of the other matter the DI had attended to while out of the room – applying for a search warrant for the Troshanis' Grove Park premises and calling in a specialist search team to find the entrance to the sub-basement. It wouldn't have done to ask Ewan where it was; better to make him think they already knew some things about the case.

"Interview resumed at 16:14, those present as before," said the DI. "OK, Ewan, you've got our attention. If the Troshanis didn't kill Katya Czwisnjowski then who did, and why did Luan Redzepi help them?"

Instead of replying, Ewan whispered into his lawyer's ear, she whispering into his in response. Mary had a good idea what was coming.

"If I'm going to give you everything on this then I want immunity in return. Witness protection, all that kind of thing."

Oh well, you may as well start big, thought Mary.

"It doesn't work like that, I'm afraid," said the DI, with the slightly weary air of someone who'd said the same thing many times before, "Immunity's up to the CPS, not us, and they'll want to hear what you've got to say first. All I can say is that the more you help us now, the better it will look for you in court."

Ewan looked crestfallen, although not surprised. It had been worth a try.

"OK."

"So, who killed Katya Czwisnjowski, and why was Luan Redzepi involved?"

"The Bristol mob killed her – I don't know their names, the Troshanis just called them that."

OK, this was an unexpected twist, assuming that it was the same Bristol mob that Katya was drinking with in TuringShroud's photo. Either that or it was a different one, in which case it really was time to hand it over to Major Crime to sort out.

"Why did they kill her?"

"Because she was trying to build up a dealer network there." Ewan looked at the two officers in turn, as if checking whether they understood. "Drugs, you know? Dope, coke, crystal meth, the full service."

"This was at the university?"

Ewan shook his head. "She already had a network there, and the mob weren't too bothered about it. Ardi said they didn't want the uni, reckoned it was too dangerous selling to rich kids, which he could understand after what happened to him at Compton. So there was a sort of understanding – she stuck to the uni and they left her alone. Plus there was her dad to think about. According to Ardi he's some sort of international drugs baron, seriously heavy guy. It was his setup really, she was like his project manager. The mob didn't want to upset him, so long as she stuck to her patch."

"And the Troshanis knew about this?" asked Mary.

Ewan looked puzzled then amused in quick succession, as if surprised again at how little they knew.

"They were part of it. Her dad organised getting the raw materials in, the Troshanis stored and processed it, her network flogged it."

Mary did her best to look as if Ewan was merely confirming what she already knew. The DI, however, didn't bother.

"Let's get this straight," he said, "you're telling us that

the Czwisnjowskis and the Troshanis were working together, manufacturing drugs in Weston and selling them around the University?"

"Yeah. Except I wouldn't really call it 'together'. It was the Polish woman – Katya – calling the shots. The Troshanis were more like the hired help. I saw her a few times at Grove Park. She was a Grade A bitch, treated them like something she'd scraped off her shoe."

"How did this arrangement come about?"

"I don't know exactly – Ardi said there was some link between the Polish woman's dad and Agron's dad and grandfather, going back to when Albania was a proper communist country. I think Ardi's family started off buying in uncut stuff from them - off the ships, you know – then the Polish lot suggested something bigger. Ardi said they were impressed with how Agron used all that police persecution stuff to make your lot leave them alone. Agron used to say that in Albania they'd have to bribe the police to keep away from them, but in England you did it for free."

A trace of the sneering smile returned to Ewan's face, but he was sensible enough to quickly put it away. Mary thought of a few people she dearly hoped would be brought face to face with the fact that their stands against "police persecution" had enabled its supposed victims to run a drugs factory supplying Bristol University students. She didn't hold out much hope of it happening though.

"And Ardi's family paid you to look after the manufacturing side of things?"

Another pause, another brief nod.

"Yeah."

They were in Buy One Get One Free territory here, thought Mary – as well as telling them about the murder, the boy was talking himself into serious trouble on the drugs conspiracy front. Still, it wasn't for her to dissuade him, and he had a perfectly good lawyer now.

"So what went wrong?" asked the DI, returning to the main shopping list.

"The Polish woman wanted to expand into other parts of Bristol. She said that if she just took a small patch at a time the Bristol mob would be too scared of her dad to do anything about it. That was what Grove Park was about. Her dad put up the cash for the Troshanis to buy it and install the lab."

"And the Troshanis went along with this?"

"Ardi's dad and uncle were dead against it, but they seemed to be scared shitless of her old man. 'Rushist' they called him – The Russian - although I thought he was Polish like she was."

"How do you know all this, Ewan?" asked Mary. There was always the possibility that a bright lad like him was making it up to increase his value as a witness.

"Ardi told me most of it. But like I said I saw this Katya a few times at Grove Park. They all talked in English because they didn't understand each other's languages. If the Troshanis tried to say no to anything she'd say 'My father will not be pleased by this' and wave her fucking BlackBerry at them, as if she was going to send him one of her BBMs. She was welded to that thing – she'd done so much messaging on it she'd worn the letters off the keyboard. It worked though - when she threatened the Troshanis with it they'd fall into line like whipped puppies, even Agron."

Mary tried to picture Agron Troshani as a whipped puppy, but the image just wouldn't come. One thing was becoming clear though; Weston CID weren't the only ones who'd been playing out of their league.

"OK, Ewan," said the DI, finishing a note he'd been writing on his pad, "let's get back to Luan Redzepi. You say he told you that he was involved in Katya's murder. When did he tell you this?"

"The night after they buried her – Wednesday, wasn't it? I was working late at Grove Park and he turned up with a bottle of vodka, proper stuff. We got shitfaced and he told me all about it. I think he was desperate to tell someone."

"Did he tell you why he did it?"

"Like I said, he told me everything."

"OK, you tell us."

Ewan took a deep breath and a swig of his coffee, grimacing as he swallowed it.

"Luan didn't want to be here, or to be involved in the drugs business. He'd been forced to come because of a debt his mother owed to Agron, money he'd sent her after Luan's dad died. It was some kind of honour thing, he had to pay it off by working for him. He hated Agron, and I mean really hated him. He didn't say it, but I reckon he thought Agron was mixed up in his dad's death, supposed to have been a road accident but Luan didn't reckon it was. The funny thing was, Agron liked him, thought he had potential."

"That must have got Ardi's back up," said Mary.

"Yeah, it did," Ewan replied, smiling, "Ardi pretended to like Luan, called him 'Cuz', but he hated him really. He was scared he was going to replace him as Agron's favourite nephew. It got worse when the Polish woman said she wanted someone to go with her on her trips around Bristol, and Agron sent Luan. All he was was her bag-carrier, and she treated him like shit like she did everyone else, but Ardi saw it as some kind of big promotion."

"So how did Luan end up involved in Katya's murder?"

"He got turned, as they say in spy books. It was the Polish bitch's fault. She said she'd just go for little patches near the uni - Redland, Cotham, bits of Clifton, that sort of thing. What she actually did was go straight to Old Market – right in the middle of the Bristol mob's territory - and set up shop there. She was fucking mad. They met a girl there, Nyesha. The Polish woman thought she was recruiting her as a dealer, but she was really working for the mob. Apparently she was a real looker. Luan had a massive thing about her, said she was like an African goddess."

From what Mary had seen in the photograph, it sounded a fair description of Nyesha Rose. And it was Nyesha's Bristol mob that Ewan was referring to, but in a different relationship to Katya from the one they'd assumed; not partners, but enemies.

"So Nyesha seduced Luan into working for the Bristol gang?"

"I don't think she needed to do much seducing. The way Luan said it he was only too glad to stick it to Agron, and to that Polish bitch after the way she treated him."

"How long did this go on for?"

"All through the summer, into October. Then Katya fucked off back to Poland and left her dealers to run things, which was a relief to everyone. By then Ardi's paranoid fantasies had come true - Agron had decided that Luan was going to be his trusted guy for dealing with the Poles. He kept him in the loop about what was going on, only of course Luan was feeding it all to Nyesha."

Mary wanted to call a timeout, long enough for her to properly take in the new landscape of alliances, betrayals and murders that Ewan was laying out for them. The DI, however, clearly didn't have that much time to spare.

"Did Luan say anything about the two students who were murdered in Bristol? We know that Katya knew at least one of them."

"She knew both of them - they were her dealers. Paying off the student loan, you know?" He grinned.

"She never touched the gear directly, just put her 'people' in contact with each other to get supplies."

Just like her father, thought Mary.

"How did that work?" asked the DI, "Did they come to Weston to collect it?" No harm in them knowing the details before the Drug Squad got them.

Ewan allowed himself a brief smirk. "No way – the Troshanis did put their foot down about that. There'd be a meet between here and Bristol, somewhere that didn't look too shady – country pubs, that kind of thing. Ardi did a lot of the delivery runs, reckoned his crewbus had diplomatic immunity." The sneer almost appeared again. Mary thought again of the people she'd like to see facing up to what they'd helped make possible.

"I met the guy – James – a couple of times," Ewan continued, "and the girl. He was OK, but she was a real little coke-head. Ardi reckoned she was the type who got desperate, if you know what I mean." The sneer came back for real now. Mary wasn't quite sure what he did mean, but she could take a guess. Women, especially pretty young blondes, had the option of paying in a way that wasn't so easily available to men. She'd probably been introduced to drugs at school, by someone just like Ewan.

"So you went on these delivery runs with Ardi?" Mary said. He must have done, if the dealers never came to Weston. He'd talked himself further into a supplying charge; she didn't feel bad about that.

"Yeah. Just a few times." At least he was bright enough to see what he'd done, and not waste their time trying to talk his way out of it. He deserved a day or two off his sentence for that.

"So these two – James Penhaligon and Amelia Foster – were their murders connected to their dealing?" It was an obvious question but the DI had to ask it for the recording.

"What do you think?" said Ewan mockingly, then seeing the DI's expression quickly continued, "Yeah, the Polish woman had picked them for expanding into the rest of Bristol. They were going to be area managers, like a fucking supermarket!" He made a noise which Mary found uncomfortably like Michael Slade's chortling. "The Bristol mob killed them as a warning, made it known they'd do the same to anyone else who worked for her. That put the willies up Agron and Ardi's dad - they wanted out, especially as she'd fucked off to Poland and left them to deal with it. She sent them one of her BBMs saying that killing her people was an insult, and that her father was going to send some specialists over to teach the Bristol mob some manners. I guess Luan told Nyesha about that and they decided to finish her off. That Polish woman was off her trolley if you ask me."

To Mary she sounded more like a dangerous combination of her father's cold ruthlessness and her mother's imperious manner. As for Ewan, he was turning out to be such a mine of information that she was tempted to ask him who'd really masterminded the Great Train Robbery of 1963. Before she had the chance, the DI asked a more pertinent question of his own.

"And you said that Luan lured Katya to her death?"

"Yeah. He got in contact with her and told her that Nyesha wanted a face to face meeting in Bristol or she was going to quit. After first two were killed she'd had to put Nyesha in charge, so if Nyesha went the whole thing would fall apart. So she got straight on a plane and flew in. She'd done it before, after James was killed – in one night, out the next. She had a false passport she used for that kind of thing, boasted about that too. Anyway, she went to meet Nyesha and that was it – they grabbed her."

"And how was the burial done?"

"Inflatable off a ship out of Portbury. Four Malaysian

crew members plus Luan to make sure they did the job right. He volunteered for it, but I think that actually seeing her dead and shoved in the ground fucked him up." Ewan suddenly smiled, as if recalling a fond memory, "They'd wiped that fucking BlackBerry of hers and given it to one of the crew as part of the deal, but he dropped it over the side as they were going back out. Luan said it wouldn't be a problem as the Bristol mob knew all about wiping phones properly."

The DI had been checking the contents of his file while Ewan had been talking. Now he looked him in the eyes across the table.

"This is all very interesting, Ewan, but there is a slight problem with the dates. Katya's mother reported her missing in Gdansk on the 26th of October, but she wasn't buried in the beach here until the night of November the third, a week later. What happened in between?"

Ewan grinned again. Mary wasn't sure he realised just how much trouble he was in, but if it kept him talking then she wasn't going to stop him.

"They missed the boat – literally. The ship they were going to put her on sailed a day early. They had to wait a week for another one."

"And what did they do with her while they were waiting?"

"I don't know – kept her somewhere, I guess. Luan didn't say."

If the pathologist's report was right then she'd been alive for most of that time, not killed until the Tuesday morning. Mary wondered how she'd spent those last few days, whether she'd known what was going to happen to her. Right now, however, she had more pressing concerns, the main one being getting enough evidence to charge Ardi Troshani with Luan's murder.

"So when did the Troshanis find out that Katya had been murdered?" she asked. For the first time she wondered whether 'Katya' was the right name to use. It was the way the police referred to innocent young victims - "Help us find Katya's killer", the posters had read - but the picture Ewan had painted of her seemed anything but innocent.

"Straight away," said Ewan, "They recognised the description your lot put out on the lunchtime news."

"And what was their reaction?"

"Fucking panic!" The ugly smile was back again. "Ardi rang me and said 'they've killed the fucking Polish bitch', he was just shouting it down the phone over and over. I went to Grove Park and it was mad there. None of them were thinking straight - they all had massive hangovers from the night before, Agron's wife's birthday, and they were just shouting at each other."

"What were they shouting?"

"I don't know - it was in Albanian!"

"You must have had an idea."

Ewan seemed to remember where he was, and the smile faded.

"Yeah. They thought the 'Rushisht' was going to come over and kill them all."

"Why would he do that?"

"Because he thought they'd killed his daughter? For not protecting her? Take your pick. The way she'd hyped him up he was the type who'd come over and kill them just for putting the wrong labels on the dope." Ewan laughed. "They couldn't have protected her even if they'd wanted to - she just did whatever she wanted, didn't listen to anyone. She was fucking mad."

"So what did the Troshanis do?"

"Agron said they should tell her dad about it, before he found out any other way. Ardi's dad didn't want to, and they had a massive bust-up about it, but Agron's the boss, so they did it his way."

The DI looked up from his notepad.

"To be clear about this, you're saying that Agron Troshani informed Katya Czwisnjowski's father of her death on the Wednesday, the day she was found on the beach?"

"Yeah. He had a special phone that he was allowed to ring the old man on direct. Use once then throw away, you know? He was only supposed to use it for something like that. Ardi knew about it."

And now they knew about it too. It meant that the Czwisnjowskis had been a day ahead of them all along. No wonder they'd turned up in Weston so quickly.

"Look, I need a break," said Ewan. He turned to Frances Holland, who nodded, then he pointed to his plastic cup, "I'll have some more of this shit if there's any going."

Mary could see that he wasn't playing games; telling them all this was taking its toll on him, emotionally if not physically. The next bit could be the toughest of all.

"Sure," said the DI, "I'll get someone to bring it to you. Interview suspended at 16:48."

Chapter 44

"Do you buy it?" asked the DI as he and Mary reached his office.

"To be honest I'm still getting to grips with it," she replied, "but basically yes. It makes sense, and he must know that we'll check it out. He's an arrogant little so-and-so, but he's not stupid enough to send us on a wild goose chase – at least I don't think he is."

"No, me neither. Let's get it clear then. We've got the Czwisnjowskis and Troshanis on the same side, the two Bristol university students working as dealers for Katya Czwisnjowski, Katya trampling all over this Bristol mob's turf, and the mob responding by murdering the two students then Katya herself. In the middle of all this are Luan Redzepi and Nyesha Rose, acting as double agents like something out of a James Bond film. Luan makes a drunken confession to Ewan about his part in Katya's murder, and two days later he's dead as well, killed by his own family. That means the Force's entire elite detective squad, not to mention Weston CID, were wrong about everything - except, that is, for a certain DS who twigged that young Ewan could have made the poison that killed Redzepi, and got a sighting of Ardi Troshani's van near the scene. You do realise how unpopular this is going to make you, don't you?"

"Yes Guv." Quite pleased though, as well.

"Still, it could be worse. From what we've just heard we're lucky we haven't been digging them out of the beach every morning for the past fortnight."

Mary was about to agree when the DI's phone rang. The conversation was short, and from the look that came over his face, it wasn't good news.

"Problem," he said, putting the phone down, "The search team are in at Grove Park, but they can't find the entrance to the sub-basement. Looks like the Troshanis spent Czwisnjowski's money on some industrial-strength camouflage."

"Probably so they could hide from his daughter, from what Ewan said."

The DI allowed himself a smile.

"Yes. Well we can't have uniform standing around all night. We're going to have to ask him, aren't we?"

"Looks like it, Guv."

"If he does that grin of his, I swear I'll put him in a cell and send Blakestone in after him."

"Blakestone?"

"Cage fighter."

"What?"

"She's a cage fighter. Bristol women's champion before she got married and came down here. You should read the newsletter more often."

"Yes, Guv." No wonder Blakestone had been able to shut Ardi Troshani up with little more than a stern look.

"Right then," said the DI, picking up his file, "let's get it over with."

"Interview resumed at 17:08, those present as before." The DI sat down and opened his file. "I'll remind you that this interview is under caution so anything you say may be used in evidence. You're not under arrest though, so you're free to leave at any time. Is that understood?"

"Yeah." Another cup of machine coffee didn't seem to have done much for Ewan's cheerfulness, but then he didn't have much to be cheerful about.

"We've got a search team in the Troshanis' place at Grove Park, Ewan, but they don't seem to be able to find any trace of this sub-basement lab of yours. Are you sure it's there?" It was a clever approach by the DI, camouflaging their need for Ewan's help as a challenge to the accuracy of his story. Ewan, however, was clever too, and threw it straight back at them.

"Course I'm sure. I thought you knew all about it, anyway?"

"We know it exists, but it might not necessarily be where you've been telling us. For all we know it may be somewhere else altogether, with Agron and Zamir clearing it out as we speak. It would be very helpful if you'd tell us how to get in." The DI glanced at Frances Holland, who in turned nodded to Ewan.

"You only had to ask," said Ewan, and Mary had to concede that he had a point. Luckily there was no grin, so she wouldn't have to persuade the DI to keep Blakestone behind her counter.

"It's well hidden. They had a guy from America come over to do it. At the bottom of the stairs into the main basement there's a big cupboard. The back wall of that's false."

"So how do you open it – a hidden button or something?"

Ewan shook his head, his expression almost pitying, the grin almost back. "Android app. It looks like a game, but swipe the screen the right way and it opens the door. It has to be running on an authorised phone."

"Does that include yours?"

"Yeah." Ewan clearly knew what was coming next. He took his phone from his pocket, switched it on and laid it on the table. "Touch that to load the app, then choose Play, and when the background appears, swipe in this direction with two fingers, like this. It's got to be two. You need to be within three metres of the cupboard wall when you do it." He pushed the phone a few inches further across the table, towards the DI.

"For the recording, Mr Taylor is passing us his mobile

phone. Can you confirm that, Ewan?"

"Yeah."

"That's very cooperative of you, thank you."

"Just remember I did it, OK?" The hint of grin on Ewan's face broadened into a smile. "The Polish woman went mental because the app wouldn't run on her fucking BlackBerry. The American guy wasn't taking any of her shit though. He told her to quit acting like a spoilt brat and get a new phone. We all loved him after that."

Ten minutes later, with Ewan's phone on its way to Grove Park, the DI resumed the interview for the third time.

"Right, Ewan," he said briskly, "I think we're into the final stretch now. We just need to deal with how the Troshanis came to kill Luan Redzepi. You've told us that they recognised police descriptions of Katya Czwisnjowski on the day she was found. When did they begin to suspect that Redzepi was involved in her murder?"

"They didn't, not at first anyway." Ewan looked uneasy.

"Didn't they wonder where he'd been on the night of the murder?"

"I told you, they were all in Marco's that night, drinking themselves stupid at Agron's wife's birthday. I doubt if they'd have remembered whether he was there or not. Anyway, he was the contact man with the Polish woman's Bristol dealers – those that were still alive, that is." The sneer appeared again. "He had an excuse to be away whenever he wanted."

"So what made them realise he was involved?"

Ewan paused, as if reluctant to say the words, although it seemed to Mary that everyone else in the room knew what they'd be. He delayed the moment further with a sip at his coffee, then spoke.

"I told them."

"When?"

"The day after Luan told me – the Thursday, I guess."

"I thought you said Luan was your friend?" The DI managed to sound more mystified than contemptuous.

"I didn't say that," Ewan shot back angrily, "I said I spoke to him a few times. Ardi was my friend, and his family had been good to me. They paid me as much for a few hours in the lab as that fucking supermarket would have done if I'd been full-time, and they didn't treat me like some fucking social experiment either, dressed up in a fucking blazer like the rich kids. I owed them."

And now you're shopping them to us, thought Mary. The boy was quite a number. Perhaps future Nobel Prize winners needed that kind of ruthlessness to get to the top. Or perhaps that was just what parents paid places like Compton School to teach their children.

"And the Troshanis believed you, did they?" asked Mary. To give Ewan his due, it must have taken some nerve to tell the family that one of their members was a traitor.

"Yeah. I told Ardi first, and he didn't take much convincing." Good choice. With Ardi it had probably been more a case of thanking the messenger than shooting him.

"And what did the Troshanis do when you told them?"

"I don't know exactly, it was all done in Albanian. I think Agron got in contact with the Polish woman's dad again, because he came back and they were talking about 'Rushist' and 'nesër' – tomorrow. Then Ardi told me what was going on. The woman's dad was arriving from Poland the next day, and they had to wait for him to give them the word, but in the meantime prepare to deal with Luan the way he'd dealt with the old man's daughter."

The DI leaned forward, over the table.

"This is important, Ewan. You say that Ardi told you that Katya's father ordered the Troshanis to kill Luan Redzepi. Is that correct?"

"Yeah. They just had to wait until he gave them the OK."

"How did Ardi feel about killing his cousin?"

The ugly smile broke out again on Ewan's face, stretching the red blotches around his mouth.

"He was raring to go! He didn't need much of an excuse to do Luan in, and he loved the idea of being an assassin for an international drugs trafficker. It was his ticket to the big time."

More like a ticket to a life sentence, as it was turning out. Still, it couldn't have happened to a nicer lad.

"And what about Agron? You said he liked Luan, and the boy was his nephew."

"I don't think Agron had much choice. If they hadn't dealt with Luan then the 'Rushist' would have dealt with all of them. Anyway, Ardi told me there was this honour thing, the family cleansing itself of the traitor in its midst, like something out of history." Ewan didn't seem to have a high opinion of history, although as a nuclear physicist that was perhaps understandable.

"Did Ardi tell you specifically that he and the others were going to do what Katya's father wanted and kill Luan?"

"Yes. He said 'We're gonna finish that cunt tonight'. That was Friday lunchtime. They'd just got the order from the old man."

Just after the "old man" had been shown pictures of his dead daughter in the DI's office. He'd probably made the call from the lobby of whatever hotel they'd lunched at.

"Do you know exactly what happened?" asked the DI. That would be hoping for too much, but no harm in asking.

"No. I didn't see Ardi again after that, but I saw that the poison was gone from the fridge. Then Ardi was supposed to be coming to the party that night, but he didn't show. I guessed they were getting it done."

"And did Ardi, or any of the other Troshanis, confirm that they'd murdered Luan?"

"Yeah, I saw Ardi on the Monday. He said they'd done the job and the Rushist was OK with it. He told me he'd wanted to make it hurt but Agron had said no, just give him the poison. The Rushist wanted it that way too - businesslike. Those fuckers are mad."

"OK, I think we're almost done now," said the DI, starting to put his papers back in their file, "One last thing though. The way Katya and Luan were both found with their arms pointing towards their home countries. Do you know anything about that?"

Ewan gave an amused smile.

"Luan got the idea from the Polish woman. Ironic, eh? She said her dad had been in the Russian army, and some of the old guys told him that when they were pushing the Germans out of Poland in 1944 there was this unit that buried dead German soldiers with their arms pointing west, towards Germany – 'Saluting the Fatherland', they called it, some kind of Russian joke. She said her old man did it with people who trod on his territory. Luan must have told the Bristol mob about it, or just decided to do it himself."

"So how come Luan was buried that way too?" Mary asked the question, although she had an idea of the answer.

"The old man ordered it. He was very specific, said it had to be done properly, not the way they'd done it to his daughter. Ardi said Agron was fine with it, because it would make it look like the same people did both burials, and he had a rock-solid alibi for the night the woman was done."

So there it was, thought Mary – the mystery of the pointing hands coming down to some Russian soldiers with a warped sense of humour in 1944. Taunting Katya's father with his own burial routine would probably have brought suspicion on Luan anyway, even if he hadn't confessed everything to the person he'd thought was his friend. As for Agron, he'd no doubt be joining his nephew in finding that things hadn't worked out as he'd expected them to.

The DI closed his file. "And you'll be willing to testify to all this, will you?"

Ewan looked shocked for a second, then was silent for three or four seconds more. Mary had seen it before; the moment when it came home to a suspect that they'd actually have to stand up in court and betray their friends in order to earn an easy ride for themselves. Many of them cracked at this point.

"I guess so, yeah, if I have to." Not Ewan though.

"Good," said the DI, as if he'd never doubted him.

"Am I going to go to prison?" For the first time the voice cracked, and Ewan the sneering genius was replaced by a small boy facing an uncertain, and frightening, future.

The DI glanced at Frances Holland. "I can't comment on that, Ewan, but the charges you'll be facing are very serious ones. We will, however, be reporting that you've cooperated fully at this stage of the investigation, and that your help has been crucial in moving the case forward. What happens later will be between your lawyers and the CPS."

It wasn't much, and Ewan didn't seem much cheered by it. Things weren't about to get better, either.

"OK, now I don't want you to be scared by this," said the DI, very effectively signalling that he was about to do something scary, "It's for your own good, as I'll explain in a moment." He took a deep breath. "Ewan Taylor, I'm arresting you for the production and supply of controlled drugs contrary to the Misuse of Drugs Act 1971, and as an accessory to the murder of Luan Redzepi on or about the seventh of November this year. You do not have to say anything, but it may harm your defence if you fail to mention, when questioned, something which you may later rely on in court. Anything you do say may be given in evidence. My grounds for arrest is information I've received from you and others, and my reason for arresting you, rather than bailing you, is that I consider you may abscond, and also that you may be in physical danger from other people involved in this case if you are allowed to go free. Do you understand all that?"

Ewan nodded.

"For the recording please, Ewan." The DI's voice was almost gentle.

"Yes, I understand."

Tears welled up in Ewan's eyes. Mary couldn't suppress the sympathy that welled up in her, despite everything he'd done. He was a bright lad; he knew that he was going to be locked up in a cell now, and that he might not be free again for years, a period of time which would seem endless at his age. His world – Ellie, their child, Cambridge, a glittering career as a scientist – had just collapsed underneath him. Not much younger and he'd still have been a minor, needing a parent or other appropriate adult with him in interviews like these, and social workers involved at every stage. Now they could bring him in and charge him with murder as if he was Agron Troshani.

"OK, well we'll take you downstairs now and get you booked into the custody suite." The DI turned to Frances Holland, "We'll be charging Ewan tomorrow, after we've completed some more enquiries." Ms Holland, who hadn't spoken during the interview, nodded in reply.

"Will you tell Ellie where I am?" Ewan's voice, still cracked, was directed at Mary now. She looked first at the lawyer, then the DI, both of whom indicated no objection.

"Yes, I'll tell her now."

"Thanks."

Chapter 45

Forty minutes later Ardi Troshani sat in the seat recently vacated by Ewan. Sitting next to him was a lawyer whom Mary didn't recognise. Hugh Jenkins had apparently left the building.

Ardi's eyes were less glazed than before, but his mood evidently hadn't improved.

"I ain't saying nuttin' to you," he said, folding his arms.

"I'm pleased to hear that, Mr Troshani," replied the DI, sounding genuinely thankful, "because it means we won't have to waste our time listening to you. You see we've been having a look round your lab at Grove Park – you know, the one in the sub-basement, swipe your phone to get in?"

Ardi visibly whitened on hearing the details that meant the police must have found the secret room. The DI pressed home the advantage.

"It's a very impressive facility. Well-stocked too. And lots of fingerprints, including yours on a container half-full of poison, of the very rare type used to murder Luan Redzepi. So really I'm just here to give you a progress report, which is that we'll be charging you and other members of your family with numerous drug-related offences plus the big one, the murder of your cousin. That can wait till tomorrow though."

Ardi kept his arms folded, said nothing. His dead black eyes stared at the wall behind the DI and Mary.

"Bit of a family gathering going on at Grove Park when we got there," the DI continued, "which was also helpful as it meant we could arrest your father and uncle without having to go chasing after them. Sometimes it's amazing how people crack as soon as we've got the cuffs on them. The drugs factory, the Czwisnjowskis, the business in Bristol, you taking care of Luan – we're hearing it all. In fact your family are singing so much that we're thinking of entering them in a male voice choir competition over the water in Cardiff. If I were you, Ardi, I'd spend this evening thinking about joining in the chorus, for your own good."

Ardi turned the dead eyes on the DI.

"Fuck yourself."

The boy was blossoming into a genuinely hard case, thought Mary. She'd seen plenty of young men like him, muscles pumped up in the gym, bloodstreams pumped up with testosterone until they were a hair-trigger away from violence that was more primitive instinct than conscious choice. For a moment she almost felt sorry for him; somewhere in there was probably an intelligent young man, must be in fact or he wouldn't have made a connection with Ewan. Still, as the DI often reminded her, she was a police officer, not a social worker. Her job was to keep everyone safe from people like Ardi, not to worry about how he got that way.

"Suit yourself then," said the DI, getting up from his chair, "we'll see you tomorrow. It goes without saying that we'll be opposing bail. I'd get used to that cell if I were you, you may be somewhere like it for the next fourteen years or so. Judges tend to go hard when we say there's been no cooperation at all. Think on that before you stick with the tough guy routine."

Back in his office, the DI dropped into his chair and leaned back.

"Well, I think that can officially go down as a day to remember," he said.

"Have we got enough?" asked Mary.

"Yes," he said definitively, "Tom says they've got

forensics coming out of their ears at Grove Park, and it corroborates young Ewan's story about drugs factories and big investments. They've found five kilos of crack cocaine, which will be enough to send the Troshanis down on its own. Apparently it's all on shelves, fingerprints everywhere. They must have been relying on that secret door of theirs to keep them safe. They shouldn't have given Ewan his own key. There's a lesson there – keep it in the family."

True, thought Mary.

"Guv, do you mind if I get off now? There's someone I want to see on my way home."

"Business?"

"Yes. Ellie Thornton, Ewan's girlfriend. I told him I'd tell her where he is."

"She lives in Congresbury, doesn't she? Can't you just ring her, rather than traipsing all the way out there?" The DI had the look in his eye that said his overtime detector had been triggered.

"I won't book it as time, Guv. She's eighteen and pregnant, I just think it needs to be face to face."

The DI's expression changed from overtime detector to one which suspected an even greater threat to effective policing.

"Don't go all Social Services on me, for goodness sake. Just remember the children young Master Taylor made his beer money selling drugs to, and the women on the streets in Bristol selling themselves to pay for the crack he made in that lab."

"I'll remember, Guv. I want to ask Ellie about something anyway."

"Fair enough then. I'll see you tomorrow, first thing. We'll have a chat with Agron."

"Thanks Guv – I'll look forward to it."

"Do we need to have our solicitor here for this?" asked

Ellie's father as he showed Mary down the corridor to the living room. She'd given them no notice, just rang and asked if she could come and see Ellie for a few minutes. They'd been cooperative, as had Ellie herself. Clearly none of them felt they had anything to hide.

"No sir," Mary replied, "There's just something your daughter may be able to help us with, purely as a witness."

The living room was large, warm and well-furnished, as was the rest of the farmhouse that Mary had come through. Ellie was sitting on a big Chesterfield sofa, next to a woman whom Mary assumed was her mother. The older woman was attractive, well dressed with expensively-styled blonde hair and smooth skin with just the right degree of out-of-season tan. She looked barely out of her early thirties; in a dim light she could have passed for Ellie's sister.

"This is my wife, and Ellie you already know."

"Mrs Thornton, hello Ellie," said Mary, sitting in the chair Mr Thornton gestured towards, "First of all, thank you for seeing me at such short notice. It's very helpful of you."

"Is this in connection with the murder at Sand Bay?" asked Ellie's father.

"Indirectly, yes."

Mary looked at Ellie. It seemed as if she'd suddenly begun to show, a little bump just below her waist. She hadn't said anything since Mary had arrived, just nodded in recognition then sat next to her mother, her expression very slightly glazed. Possibly she knew that they'd taken Ewan in for questioning; Mary didn't know if she did, and wasn't sure whether to tell her yet.

"Ellie, I want to ask you about the night you and I met in the Brit. That was the Sunday, the day after Sand Bay."

"Yes, I remember," Ellie replied. There was a

dreaminess to her voice that Mary remembered from the Brit, only now it seemed more sedated than relaxed.

"You and Ewan left together, after he'd joined you there."

"That's right, yes."

"Did Ewan contact anyone, call or text them, after you left the Brit? You were meeting your friends in another pub, weren't you? Did he speak to anyone on the way there?"

Ellie said nothing. There were no tears, just an unnatural stillness as she sat there, all expression gone from her face.

"Darling?" said her mother, squeezing her hand.

"When we left Ewan said he needed the toilet. They're outside, by the courtyard, you know?"

Mary nodded.

"I waited for him, it seemed like ages. It was freezing cold out there, and I began to get worried, you know, with the baby. So I went in to find him."

"Into the men's toilets?"

"That's right. I won't get into trouble for that, will I?"

"No, of course not. Did you find him there?"

"Yes. He was standing there talking on his phone. When he saw me he said 'Got to go' and ended the call."

"Did you ask him who he'd been talking to?"

"Yes, he said he'd rung Zac to tell him we were on our way. I got annoyed because he could have done that from the car without leaving me to freeze outside, then he said no, it was Zac who'd called him and kept him talking."

"And did you ask Zac if that was true?"

"No, I didn't think I needed to check up on him like that."

It occurred to Mary that Ellie might think Ewan's call had been to another woman. However something in her manner said she didn't.

"Is Ewan in trouble?" Ellie asked, glancing round quickly at her mother and father.

Mary wanted to take Ellie's hands in hers, but she was too far away from her.

"That's the other reason I'm here. Ellie, we've arrested Ewan, in connection with serious drug offences and the murder of Luan Redzepi. He's been interviewed under caution, and he's told us everything. He's in custody now at Weston and we'll be formally charging him tomorrow. He asked me to tell you where he was."

There was no reaction, save a moistening in Ellie's eyes.

"Is he going to go to prison?"

"Probably, yes. But he's being very cooperative, and that counts for a lot with judges and the CPS. It's not up to us what happens from here on."

"Does he have a lawyer?" Mr Thornton asked.

"A duty solicitor, yes."

He turned to his daughter. "We'll get him a good lawyer, darling. A really good legal team can work wonders – don't worry." He turned back to Mary. "You may disapprove of that, Detective Sergeant, if he's been involved in what you say he has, but I make no apology for it, I'm afraid."

"None needed, sir. Everyone's entitled to representation. Ewan's the father of your grandchild, and he certainly needs people who'll stick by him right now."

Mr Thornton nodded. Mary looked at Ellie again, still sitting motionless next to her mother. Ewan's wasn't the only world that was collapsing.

"Ellie, thanks for being so honest with me," she said, as soothingly as she could, "I know things must seem very bleak right now, but with your family to support you you'll get through it, all of you." Now she did sound like a social worker – good job the DI couldn't hear her.

"It's OK," said Ellie, her eyes still focussed on the middle distance. She'd known, that was obvious now. Perhaps not the details, but that Ewan was mixed up in something. Mary decided on the charitable interpretation, that she'd probably tried to persuade him to stop it. She could imagine Ewan's response.

As Ellie's father showed Mary back along the corridor, he paused.

"The phone call you were asking Ellie about – that happened after the murder in Sand Bay, didn't it? Are they connected?"

"Not directly, sir, no. The call may be connected with an assault on someone who'd been helping us on the Sand Bay case, which happened later that Sunday evening."

"Will Ewan face charges over that?"

"Probably not. It's just tying up loose ends really."

"Is that you, Love?" Don shouted from the living room as Mary closed the front door and put her coat on the rack.

"Yes – who else were you expecting?" she asked in mock accusation.

"One of my many lovers, of course," he said, joining in the joke.

"Yeah, right – love you for your dirty overalls, do they?" She bent over the back of the sofa and kissed him, softly and for a second longer than had become their norm. It was the kind of start their evenings hadn't had for some time.

"I haven't done anything about dinner yet." Don said apologetically.

"Good, because I'm doing it. My turn, I think. I've got us steak, chips, peas, onion rings, trifle for afters and these," she pulled a four-pack of premium lagers from a carrier bag, "for you."

Don's eyes lit up, whether at the sight of his wife, the lagers, the dinner menu or all three wasn't clear. Mary didn't care – it was just good to see them lit.

"Right – I'll put the oven on then I'm going upstairs for a shower. You're not desperate to eat in the next half hour, are you?"

"Not at all, Love, no." said Don, his eyes still gleaming.

Mary went upstairs to their bedroom, switched on the bedside lights and began to undress. When she was naked she went into the en suite and turned on the shower. The hot water came quickly, and she stepped eagerly under it, welcoming the warm jets onto her skin. She'd only been there for a couple of minutes when she saw the bedroom door move, and a figure come in. Smiling, she pushed the cubicle door open, and saw her husband in front of her.

"Room for another in there?" he said, grinning like the Don who'd grinned at her sixteen years ago in the flat above the off-licence.

"You bet there is. Oh Don, I really love you." She reached out and pulled him to her, felt his arms around her, his body against hers.

"Me too, Sweetheart, me too."

Chapter 46

Mary was in the office at 8am the following morning, bright and keen to get started despite having had not quite enough sleep. The DI was already there, but didn't look quite so bright.

"What time are we interviewing Agron, Guv?" she said, leaning into his office doorway.

"We're not – not yet, anyway," he said, "Come in and close the door." There was a trace of weariness in his voice. Clearly something big had happened, and clearly it hadn't been good news.

"We've had a message from Bridewell Street," the DI continued, "We're to wait until DSI Kopacz gets here before interviewing Agron or Zamir, or charging them."

"Do you think it's a takeover?" It wouldn't be the first time Major Crime had swooped in to take the glory after a local team had done the work.

"Might be more than that. He's bringing a CPS man with him. That's probably why he's been delayed – waiting for the CPS chap to get out of bed."

Mary smiled at the joke. Crown Prosecution Service staff, most of them lawyers, were notorious for their reluctance to make the kind of early start that every police officer accepted as part of the job. The smile didn't last long, however; nor did the DI's. The presence of the CPS this early in the process usually meant one thing - a deal. And deals made by the CPS often left a bad taste in the mouths of the police.

Kopacz arrived at 9.35, slightly out of breath from the effort of bringing his bulk and large document case up from the car park. With him was the CPS lawyer who, it turned out, wasn't a chap after all, but a rather glamorous woman of around thirty who introduced herself as Fazila Khan. Ms Khan's accent said that she'd probably been to a school not unlike Compton before attending a university not unlike Cambridge. She had looks, a privileged education, a high-flying career and plenty of money if her clothes were anything to go by; Mary's first instinct was to dislike her on principle, while the DI clearly struggled to keep it professional as he shook her slender hand with its jewel-encrusted fingers. As Ms Khan spoke, however, apologising for keeping everyone waiting and thanking them for letting her sit in on this, it became clear that she was, in fact, more down to earth than some of the CPS staff they'd had to deal with in the past. Mary decided to give her the benefit of the doubt, for now at least.

"First of all," said Kopacz as they settled round the interview room table, "well done to you and your team, Steve. This is a major result. Quite apart from solving the beach murders, I don't need to tell you what a big political issue the student murders have been. I've had the Chief Constable on this morning expressing his satisfaction, and he'd had the Mayor on to him."

"It's DS Miller's collar, sir," said the DI, "We were all barking up the wrong tree but she put a couple of minor clues together and came up with the answer – and, I should say, without a computerised investigation management system in sight. Good old-fashioned policing."

"DS Miller will get the recognition she deserves, I can assure you of that, but I'm sure she'll agree that officers like her need backing from senior officers like you, who are willing to trust them. Isn't that so, DS Miller?"

"I couldn't agree more, sir." said Mary loyally. She meant it, too.

The meeting was quickly turning into a mutual appreciation society, no doubt partly, at least, for Ms

Khan's benefit. That was nice, but Mary had seen enough of Kopacz in action by now to know that the pats on the back were probably a softener for something less enjoyable to come. It didn't take long to arrive.

"I expect you know what we're here for," said Kopacz, shifting his body uncomfortably on the small chair, "We're going to take over the interview with Agron Troshani, I'm afraid. Mary, I'm sorry but there won't be room for you. I seem to make a habit of this, don't I?"

"No problem, sir."

"And you can also probably guess what comes next. Ms Khan is here with authority to offer Mr Troshani a deal, up to and including immunity from prosecution, in return for full testimony against the Czwisnjowskis. Now I realise how galling that may be for you, especially after all the trouble you've had with the Troshani family, but Czwisnjowski is a genuinely big fish on an international scale, and this may be a once in a lifetime chance to get him into jail."

"We wouldn't do this lightly," said Ms Khan, "but as I believe Mr Kopacz has already outlined, Czwisnjowski is a major target criminal in at least eight European countries, and removing him would strike a significant blow against the drugs trade all over the continent. Not least, he's a major conduit for drugs to and from Russia, and that's a trade which it's generally accepted can only be dealt with from the Western end."

Perhaps it was just her good mood after the previous night, but Mary found herself thinking that it all made sense, and that it was actually quite good of Kopacz and the CPS lawyer to take the trouble of explaining it to them in person. There was no harm in checking the fine print though.

"You say the deal's for Agron Troshani? What about Ardit and Zamir?"

"Strictly Agron only," said Ms Khan, "He's the one who struck the deals with Czwisnjowski, Zamir doesn't know enough about them. As for Ardit, he's not in the picture. If Agron demands immunity for his brother and nephews, then the deal's off. I'll be frank with you – we're under pressure to make this deal, from our own agencies and partner countries. However the decision has been made that we can't start giving immunity to entire families – and that comes from way above my pay grade."

Mary considered herself a pragmatist. She'd heard enough from Ewan the previous day to know that it would, in fact, be worth letting the entire Troshani clan go if it put Czwisnjowski behind bars. If Fazila Khan could keep it to just Agron then that would be a bonus. She looked across at the DI. As far as she could make out he was thinking much the same thing.

"Thank you, sir, and Ms Khan, for explaining the situation. I appreciate it." The DI nodded in agreement.

"Good," said Kopacz, "Well we'd better get on with it. We'll see you again before we go – and well done again. First-rate collar."

"Thank you sir. I'll have Agron brought up, shall I?"

Just 90 minutes later the DI emerged from the interview room and called Mary over to his office.

"What's happening, Guv?" she said as she pushed the door closed.

"It's all over," he said, "Agron gets immunity, no-one else, and in return he gives us the whole story against Czwisnjowski, written statement, testify in court, the lot. We even get to keep him on remand until the case is over, then the CPS drop the charges when he's delivered what was agreed."

"That was quick – did DSI Kopacz give him the full treatment?"

"It wasn't Kopacz," said the DI, "it was Ms Khan. She may look wet behind the ears, but believe me, she knows what she's doing. Agron demanded that Zamir got immunity with him, but she just laughed at him – and I mean actually laughed, out loud." The DI looked around to check that no-one would overhear them. "This is just between us. At one point she turned the recorders off, then told Agron not to have any romantic ideas about British justice, that the Government wants to send a message to foreign criminals that they aren't welcome here, and if the CPS wanted to they could make sure he went in front of the right judge and got a 20 year minimum. I didn't know they could still do that."

"Speak softly and carry a big stick, eh Guv?"

"Very big. Ms Khan isn't from Bristol either – she's from a special CPS unit in London, normally works on NCA cases. The reason she didn't arrive until 9.30 is that she caught the 7am from Paddington and it got into Weston at 9.20. A CPS lawyer on the 7am train – I never thought I'd see that."

The DI was clearly just a little bit awestruck, which was something Mary had never thought she'd see. She thought it best to check the small print again.

"Did Agron try to get a deal for Ardi?"

"No, in fact he seemed glad to see the back of him. Young Ardi's going down for his full entitlement, with help from his uncle."

"What, Agron's going to testify against him?" Now she was awestruck. She'd have imagined the DI tap-dancing on a filing cabinet before one Troshani giving evidence against another.

"Ms Khan again. She said she'd personally fly to Tirana and make sure Luan's mother knew that Agron had agreed to kill her son. That would have reignited some blood feud with the Redzepi family going back to the 14th century. The alternative was that they presented it as Ardi acting off his own bat while Agron was still negotiating with Czwisnjowski."

To Mary the story had a familiar ring to it. She remembered her father telling her about the terrible blood feuds among the Camorra clans around Naples, one of the reasons why her grandfather had stayed in Britain after the war. Perhaps the Troshanis, in their own crooked way, were here for the same reason. Sacrificing Ardi might buy off the Redzepi family; she hoped it would. Better that than having the local beaches full of dead Albanians for the next seven centuries.

She was about to voice this opinion when the Squad Room door opened and Kopacz came in, closely followed by Fazila Khan. They made their way straight across to the DI's office, where Kopacz opened the door without knocking and leant in, his bulk filling the doorway.

"We've got a problem," he said, "The Czwisnjowskis have gone AWOL. We were supposed to be watching them but somehow they gave us the slip at their hotel. The diplomatic car's still there but they've gone, along with their minder."

"Presumably they'll be trying to get out of the country, sir?" said the DI.

"Looks like it. We've put a watch out at the docks and we're checking the passenger lists at the airport. We're trying to get the minder's phone number from the Polish embassy, but no joy so far."

Fazila Khan had been waiting patiently behind Kopacz's one-man door blockade, but now she pressed her way, politely but firmly, into the gap.

"We really can't afford to lose Czwisnjowski," she said, "If we do then this whole thing falls apart, and the repercussions will be dire, believe me. Do you have any idea where he might go to lie low for a while, until we've relaxed our watch on the exit points? Would the

Troshanis have a suitable place?"

"That was Grove Park I'm afraid," said the DI regretfully, "and I don't think he'll be turning up there. Other than that, I...."

The DI was interrupted by a phone ringing, softly at first but quickly getting louder. Pushing back a mild panic, Mary reached into her jacket pocket and felt the phone vibrating, heard it even louder as she pulled it out. Throwing an apologetic glance around the office, she held the phone in front of her and read the caller's name on the display.

'M Slade'.

Chapter 47

Mary's thumb hovered over the phone, midway between the green and red buttons. Red was the simple option, a chance to show the DI and Kopacz that she was obeying the Force's instructions to have no contact with Michael. But in the second and a half she had to consider it, one thought filtered through; every time Michael had called her, every time she'd contacted him, he'd come up with something big. Without thinking any further, she decided on a compromise. Her thumb came down on the green.

"Hello Mary, it's Michael here."

"Michael, you know I'm not allowed to have any contact with you. I'm going to have to end this call. Sorry."

"Actually you can talk to me, Mary – that's why I'm ringing. I've got something that may be of interest to you, as well."

Mary gave a look of puzzled exasperation, hoping that the others in the room would understand.

"No Michael, I can't talk to you. You know that." It occurred to her, suddenly, that he might have lost patience with the TuringShroud subterfuge and decided to blow it wide open. If so, then he'd be blowing her career apart with it.

"Yes you can, Mary. I've had a meeting with the Chief Constable and the Police Commissioner, extremely nice people, both of them. They've given me a written assurance that no police officers will face any disciplinary action over the assault on me, and agreed that I am free to act as a technical advisor to the police as and when requested, with immediate effect. They were a bit resistant at first, but when I pointed out that the current situation rather flew in the face of last year's "Citizens Assisting Justice" campaign, they came round fairly quickly." A chortling noise came through the earpiece. "They've also agreed a modest ex gratia payment which I shall, of course, be donating to the Save Birnbeck Pier appeal."

Mary struggled to take it all in, then realised that she was surrounded by senior officers, plus a very senior CPS lawyer, who were also struggling to take it in.

"Hang on please, Michael," she said, then covered the phone's mouthpiece with her hand. She turned first to Kopacz. "It's Michael Slade, sir, the man who gave us the lead on Katya Czwisnjowski's phone," then to the DI, "He says he's had a meeting with the Commissioner and Chief Constable, and they've authorised him to have contact with us again."

The DI shook his head sadly. "It sounds like Mr Slade's finally lost the plot, if he's having imaginary meetings with the Chief Constable. Give me that phone, I'll deal with him." He turned to Kopacz, "Sorry about this, sir."

"Actually I think he has had a meeting with the Chief Constable," Kopacz replied, "at least that's what I heard was happening. Why's he ringing, Mary?"

"He says he's got something for us, sir."

"Does it concern the Czwisnjowskis?"

Mary took her hand from the mouthpiece.

"Michael, this something you've got for us, is it about the Czwisnjowskis? Can you tell me what it is?"

"It could well be relevant to them, yes. But I need to show it to you really. If you're at the police station I could come and see you."

She covered the mouthpiece again. "He says it could be relevant, sir, but that he needs to show it to us. He says he'll come here."

"Better get him in then." said Kopacz.

Mary saw the DI's face in the corner of her eye as she took her hand from the mouthpiece again. This had better not be a waste of time, or her life was going to be difficult for the next few weeks.

"Michael, where are you – Bridgwater? We can send a car for you, it'll be quicker."

"No, I'm in the cafe opposite the Town Hall, just along the road from you. I can be there in two minutes."

Mary ushered Michael into the CID office, explaining the various teams dotted around it as she went. He was still proudly fingering the Visitor badge he'd been given at reception. It had been a very slightly emotional reunion at the front desk, with Mary shocked to see the marks of his beating still clearly visible on his face, and the wince of pain he gave as a movement disturbed his bruised ribs. It hadn't been until they were safely in the lift that she'd thanked him for all the help he'd given her recently, commenting in passing on the high quality of the coffee in the Orchard Place Internet café. He'd replied, with a slight chortle and another wince, that he'd heard it was good too, indicating that the mystery of TuringShroud would remain just that.

With three people already in the DI's office it was standing room only. Still not quite sure that this wasn't a particularly surreal dream, and that Don was going to wake her up any minute, Mary began the introductions.

"DI Jones you already know of course."

The two exchanged nods, not exactly those of long-lost buddies, but not of two rutting stags either. It seemed to Mary that she wasn't just projecting her own feelings in seeing a hint of guilt on the DI's face as he saw the marks on Michael's.

"This is Ms Khan from the Crown Prosecution Service," she said, "and this is Detective Superintendent

Kopacz, from our Major Crime Unit."

"Pleased to meet you, Ms Khan, and you, Detective Superintendent." Michael looked at Kopacz with undisguised admiration, "I've read a lot about you."

"Have you, sir?" said Kopacz.

"Yes. In 1987, despite being unarmed yourself, you single-handedly kept the heavily-armed St Anne's payroll gang trapped in an alleyway until backup arrived, earning a commendation and effectively ending the era of the great Bristol wage robberies."

"I did indeed, sir, yes."

"I'm honoured to meet you." Michael stuck out his hand, for all the world as if paying his respects to a great war hero, which, Mary reflected, Kopacz arguably was.

"Thank you, sir," said Kopacz, shaking Michael's hand, "Now we have a missing persons problem, which is somewhat pressing as we're keen to arrest the persons in question for a number of serious offences."

"The Czwisnjowskis, I assume?" said Michael.

"That's correct. They left their car at the Avon Gorge Hotel this morning and took off with their diplomatic minder, one Otto Borowski."

"We gather you've made some extremely valuable contributions to this investigation, Mr Slade," said Ms Khan, "I wonder if you might have any insights now as to where the Czwisnjowskis might have gone?"

"Actually I think I might, as it happens," said Michael, reaching into his inside jacket pocket, "that was what I wanted to show you."

He took out his phone, the one he'd used as a map and compass at Sand Bay. A few presses and swipes turned the screen into a plan of an airport, the runway and parking aprons clearly visible. Superimposed on it were a number of tiny aircraft shapes, pointing in different directions. He pointed to one, in blue, parked with its nose towards the runway.

"This is Bristol airport, and that's a Gulfstream G650. Top-end business jet, capacity up to 18 passengers, range 7,000 nautical miles, top speed of over 600 miles per hour. Registered to a Russian mining company based in Kazan, in the Volga region. This is its second visit in the past month – it flew in on the 6th of November, flew straight back out, then arrived again three days ago. It's been on the tarmac since then, which seems rather a long time for such an expensive aircraft to be sitting doing nothing."

"Indeed it does, doesn't it?" said Kopacz, as he and Ms Khan peered closely at the screen. Indeed it did, thought Mary. They'd assumed all along that the Czwisnjowskis had driven down from London with Borowski in the embassy car, whereas in fact Borowski had picked them up from Bristol airport after they'd arrived in a private jet – which, no doubt, had been ready to pick them up again at a moment's notice, and was hopefully still waiting for them now. Borowski, of course, hadn't mentioned the jet. To be fair there was no reason why he should, although she doubted if he'd have told them even if there had been.

Standing back, Mary saw that the DI was excluded from the group around the phone, barred from entry by his own desk. Then she saw that Michael had noticed it too. He swung round and held the phone out for the DI to see. "Here it is, Inspector, the blue one. As you can see, it's on the side apron at the moment, but if it's fuelled then it could be ready to take off at 20 minutes' notice."

"Thank you." said the DI.

"You're welcome," Michael replied. For a second Mary had an insight of what it was like to be a mother whose two small sons had finally learned to share. She quickly put the thought away.

"Right," said Kopacz, his voice deepening to what

Mary imagined was that of a Flying Officer heading out to his Hurricane, "we'd better get across to that airport, hadn't we? Ms Khan, you come with me. Steve, I'll get on to uniform as we go. What's the best route from here?"

Before the DI could reply, Michael jumped in.

"Out to the M5 junction, straight over onto the A370, through Congresbury, turn right into Brockley Wood, over Brockley Coombe and you're there," he said, without taking a breath, "It's a good fast road all the way, especially in a police car. The other way you can't avoid Banwell, and if there's a lorry stuck in the narrow bit you'll be there for 10 minutes, even with lights and sirens."

"Er, that's right sir," said the DI, allowing himself a brief murderous glance at Michael.

"OK, let's go," said Kopacz, "We'll see you there."

The DI was already filling his pockets with phone, notebook and keys. Now it was Michael's turn to be the outsider, his status uncertain as everyone else prepared to leave.

"Guv?" Mary said, inclining her head towards Michael.

"What?" he said, then looking in the direction of Mary's gesture, "Oh, yes. Do you think you'd be up to a high-speed car journey, Mr Slade? It can get a bit rough over the bumps. We wouldn't want to aggravate your injuries."

"I'll be absolutely fine, inspector," said Michael, his eyes gleaming so brightly that in other circumstances Mary would have considered arresting him for possession.

"Right then," said the DI, "we'll take my car. You go in the back, Mr Slade. Keep your seatbelt on, don't touch anything and no talking while we're on the radio. Is that understood?"

"Absolutely, Inspector, absolutely!"

The DI's Audi touched 70 as they hurtled up the dual carriageway towards the motorway junction, other vehicles pulling aside at the sound of the siren and the blue lights flashing behind the radiator grille. Ahead they could see Kopacz's big Vauxhall having the same effect. They caught up with it just before the M5 roundabout, taking the lead as they swept over the motorway, through red lights at the junction with the slip road, and down the A370 beyond it. As they went over a bump Mary heard a muffled 'ouch' from the back seat, turned and saw Michael holding his ribs. Then the car veered slightly and hit another bump, and she saw the DI look in his mirror, a grim smile on his lips. She gave him her best withering look, and the car found smoother tarmac.

Michael had been right about the route; the road was just two lanes, but wide and with good visibility, allowing the DI to keep up a good speed as other vehicles pulled aside to let him through. Soon they were at Congresbury, flashing past the car dealers and into the village centre, slowing to 45 mph as the buildings became more closely packed. Mary looked at the turning that led out to the Thorton's farm. She wondered what Ellie was doing, whether her father was on the phone to a good firm of lawyers.

As they left the village Mary's phone rang, the screen showing a number she didn't recognise.

"DS Miller."

"Mary, Kopacz here. Put me on speakerphone, will you?"

"Yes, sir. DSI Kopacz, Guv," she said, pressing the button and holding the phone up in front of them.

"Steve," Kopacz said, shouting to make himself heard over the sound of the sirens, "Uniform should be there just before us. Flights have been suspended and the

Gulfstream has not taken off, repeat not taken off. Head for the Tall Pines Golf Club, which is a right-hand turning off Downside Road. Do you know it?"

"Yes, sir."

"Good. There's an emergency access gate just past the club – airport security will be ready to open it for us. That leads straight to the parking stands. The Gulfstream's on the left when you come through onto the apron."

"Got all that, sir."

"Good. Let's hope they haven't smelt a rat and done another runner."

"No sir."

Kopacz's voice came through again, even louder now. "How are you doing, Mr Slade? DI Jones not driving over too many bumps I hope? I hear those Audis are stiffly sprung."

Mary looked through the back window and saw the Vauxhall the regulation distance behind them, a Squad driver at the wheel, Kopacz in the passenger seat. She suppressed a smile. Nothing got past Stan.

"I'm fine thank you, Detective Superintendent," Michael shouted back, "For a large car it shows remarkable agility in the corners."

"I'm glad to hear that, sir," said Kopacz, "Right – we'll see you there." The phone went dead.

They raced on up the hill, into the countryside and through the village of Cleeve, strung out along the roadside for what seemed like miles. The DI straddled the painted-off central area where possible, pulling smoothly back in to miss bollards by a safe distance. During a stretch of clear road, Michael leaned forward between the front seats.

"You're a very good driver, Inspector. Most impressive."

"Thank you, Mr Slade. Police training, one of the

better uses of taxpayers' money."

"I agree."

The traffic lights at the junction into Brockely Combe Road were red, with a queue in the central lane waiting to turn; the DI cruised smoothly down the left-hand lane then did a hard right around the front of the line of traffic, Mary looking back to see the Vauxhall doing the same. Michael winced again, but this one had been unavoidable.

The road was much narrower here, with trees each side ready to provide an unforgiving run-off area if they made a mistake. The DI kept it to 50, and kept his cool when a hapless driver in a small Mazda did exactly the wrong thing by slowing down to 25mph, just too fast for them to safely overtake him on the approaching blind bend. They were soon past him though, thankfully before the road narrowed to barely two-car width as they came down from the Coombe, the Vauxhall closing up tightly behind them to make sure it got through as well. As their speed increased again, Mary turned to the back seat.

"Are you OK, Michael?"

"Yes, fine thanks." He did seem fine too; eyes still bright, peering eagerly through the windscreen and side windows.

"You're a very good passenger. Some people get a bit queasy on rides like this."

"No, this is great – it's like rallying with sirens!"

Even the DI cracked a smile at that one.

The lane down to the golf club was single track but also arrow-straight, and they hit 50 again, alternately-flashing headlights bouncing off the hedges in the mid-day November gloom. Beyond the club entrance the lane dipped steeply down and back up again, then swung round to the right. On the bend was the gate in the airport perimeter fence, three men in hi-vis jackets standing guard in front of it. Mary reached for her bag to find her warrant card, but the gates were being swung open when they were still 50 yards away. The DI slowed nevertheless, wound his window down and shouted "Which way?" to the man nearest him.

"Left here – that takes you straight to the stands" the man shouted back. The DI thanked him and accelerated hard up the access track, stirring up a cloud of dust from the loose gravel surface. The track ran alongside the runway, and for a moment they were deafened by the noise of reverse thrust from a jet that had just touched down. The DI hit his window button, but before it had finished closing they were past the maintenance shed, off the loose surface and onto concrete. And there, on the left, stood the Gulfstream G650.

A marked car was already on the scene, parked strategically in front of the plane's nosewheel. A uniformed officer jumped out as the Audi came to a halt, pulling his cap hastily on.

"They're in the plane sir. We've told the ground crew not to bring the steps back until armed response have arrived."

"Good," said the DI, jumping out of the car, "Do we know who's in there?"

"Three crew, two passengers is all we've heard so far, sir."

"OK – thanks."

"What's the story, Steve?" Kopacz shouted as he lumbered towards them from the Vauxhall.

"Three crew, two passengers, sir. Either it's them or we're very unlucky. Uniform have had the steps kept away until armed response get here."

"No need for that," said Kopacz, panting slightly, "Not Czwisnjowski's style. That plane will be squeaky clean, I'd bet my pension on it."

The DI looked worried, and a little embarrassed. "Best

not to take the risk though, surely sir?", he said, lowering his voice so Mary could barely hear him.

Kopacz shrugged. "No, you're right. They're not going anywhere, are they?"

Thankfully they didn't have long to wait, as the sound of sirens from the access road heralded the arrival of two personnel vans, riot shields folded up above their windscreens. As the first one stopped a black-clad officer, in bullet-proof gear and carrying a semi-automatic rifle, jumped out and ran up to Kopacz.

"What have we got, sir?" he said.

"Hello Gerry," replied Kopacz, "Aircrew plus two suspects, not known to be armed but potentially dangerous all the same."

"Shall we get them out?"

"Yes please."

The steps were put in place by two rather nervous-looking airport staff, and a message was relayed via the control tower telling the plane's occupants to disembark. Firearms officers took their positions in a semicircle, covering the door and emergency exit hatch. After a brief wait, the door swung inwards, then open. At the top of the steps, like a visiting world leader and his wife on a newsreel from the 1960s, stood Mr and Mrs Czwisnjowski, he impeccable in his perfectly-tailored suit, she magnificent in her sable coat.

Kopacz went forward to meet them, looking himself like part of an official reception party. He didn't, however, have any words of welcome.

"Wiktor Czwisnjowski, I'm arresting you for conspiracy to murder Luan Redzepi, and also for conspiracy to import, manufacture and supply controlled drugs. You do not have to say anything, but it may harm your defence if you fail to mention, when questioned, something which you may later rely on in court. Anything you do say may be given in evidence.

Do you understand?"

"Yes, Superintendent Kopacz, I do," said Czwisnjowski, and allowed himself to be led to the waiting squad car. He was soon joined by his wife, whom Kopacz arrested, with impeccable courtesy, as an accessory to her husband's activities. As she was being taken to the car, she passed near to Mary. Their eyes met, as they'd done in the mirror at Bridewell Street. "When you have your own children, you will understand," said Mrs Czwisnjowski, and moved on.

"Excellent work, everyone!" said Kopacz, as the squad cars began to drive off, taking their prisoners with them. He turned to the DI, "You've done a great job in Weston, and don't worry, it won't be forgotten. Well done to you especially, Mary. I'm sure your DI here knows what an outstanding officer he has in you. And to you, Mr Slade. It's been very good to meet you at last, and I expect we'll meet again." He held out his hand.

"I hope so, Detective Superintendent," replied Michael, eagerly shaking it.

"Stan will do, if we happen to be having a drink. Talking of which, Doc Singh was asking after you, wondering when you'd be well enough to meet him for some more discussions on cryptographic matters."

"I'm well enough now!" said Michael, clearly keen to renew his acquaintance with the Doc.

"Yes, I can see that, sir. I'll let him know. Incidentally, some people in Cheltenham are very keen to talk to whoever sent us some emails which they haven't been able to trace. You wouldn't have any insights for us on that, would you?"

"No I'm afraid not, Mr Kopacz."

"But you work developing high security online systems, is that right?"

"I'm more of a middleware man, really."

"No doubt you are, sir, no doubt you are. Goodbye then."

As Kopacz walked back to his car, it occurred to Mary that she and the DI hadn't actually done anything at the airport; they'd been spectators at what had quickly become a Bristol operation. That was understandable, but something of an anti-climax all the same. Still, it was her choice to be part of the Weston team. As she turned away, however, she was surprised to see what looked like a local patrol car heading towards them from the main terminal building. It drove up to them, a back door opened and to her surprise, PC Durham emerged. Then, to her complete astonishment, she saw that he had someone handcuffed to him, and that the person in question was Otto Borowski.

"Sir, Sarge, we caught him in the car park, getting into a hire car. Airport Security spotted him on CCTV bringing the suspects in – the woman stuck out a mile in that fur coat – and we just managed to get to him before he drove off. He says he's a diplomat, but he hasn't got any ID."

"Well, well," said the DI, his eyes lighting up, "Mr Borowski. Fancy seeing you here."

"Tell this boy to release me at once!" Borowski spat out the words, "As you know full well, I am an accredited member of the diplomatic corps."

"Actually I don't remember ever seeing your accreditation, sir. And you don't have any official ID with you now?"

"I have left it at my hotel." Borowski said, a little less stridently. He could obviously see where the DI was going with this.

"Just like you left your embassy car and driver, eh? I wonder why that was?"

"I have done nothing wrong. My job is to assist Polish citizens in this country. Mr Czwisnjowski is a prominent businessman in Poland. He asked me to take him to the airport, that is all I did."

"And the fact that he told you to leave the official car out front and collect him from the back door in a hire car didn't ring any alarm bells?"

Borowski bristled now, the buttons of his suit straining as he puffed out his chest.

"I don't need to remind you, Inspector, that I have diplomatic immunity. I don't need to answer any of your questions. Now release me, or my ambassador will be making life very hard for you."

"No ID, no diplomatic immunity, I'm afraid." The voice came from behind them. It was Fazila Khan's. "Not until someone comes from the Embassy to verify your status, anyway. And I wouldn't bank on keeping your posting here for very long once we do let you go. The Polish government is fully committed to playing an active part in the fight against organised crime across the EU – in fact I was at a conference in Warsaw on that subject only last month. You may have acted in good faith, Mr Borowski, but that won't lessen your government's embarrassment if it emerges that not only has one of its most prominent business figures been arrested for drug running but one of its embassy staff assisted, albeit unwittingly, in his attempted escape. I'm sure they'll find something more suitable for you in another part of the world. In the meantime, best to lock him up I think, don't you Inspector? We can't have people running round the West Country with no ID claiming to be diplomats, can we?"

"No, I don't think we can, Ms Khan," said the DI, "Take him in, Durham, and if he won't go, arrest him for aiding a suspect to escape. Good work."

"Thank you, sir." said Durham, "Come along sir, Sergeant Blakestone will explain your rights to you when we get to the station."

Epilogue

The Pink Flamingo Room, Weston's premier cabaret and live music venue, was gratifyingly full for such a cold early December night. At a table near the stage sat a party of six: Mary and Don, Michael and Mrs Slade (a pretty woman with fair hair and a kind but permanently worried expression), the DI and the ever-cool Karen, looking more than ever like a Scandinavian princess on a trip to southern latitudes.

The tickets had been waiting for Mary on the front desk when she'd arrived back from Bristol Airport two weeks earlier, with a note that read "Thanks for looking after Stevie – J". The evening was going well, with members of the party finding common ground to share. To Mary's intense relief, Don and Michael had hit it off, largely due to an apparently genuine interest on Michael's part in gas boiler technology and heating system design. Mrs Slade, it turned out, was a district nurse, so a healthcare professional like Karen. That left the DI and Mary, occupiers of large tracts of common ground, but content to put them aside for tonight and enjoy the evening.

Both were, in fact, particularly glad to be away from the station. The previous night BBC reporter Jane Thomas had broken a story on the regional news about secret memos from Constabulary HQ, leaked to her by anonymous email, which said that intelligence received from the NCA about a criminal family setting up a drugs factory in Weston-super-Mare should not be pursued or shared with the local CID, due to "sensitive political considerations". The story had appeared again that morning in a national newspaper, and all hell was now on the loose in the upper echelons of the Force. As the DI said though, it was Portishead's problem, not theirs.

The house lights dimmed, a spotlight came on over the stage, and into it walked the compère. He tapped the microphone, then addressed the room.

"Ladies and gentlemen, it's with great pleasure that I introduce tonight's star act, a local-born lady you all know, a tribute to one of the greats of Country Music but also a fine artiste in her own right. Put your hands together please, as Miss Jolene Buller is Dolly Parton!"

The room filled with applause, a full contribution coming from the table at the front, with Michael managing a couple of whoops. The curtain parted, and into the spotlight walked Jolene, in the same outfit she'd been wearing on the night Mary and the DI had called in to see her at Between the Lines; pink leather boots, fringed suede skirt, rhinestone-studded blouse with generous décolletage, her blonde hair now topped by a large Stetson hat. She was carrying an equally large acoustic guitar, of a make which Mary knew to be expensive and high quality, such items appearing regularly in lists of stolen goods in the Weston area.

The applause died down, and Jolene took her place on the high stool in front of the microphone. When she spoke, however, the voice wasn't hers but instead that of a woman from the southern states of the USA, the accent perfect, the mannerisms precise.

"First of all I'd like to thank y'all for coming here to see me tonight, I'm honoured to be playing for you," she said, plucking lightly at her guitar strings and adjusting the tuning on one of them, "My Daddy has a joke that this first song is named after me. I don't know if that's true, but I'd like to play it for you anyway. This is called 'Jolene'."

And then something miraculous happened. In a few opening notes the last traces of Jolene Buller

disappeared, and in their place was the Southern woman, her soul laid bare, her voice breaking as she pleaded desperately with her friend not to steal her man away from her. The song had been played a million times, people groaned from over-familiarity when it came on the radio, but in the hands of Jolene it was devastating. Mary felt tears welling in her eyes, then Don's hand squeezing hers, and his voice in her ear, "No-one's taking me away, you daft thing, I love you."
"Me too," she smiled, and squeezed his hand back.

The song ended and the applause erupted, even cool Karen raising her hands high to show her appreciation. Still clapping, Mary leaned across behind Mrs Slade.

"Did you know she was this good, Guv?" she asked.

"She was rubbish when she 14," he replied, "She must have been practising."

As the applause ended Jolene sat up to the microphone. "Thank you, thank you y'all," came the amplified voice, "for making me feel so welcome here in this very special cabaret venue. I sure do appreciate it. Now we have some very special people in the audience tonight. Sometimes, I know, we don't take too kindly to those who have to enforce the statutes, but tonight we have with us two of the brave law enforcement officers who apprehended those responsible for the terrible murders that were perpetrated here in Weston just last month, and made the streets of our town safe for our children to walk again. I'd like us all to show our appreciation to them now."

Jolene began to clap, and to Mary's surprise the whole room began to clap with her, heartfelt applause with no irony, Don's so loud that she feared for her eardrums. She and the DI sat, embarrassed, not knowing whether to clap too, but knowing also that it was a moment they were unlikely to experience often in their careers. She'd made a difference, and these people all recognised it.

The room fell quiet again, and Jolene took the microphone. "Now there's another good friend of mine in the house tonight. He sure is a very talented musician and I'd like to invite him to come up here and sing a duet with me now. Michael?" She extended her hand towards Michael, who jumped up from his seat so quickly that he almost spilled his drink. "I know that Michael knows this song," she continued, "because my Daddy ejected him from the stage in his bar just last week for trying to sing it at the Country and Western karaoke night." As Michael reached her side she unhooked her guitar strap and passed the instrument to him. "This is a song by a man called James Taylor. He's not a real country singer like Waylon Jennings or Hank Williams, but he does his best, which is all any of us can do." Standing next to her, an expression of pure joy on his face, Michael played the introduction to the song. As he approached the first verse, Jolene smiled and turned back to the microphone. "I hope y'all enjoy it – it's called 'You've got a friend'."